Praise for *A Thing*

"Paik's inspiring debut novel is an assured look at how and why it's imperative to change traditional definitions of failure and success... Paik successfully makes readers feel invested in every character... A fascinating exercise in exploring camaraderie and hard work without a particular reward in mind. This rich character study of a man dealing with a mid-life crisis through coaching is full of small, resonant details."

—*BookLife Reviews*

"An involving book that will appeal to a wide audience... Anyone looking for a read that is ultimately about a quest for purpose, meaning, and achievement will love *A Thing or Two About the Game*."

—D. Donovan, Senior Reviewer, *Midwest Book Review*

"Paik's writing is succinct, easy to follow, and the pace of the book moves along perfectly... On the surface, *A Thing or Two About the Game* appears to be about girls' softball, but the story encompasses so much more than simply that. It incorporates friendships, rivalries, sportsmanship, teamwork, kindness, competitiveness, and perhaps most importantly, the ultimate, deep-rooted human desire to find meaning in the mundane."

—*Feathered Quill*

"Even if you are not into softball, there's plenty to enjoy in *A Thing or Two About the Game* for anyone who loves slice-of-life stories."

—*Readers' Favorite*, Five-Star Review

"A fun and engaging sports novel about giving your all for the love of a team."

—*Independent Book Review*

A THING OR TWO ABOUT THE GAME

a Novel

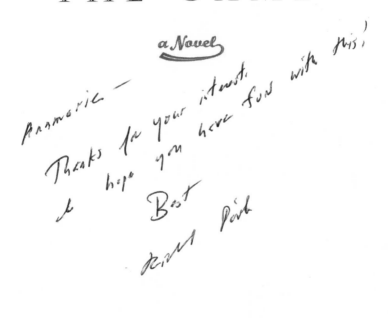

Annmarie —
Thanks for your interest,
& hope you have fun with this!
Best
Richard Paik

RICHARD PAIK

atmosphere press

Chapter 1
SEEDLINGS

Brad rakes the dead thatch from the backyard, working up a sweat in the March chill.

His cell phone rings.

His hands are black with grime; callouses ripening to blisters. When he's done with the thatch, he'll start hacking away at the bleached and brittle stalks in the garden beds. Raking, clearing, mulching. Then planting.

His cell phone rings.

He drops the rake and fishes the phone from his coat pocket.

It's Stephanie. His ex.

What the hell? It's been six years. They're all sorted out. But, what the hell?

She starts into a long explanation about something. Brad holds the phone with his fingertips, so it won't get too dirty. *Uh huh. Uh huh.* Why did he even answer? Now he's stuck and he doesn't know that he's got the time or patience for whatever's coming. Through the jumbled clatter of words, he makes out that she's signed on to coach her friend's daughter in softball—*great, whatever*—they've just picked their teams and it looks like a nice group of girls—*okay, great*—and they're going to have a lot of fun and Brad misses some other stuff and he's pretty much stopped paying attention until a few phrases and syllables interlock and make themselves plain: "Can you take my place? . . . As coach?"

"What? Wait. What?!"

"I know. I know."

Does she think he's got nothing to do? He waits for her—dares her—to say something about "not working." It's taken some time, but he's getting back on track and he's got stuff going on now. She has *no idea.*

She reminds him that he coached his nephew Ben, not that many years ago. "You liked that."

That was because his nephew Ben was on the team. And it was hockey. *Boys'* hockey. And it was a lot of years ago; like eight.

But didn't he enjoy it?

And he was only an assistant.

But doesn't he just love . . . coaching?

Boys' hockey. He *liked* coaching that season. *Loved?* That word doesn't seem to fit *anything* anymore. "Different game, Steph. Different time. Different life." He doesn't bother to mention that he'd done that as a favor to his sister, not his ex-wife.

But doesn't he *enjoy coaching?* And besides, it's just temporary.

He missed that part.

"It's Conner."

"Who?"

"Conner. My boyfriend. He's the real . . . the *official* coach. Something's come up for the first month or so and we just need somebody—hopefully you—to fill in."

Conner. Boyfriend. Yes, he recalls hearing that name. So, he's doing his ex-wife's *boyfriend* a favor. Not that he has some kind of "ex's boyfriend" problem, but it makes easy material for bitter affectation.

"Brad. No. I didn't mean . . . please . . ." Apology, mixed

with plea. Her friend Gwen had a daughter signed up for softball. Their team needed a coach. Gwen knew that Stephanie had played a lot of softball in her time, and wondered if she might consider coaching. Stephanie didn't have time for that kind of commitment and she was recovering from an injury, but Conner, whose daughter had played softball and who had himself actually played *college* baseball, had reacted positively to the idea. Eventually they'd arranged for Conner to coach, with Stephanie as assistant. But now Conner has a nightmare month of overseas work coming up, and everything's hitting the fan and he just can't do it for a month or so.

So why doesn't *she* just take over?

She broke her leg skiing. She's still on crutches for another week. Even if Conner were in charge, she would only barely be able to participate and might have to find somebody else to help out. "I really don't have time for it anyway," she adds.

"And I do?"

She pauses. He can picture her blinking, biting her lip.

He waits. He's not trying to be a jerk. Part of him realizes that it might be a good thing to get out, back out into the world. On the other hand, why is he even humoring this discussion? Shouldn't this be a short and simple no? He can feel his gears turning; wheels spinning. Spinning in too many directions, wobbling, flying off. *I know what you might think but I've got stuff going on every day and I'm getting clear on things and no it has nothing to do with our divorce, you don't understand at all and I know your adopted kids take a lot of time but that's what you signed on for, along with your new ex-jock boyfriend and this coaching gig and I'm sorry about your broken leg but your problems aren't my problems.*

He *does* feel bad about her injury: He backs off a notch. "How old are these kids anyway?"

Eleven and twelve.

Jesus. "That's got to be the worst age."

"Uh . . . No. That's not such a bad age. No, I don't think so."

The wary circling continues. At some point, Brad realizes that he's dodging. Not refusing.

She certainly didn't make this call lightly, she says. She's desperate. She's tried all the parents. Only one parent said she could help out at all, and that was only after being promised that she would not have to be at practices.

They end the call, trying to balance civility with resentment, reconciling ever-present urges to accuse and gain advantage.

Stephanie extends herself: "You were a great coach." And a few last blurts: "And I *know* you loved it. I remember how upset you were that *one time* you had to miss a practice."

"Assume it's a no."

Brad hangs up, wipes the phone screen with his sleeve.

He contemplates the garden. It sits in a pretty good patch of sunlight. He tries to envision eggplant, beans, maybe melons. He'll finish the raking and then pull and chop and whale away at the dead but stubborn matter in the beds. Then he'll put plants in the earth. Nothing fancy. The simplicity is part of the charm. It's not some huge commitment. If he were to invest time . . . in soil treatment or carpentry—if he were to strive for precision, then he would want results. And then it would start to matter. A meager crop would feel like failure.

* * * * *

Finally Mom's car appears. Meghan remembers to thank Anna's mother as she heads out the door.

Mom apologizes for being late.

Meghan fastens her seatbelt. "It's okay," she says. Nothing *bad* happened. Mom is always looking for something bad to fix.

"Well," Mom says. "How was it?"

"Fine."

Is she happy with the project? What did they decide on?

"Turtles."

The wrinkles in Mom's forehead look like the rows of bacon strips in the vacuum-sealed package. "Sea turtles? Or freshwater?"

Meghan does not know.

"Let's see. I can remember box turtles. What they look like. Painted turtles? Have you heard of painted turtles?"

"Just turtles."

What *about* turtles were they going to study?

"About evolution." Meghan can see Mom warming to more questions. "About how they were evolved."

"How they evolved," Mom auto-corrects. But she seems content with this answer. "And how do you like your group?"

Meghan doesn't know. Three girls, plus her, from class. They're all nice enough. She volunteers that one of them— Lily—is going to play softball.

"Well that's nice. Are you going to be on the same team?"

Meghan doesn't think so. "Lily is on the Cardinals." And then she can't remember the name of her own team. She concentrates, searching her memory, and then comes up with it. "Marlins," she says. "I'm on the Marlins."

Mom smiles. "That's right. I think you have your first practice next week."

Yes. Right.

Meghan looks forward to softball season. But she looks down at her feet, wary of conversation. She remembers sitting at the dinner table, asking if she was signed up for softball. Mom was surprised that she wanted to play and asked— twice—if she was sure. Yes. Meghan repeated it twice: She wanted to play. She'd be fine.

Softball is the one sport where everybody takes turns. She gets her turn at bat, same as the best players. The uniforms are bright colors, the hats are cool, and they make most of the girls look just about the same, which makes it feel safe. When she's in the field, the ball is not hit to her often, and by the time she gets to it she usually knows what to do.

Despite her concerns, it makes Mom happy that Meghan wants to play. And playing softball, Meghan's learned, protects her from other unwanted activities, like soccer and violin lessons. It protects her from other as-yet untried activities, like chorus or math tutoring.

It will not bother Meghan if she's the worst player on the team. Nobody has been mean to her in softball. There are no bad grades. When she bats, she can hear other girls—even popular girls—yelling "you can do it, Meghan, let's go Meghan, you can do it!" And she believes them because, lo and behold, she has brandished her bat the way her coaches told her, and in fact used it to strike the moving ball. She has never made the ball fly out over and past the infielders, but she has felt the joy of contact, seen other girls scurrying after the ball that she has launched into urgent territory, and felt—yes!—the thrill of success upon reaching first base. Once there, she can run. She has the same running skills as everybody else; she can do it. She does not run very fast, but as long as she can run, that's basically the same thing that all the other girls do.

"When's the practice?" Meghan asks.

"Next Wednesday."

Meghan considers that. "Do I have an appointment with Dr. Himmelman?"

Mom sighs, casts her eyes down for a moment. "I think you might have to leave practice a few minutes early."

This is disappointing, but at least she'll make most of the practice.

"Anyway," Mom says. "What are you doing for the turtle project?"

They have to read some stuff, find some more stuff online, and learn about how turtles evolved from something else.

"Evolution is very interesting," Mom says.

"Yeah. But it's scary."

"What's scary about it?"

"I didn't mean scary," she says. But if only the fittest survive, Meghan suspects that she—her wispy strain of her species—would go extinct. "I just wonder how I might adopt."

"Ada*pt*."

"Adapt," Meghan repeats.

Mom looks at the road. Her shoulders slump and she looks a little disgusted. Meghan guesses that she probably should have known the difference between "adopt" and "adapt." Then she follows Mom's gaze and realizes that it's the suddenly slowing traffic—not something about her—that's bumming Mom out. After a moment, Mom says, "You know, Meghan, every single living thing adapts."

Meghan looks at Mom. She looks at the stalled line of SUVs in front of them, and then looks back at Mom, who's muttering something about the traffic. Meghan's confused about what Mom said about adapting. They've just started the evolution unit, but Meghan's understanding is that it's not *people* that change, it's the *species* that changes over really long periods of time.

"Every animal, every human, and even every plant has to adapt—or adjust—to the world around it," Mom says. "We all have to adjust how we deal with things. Every one of us."

"Oh," Meghan says. She realizes that she herself has adapted; adjusted. After Dad left. How she acts around Mom. These things have something to do with why she has to see Dr. Himmelman. Because these adjustments are not easy.

* * * * *

Pitcher's Pub. Brad and Mike sit at the dark wood bar. They've got a spring training game going on the TV overhead. The Red Sox are making a pitching change, bringing in one of their young prospects.

Mike keeps grinning sarcastically, making dismissive

comments.

Brad explains that this pitcher had not been a highly regarded prospect until the second half of last season, when he developed a wicked changeup. "After that," Brad says, "he dominated. He's got a ways to go, but he's shown some potential."

Mike sighs with pitying patience. Prospects are prospects.

"Sure," Brad says as he watches. "But every major league star was a prospect at some point."

"For every major league star, there's a hundred failed prospects," Mike retorts.

Of course. But Brad is optimistic, or at least hopeful. He likes trying to figure out which kids will make it. It doesn't seem to follow set patterns. Talent is involved. Luck is involved. Circumstances—who's ahead of you or coming up behind. Biased preconceptions: "The kid just looks like a *ball-player.*" "When he hits the ball it just *sounds different.*" A lot of times it's about how a player adjusts to failure. Once in a while somebody makes the big leagues on sheer willpower and persistence, struggling along even as they're passed over, in the face of injuries and failure. Brad loves those stories.

The batter steps in. Brad watches the pitcher. "Hey," he says. "Look where he's standing on the slab. Way off center, first-base side." When the pitcher stands on the end of the pitching rubber instead of the center, Brad can see how the pitch comes at the hitter from a slightly different angle.

Mike spreads his hands. Big shrug: *Whatever.*

But Mike heard. He'll probably remind Brad of it someday.

Mike and Brad grew up together. After not seeing each other for decades, as grown-ups they rediscovered each other living in the same town. Not that they'd been best buddies. In fact, there had always been a certain wariness between them. The first time they went out together as adults, they got drunk and started buying each other *one more round,* saying stuff like "I *hated* you" but balancing it off with talk of people they used to know and some of those almost-if-only tales about girls they'd had crushes on.

At this point, any odd issues between them have fallen away. They get together every few weeks. In the suburban world of two-child families, they serve as social life for one another. Together they weigh the merits of craft beers and stock investments. They watch ballgames, banter about women, and bask in the easy fit of a relationship that's broken-in like old jeans.

Von, the perpetually congenial bartender, collects coasters and wipes down the bar. He looks up at the TV as he dunks a pair of pint glasses. He nods at Brad. "I see what you're saying about the kid's delivery," he says.

"It's a little different," Brad says.

"Good observation," Von says. "Pitching coach."

"Well. Get this," Brad says. "I've been asked to coach a *girls' little league softball team* this year."

"No shit." Von dries a pint glass with a towel. "You know I ump. You knew that, right?"

Brad had not known that. Umpiring girls' softball? Well. *Somebody* has to do that.

"Yup," Von says. "I ref youth basketball, baseball and softball." He punches an imaginary strike in the air: *"Strahh!"* Von looks at Brad, cocks his head to one side. "You're Stephanie's ex?"

Brad starts to say yes, but stops: "How did you know?"

Von knows most of the players. He knows the coaches. When a team needs a coach, he knows about that, too. "I was wondering who this new guy was—who you were."

"Huh." Brad doesn't want to look too interested. "Are these girls any good? Can they play?"

Von looks up at the TV as he structures his answer. "At this level—'Majors'—they're all over the map. Out of twelve girls, most teams have about four or five girls who can throw the ball across the diamond and hit line drives to the outfield."

He pauses, recalling his impressions of last years' teams. "A few of them understand the game pretty well. Most of the girls can at least play catch and make decent contact at the plate. They'll catch popups, maybe catch a line drive and get a big thrill. About half the girls still throw . . . like . . . girls."

Brad listens carefully, trying to process images.

"And then every team's got three or four girls that might have been playing for a few years but you'd never know it; you wonder why they signed up. Sometimes it's just—their parents are making them play. And some of them just want to hang out with a friend who plays. Some of these kids improve; some of them don't. Every team's got at least one hopeless case."

Brad nods thoughtfully. He wonders if he could stomach it.

"Wait a minute." Mike turns to Brad. "You're not actually considering this?"

Brad shrugs. "Might be."

Mike laughs. "Un. Fucking. Believable."

"What?"

"Believe it or not," Mike says, "I, too, have been asked to coach girls' softball."

Mike's got no kids. Never been married. Hasn't played organized sports since about tenth grade. That was the year he pissed everybody off by quitting the hockey team. *Pissed everybody off*: Brad remembers it being something about the *way* he quit: so indifferently, without angst.

Over the winter, Mike says, his girlfriend asked him if he might want to coach her daughter's team. He corrects himself: "*Help* coach."

It occurs to Brad that Mike looks the part. Thinning hair under the ball cap, small beard and goatee, just enough belly for a suburban dad.

"That discussion didn't last long," Mike says. "*Nooo* thank you."

Von listens as he mixes a drink. "I'm guessing that was

through Phil Braden," he says. "He was looking for another assistant."

Neither of them knows Phil. Brad nods at Von, turns back to Mike. "You didn't even consider it?"

Mike throws up his hands. "I'm busy. The last thing I want to do is get into something with my *girlfriend's daughter.*"

"You don't like the kid?"

"That would be Claire Boniface," Von says. "Good kid. Awesome pitcher." He windmills his arm loosely, forward and up and around, approximating the softball pitching motion. "She should be the star of the league this year."

Mike has no problem with Claire. But. On his fingers he starts ticking off the obvious pitfalls that make coaching a dumb idea. "A: Me and Joanne. What if we break up? Now there's a shit show. B: What about Claire's father?" He holds up a finger to keep Brad from butting in. "And before you start telling me how much *fun* it's going to be, C: I don't give a shit about softball. And I'll throw in D: I don't give a shit about a bunch of little girls I don't know, and who will whine, giggle, not play well in most cases, and probably not care." He sits back, and actually rubs his hands together like he's washing them. "I've got better things to do."

Mike's probably right. But his couldn't-be-bothered breeziness annoys Brad. "You'd be a good coach," Brad says. He believes that. As a kid, Mike always had good 'game sense' in whatever sport they were playing, whether it was baseball, soccer, or hockey.

Mike waves it off. "*You* wouldn't be."

"Excuse me? Asshole?"

Mike shakes his head. He grins—*marvels*—at Brad's cluelessness.

"Come on," he says. "Knowing you, you'll have a bunch of clever ideas and creative drills. But these kids won't get it, they won't care, and you won't know how to deal with that."

For some reason Brad lets him go on.

"You were probably one of the best scientists at Rylix. And where'd that get you?" Mike holds up his index finger: *point coming.* "It'll be the same deal with this coaching gig," he lectures. "You'll have all these ideas, but they won't take, and you'll spend all spring in a frustrated funk. Just like your fucked-up Rylix situation. You're Brad the talented biotech scientist with the great ideas. Go ahead. Feed them into the machine. See if anything comes out." He pauses. But he's still not finished. "It's not like you're going to be *recognized—*"

"*Geez.*" Brad holds up his hands. "I *get it.* Dumb idea."

On the tube, the kid pitcher works from the stretch position, checking the runners. Hands to the belt. Windup. A line drive jumps off the hitter's bat. Into the left-center field gap. It hits the wall on one hop. Opposing runners race around the bases.

"There goes the two-run lead," Mike says, almost triumphantly.

"Spring training," Brad says. "Give the kid a break. Tough hitter. Bad pitch. It happens. Lesson learned."

"Well. Let's hope so." Mike looks back at the screen. "We need results, baby. Not potential."

"I don't know anything about your biotech work," Von says. "But this coaching gig—it's easy. It's fun. Some coaches really get into it. You know, yelling at the umpires." Von thrusts his head forward in exaggerated pantomime: "*Come on—that pitch was low!! She was out of the baseline!!*" Von shrugs. "Whatever. You wanna do that, it's all good. But if you just want to toss the balls out there and assign positions and cheer a little bit, that's okay, too. You get outside, work with the girls, teach a thing or two."

Brad takes a long pull from his glass.

"Personally, as an umpire, I just like being around the game. Even at this level of play. It gets me out; gives me— well—a change of eye level, so to speak."

Brad feels his hand at his chin. "Do the girls at least—do

14

they care?"

Von keeps an eye on the head of foam as he pours a pint from the tap. "Some take it seriously, some don't. I've got a T-shirt," he says. "On the front it says: 'Girls' softball.' On the back it says, 'it's all about the ice cream.'"

"Ha," Mike says. "That's good."

Two guys take stools down the bar. Von takes note, reaches for coasters and menus. Before heading down the bar, he looks at Brad. "But yeah, they care. I mean, they cry. If that's what you mean."

* * * * *

The tomato plants are in. Nestled in their cages, green against black mulch, tiny and frail but orderly for the time being.

Brad sits on the deck in cold sunshine. It should be out of the question: coaching a bunch of girls; eleven- and twelve-year-old girls he doesn't even know. What a mess. It's not spite; it's not about Stephanie. Although he does wonder about Conner. And she'd once called him a *loser*. So maybe he doesn't feel like helping her out.

Stephanie denies that she ever said that. "I said you would be a loser *dad*."

Same thing.

"No, it is *not* the same thing." Maybe it was Brad himself, Stephanie said, who wanted to hear Stephanie call him a loser.

"Why would anybody want that?"

To justify resentment. Because it was simpler. How should she know? She did question how good a father he'd be: Every-thing seemed to be about *him*. But that was an entirely different issue. Whatever it was that he thought he'd heard, she insisted that she had *never* called Brad a loser.

From the deck, Brad looks over his garden. The tomato seedlings quiver in the air currents. He's tried growing them from seed. It took a little extra work, a little indoor time in the winter, sprouts coming up in paper cups. For whatever reason, he didn't get far with that.

So he plants seedlings. There's enough challenge in that. It's hard to envision, but in a month or so they'll be climbing their cages, getting unruly. Production is unpredictable. Last year he got a good crop from four of his six tomato plants, but it was very uneven. It was still June when one of them exploded with clusters of small green globes. He should have pruned some of them off. Most of them just hung there and cracked and withered and came to nothing. Another plant produced very little volume, but the tomatoes it did produce swelled up and hung heavy and red over the bars of their cages. Two plants were anemic all summer, but then in September they busted out. Those plants produced a late bumper crop. On misty mornings he'd go out and find them; big blotches of vermilion hiding under leggy stalks and leaves. Nearly overlooked, each one of these was a surprise and gave his hands the fuzzy sweet smell of high summer all the way into October.

He still needs to get back to Stephanie.

Brad remembers his youth hockey coaches. Most of them yelled, loudly and frequently. The perception back then was that coaches who yelled were coaches who demanded excellence. Good coaches intimidated. They did not hesitate to make public displays. Mostly, Brad thought, they yelled about the bad play that had just happened; they yelled what spectators were thinking. And they favored the kids who *fit*, who carried themselves like they deserved to shine.

Brad remembers the dingy rinks. He remembers six a.m. in the locker rooms: scarred benches, fluorescent lights wavering nervously, cinder block walls.

He remembers Coach Dub. "Dub" was short for 'W.' His last name started with a 'W,' followed by an impenetrable jumble of consonants. With his crew cut and thick, black-rimmed glasses, Coach Dub did not look like a coach. But

Coach Dub knew hockey; a lot more than most Pee-wee-level coaches.

His players—other than Mike—feared Coach Dub's wrath. Not being among the team's presumed future stars, Brad especially feared Coach Dub's wrath. During games, Coach Dub kept calm, standing stoically behind the bench, tapping players on the shoulders with quiet confidences. In practice, though, he let fly with full fury: "Look—look—*look up!*" he'd yell. His face would turn red and he'd flail at the air like a sleeping man having a nightmare. "Be aware! Be a*ware*! What the hell are you *looking* at?! You have to *see* the defenders, *see* your line-mates; ya gotta see the play *developing.*" And then: "You *freakin'* guys! You gotta *read the play!* I swear to God, some of you nitwits couldn't read a play if it was *Go Dog Go!*"

After the last practice of the season, Coach Dub kept Brad late. This meant stops and starts. Brad wasn't sure what he'd done to deserve the punishment, but he knew he'd be gulping for oxygen as his legs turned rubbery. *Whistle: Go! Whistle: Stop! Whistle: Change direction and go! Whistle: Stop! Go! Harder!*

Coach Dub brought a puck onto the ice. He passed it to Brad. Brad passed it back, waiting to begin the drill. Instead, Coach passed the puck again, and they skated up and down the rink at a leisurely pace, slinging the puck back and forth. The empty rink rang with stark reports of puck striking wood.

Coach Dub talked. When he was Brad's age, he said, when he had the puck, he'd tried to anticipate the defense and understand his teammates' tendencies. Sometimes he'd tried to nod them toward passing lanes that looked clogged but were *just about to open up.* Sometimes these improvisations confused his linemates, who did not see what he saw.

Brad wondered when the stops and starts would begin. He kept skating, passing, skating, passing.

"I've been hard on you," Coach Dub said. "That's because your game is *my* game. There are times when you play the way I *wished* I played when I was your age. I've been trying to get you to play like that every game." They'd been around the rink twice. "Eventually you'll get to play with guys who see and think more like you do," he said.

At the far end of the rink, the Zamboni engine coughed and roared to life. Coach Dub came to a stop. He bent down to pick up the puck. "I hope you keep playing this game." He raised his voice to be heard over the Zamboni. "You've got a lot of potential."

In the locker room, Brad peeled the tape off his pads and balled it up. He didn't talk to anyone. He replayed Coach Dub's words in his head, as if to check and make sure he'd heard them. The locker room seemed like some newly discovered and fascinating place. As he slipped off his shoulder pads, and then the sweat-soaked T-shirt, the sweat on his body shimmered strangely. It glowed.

That moment didn't change a thing in his life. To finish out the season, he played sluggishly in the next game, then had to miss the last game . . . and nothing came of it. Looking back on it, Brad realizes that he didn't really believe Coach Dub's words. They made Brad feel good, but he didn't *believe* them or feel like he deserved to be anything more than a respectable second- or third-line player.

So, none of it matters. Didn't lead to anything. But Brad remembers it. It was a good moment. There are few enough of those.

Cold shadows slant down on the yard. He's got tomatoes and cukes in the ground; eggplant next. He hasn't planted eggplant before. Other than tomatoes and cukes and squash, he's tried peas, peppers, beets, and beans, all with limited success. This year he'll try something different.

Chapter 2
AGENDAS

Hi Brad

I really appreciate your doing this. I know it was an unusual request and it doesn't provide any real benefit for you (nothing for the resume here! ☺). I really didn't want to ask you for this, but I honestly think you'll have fun with it. Thank you thank you thank you. Conner and I will relieve you as soon as we can.

Steph

The part in parentheses bugs him.

A few days later she comes by to drop off the coaching stuff. The equipment bag bulges and clanks. On the porch she lays out helmets, bats, catcher's gear, and a protective mask for the pitcher. There's a bucket of scuffed practice balls. Two boxes of brand-new yellow-green game balls.

The team—Brad's team—is the Marlins. There are six teams in the league. They'll play fifteen games, and then playoffs. Every team makes the playoffs. She walks him through a sheaf of papers: an official safety handbook, players' medical forms, team roster, parents' contact information.

Does he need contact info for the other teams' coaches? She'll e-mail it.

Who are these coaches? What are they like?

All the head coaches are dads. Except one: this guy who coaches every year even though his daughters are grown up.

No moms?

No moms this year. Except—she remembers something. She takes the pen from behind her ear and on the safety manual writes "Diane." Diane is the lone parent volunteering time for the Marlins. The only mom-coach in the league. She'll do her best to be available, but she can't promise full participation. She's coached before.

Brad's head swims. He's too tired to ask questions; too tired to process answers. He'll contact Diane soon.

Steph's ready to go.

Brad folds his arms. He wants to know: What did she mean in her e-mail—the part about there not being anything for his resume?

"Huh? Oh. Well. Nothing."

Does she think that's the only reason he does things?

She gives Brad a weary look. "I really don't remember. It was just a quick e-mail. So, Brad. Whatever I wrote, I didn't mean anything by it."

Brad nods without looking at her. Drops it.

"Hey," she says. "I'm not—let's not—this isn't about you and me." She starts down the steps, limping slightly.

"Right. I'm good."

She stops and looks back at him. "I think you'll be good at this."

"Why do you say that?"

She shrugs. "You like to think about these games. You're a scientist."

Scientist. Brad wonders what that has to do with anything.

They wave to each other as she gets into her SUV. It's not about them. And it's not about Brad and some "coaching accomplishment," which he suspects is what Stephanie meant in her e-mail. Whatever the case may be, he will keep this in perspective: It's softball for eleven- and twelve-year-old girls. At the same time, he doesn't want to just toss balls around, pitch batting practice, and lead the cheers. There has to be *something* worth accomplishing.

* * * * *

Ashley's telling Jamie about how much she hates her mom, who's always making her do stupid things. Like sign up for softball. Again. Which she played last year and it was actually not bad, but wasn't that enough?

Jamie nods along. They're hanging out in the shed behind Ashley's house, which is actually a sweet arrangement, out-fitted with an old sagging couch, a string of white lights snaking around, and a collection of spattered plastic pails turned upside down. It beats hanging out at Jamie's house, where her 24-year-old brother Greg parks himself in front of the TV with Cheetos and cigarettes and beer and tosses the empty cans and then a few half-empty cans in the general direction of the garbage pail.

These days Ashley mostly likes to sit around and talk shit about other people and smoke cigarettes and talk about weed and how she's pretty sure she knows where her sister keeps her stash. Jamie knows how Ashley likes to talk. It doesn't mean anything. To humor Ashley, she accepts a drag on a cigarette, and then she has to squelch a cough and ends up doubled over in a cloud of smoke. "What the fuck," she says.

Ashley taps the ash off the end of her cigarette and blows out a plume of smoke.

Jamie slouches down into the couch. Up until last year, she didn't even know there was a softball league to sign up for. She starts tossing a tennis ball off the plywood wall, catching it on the return.

Ashley watches the tennis ball traveling back and forth, Jamie catching the ball with one hand and sending it back with deft wrist flicks. *Thunk*, return, *thunk*, return. Every toss goes to the same spot, a red circle drawn in red sharpie between two studs.

"Did you draw that circle?"

Jamie shrugs.

"You know." Ashley takes another drag on the cigarette. "*You* should play softball."

Jamie keeps on tossing and catching.

"I mean it. I bet you'd be good."

Jamie's second brother Roy was a pitcher in high school and when Jamie was *nine* years old he'd made her play catcher while he fired fastballs and worked on his curve ball. His errant pitches tore at the dirt like strafing fire, and Jamie learned soon enough how to scoop them up. When Roy had had enough, he'd say "thanks, punk," and they'd play catch and he'd toss grounders and fly balls to her.

"We could hang out," Ashley says.

"Who says we'd be on the same team?"

They could make a request, Ashley says.

Jamie hasn't actually played in a real organized game, but her brothers used to let her play in their pickup games— sometimes softball, sometimes baseball—and her brothers' friends told her she was good and let her try some of their beer afterward. She's sure she'd be better at softball than most of the girls her age. But last year when she asked, her mom sighed and ignored the question. Jamie pestered her, but her mom said that she'd paid for both of the boys to play baseball, she'd paid for all that equipment, and that was enough.

"Roy got good enough to play for the high school team," Jamie said.

Her mom closed her eyes, measuring her words. "And that got us where? That came to what?"

Jamie stops tossing the tennis ball. She waves the cigarette smoke away. "Already tried asking. Remember?"

"Oh come on." Ashley laughs. "Tell her you wanna make some new friends."

Jamie fidgets with the tennis ball, squeezes it. "I don't need any fucking friends."

* * * * *

Mike usually has about three monitors on, each layered with an array of overlapping displays. He alternates among computer-animated images: American colonists in farm garb with muskets and pitchforks; red-coated British laden with ammunition and firepower. Winter camp in stunning realism: smoke rising from the embers of cooking fires; barefoot colonials in rags and bandages.

Mike's job is to define the behaviors of these characters amid changing circumstances. His clients produce computer games. Usually war games. They need Mike. They love him. They regard him, he's heard, as a unique, important, and hard-to-find resource. He approaches his assignments with calm confidence.

Right now, though, a stray thought hovers, gnat-like, and won't go away. *Goddamned Brad*, he thinks. He should have known better than to talk to Brad about work.

Desertion. Would these soldiers desert?

Well, of course: *duh*. Desertion happened. In the Revolutionary War; in all wars. No matter how compelling the cause, soldiers quit and went home. But his product—*why can't Brad get this?*—is a *computer* game. Computer games are fun. Players engage in combat and strategy. They do not care about morale issues.

Mike tries to reconstruct the tortuous path that led— somehow—to this horribly stupid *Brad* idea. At the pub they'd started out talking about Brad's softball coaching gig. Brad was pestering Mike to help him coach softball. He wouldn't let it drop. After they'd left their money on the bar, he continued to pursue it, from their barstools to the men's room urinals to the sidewalk outside, where they stood arguing under the streetlight. *"Come on,"* Brad said. "You don't want to deal with the girlfriend's-daughter issues? Fine: Don't coach that team. Help *me.* I need help. And it would be fun."

Mike grinned and held up his palms, impervious as always to Brad's circling and jabbing. He knew how to humor Brad.

But Brad was really irritated. "What is it with you? Can't step outside your little gated-subdivision life?"

What? Mike's neighborhood did not remotely resemble a gated subdivision.

"You're all set up, aren't you? Everything just *so* cozy comfortable and peachy."

"Well, yeah," Mike said. *This is weird*, he thought. It occurred to him that Brad was still sore at the world for losing his job, but there was no reason to be sore, since it had been his own decision to resign. Mike wondered if they should go back inside. Sometimes, things flowed better amid ambient chatter.

Brad kept pushing. "Why don't you just take a chance on something?"

This made no sense at all. *Take a chance? Take a chance?* What was he talking about—coaching softball for a few short months? They *were* talking about softball, weren't they? "Take a chance on *what?*"

"Why don't you—for once—just try something where you're not already an expert?"

Now, why would anybody do that? The way Mike saw it, Brad ought to stick to things where he *was* an expert. *Why don't you, for once, just try something real world? . . .* was the response that he chose to keep to himself.

"Even in your main gig you don't use your creativity," Brad said.

How would Brad know? Mike hunched against the chill of

the night, hands retracted inside his coat sleeves. The bar would be better for this. In the bar there was more freedom to toss insults: Words tended to land harder when there were just two of you in a narrow cone of light on an empty sidewalk.

"Everybody knows your video games are cool, and your job is glamorous and you're your own boss, but you're just so safe and unengaged."

Mike knew well enough to let Brad rant along, but he was utterly bewildered. "Are we still talking about coaching soft-ball?"

Brad continued his onslaught. "You just never get outside the formula zone, do you?"

That was correct. The formula zone was the comfort zone. It paid the bills. These, Mike explained, were mass-market games. Not indie movies. The object of the game was to win the battle. Kill the other guys. Mike's job was to shape behavior profiles of characters in combat. "It's not about philosophies and artsy stuff. You know? It's not about some soldier being reminded of home when he hears a warbler in the spring. It's not about some piano player guy getting his fingers blown off."

Brad seemed to be listening now, a bit less agitated.

"I'm freezing," Mike said. "Let's hit this another time."

Brad's e-mail—"re: desertion!"—came the next day.

Desertion. Think about it. You would have a more authentic and original game. Come on. Wouldn't some of your soldiers and warriors desert, or change sides, or at least think about it? Does that rock the boat too much? After freezing your butt for three months 'why am I here?' gets to be a tough question, doncha think? YOU should appreciate this better than anyone.

Mike looks over his ragged characters. Okay Brad, he thinks, why should *he* in particular appreciate this? And why,

Mike wonders, does he let this bother him?

He sizes up the colonial army. Sure, the prospect of desertion would probably change the campaign strategy. But it would complicate the game. His client would hate it. It's a long shot at best. So typical of Brad. When they talk sports, Brad constantly envisions successes that have no real chance. He especially likes the improbable story—some washed-up minor league pitcher regains his health after eight surgeries, learns a new pitch, makes a sudden splash. *Yeah right.* This is so . . . so *Brad.*

* * * * *

At the pub, Von hands Brad a rule book and a stapled handout. They've already held the pre-season coaches meeting, where league protocols are reviewed. Von tells Brad not to worry: It's all covered in the handout. "The one thing from the meeting that's not in there," Von says, "is that this is supposed to be a fun league. Teach the basics of the game, help the girls learn, let them have fun. It's not about winning."

The rule book is filled with fine print and codifications with letters and lower-case Roman numerals. This, Brad thinks, will take some review. His team will have to know the rules. *He* will have to know the rules.

He takes the rule book home. He studies it. At the kitchen table. At his desk. On the toilet. In bed. He tries to digest in small installments:

- Mercy Rule: Games are six innings long. If one team is winning by ten or more runs after four innings, that team is declared the winner, and the game is over.

- Ten girls play the field each inning. Four players must be positioned in the outfield. Regardless of who's playing in the field, the batting lineup includes every player, and remains unchanged for the entire game.

- Pitcher's circle: there's a white circle around the pitcher's slab. Runners on base cannot start to advance while the pitcher possesses the ball inside the circle.

And then there's the infield fly rule, the dropped-third-strike rule . . . the definition of a legal versus an illegal pitch.

It's a lot. Even for him. Certainly it will be a lot for the girls. Maybe they can go over a few rules at each practice. Practice: ninety minutes? Is that standard? What can they accomplish in ninety minutes?

He needs a plan. He takes up a pen and a yellow lined notepad.

Individual drills: ground balls, fly balls, maybe just long toss for a while. He wonders: Can he actually teach them how to throw better, hit better, catch better? Team drills: They need to understand cutoffs, where to throw the ball. They need to cover bases; they need to back up bases. How about sliding? Will he have to teach that? Bunting? Maybe just making contact at bat—maybe that will have to do.

Sheesh. Simplify: They need to know the rules.

Brad tears the sheet off the pad and crumples it into a ball. He sits, resting his chin on his hands. He needs an objective. As a coach. Truth be told, he'd just as soon win, but if it's not about winning he still wants to . . . accomplish. He wants to accomplish *something*. If he's going to do this, he needs to know why he's doing it. He will not allow another situation like he had at Rylix, where it all got fuzzy. Not that his livelihood is at stake this time. But still: At some level of understanding, the point of it all needs to be clear.

He squares himself at the notepad. "Rules," he writes. And then: "Improve."

Across the room, the television's showing some documentary about horse racing. He's not paying attention—it's horse racing—but he glances over for a moment and notices the grainy footage of some historic finish, all the jockeys flailing their whips, flogging the *crap* out of their horses and he wonders if this leaves marks on the horses, scares the horses, whether it makes the horses run faster at all, or just gives the jockeys something to do.

And then it comes to him: base running. Surely some of his players will be slow runners. No matter—the Marlins will know how to run the bases. Even the least-talented player, Brad reasons, can run the bases, alertly if not swiftly. Therefore, even the least-talented player can contribute. And base-running is not scary; it does not induce fear, as in the fear of striking out, or of failing to catch a fly ball. It's about awareness, which can be improved more easily, he thinks, than hitting or throwing. And finally, if they understand base running, it will help them—hopefully—understand the game.

He's happy with this thought progression. Then it occurs to him: He knows nothing about almost-teenage girls. He's seen them hunched to their cell phones like nodding pigeons. He's seen their blank, sealed-off expressions.

Well. He'll deal with them. He'll just be himself. Or, wait. He can't be too nice. He can't give and take; he can't explain nuances and exceptions and underlying reasons. He needs to be simple, with clearly stated rules.

Maybe they'll be afraid of him. Brad the all-seeing and imperious: dark shades, arms folded. Trucker's tug at the cap visor. Shoes: Coaches have special shoes, right? He recalls coaches in combat-ready black shoes with razor-ridged soles designed for the mud-eating, jeep-spattered rigors of *coaching*. Brad has a pair of tattered tennis shoes. They're *white*. They'll be fine. Right? Or not? Will they signal inadequacy? Invite ridicule?

It's very possible that he'll just suck at this; that he'll never command their attention. That his words will never make it to the far side of some vast chasm between them. He can picture a bunch of girls giggling and whispering among themselves while he explains drills. If they do, then what? *Girls, come on. Please.* Or, maybe a little sharper: *Hey, listen up!* Disciplinarian mode: *If you think it's funny, you can leave right now.*

He looks over the roster. Twelve names, in the order in which they were drafted. Brad focuses on first names.

1. Kelli
2. Jamie
3. Lissa
4. Emmie
5. Renni
6. Courtney
7. Maddi
8. Colleen
9. Ashley
10. Kacie
11. Lori
12. Meghan

He'll need to get off to a good start. He'll need to get past this uncertainty. The practice fields are still soggy, so the first few practices will be on a blacktop. Not good for hitting practice or infield practice. Good, however, for base running drills. It still gets dark early, so the first few practices will be short. For the first practice, Brad thinks, if he can introduce some base running drills, after that it might be enough to just throw the ball around and learn a few names.

Chapter 3
PAVEMENT

Brad shivers under two sweatshirts. Wind skids over the puddles on the blacktop. He makes a point of meeting the parents, mostly mothers wearing goggle-sized shades against the harsh slant of the sun.

The girls start tossing balls to one another. Some of them throw with their elbows snugged up against their ribs, like they're keeping their cell phones there while they throw. Most of them can catch. Some of them reach out, snatching at the ball before it gets too close. They giggle at bad throws: "Sorry." Balls bounce away over the pavement like eager puppies. Girls give futile chase until the balls come to rest, twirling slowly in icy puddles.

He counts the girls: ten. Out of twelve. He watches them, trying to match names with faces. There's one easy one: Kelli. She introduced herself to Brad, came up to him straight out of the car like a confident colleague. She was the top draft pick, assistant coach Diane's daughter. He looks for her, spots her in a red sweatshirt, light brown hair, tossing easily. Maddi, Stephanie's friend's daughter—Brad swivels his head to find her—she's the compact-looking girl with the dark complexion. She's throwing with a girl in a purple jacket, whose name is—Brad checks his list . . . Kacie. And in the blue ski jacket: Renni, who might miss a few practices for medical appointments, but who will be available most of the time.

Brad checks the time. He'll give it a few more minutes. And then it will be time to introduce himself and say something: Something.

As he waits, he introduces himself to a round and rather unathletic-looking girl: Lori. "Your Mom tells me you're new to this game."

She nods. Brad looks her in the eye. She seems mildly curious about him, as if he may or may not be a friendly extraterrestrial. She has a big horsey jaw and chubby cheeks, made pink by the wind.

"But you've been working on it, I hear."

She nods again. "I'm good."

"Let's throw a bit."

Brad lobs at first, gradually backing up to increase the distance between them. She snatches at the ball with one hand, but she catches it. She does not seem to be afraid.

Her throwing is not as good. She raises her arm up like a question mark, wiggles it about, and then casts the ball, which plops forward like a shot-putted raisin.

Brad talks to her about snapping throws: snapping at the shoulder, snapping at the elbow, snapping at the wrist. No brilliance imparted, but it feels okay: He's instructing. He's talking, demonstrating. Like a coach.

She tries again. The ball drops like a cork out of a pop-gun.

There's no *snap*—she doesn't connect that word with the act of throwing a ball. Brad flexes his arm and elbow back and forth, talking about snapping. Lori takes the ball and launches another weightless shotput, exactly as before. Brad feels his voice getting louder. He checks himself: It's the first practice. He remembers sitting at the table thinking about why he was coaching and what he wanted to accomplish, and right here he can see that he'll need patience, and then he remembers something about that horse racing documentary on the tube.

He takes off his belt. He holds it up for her. "This is a whip," he says.

Some of the other girls stop throwing to watch. Brad hears a few giggles. He's gained their attention. Which is good: He wants them to remember.

He takes the tip of the belt, flaps it against the pavement. "Wouldn't hurt much if I hit somebody like that."

Lori nods.

He push-tosses the whole belt to the pavement. "That wouldn't hurt, either."

He whips the pavement with it. The sound of it zaps the air. "But if you snap it, the end of that belt stings. And if you throw the ball like you're cracking a whip, you can make it go really far."

He hands the belt to Lori, urges her to "crack the whip" on the ground. Lori accepts it warily, glancing uncertainly at Brad.

He demonstrates how she can use her arm like a whip, snapping at every joint. "Go ahead," he says. "Hurt the ground."

Lori raises the belt and brings it down as fast as she can. The belt wags along behind. No miracle occurs. But on her second try she steps forward with her arm coming down more slowly at first, and then there's some slight snapping action, and the whip makes a sharp sound on the pavement.

The other girls gather to watch.

"Okay." Brad raises his voice. "Bring it in. Everybody."

The girls crowd around. The little huddle actually feels sheltering.

"Did everybody see that?"

Heads nod. About half of them have braces.

"Every one of you." He puts his belt on as he speaks. "Snap those throws. We'll work on that as we go along."

Maybe they think the whip thing is weird, but they seem to be listening.

"Thank you, Lori," Brad says. "You'll be fine."

They go around the huddle with introductions. Brad sets out objectives for the season: Have fun. The Marlins will have fun by (1) learning the game, (2) improving skills, and (3) always doing their best.

A hand shoots up. The dark-haired girl wears a serious expression, thin lips gripping each other.

Names tumble through Brad's head. He nods at her to proceed. "Yes."

"What about winning?"

"Yeah," Lori joins. "Are we going to win?" Brad looks at her; pink-faced, hopeful.

It feels like two different questions. Lori's question seems to be about what will *happen*. As opposed to . . . *Jamie*. That's it: Jamie. Jamie's question is about what they will *do*. "Well," Brad says. "If we can take care of what I just said—learning the game, improving skills and doing our best"—he surveys the faces—"then we'll see if we can win a few games, too."

The words twist away on the wind. Inside a gymnasium, the words would have sounded bigger. Possibly momentous. The girls shiver in their sweatshirts.

They start with a few simple throwing drills. The girls follow instructions.

Then it's time for a base running drill. Brad paces off an imaginary diamond, setting rags on the blacktop to mark the bases and the spot where the pitcher stands. He's taken great care to think through his instructions. He's written them down. He pulls out the folded piece of paper.

- *Coach stands in the pitcher's circle. A fielder stands on each base. Everybody else is a baserunner. The first runner starts at first base. The rest line up behind her. As long as the pitcher has the ball in the pitcher's circle, a runner cannot leave her base.*

- *From the pitcher's circle, the coach throws the ball to the fielders covering the bases. Fielders throw the ball back to the coach.*

He scans their faces. They're following his gestures; they seem to be paying attention. "When you're the baserunner," he says, "you have to look for opportunities to advance—to get to the next base. That's not just when the ball is hit." He reminds himself to go slowly. "When the other team is throwing the ball around—any time the other team throws the ball anywhere other than the runner's next base, it's an opportunity to advance." He moves to the pitcher's circle and points to first base. "So, if you're the baserunner and you're on first base and the pitcher—me—throws the ball to second base, that is *not* an opportunity to run. However,"—he holds up his index finger—"if the throw goes to third base, the runner on first has an opportunity to run to second. When you see an opportunity like that, *do not hesitate*. Run as soon as the ball leaves my hand."

Again he scans their faces. Their expressions give away nothing. Nobody wants to ask a question. He's doubtful of their comprehension. *Just start*, he thinks.

It takes several tries for each girl. With a runner on second, Brad throws home, listening for the patter of sneakers on the pavement behind him. He stops the drill several times to point out missed opportunities. Are they getting it? Do they think it's fun? It's about stealth, after all; a game of stealth. After just a few turns, he's pleased: Most of the girls are getting the hang of it. "A little quicker," he urges. "That's the right idea, just start going as soon as the ball leaves my hand."

He wants this to be automatic. "Any time you see that ball getting thrown around and it's not going to the base ahead of you, you're on your way to the next base. Don't wait for me to tell you."

For a last drill, they throw the ball around the rag-marked

diamond. Outfielders back up every throw: another habit to instill.

And that's it.

Brad calls them in. He quizzes them about a few rules: force-outs versus tag plays. Most of them know this one. Then, the dropped-third-strike rule, and he thinks it should be simple, but he talks slowly: "If you strike out and the catcher doesn't catch the third strike—or catches it after it hits the ground—you can run to first base."

Two rules: enough. He points his finger around the huddle, reciting names. Kelli's an easy one to remember, Lori's an easy one for him, since they've had some one-on-one interaction. That's Kacie in the purple, Jamie with the serious look, one of the more athletic ones. In the darkening parking lot, cars assemble: Time to quit. Not a bad first practice.

* * * * *

Diane was pleased when she received Stephanie's e-mail asking her to help coach Kelli's softball team. Back in high school, she'd been a sure-handed, scrappy third baseman. She's been throwing a ball around with Kelli since she was three, and she'd coached Kelli's teams in the lower levels. She's done with that. But yes, she offered that she could help out a little, and she also mentioned that her niece, Heather, would probably be willing to help out on the bench during games.

She couldn't make it to the first practice. Before the second practice, though, she and this new coach Brad arranged a "coach meeting" at Pitcher's Pub.

She identifies him at a high-top table along the paneled wall. Slight of build, sort of mild and studious looking, surprisingly youthful. No ball cap, no facial hair or stubble, no square-chested swagger. There's a bit of a substitute teacher look. She wonders how the girls will react to him.

She slings the strap of her bag over the corner of the

seatback. She decides to keep her leather coat on, slides onto the high stool beside the vintage photos and framed jerseys.

They have a lot to talk about. Brad wants to know how much the girls know. Can he assume that they all know the basic rules? Tagging up? Force plays?

"Assume that they don't know," Diane says. "If they already know, it won't hurt for them to hear it again."

A waitress takes their beer orders.

Brad asks for clarification on some rules. How soon can a runner leave the base when the ball is pitched? Do outfielders have to position themselves on the outfield grass, or can they sneak in to play shallow?

Runners are allowed to leave the base as soon as the pitcher releases her pitch. Outfielders must be positioned on the outfield grass.

He asks about how girls this age behave in practice.

She notes his manner: questions delivered in carefully wrapped packages. Which might be okay, but she's not sure how it will play: These girls take direction from the big barking voice. She brings her head forward, lifts her eyebrows. "They're girls and they will get gabby. You—we—just have to keep them busy."

Do they care about winning and losing?

Diane wags her head lightly. "Some do. A lot of them, though, won't know what the score is. It's not about winning and losing anyway."

"I get that," Brad nods. "I also—I might need to remind myself that it's also not about me."

Diane chuckles slightly, and then lets a broad smile unfurl. She leans back in her seat.

"Which means that it's about these girls," Brad says. "None of whom I know."

"Aren't you glad you got yourself into this?"

Brad's small whimper makes Diane laugh. The waitress sets down pints of beer and water. Brad asks about Kelli.

Kelli likes to win, Diane says. But mostly she wants to have fun. "Which is really what it's about. Have fun and learn the game. You know?"

Kelli will probably be the main pitcher, is Brad's understanding from Stephanie.

Diane shrugs. "Kelli can pitch. She should probably—she likes to play other positions, too, but she can pitch."

Brad knows nothing about the mechanics of this underhand "windmill" delivery. He's curious: How advanced are the pitchers? How advanced is Kelli?

Kelli can hit the strike zone with pitches travelling at a medium-fast rate. She's no Claire Boniface, Diane says, but last season in the younger "Minors" division she was probably one of the better pitchers. Like every pitcher, she has spells where she'll get off track.

Brad will have to learn about the softball pitching motion— the windmill delivery. Diane knows a little about it. Not a lot.

Brad nods thoughtfully. Diane can see him filing away mental notes.

"And how about you?" he says. "Did you play . . . high school? College?"

"High school." Diane can barely remember being an athlete. She can still fling it, but she's a little plump—not fat but no longer slim—and can't spring about the way she used to. She wonders if she still looks like an athlete. "Third base. I was no star, but I had my moments."

Brad gives credit: "But you played. Which means that you know the game."

"I guess."

"Were you . . ." Brad gestures uncertainly. "What were you best at?"

"Truth be told, I had a bit of a mean streak." She sees Brad tilting his head, weighing various interpretations, and she laughs, waving it away like a bad smell. "I just needed to make up for my deficiencies."

Brad smiles. There's one other thing he wants to know: Why are all the coaches *guys*?

Diane eyes a platter of nachos on its way to another table. "Dads like to coach. They like to be coaches. You know"—she stiffens into a manly pose—"*coaches.*"

Brad breathes out slowly. "Mansplainers?"

"Well." Diane looks up at the ceiling as she considers the word. "I guess you have to be. I mean, it's part of the gig. Like I said, when in doubt, assume that they don't know." She flicks at the air. "But anyway—as for moms? More moms coach in the younger age groups. They're more like party mothers." She glances at her beer. There's also the issue, she adds, of experience. Girls' sports weren't a big thing when these moms were kids. So, not many of them have played much softball.

Makes sense. Brad nods.

"By the way," she says, "what age level—do your kids play ball?"

Brad shakes his head. No kids.

Diane hesitates. She's heard about how Brad came into this coaching gig. The original coach, Stephanie, is his ex-wife.

"Stephanie adopted two kids," Brad says. "They're not mine."

Simple enough. Got it. Diane's feeling is that they can have a good season with this guy. "We'll have fun," she says. She lifts her glass. "To the Marlins."

"To the Marlins." Clink.

* * * * *

Practice number two: still on the blacktop. Windy again. Chilly again. The girls arrive and start tossing back and forth. Brad walks behind them, watching. He urges them to increase the distances between them. He wants them to get used to longer throws. Throws go astray, as they did at the first practice. He's not sure if it's less frequent or not.

He stops to watch Meghan. Spindly, freckly, wrists dangling in classic prairie dog posture. In correspondence, her mother indicated that Meghan is not a good player, but she's played before and likes to play catch. Brad can see, though, that Meghan wants to catch the ball with her pink glove facing upward, palm-to-sky. Elbows stiff, straining back to look away. Like she's catching a ripe melon from an upper-story window.

Brad takes her aside. He doesn't want to make too much of this right here in front of everyone, but he's afraid that a line drive might bounce into and out of the open pocket of the glove and hit Meghan's face. "Unless it's a low throw—below your waist—get that glove up; fingers up," he says. Meghan nods blandly. Maybe she's heard this before.

Once they get warmed up, they're back to base running. It's easy to see who can run and who picks things up quickly. Jamie is one of the bigger girls, very athletic. She might have a bit of an attitude, or maybe, with her dark hair pulled back tightly, she just naturally looks slightly cross about something. She gives short, grunting answers when Brad speaks to her. Yuh. Yuh. Head nod. *Is that all?*

Kacie and Lori have the hardest time with the base-running drill. Kacie—Brad notices that she's worn all purple for both practices—is chubby like Lori, but unlike Lori, who never sheds her pink-faced lost-in-a-dream smile, Kacie looks at Brad with a furrowed brow: *You mean, now? Me? Where?*

Several times, Brad listens for the sound of sneakers pattering behind him, but then turns to see Kacie still standing on her original base. "That was your chance, Kacie," he says. "If I throw the ball to one of these other bases, you need to run to the base ahead of you." He grins, reminds himself to stay loose. "Don't worry; you'll get it. Just get those purple shoes moving!"

Kacie nods, and her face shows signs of comprehension, but Brad's not sure if she understands the base-running concept or just the reference to her purple shoes.

On Jamie's turn, she advances alertly from second base to third, as instructed, as Brad throws to first base. Then, as the fielder throws the ball back to Brad, Jamie runs again, dashing across home plate. That's more than he's instructed them to do. Brad loves it. He loves the *way* she runs, like she's out to punish the fielders. He worries, though, that if the other girls start doing this, the drill might get crazy, with too many baserunners getting silly without really knowing what they're doing. "Great idea," he says, "but for now, stay put on the return throw."

"Okay."

He nods to himself slowly. "But you're onto something."

More of them start to get it. Head-nods increase in vigor. They get to a base and then get ready to go again, leaning toward the next base, hands resting on forward knee.

But Kacie—Kacie continues to hesitate. She waits, starts, stops, retreats to her original base—*her* base—and Brad can see that the base means *safety*: a raft amid unkind seas.

"Look," he raises his voice to address the group. "Always look for chances to run. Our team—the Marlins—we're going to run the bases *aggressively*. That means you're going to be tagged out once in a while. But we're going to make the other team *throw that ball*. And we're going to make them *catch* the ball. We'll give them as many chances to make mistakes as we can. I want you to learn judgment—I don't want you to wait for signals and commands. And I will never criticize any of you for running the bases aggressively."

"But—" Kacie raises her hand.

Brad nods "Kacie?"

She looks down, grins to herself. "Never mind."

He gives her a chance to say whatever it was. It occurs to him that Kacie is a lot less interested in becoming a baserunning heroine than she is in not getting tagged out. Maybe she doesn't feel confident about her speed, but he's *just said*—

or, no he didn't actually say it, but don't they *get it?*—that it's about alertness more than speed. The starkness of the contrast confounds him: In Little League baseball, he and his friends strove to be fearless and daring. They strove for glory; they strove to be big leaguers someday. The Marlins feel no such motivations.

He checks the time. They've taken ten minutes for warmup and long toss, fifteen for base running. It's time for cutoff drills.

He's taken pains to think of instructions that will be clear and simple. And precise. And not too long. Knowing how confusion will find its way, he's chosen just a few points of emphasis.

- *On long hits to the outfield, outfielders have to get to the ball as fast as they can, and then get it back to the infield.*

- *When the outfielders get to the ball, an infielder must present a "cutoff"—or relay—target for the outfielders to throw to.*

"Without a cutoff," he explains, "the outfielders have to figure out the correct base to throw to, and they have to make long throws, which are hard. This way"—he gestures at the empty blacktop with its rag bases and imaginary players—"the outfielder's throw to the cutoff is relatively easy, and then the cutoff player can make short throws to other infielders covering bases." He couldn't help elaborating. But it feels like a speech. He needs to wrap up, and then just start. He points to various spots on the blacktop as he reads from his written instructions:

On a ball hit to left field, the second baseman covers second base; the shortstop takes the "cutoff" position in the shallow outfield between second base and the outfielder throwing the ball. On a ball hit to right field, the shortstop covers second base and the second baseman is the cutoff.

There's more to it than that, but that's enough for now.

Brad stations players at the four outfield positions: left field, left-center field, right-center, and right. He makes the outfielders turn their backs to home plate and then scatters balls all over the outfield. The idea is that the outfielders will have to run to retrieve a ball, but without being able to see what's happening on the basepaths, they will have to rely on the infield cutoff players—correctly positioned, he hopes—to present obvious and easy-to-find targets. In the infield, he stations Colleen at second base, Maddi at shortstop, Jamie at third. He's getting their names down.

Ready? Okay. "Ball is hit deep . . . to . . . LEFT-CENTER FIELD!"

In left-center field, Lissa springs into action. She runs to the nearest ball, turns, straightens, and steps easily into her throw. From her position at shortstop, Maddi has ventured a short way into the outfield: She's the cutoff. She takes the throw from Lissa and looks to second base. Where she finds nobody covering.

"Okay. Colleen?" Brad points at second base. "That's your base on this play. Gotta cover that base."

Colleen is a serious but frail-looking girl, small enough that her baseball cap comes down over the outside of her ears. Dark hair, freckles. She's paying attention. "Got it," she says.

It's Renni's turn in the outfield. Renni: small and freckly like Colleen. She's poised to pounce, like she's found the perfect position for an ambush. She bounds eagerly after a ball in left field. Maddi runs out for the cutoff. Third baseman Jamie's also there; another cutoff.

Brad stops the play.

"Jamie. You're playing third base. Who's covering third?"

She turns around, sees the vacated base. Her face reddens.

"Girls. One cutoff. Don't confuse the outfielder. If you're not taking the cutoff, there's a base to cover. Gotta cover the bases."

Colleen stands on second base. Where she's supposed to be. "Colleen," Brad says. "If you're the baserunner, and you're coming around second base and nobody's covering third, what do you do?"

"Keep running."

"Correct!"

Jamie nods. "Got it."

He calls out hits to center field, right field.

"Coach?" Courtney raises her hand in right field. "What if I can just throw it to the pitcher?"

Brad nods, repeats the question, shouting so they can all hear. "Don't do it. From the outfield that's a long throw. Let's say the baserunner has just rounded first. If you throw the ball all the way from right field to the pitcher's circle, then the ball's in the air a long time and it's NOT going to end up at second base. So what would a good baserunner do?"

Silence.

"Hey—girls—let's say you're running the bases and you've just come around first base and the right fielder throws it all the way from right field to the pitcher. What do you do?"

A few seconds pass.

He starts to repeat the situation, louder, and then stops. He wonders if he's force-feeding, trying to do too much. He wonders why they don't get it. Somebody behind him says *"Oh,"* another voice says *"Um."* They're all looking at each other and Brad hears a few cautious voices, but it sounds like they're trying out a new foreign language until Renni boldly and impatiently presents the answer: "Go to *second!*"

"Thank you, Renni. That's why we need to throw to the relays—or cutoffs. Get the ball back into the infield. The cutoff fielder takes the throw, and now it's a short throw to second, short throw to the pitcher. That's how we keep that runner from advancing."

Next ball is to right-center field. Colleen's the cutoff. So, apparently, is Maddi, who joins Colleen in short right field.

"Maddi! Second base. Who's covering second base?"

"Oh." She grins sheepishly. "Yeah."

Third baseman Jamie raises her hand. She'd started toward second, then stopped. "If that happens, should I cover second?"

"No. You HAVE to stay at third. That's great alertness by you, but you have to rely on your teammates"—he gestures at Maddi—"to cover second."

On the next play, the girls position themselves correctly, but the throw from Kelli bounces away from Maddi and races, rabbit-like, for a patch of brambles at the edge of the blacktop. Colleen and Maddi give chase and start poking at the scratchy fortifications of shrubbery.

"It's okay," Brad calls. "*Leave it*. We'll get it later."

Two girls join the search.

"Girls—"

"We got it!" They hold the ball aloft in triumph.

The girls rotate positions.

Renni gets it. She gambols through drills, grinning— almost laughing—as she positions herself quickly and correctly every time. Brad remembers an e-mail from her parents about some medical issue that might get in the way this season. He watches her accelerate, change direction, grin. She's got an enormous glove—probably her dad's—that she uses to gobble up ground balls and snare line drives. She slings her throws with a confident hop, turns and lopes back to her position. She can play.

Next turn: "Right field!"

Courtney runs to pick up a ball. She runs with long, elk-like strides. She gathers a ball, cocks her arm, threatening and loaded to fire. Like a sharpshooter she scans the array of girls who might be waiting for her throw.

Then she repeats her survey: *eenie . . . meenie . . .*

"Gotta get that ball in! Courtney!" Brad says. "Is something confusing?"

"I wasn't sure whether to throw it to Renni or Lissa."

"Who's the cutoff?"

"Lissa."

"There you go. Throw goes to Lissa."

"But isn't she supposed to be in a straight line between me and second base?"

Lissa plays with her hair, twists herself around. She's positioned generally between Courtney and second base, which is correct . . . but she's not, Brad realizes, in an *exact* straight line. *Geez, it doesn't have to be EXACT . . .* "Lissa!" Brad jumps up and down, waving his arms over his head like he's signaling a distant ship. "Make yourself obvious! Beg for that throw!

"Girls!" he says. "No matter what you do, please do *not* hold the ball in the outfield. Get it in. From out there you're a long way from the runners and the bases. Get it in to where somebody can make a short throw to a base."

Courtney looks down and sighs. *Shoot,* Brad thinks. "It's okay, Courtney," he says. "We'll get this. This is why we're practicing it."

Time's up. They've been able to run just six repetitions. Not one was executed correctly. *Patience.* They haven't even had a practice on a real field yet. And besides, what difference does it really make?

Chapter 4
TREES

Just days before, the park grass was burlap brown. Almost overnight, a green singe has appeared. It's past dinner time, but the light lingers in the clear spring air. Joggers huff along the paths. Shouts and laughter drift over the fields. Basketballs spring off the court. High school dudes go three-on-three at one end, and at the other end an older guy shoots free throws.

Brad's seen this guy before. From across the field, Brad can identify him by his shooting form: There's a slight one-footed hop, and then, as he releases the shot, his non-shooting hand flicks backward along his side, like the follow-through on a swim stroke. He's good: Swish. Retrieve. Shoot: Swish. Retrieve. Shoot: Swish.

* * * * *

On the walking path ahead of him, a familiar figure moves along the edge of the forest, passes behind a tree, pauses, looks around.

"Mike!" Brad picks up his stride, then breaks into a jog.

Mike waits for Brad to catch up. "What are *you* doing here?"

"Well, *I* live here," Brad says. A block away, anyway. Brad has never run into Mike in the park before.

"I'm just"—Mike affects a theatrical tone—"taking the air."

"What a great time of year," Brad says.

Mike shifts from side to side, hands in pockets. He used to hate how long it took for spring to establish itself, he says. Now, though, he likes it, even with the muck and everything still dead in the woods.

Brad thinks about that. Okay. Sure. Plenty to like. He walks Mike to his car. As Mike gets into his car, Brad hoists an imaginary mug. "Pub?"

Not necessarily tonight, Mike says. But, soon. They're due for a couple. Mike buckles himself in and brings down the window. His client, he says, has just released their new computer game.

"War game?"

"Of course. That's all they make anymore."

"Really?"

"Not entirely. But that's where the money is."

"Deserters? Did you get them in there?"

Mike grimaces apologetically.

"Well," Brad says. "Next game, right?"

Mike chooses to not answer.

Brad's not completely serious, but it disappoints him that Mike won't even *consider* a new idea. Maybe, he thinks, it's because Mike hasn't exchanged a whispered syllable with his parents or siblings in ten years; he knows all too much about desertion. Brad stifles the thought. "I'm sure it's a great game," he says. "I guess these games don't have many characters who take behavior patterns from me."

Mike laughs. "Those ones always get killed early."

* * * * *

On a stretch of open field, a dad tosses a softball; gentle underhand deliveries to a girl with a bat. The mom catches, calling out encouragement in a high-low sing-song: *"There you go!" "That's it!"*

The father speaks more seriously. "Watch the bat hit the ball."

Brad smirks. *Huh?* Watch the *bat* hit the *ball?* He's heard this so many times and wondered how something so stupid could ever gain currency. How about: *"Keep your eye on the ball?"*

"Not like that," Dad continues. "Keep your hips back, and then rotate them when your hands are here." The dad demonstrates in slow motion, moving the bat slowly through an imaginary strike zone, talking fast about feet, hips, hands, arms.

The girl swings again, exactly as before.

A couple more pitches go by. The girl lunges at the ball—almost leaving her feet, landing on her front foot, with her back foot in the air. One good thing, Brad notes: She's going after it with bad intent; she wants to *smack* the thing.

"No . . . no . . . not like that," come the corrections. "Start with your shoulder higher. Line up your knuckles."

Brad can't hear the girl's response. Pitch after pitch manages to elude the shiny metal bat. After each pitch, she prepares for the next one, checking her knuckles, checking the bat position.

"Higher, get your back elbow higher."

Brad makes a mental count: Elbow, shoulder, knuckles, hands, hips. Is he *trying* to confuse her? Or is he simply trying to impress his wife—or maybe himself—with his technical expertise?

Brad stops and squints: It's Lori.

She's smiling, even as she seems to pay no heed to her father's instructions.

Swing. Miss.

"Watch the bat hit the ball."

Swing and miss. Swing and miss. Ground ball, back to the

pitcher. Swing and miss. "Sorry, bad pitch. My fault." Swing and miss. Foul ball, clipped onto the grass just to the side.

Dad begins to lose patience. "Listen buddy," he says. "If you want to get good at this, you need to listen."

Mom rises up to defend. "Honey. Maybe we can just let her—she'll figure it out. She's just having fun. Let's just—"

"It'll be more fun if she's good at it," Dad snaps. He pauses to recompose, then continues with the girl. "If you want to learn how to hit the ball, then you have to do what I say. You can't just do the same thing over and over. You need to *listen*."

"Lori," Brad calls.

She glances over, recognizes Brad. "Oh. Hi."

"Hey!" her mom shouts.

They've met. Brad scans his memory for her name. Lauren, he thinks. Lorraine, possibly.

"Just who we were looking for!" she cries.

The dad gives a sullen look.

Brad waves and moves quickly to introduce himself to . . . "Brian."

"I love this," Brad says, nodding in Lori's direction.

Brian stands a little stiffly, flicking the ball into his glove. "She seems to like it okay."

Brad calls to Lori: "What's your favorite part of this game?"

She swishes the bat back and forth. "Catching. Hitting."

"How come you didn't play before this year?"

"I don't know."

Brad looks at Brian, who shrugs. "It just never occurred to her. And she"—he lowers his voice—"there are some issues to consider with her."

Brad is not ready to get into that. He looks from one parent to the other. "Mind if I put in my two cents?"

"You're the coach," Lorraine says eagerly.

Brad walks to Lori, keeping his voice low. "Let's keep it simple," he says. "First, I love it that you're really hacking at that thing. That's what you're doing right."

Lori studies her knuckles gripping the bat.

"Now," Brad says. "Two things. Only two things. Number one: Keep your eye on the ball. Look only at that ball. Second: snap your wrists. That's what makes your bat go fast. Which is what makes the ball go far."

Brad demonstrates a few swings, comparing the quick swing driven by wrist snap versus the lazier, looping swing driven by outstretched, arcing arms. He wants her to understand: The wrist snap is what makes the bat go fast. He pauses. He wants to tell her not to lunge after the ball, but stops himself: *two things.*

Lori smiles as Brad hands the bat back to her.

He lingers for a few pitches. She lunges, misses. He offers a few reminders as the pitch count rises. *Good eye. That one was outside.*

"Sorry," Brian calls. "My bad."

Lori gets in a few good swings, along with some not-so-good swings. A ground ball shuffles over the turf. The next pitch comes in over her head; she lunges and swats. Brad moves his hand in a chest-high plane. "Remember: The strike zone ends here. Those high ones are close to your eyes, so when the ball looks big and tempting, it's probably too high."

She nods, and this time she looks Brad in the eye. On the next pitch she raps a line drive over her dad's head. Lorraine yelps enthusiastically. "There you go!" Brian says as he watches the ball land.

Darkness is creeping in, welling up under the trees. Brad realizes that he's interrupting their family time. He nods at Lori's parents. "You keep working on it, Lori. I bet you'll get some good hits this year."

"Hang on." Brian motions him over. He wants to know what Brad was telling Lori.

Brad explains: She might keep it a little simpler for a while.

Brian looks at Lori, who's swishing her bat at bugs. He

looks back at Brad, one eyebrow raised. "You play a lot of ball?"

Brad shakes his head. "Not really."

"Any?"

"Little League, a year of Seniors. A lot of rec league softball."

Brian considers this.

Brad returns the question.

"I played in high school. Third base and center field."

"You were a *real* player," Brad says.

"So . . . How'd you get yourself into this gig?"

It's a long story: Brad gives him the quick version.

"So you're subbing?"

Yes.

"For Conner."

"Do you know him?"

"Oh, sure," Brian says. "Great guy. He'll be a heck of a coach. Once he gets freed up from this biotech deal over across the pond."

"How do you know him?"

Originally through work. Brian's a venture capital guy. Mostly biotech startups. His firm provided some late-round funding for Conner's company. He shakes his head, grinning. "Poor Conner," he says. He's trying to salvage a mess of a deal. Conner stepped in, Brian says, when the deal was falling apart, and he's over there trying to rally the troops with the shit flying all over the place.

"I don't envy that," Brad says. He is eager to avoid any discussion of biotech deals or biotech companies. Or Conner.

"Anyway, Conner's played some serious ball. He'll bring a ton of experience. And he's a great guy."

Brad nods at Lori. "Well, he's got a good group of girls to work with."

Brian nods. "I appreciate your making time for this."

They shake hands. "Gotta go!" Brad calls to Lori and

Lorraine. "Great job, Lori. Keep at it!"

He walks on in the dimming twilight.

* * * * *

When he gets home, Mike checks his new photographs. There are a few dozen.

He thumbs at the photos on the smartphone screen. Trees. Clumps of trees. Dark stumps. Fallen limbs. Smooth bark; rough bark; gyrating shapes. He finds a few striking poses, a few interesting perspectives.

Back in the fall he'd bought a sketch pad, a box of vine charcoal, an assortment of drawing pencils, and a gum eraser. He's been sketching most every night for about four months now. He fills the sketch pad with swift, carefree strokes, tortured scrawls, delicate pencil lines. He roughs out shapes, blocks in dark areas, smudges with his fingers, cross-hatches, erases.

There's something about the late winter forest. This time of year, the trees are not just trees. They are rotted stumps, flailing limbs, fallen soldiers, neighbors squabbling, bitter intertwined couples stabbing the ground. Winter, he thinks, is when the trees really show themselves.

In just a few weeks, though, from the cranky and crooked joints, new buds and shoots will emerge in a gassy, olive gold haze. The haze will curdle; the tangles will simplify. Shapes will start to make sense. From random and ragged, they'll transform to bristling and uniform, ready for parade grounds.

He needs time in the woods before that happens. If drawing, as they say, is all about seeing, then he needs to get out in the woods and see.

He doesn't understand this interest—this new fascination: What *is* it about the bare forest? He contemplates the question as he thumb-flicks through his photos. Every tree seems twisted and broken; cadavers wading in the scabby debris of the forest. But each one manages to keep growing in its own odd and defiant way. Mike imagines that each tree is trying— straining—to get back to the form that it would have taken if only it had been planted in a planned arboretum landscape, then nurtured by arborists: if it could be the tree that it was *supposed to be.* If such a thing could be imagined.

Chapter 5
MOTIVATION

It's Phil Braden's tenth year coaching girls' softball. He knows what he's doing. He knows details of the game that are often overlooked. And he loves it. Even with the frustrations and the bewildering behavior of young girls who don't understand the game, he loves it. He loves the process: instilling fundamentals, teaching the game, deploying strategies, and— probably most important of all—motivating girls.

Phil knows all the girls. He's coached them or coached against almost all of them.

This year he has Claire Boniface as his pitcher. Claire is a bona fide star, a big athletic girl who loves softball and works at it year-round with a personal coach. She is one of the rare ones who might someday go on to play college ball.

Over the winter Phil spoke to Claire's mother, Joanne. He ran into her in the produce section of the grocery store. She was prodding at a nectarine, peering over the top of her reading glasses.

Phil was not surprised that Joanne knew who he was. She seemed pleased that Phil was interested in Claire.

"I'd love to coach her," Phil said. "And I think I can help her." He hesitated. "Do you or your husband have any interest in coaching?" If so, she or he could be Phil's assistant. That would put Claire on his team.

Joanne was divorced.

"Oh, sorry," Phil said. "Well, do *you* have any interest in coaching?"

"Me?" Joanne let out a spluttering laugh. She had no experience, no knowledge, and no interest. She paused. It was possible, she said carefully, that if the team really needed somebody, her boyfriend might be interested. Mike had a hectic schedule, but he might be persuaded to help out to some extent.

"Does he live with you?"

Joanne interrupted her nectarine inspection, eyed Phil over the top of her glasses.

"None of my business," Phil said quickly. But, he explained: Daughters of head coaches and assistant coaches were assigned to their parents' teams. Mike was not Claire's father . . . but if Mike were a part of Claire's *household*, that just might be sufficient.

* * * * *

Over the winter, Brad used his idle time to brush up on his investment skills. He's been managing his IRA investments, along with some brokerage account money, for a good fifteen years. During that time he's accumulated knowledge and experience and achieved some success. He's sifted among various approaches and identified a few principles that have helped him understand the value of companies. He's had disappointments, but he is proud to have completely avoided disasters like Enron. During the Great Recession, he was able to stomach a couple of sickening losses without selling, and he picked up a few names that he'd been tracking for years. His investment accounts swelled, putting him on track for a comfortable retirement—if he doesn't spend down too much during this dismal period of unemployment.

He's done particularly well with biotech stocks. Here, of course, he brings personal knowledge. He knows people. He knows some of their businesses. He knows what he's doing.

Over the winter he undertook a full review of his holdings, at the same time prowling through literature for new ideas. He read through SEC filings and spent weeks researching the industries and their competitive landscapes. He did not fully grasp the nuances of balance sheets and pension plan obligations, but he set up a course of study for himself, and learned how to flag and understand the important issues. Much to his surprise, he enjoyed it.

The winter went by, intermittent snowfalls followed by spattering rains. Broken branches and plastic bottles nested atop the street drains. Brad spent the bleak days by the window, hot cocoa in hand, poring over annual reports, reconciling balance sheets with cash flow statements. He watched the white flakes plummet and drift, wondering if anything was going to stick. It occurred to him that he might parlay this pastime—investment—into a new career. But it seemed so far removed from anything he'd done before. So far removed from the mysteries of cells and proteins and the workings of the human body. So far removed from how he thought of himself. He wondered if that might be a good thing.

* * * * *

The fields have dried at last. The ball makes a frizzy, rug-burn sound as it skips over the turf. The Marlins will hold practice on a real softball field.

Emmie has missed three of the first four practices. She's not completely sure that she even wants to play, but she'd insisted on it and now her parents will not be happy if she wants to quit. The truth, she realizes, is that they might have been right: There are plenty of reasons not to play. She doesn't know much about the game. She's never played before. She goes to a small private school and doesn't know anybody on the team, or maybe even in the league. With the school play and gymnastics every day, she's got too much going on.

But this was *her* choice.

Coach Brad takes her aside at the start of practice. He needs a favor. "Would you remind your parents to watch for e-mails and let me know when you can and can't be here?"

Emmie nods.

Coach explains that he has to plan out drills and practices and it's hard to do that if you don't know how many players to expect.

Emmie nods and turns toward the field to warm up.

"Emmie."

"What?"

"So will you please remind them?"

"I said 'yes'."

Coach Brad looks at her, head tilted.

"I'll remind them," Emmie says.

She can see that Kelli and Jamie are good players. Especially Jamie. She throws the ball hard. She likes her throws to make that loud popping sound in the other girl's mitt. When they practice batting, Jamie swings hard; it looks like she wants to *hurt* the ball. She takes every drill seriously and runs as hard as she can. She doesn't gab with the other girls, except once in a while with her friend Ashley.

Ashley, on the other hand, can play a little bit, but when Coach Brad talks to the team, she plays with her hair, chews gum—she seems to really *work* on it because her face makes all these stretchy contortions—and blows bubbles.

Emmie knows she shouldn't judge too quickly, but she's taken an instant dislike to Lissa, who constantly fiddles with her earrings and her hair. Lissa thinks she's pretty. But could she please leave her hair alone for two minutes? And those shiny dangly earrings: It looks like she's listening to them, the way you're supposed to listen to conch shells that somebody brought home from their beach vacation. At the same time, Emmie can see that Lissa is a pretty solid player. She catches every throw, and she can throw it all the way across the diamond from third base to first.

From her one practice, and after playing catch with a few other girls, Emmie is relieved to find that she won't be the worst player. She'll be better, she thinks, than at least some of them. Like Kacie, the girl who always wears purple. Kacie can throw and catch and even hit a little bit, but she doesn't get the base-running and either she isn't paying attention or she might have one of those attention problems.

Lori is not very coordinated, but at least she tries. She can't hit—she keeps taking these wild swings like a blindfolded second-grader going after a piñata—but she actually catches the ball most of the time.

And then there's Meghan. Coach reminds her over and over to get her glove fingers up. Emmie sees what he's talking about, how Meghan always tries to catch with the *palm* of her glove facing up. Meghan nods her head like she understands, but she won't do it. Emmie's seen this before, in gymnastics and in other sports: Kids are afraid to try something different, so they just keep doing it their own way and eventually the nagging goes away.

Emmie worries about how well the Marlins will do, but she takes comfort in seeing that she's not that far behind, and maybe even a little ahead of some of her teammates. Also, Emmie can follow what Coach Brad says. All the drills about where to throw: It makes sense that you need to know what you're going to do *before* the ball is hit. She finds herself getting impatient when Kacie or Lori or Meghan don't get it, but then she reminds herself not to be that way.

At her first practice, Renni asked her why she'd decided to play after not playing before, and she said, "Because it's fun. I hope."

Renni laughed. Renni always seems to be thinking of some

funny secret joke. She reminds Emmie of that "thing" character in Dr. Seuss books. "For someone who's never played," Renni said, "you're doing great."

"Thanks," Emmie said. Emmie knows that she's athletic. She'll pick it up quickly enough. And there's no pressure. That's the best part.

* * * * *

Brad keeps Kelli after practice to work on pitching. Brad has asked around, watched some YouTube, checked out a library book called *Softball Pitching: Secrets of the Windmill.*

Kelli's happy to stay late. If she's going to pitch, she says, she needs the practice.

They begin with some simple warmups. Then Brad introduces a few wrist-flick exercises and striding routines. Kelli tries them and nods cooperatively. Her motions are fluid and instinctive. She looks well-accustomed to playing fields, comfortable in sweats and cleats, brown hair in a perpetual ponytail. She's got the sturdy, semi-bow-legged walk of a boy jock.

She starts to pitch. Her pitches have a bit of an arc, but they're faster than Brad expected. She bounces a pitch now and then, but most of the time she's around the strike zone.

Pretty good. What would she like to work on?

She tosses the ball into her glove a few times as she thinks. "Everything. Throwing faster. Throwing strikes more consistently."

Brad has a few minor suggestions. She's been starting her windup with her feet together. Brad wants her to start with her feet about shoulder-width apart. That way her delivery starts from a balanced base.

She nods. Simple enough.

Next, he asks how she grips the ball. She hasn't thought much about that.

"For now, just try to be aware of how you're holding it. If you want, try adjusting it; try your fingers on the seams in different ways. Just to see what works. See what feels good."

Kelli resumes her pitching. After about twenty pitches, she seems to lose her feel and starts firing bouncers in the dirt. Brad picks some of them up on the short hop. Some of them skid by.

It's better to miss too high than low, Brad says. Batters will swing at high pitches. Low pitches look far away, and if they hit the dirt, both batter and umpire know for sure that it's a ball. Plus, they're harder for the catcher to catch. Finally, since the pitcher releases the ball low—just off her hip—a ball traveling upward has a bigger change in its elevation, and that makes it harder for the hitter. He's talking too much.

The next three pitches skip in the dirt. Brad scoops two of them; the third one bounces crazily and whacks him in the shin. Brad has told himself to never show pain; he doesn't want girls to think it hurts and become afraid of the ball. But he can't help it: He slumps forward, shuddering.

Kelli stomps on the ground.

"It's okay," Brad gasps. Deep breath. The pain starts to subside. "This isn't easy," he reminds her. When she misses low, he says, it's probably a problem with the release point. They may tinker with strides or wrist snaps or follow-through, but the release point will be the hardest thing. He stands up, cautiously puts weight on the leg.

"Are you okay?" Kelli asks.

Brad nods, holds up his hand. He'll have some ideas for next practice. He'll think of something.

*　*　*　*　*

After dinner, with the dishwasher running, Brad stands in his kitchen, trying to envision Kelli's delivery. Trying to match it with all the terms and sequences he's been learning. In order to teach this windmill motion, he has to be able to demonstrate it. He tries to step through it in slow motion. He stops, glances again at the difficult sketches in the book.

It's like trying to learn the Lindy Hop blindfolded. He struggles to splice the sketches together into a flowing image; to understand the coordination among the moving body parts. He starts and stops and starts again, going slowly, picturing the movements. *Okay. Now fast.* His hand, windmilling upward, connects with a chairback. *Jesus Christ!* His fingers buzz like angry hornets. On inspection, he's almost disappointed that there's no blood. Blood would have validated the pain.

What am I doing? This is ludicrous. If he can just hang on for a few weeks, Conner will come riding in to save the day. Riding gallantly: university-logo ball cap on handsome head. Brad builds the shining hero image sarcastically. Bitterly. His thoughts about Conner, though, remind him that he does know somebody who knows about softball pitching.

Steph:

Sorry to bug you. It's about this mess that you got me into. I'm trying to teach girls how to pitch. I've been reading about it but it's a little overwhelming.

Here's what I've been "teaching": start with feet apart for good balance; stride toward the plate; swing the arm in a straight 'arm slot' that goes up and around and then almost brushes against your leg; understand that during the delivery the shoulders should start facing forward, then "open" to face to the 3b side and then come back square to home plate.

My main pitcher wants to throw harder, and I do not know how to help with that. Can you help me?

Thanks (a lot)
Brad

PS—and btw when's Conner coming back?

Her reply comes almost immediately.

Brad:

Where'd you learn all that? Sounds like you're on the right track with your pitcher—pitchers? Don't give them too much at a time. Release point will be the hardest part. One thing to remember is that it's not always a good thing to focus on "I'm going to throw a strike"—it's usually more helpful to be aware of the mechanics of your delivery—what your arms and legs and wrist and torso are doing. That's not an easy thing, but if you can help them be aware of their mechanics that can help a lot.

As for speed, your pitcher should just concentrate on throwing strikes first, get her delivery down. Once she's good with that, she should just do the delivery a little faster, and push off harder.

It won't be easy. You'll need a lot of patience. Btw I don't mind e-mailing about this stuff.

Steph

PS—Not sure about Conner. Things look pretty hectic. I'm not expecting him back for at least a few weeks.

* * * * *

Practice is just starting. The first girls arrive, and Brad gets them to warm up as they chat. He finds Courtney and they start tossing. Brad throws it; Courtney catches it. Her return throws thump into Brad's glove; he doesn't have to move it. With each throw he steps a little farther away.

"That's too far," she complains.

Brad considers this as he gets ready to throw. "Courtney," he says. "You're doing great. These throws are not hard for you."

She slumps forward, exasperated.

Brad throws. Courtney slings it back. It smacks solidly in his glove. "Great throw."

Ground balls: She catches them. Her long strides look lazy, but it's just her way; she can cover some ground.

Fly balls: She wavers unsteadily as she settles under them, but she catches them, using both hands.

"Looks like you can play just about anywhere," Brad says. "What's your favorite position?"

She doesn't know. First base. Second base. Right field. "I like it on the right side of the field."

Huh? "How about shortstop?"

"I can't play there."

"How about third base?"

She looks down, shakes her head. "I don't think so."

"You caught everything I threw you. Can you make a running catch on a fly ball over your shoulder?"

She shakes her head at the apparent lunacy of the thought. "Nooo."

"Neither can anybody else. Let's try a few."

"But I can't."

"Courtney."

"I *can't*."

"Yes you can."

"Really. I can't."

The other players arrive.

Brad runs them through infield drills, hitting, and cutoff drills. Then it's time to go over rules. For today he's picked a hard one: *When's the play over?* The girls look at each other. He sees a hand raised and then withdrawn. "The play is over," he says, "when the pitcher has the ball in the pitcher's circle, or when the umpire calls 'foul ball' or 'dead ball' or 'time out.' Until one of those things happens"—his hand cleaves the air for emphasis—"the play is not over. Until one of those things happens, you're still playing."

At the end of practice, he introduces a new drill: over-the-shoulder running catches.

Courtney sags in protest.

Brad makes it as simple as he can. Line up next to him. Run away from him. He will loft throws ahead of them, leading them, so they have to keep running to catch it over their shoulders. As he describes the drill, he sees their mouths open, faces crinkled in confusion, or maybe despair.

He decides that, for their first turns, they will line up like football receivers and run at a slant, which feels a little easier. He asks if any of them watch football, if they've seen receivers make running catches. Nobody raises their hand. No matter.

They take their turns. He finds himself trying too hard to make easy throws, calling out "bad throw" when they don't catch it. Only Renni and Colleen manage to catch their throws. The second time through, Jamie and Courtney catch it, but most of his throws land on the ground.

But Brad *knows* they can do this. He stops the drill. "All right," he announces. "I'll have something—some small gift—for you at the next practice—"

What? Like what? Candy? Let's get ice cream!

"—if Courtney—right now—can catch one over her shoulder, running full speed, straight away from me."

The pretty-please pleading drops off. The girls look thoughtfully at Courtney.

Courtney shakes her head, starts to protest, but Brad

wants none of it. "You can do this. Courtney. You can do this."

"But I . . . can't . . ."

"Yes you can. Courtney. This is not punishment. You have a chance to win something for your teammates, and if you don't catch it—hey, nice try, no harm done."

She sighs in resignation. She readies herself. Okay.

"You can do it," someone says.

Courtney starts running, about half-speed, looking back at Brad, then turning around to face Brad, running backwards.

"Courtney." Brad motions her back, to start again. "Run forward, away from me, show me your back. While you run, look back over your shoulder. Just look for the ball," he tells her. "Don't try to peek at your glove."

"Why can't I look at my glove?"

Brad's ready to throw. He stops. "Courtney. Do you look at your glove when you play catch?"

Courtney thinks about that.

"Come on. Just look at the ball. Your hand will know where to go."

The girls watch. "Come on Courtney, you can do it."

She starts running, a little faster than half-speed. He can't make it too easy. He lofts a casual throw over her head. A bit too far.

She runs; she sees the ball; she's getting under it; closing on it. As she reaches for it, she sneaks a look at her glove, taking her eye off the ball. At the last moment she lunges slightly. Running girl and ball trajectory converge. The ball contacts the palm of her glove—and a few cheers discharge as the ball bounces to the fingers of the glove . . . and then out.

A collective groan goes up, quickly overtaken by protest. *That was too far! That wasn't a good throw! She had it in her glove! Let her try again! Let me try!*

Brad thinks: Compromise. Great try, maybe not the greatest throw. "I tell you what. Next practice, I'll have something for the team. It won't be any super *grand* prize, but that was a good enough try that I think you won something."

Cheers erupt. He sees a fist thrust in the air.

All for the promise of an as-yet unidentified treat. Brad remembers the T-shirt Von told him about: *It's all about the ice cream.*

Brad pats Courtney on the head. "I bet you would have caught it if it had been a Klondike bar, or maybe a candy bar."

She smiles. "I love Klondike bars."

"What's your favorite treat?"

"Gummi . . . uh . . . maybe Skittles."

"You gonna catch a bag of Skittles?"

"Do I get to eat them?"

"Sure."

Certainty emerges: "I'd catch a bag of Skittles if you threw it over a *cliff*."

"Over the shoulder?"

Yup.

Renni chimes in: "Would you catch it if he threw it over a snake pit?"

And others: *What if he threw it over boiling slime? What if it was like a whole bag of Reese's? How about . . .*

For Brad, it's a relief: They're not too grown-up or too cool for this. He snaps his fingers, points at Courtney. "Next time, Courtney," he says. "Bag of Skittles."

* * * * *

Home Depot: Brad steers the cart, heavy with fertilizer and eight bags of mulch. He navigates the parking lot, opens the back of the car, then whumps the heavy bags in.

A woman retrieves a shopping cart from the cart station. Two girls stand by, huddled over cellphones, unaware that they're blocking the woman from extracting the cart. Something about the woman looks familiar. She scolds impatiently: "Girls, you need to move so I can—"

"Hey." Brad waves. "Colleen!"

The three of them start toward the store. The cart rattles loudly over the pavement. Brad calls out again; he's pretty sure it's Colleen.

Colleen's mother looks back; recognizes Brad. She stops to smile and wave. She bends down to Colleen, gestures toward Brad. Colleen follows instructions; looks up from her phone. "Oh." She sees him. "Hi." She waves, and then resumes her cellphone interactions.

Chapter 6
ODDS

It happened back in November. Rylix was feeling the heat, in the lab and on the balance sheet. The company needed capital. They needed to show progress. Backers and partners were losing patience. The company started eliminating promising new projects in favor of treatments that made incremental improvements to existing medicines. The ability to attract immediate cash infusions—preferably from major pharmaceutical companies—was what drove decisions. Rylix, it seemed, was no longer about science, or discovery.

Every eliminated project dealt a blow to Brad and his team. Their ideas were their babies. They believed that they could find their way to the answers. The money would follow.

On Friday afternoons they gathered at the brewpub, where they drank craft IPAs and sneered at the prospective partners; these big pharma companies that had hit it big fifteen years ago selling pills that helped kids lose their zits or something. Now they fiddled around with new flavors for the pills, or half-doses or new bottle caps, or Version II and then fast-acting and then Version III Extra Strength.

Nobody on Brad's team wanted any part of that. They were all about new science. They were about innovation. They were about new medicines that would ease pain and cure disease.

Before any of that happened, Brad got fired. Technically, he resigned. But he got fired.

The globetrotting Rylix executives had finagled a series of meetings with a company based in France. It got picked up in the gossip around Biotech World corridors, and it made sense. Except, Brad knew, the French partners were under false impressions about one of the key drugs in Rylix's pipeline. Rylix had actually shut the project down, but when it attracted interest, that changed quickly. As did the results of an early-stage trial. Not the actual results, but rather the recipe of molecules administered. It was a minor change. But Brad knew.

The French pharma sent a team to tour Rylix's lab. Brad said nothing about the altered tests. But somebody did. Red-faced Rylix executives leaped to their phones to squelch the "false rumor."

Brad knew who had spoken. But he could not bear the thought of Mia losing her job for telling the truth, for doing the right thing. He should have been the one. He was the team boss. And he was the one who, in some sloppy happy hour conversation, had let it slip: If he'd kept his mouth shut, she never would have known. So he stepped forward, claiming responsibility for the statement.

The merger fell through. And Rylix was in trouble.

Rylix handled Brad's resignation in the media with smooth public relations, in the office with shunning shame. In the aftermath, among the company executives, he heard only from Lou Disetovich, the COO. Lou said he was sorry; he knew what the company was losing. But. "Damn, Brad. It's what I've been trying to tell you. All the political BS—okay, maybe it's stupid, maybe even dishonest, but you gotta deal with it and you just wouldn't. You play that game, just a little, and your friend Larry Tarlton bails you out of this mess. But you never played."

It certainly was stupid, Brad thought. Some of these

assholes didn't know DNA from RNA, and yet there they were, acting knowledgeable; getting loud and critical like drunken slobs in an art museum.

"You can't dismiss it," Lou said. "Those guys know their part of the business and it happens to be a big part of the business. The money's gotta flow. If those guys don't bring it in, we're done. You didn't want to get with the program, so this had to happen."

Brad had not expected to feel so wounded and lost.

Only Mike could see it. And so, on an unseasonably warm late-autumn evening, Mike invited Brad to his condo. They set two directors' chairs on the little balcony with a view of the river through bare trees. They propped their feet up on the metal railing and drank cans of Dale's Pale Ale. The crank and pop of opening cans broke the stillness of the evening.

"I'll have more time for hockey," Brad said.

Sure. There was that, Mike agreed.

"You should play," Brad said.

Mike made a sour face.

"You were good."

"I'm not good now. And what would be the point?"

"There's no *point*." Brad regretted the edge in his tone. "It would be fun."

Mike didn't reply. A great blue heron winged silently toward the river, a dark silhouette against the twilight sky.

Brad was going to take some time before jumping back into a new job.

Mike thought that was a good idea. His suggestion was to get out of biotech.

Brad shook his head. It's what he did. He'd chosen it.

"Unchoose it," Mike said.

Brad fell silent. Once upon a time, he'd loved his work. He still loved the *idea* of it. He loved the processes: envisioning new medicines, designing experiments. Observing the behaviors of protein molecules; figuring out how to teach them new tricks. Even the delivery systems: They required a sort of creativity that was almost as fun as the development of the medicine itself. Staggering potential sparked their imaginations and hovered behind every project. *That* was what it was all about.

"Okay. But. Tell me something." Mike took his feet down off the rail. "How many of these drugs ever get to market?"

Different numbers got tossed around. Not a lot: one out of three hundred. One out of three thousand. Depending on how you counted the denominator, which might be projects that actually made it into pre-clinical testing, or just nice ideas that had just survived some initial scrutiny.

Mike let out a low whistle.

Brad felt like he should explain. Many—most—biotechs didn't bring drugs to market; they researched and formulated drugs and therapies. Which brought in new capital, which provided licensing rights, partnership rights, shared revenue streams. Or sometimes their knowledge just created value, to be realized when the whole company got bought by some big pharma company. Those were the companies that actually brought medicines to the market.

"Gotcha. It sounds like the whole industry is about failing. Or at least, not about succeeding," Mike said. "Not the greatest setup for you."

It wasn't about failing, Brad said. It was about possibilities.

Mike nodded slowly. And Brad knew what he was going to say. That Brad was talking about *potential*. Once again: minor league pitching prospects, vegetable gardens, drug discoveries. That Brad loved potential; that Brad *protected* potential.

But Mike said nothing. The dusk thickened. The last light shimmered on black water. Windows lit up in the buildings along the river.

"Shit." Brad slumped forward, examining his beer can. "Seems like everything. Is about failing."

Mike weighed possible responses. He looked out over the

dark trees. Brad's comment had started as a casual toss, but then a few words might have gotten a little stuck in some constricted passageway.

Brad plowed on. "Yup," he said. "About." He tucked his chin down against to his chest. "Failure."

"Remember," Mike said gently. "*You* were the one who didn't have your head up your ass."

Brad knew this. But he was not wanted, and it stung.

"You resigned, remember?"

Brad remembered. But he also remembered the punched-in-the-stomach grimness of that day. He remembered turning in keys and badges. Finding his desk emptied out. A few paper clips, loose pennies and sticky notes presented the only evidence of Brad. Boxes packed and stacked. It had been his choice. It hadn't felt like it.

Chapter 7
WHY COACHES COACH

It's a bright April day: a day for dark shades and windburn. A regatta of high clouds maneuvers smartly in a spanking breeze. The schools are on spring break. With many of the girls away with their families, three coaches have agreed to combine teams for a joint practice.

Phil Braden introduces himself to Brad. They shake hands and start comparing their outlooks for the season. Brad nods along, keeping an eye out for arriving Marlin players.

The girls have taken positions in the infield, fielding ground balls from Phil's assistant, Bruce, who slaps ground balls and shouts instruction with a drill sergeant's bark.

"I'm still sort of wondering why I'm doing this," Brad says.

Phil points his finger emphatically at Brad. "That," he says, "is a very important thing.

"What is?"

The first thing every coach *must* know, Phil says, is why he's coaching. It is one of the first precepts in his book.

Precepts. Book. Is there a coaching bible, Brad wonders, that he should have?

No—not yet. But soon, Phil says. Phil is writing a book for softball coaches. It will teach fundamental skills, strategy, advanced skills. It will present team drills as well as individual skill drills for each position. It will present ideas about how to run practices, how to make it fun.

"That's great," Brad says. "I tell you what, I could use it right now."

"I'm finishing up the cover design," Phil says. "It'll be out next . . . probably next fall."

"I'll look for it," Brad says.

"*Coaching Winning Softball.*"

"How about 'Softball Coaching for Dummies'?"

Phil is momentarily distracted by something going on in the outfield. "What's that?"

Brad shakes his head. "I'm sure I could learn something."

There will be chapters, Phil goes on, covering every aspect of the game. People don't realize how much is involved. One of the most important secrets, he says, is how to motivate girls. One year he told his girls that if they kept showing up and practicing and doing what he said, that they could accomplish something special.

"You mean go undefeated?" one girl asked.

"Yup," he'd replied.

And they had.

"Okay," Brad says. "So why do *you* coach?"

Phil spreads his hands. "Originally I coached to coach my daughters. That was years ago. Now I coach because I have a lot to impart. I can help these girls."

"That's a good reason," Brad says.

* * * * *

From his catchers' squat, Brad tosses the ball back to Kelli. "Try a few with your eyes closed," he says.

Kelli cocks her head doubtfully. "With my eyes closed?"

He repeats it with firm confidence: "Eyes closed." A command, not a suggestion. He'd promised a new idea: This is it. With her eyes closed, she'll be forced to think about what her legs and arms are doing, where they are. Arm slot, stride. Release point. She'll have to feel it. "Whether it's you or Jenny Finch or Pedro Martinez," he says, "there's going to come a time when you just can't throw a strike. Can't find the strike zone. Five straight pitches; eight straight. It happens to every single pitcher at every level. When that happens, you'll have to adjust. You'll need to know what your arms and legs are doing wrong. You can't just stare at the catcher's glove and get mad"—he presses his fingers against his temples—"and think *'strike-strike-strike-I'm-so-intense-I'm-going-to-throw-a-strike'* and expect to throw a strike. You have to be able to know what your correct stride feels like, and what your release point feels like and what your follow-through feels like. That will help you adjust and get back to throwing strikes."

Kelli looks skeptical, but she takes in a deep breath, closes her eyes, takes a moment to gather her awareness. She delivers. The pitch comes in about knee high, just a bit off to the side.

"Not bad."

Her face lightens in surprise.

"Next pitch will be a strike."

The next pitch comes in a little bit higher, just off the plate on the same side.

"Not bad," Brad says. But both pitches have been off the plate on Kelli's glove side. She'll need to make an adjustment.

Kelli nods.

"What adjustment would you make?"

She tosses the ball into her glove, wrinkles her face: "My stride? The direction of my stride."

Brad agrees. That's probably the first one to try.

Her next pitch comes in high. Brad has to reach over his head for it. But it was right down the middle.

"Good adjustment!"

"Should I still keep my eyes closed?"
Brad nods. "A few more."

* * * * *

Jamie does not have very many friends. Not on the Marlins. And not in school, where most of the girls keep their distance. This is probably because she lives with her mother and older brother and sister and their toddlers, and sleeps in the den in the apartment. She's pretty sure the other girls whisper things behind her back.

At the beginning of practice she usually hangs out with Ashley while the others start playing catch. Ashley has some sort of attention problem, and she's not very confident or pretty or popular, but she lives just down the street, so they hang out sometimes.

At their fifth practice, Coach Brad introduces bunting. Once you get your feet squared around, facing the pitcher, he explains, it's like using the head of your bat to "catch" the ball. To start, he tells the batters to not even use their bats. Instead, Coach makes a couple of soft tosses that the batter has to catch bare-handed with her right hand, which is normally her throwing hand. After a few tosses, he tells them to take the bat and hold it down near the end—the head—with just that same hand, just like it's a glove, and then act like you're catching the toss, letting the ball bounce off the bat head.

Jamie hasn't bunted before. It sounds weird. It feels awkward at first, but when Brad tosses the ball, it's not hard to catch it with her right hand. "Your throwing hand is your more coordinated hand," Coach says, and Jamie guesses that he's right. After that, Coach hands her the bat, and it's not hard to use it like you're catching, even if the ball just bounces off. When he finally lets her try it for real—like it's a game— she holds the bat with both hands, squares around to face the pitch. The ball hits the end of the bat and plunks down onto the dirt in front of home plate.

She can't believe it: It's easy. At the same time, she does not want to bunt. What's the point? The idea is to hit the crap out of the ball, which is how you win softball games. Coach says they won't have to bunt very often, but he wants everybody to know how. "It's something we can use to advance a baserunner. And good things can happen: A good bunt makes the other team's players move around, cover different bases, and make a play. There will come a time when we need that."

Ashley rolls her eyes. Jamie sees this and grins. Ashley did not do well in the bunt drill. She kept stepping across home plate, and she mostly missed the ball. In the huddle, she snickers. "Bunt," she whispers. "What does that rhyme with?"

Jamie grins, but keeps paying attention.

Near the end of practice, Coach calls them in to introduce a new drill: the pickle drill. Where an opposing runner is caught between two bases, and they have to tag her out. It's an exercise, Coach says, in covering bases, handling tricky throws, making judgments. It will be hard at first, he says. But they *have* to know how to do this.

He takes a deep breath. "To do this right," he says, "we need three fielders." Coach gestures at two rag bases. "Now, the way it works, is, there's an opposing base-runner between the bases—let's say she's between second and third. One of our fielders has the ball. Let's say it's the shortstop, who's just taken a throw from the outfield. She chases the runner, to tag her. The runner has to choose a base to run to."

Jamie tries to envision the imaginary player chasing the imaginary baserunner. "So we need fielders covering both bases," Coach says. "When the runner gets close to the base, the fielder chasing her has to throw to that base. The fielder at the base takes the throw and tries to tag the runner, but if she can't—if the runner turns around and runs toward the other base, this fielder becomes the new chaser. The original chaser has to cover the base that the new chaser just left."

Jamie thinks she gets it. She looks at her teammates. Renni looks confident, as always. Kacie looks confused, as always. Lori looks like she's listening to something else. Emmie and Colleen look like they're trying to figure out a hard math problem.

"Just remember," Coach says: "If you're not covering a base and you see your teammate chasing the base-runner, you've got to cover the base that she's just left uncovered."

They start the drill; Ashley's the first runner. She positions herself between the bases. Renni's the chaser, with Courtney and Lissa stationed at the bases.

"Go!" Coach Brad calls.

Renni jogs toward Ashley, grinning and ready to throw. Ashley watches her approach. Jamie yells at Ashley to run, but Ashley just stands there. Renni tags her and holds the ball aloft in a victory pose: like, *that* was easy.

"Same group, again." Coach Brad calls. "Ashley, run. Choose a base and run."

Renni approaches again. This time Ashley runs. She runs toward Courtney's base. Renni's throw sails over Courtney's head. Courtney takes off after it as it bounds away. Ashley runs to Courtney's uncovered base, then to the other base, where Lissa is stationed. Courtney gets the ball and starts jogging back. Ashley keeps running, back toward Courtney's base. Courtney grins, confused about why Ashley's still running, and then tags her out.

Ashley keeps running, back to Lissa's base.

Courtney tosses the ball to Coach Brad. Everybody watches Ashley, who smiles as she continues at an easy jog, back and forth between the bases.

Jamie wonders if Coach ever gets mad. At school, a lot of their teachers let Ashley get away with stuff because she doesn't do anything *that bad*; she just always seems to be testing, figuring out what she can get away with.

Coach folds his arms. "Ashley," he says.

Ashley bounces along.

"Ashley."

"Yessir."

"We're trying to accomplish something here."

"Oh." Ashley stops running. Instead of returning to the end of the line, though, she sits down on the grass. The rest of the team keeps going with the drill. It's actually not complicated: One girl at each base, a base-runner in the middle, a fielder approaching with the ball, chasing the runner.

Jamie takes her turn as the base-runner. Meghan takes her position at one of the bases. Courtney has the ball. She runs at Jamie, who runs hard toward Meghan's base. Courtney's throw comes at Meghan over Jamie's shoulder. Meghan reaches, holding both palms up, averting her face from the ball like she's been blinded by the sun. The ball glances off her glove and dribbles away.

"Same group. Again!" Coach calls.

"Step out," Jamie says. "Meghan."

Meghan hears her name; looks at Jamie.

"Step out of the baseline. That way you and Courtney can see each other. You're the target. And you can see the ball better, because the runner—me—I won't be in the way."

Meghan looks down at her cleats. She's standing on the base. She tries a step—just a small step—to one side.

"Right there," Jamie says. "Can you see Courtney now?"

Meghan nods: She seems pleased. "I can see her better," she says. She looks down at her glove, flexes it open and closed. Then she opens it and holds it up. Like a target.

Jamie notices that the glove is pink, but as long as Meghan shows *some* target, she's doing better, and the color of the glove doesn't matter.

The next week, the Marlins have two practices. For the first practice Jamie arrives early. She waits for Ashley, but she's absent and Jamie ends up warming up with Maddi. At the next practice, Jamie looks for Ashley again, but she's not there. Again. Even though she'd been at school.

* * * * *

Mike sits at the bar. To his left, Brad and Spence, another pub regular, look up at the Bruins' playoff game on the tube. Mike gazes up absently. He could barely give a crap.

Things have been going nowhere recently. His drawing has not progressed: He keeps drawing the same scenes, and they all seem to come out the same. And for work, he's found himself weighing Brad's suggestions about soldiers deserting the Colonial army. Dumb idea: Why would he consider it?

He muses over these thoughts, even as he gazes up at the hockey game, and realizes that he doesn't need to be there at all. At that moment, though, he sees Von behind the bar, nodding past him, and he notices the bare and slender arm extended between him and Brad, and realizes that there are two women just behind his shoulder blade, trying to order drinks.

It surprises him when one of them—the taller one, a little plump, but still cute—taps Brad on the shoulder: "Coach? Brad?"

What's this? Mike thinks. Brad *knows* somebody? Brad's talking to a *woman* in a *bar*? It turns out that it's the mother of one of Brad's softball players. But the other one—the cuter one—does not seem to know Brad.

Mike jumps in. "Are you also a softball mom?" He's ready to say that he knows a star softball player, but is not sure how he'll talk about Claire: *My friend's daughter? My girlfriend's daughter?*

The woman shakes her head, but smiles. "Are you? A softball dad?"

He makes a flat, wiping motion with his hand: "Not even

a dad."

"I played as a kid," she says. "I loved it."

So: She's willing to engage.

She extends her hand. "Suzanne, by the way."

Von sets drinks on the bar, and the ladies return to their table.

Brad turns his attention back to the hockey game. Mike knows that Brad is actually excited to have had the "action" of talking to a reasonably attractive woman for a few minutes, but he acts like nothing happened.

So, if anything is going to happen here, Mike can see that it's going to be up to him. During a commercial break, he looks back toward the ladies' table, and just happens to catch the eye of his new friend—Suzanne—and smiles and waves. A few moments later, they seem to have a question about something, and Suzanne raises her hand to signal him over.

"Me?" he mouths, pointing to his chest.

Both women nod in vigorous confirmation: *Yes!—you.*

Mike steps down off his bar stool. He goes over to join the women. It turns out that they have a question about hockey; about defensive strategies. Mike's answer moves from fundamental explanation to for-instance hypotheticals. The women nod, grateful for their new understandings. This leads to more questions, and then other subjects.

They order another round from the waitress, and Mike figures that Brad and Spence are happy enough without him. He thinks about Joanne, but reassures himself: It's all good. They're adults, and they've always understood that they're going to give each other plenty of space. Jo, after all, is a single mom: Mike is far from her top priority. Lately that's been obvious.

After another drink, as the hockey game ends, as it gets to be 10:30, the three of them divide up their tab and get up to leave together. Outside, he and Suzanne find that they're both parked down the block, in front of Bellinger's Tavern, so they bid goodnight to Brad's player's mom and walk together. When they get to Suzanne's car, she starts fishing in her purse for keys, then stops. She tilts her head to one side, tosses a nod at Bellinger's. "It's not that late," she says. "We could go for one more."

* * * * *

GAME 1

Brad tries to remember the list of pre-game duties. Warm-ups. Work with Kelli—his starting pitcher—and the catchers. Rake and line the field, pound in the pitcher's slab. All new to Brad. Listen to forty-five different questions from the girls, and *hey, put those cell phones away!*

Time to meet with the coaches and umpire. Exchange lineups: Where's the scorebook? Run to the equipment bag. *"Where's the scorebook!?"*

He hears a pleasant voice: "Right here." She's walking toward him, pencil tucked behind her ear, neat swirl of copper hair like a ribbon on top. She's Heather: Diane's niece. She's volunteered to keep score for most games.

"Thank you, Heather. I am very glad you are here."

Cradling the scorebook, she walks with Brad to home plate to join the Mets' coaches and exchange lineups. She angles her slender neck to see the names in the Mets' scorebook, and everything's jocular and sportsmanlike as they go over ground rules. Heather looks to be in her mid-twenties and Brad's a little bit startled and off-balance because he'd forgotten about Diane's niece. As they head back to the dugout, Heather addresses the girls, reads out their position assignments. The Marlins listen dutifully and form a neat row on the bench, as if their beloved and beautiful governess has just beckoned a woodland thrush to feed from her hand.

Amid the clutter of concerns, Brad derives comfort from

two things—now three, with Heather's presence. First: Kelli. His pitcher carries herself with confident, athletic strides. She's ready.

Second: The uniforms. He's grown familiar with the girls and their bulky ski jackets and frayed sweatshirts. None of that today: They're all in Marlins' teal blue. Bright teal with matching teal socks and black pants. They look like they belong together. Watching them playing catch, and running to retrieve stray throws, he wonders if in some subtle way they think so, too.

He knows it's a false impression. But it helps. It obscures his knowledge: that one of them will forget the signals, that one of them will get flustered and make an inexplicable throw to a wrong base, that somebody will lose track of how many outs there are.

Kacie and Meghan wear their shirts untucked. Brad tells them to tuck them in. Kacie complains, but Brad insists. Meghan has a problem because her shirt is too big for her, but it's okay, Brad tells her, just tuck it in. Colleen, he notes, has the same problem; she's tucked her shirt in so far that about half the number on the back is hidden in her pants. Colleen is also in minor non-compliance for the way she wears her hat like sort of a bonnet, with her ears tucked inside the hat band.

Good enough. They look reasonably orderly. For the moment, in fact, to Brad they look like a sharply-creased *unit*. Are they prepared? Of course not. Brad needs to remind Maddi about something, but stops himself. He doesn't know what will happen. He'll just have to let them play and do what they do.

The game starts cleanly. The Mets' leadoff batter hits a weak ground ball to Lissa at first base, who fields it and steps on the base. One out. The next batter strikes out. Walk. Then, on a slow grounder to the right side, he watches first baseman Lissa and pitcher Kelli converge on the ball. To his surprise and delight, Kelli lets it go and runs to cover first. Lissa fields it cleanly and flips it to Kelli. Brad smiles: It almost looks like some coach had shown it to them. Three outs.

The smooth inning seems to build confidence. The Marlins play better than they do in practice. At shortstop, Renni runs, lunges, and her glove swallows a line drive headed for the outfield. There are bad throws and a dropped throw, and a line drive that squirts out of Colleen's glove, but pop-ups are caught, ground balls fielded.

Brad tries to notice girls covering bases, throwing to the right places, getting their cutoffs right. He feared that the girls would forget, that they wouldn't make the connections between abstract practice drills and game situations. But then, with an opposing runner on second base, Kacie—and Brad realizes that it's the first time he's seen her not wearing purple—ventures in from left field to back up third base. The runner on second makes no move toward third, but Kacie has remembered: A steal is possible, a throw might happen.

"Way to go, Kacie!" Brad pumps his fist as if she's just turned a triple play. "That's exactly what we want. That's how to be alert!"

After the inning he takes her aside. "Make a habit of that. There will come a time when that throw comes and it gets past the third baseman, and you will be there and you will be a hero."

She smiles, breathing hard. "Am I up this inning?"

After the game, Brad sits at the kitchen table with the scorebook. Despite their loss, Brad feels a quickening energy coursing through him. He finds himself replaying moments in his head. There's plenty to feel good about. For all of them. He turns on the computer.

Hi all:

Mets 9, Marlins 6. Pretty good game, though. I was mostly pleased. Nice pitching by Kelli, a couple of big hits for Jamie and Lissa. The girls ran the bases reasonably well. Big lunging grab by Renni! Shout-outs to Lissa and Courtney, who caught well and blocked some tough pitches in the dirt. There were errors, of course, but those happen. The game was competitive and mostly clean. We'll get better. I hope the girls had fun.

* * * * *

Mike brings his sketchbook out onto the balcony. His drawing has grown more accurate, even as he works more quickly. Without quite mastering anything, his progress has been satisfying.

From the balcony there's a view of the trees along the river. He's studied his field guides, matching their photos and illustrations with photos from his forest walks, and at this point he can identify species even from a distance. From where he sits he can make out paper birches, river birches, beeches, sugar maples, white pines, cedars, and elms. But the species, he's learned, does not always define the way the tree grows. One elm tree grows skinny and sparse; another full and graceful. Some trunks curve in smooth arcs. Some split apart like sundered families. Others simply divide, agreeing to part in gradual farewells.

Charcoal, pencil, and compressed graphite sticks make scratchy, satisfying sounds as they mark the paper. He varies the strength of lines, works the eraser where the light falls, slows the pencil for fine details of bark and leaf. He fills sketchbooks with broad compositions, small detail sketches, and quick, loose studies.

Mike wonders if he's *good* at this. He's shown Joanne a few of his sketches. The subject matter—all those broken trees—did not appeal to her, but she complimented him on his progress.

Other than Joanne, nobody knows about his drawing. He's thought about telling Brad, but if he were to do that, then suggestions and questions would inevitably follow. Probably good ones. But Mike will not be ready with answers. He is not ready for Brad.

* * * * *

Brad ponders position assignments for Game 2.

In the first game, the Mets played their best players at the most important positions: pitcher, catcher, shortstop, first base. Sometimes third base. The weaker players played the outfield; one or two of them got an inning at second base.

For the Mets' coach, it was simple. But Brad sits at the laptop entering, deleting, re-entering, tinkering.

Courtney. Why does she think she can't play shortstop or third base? He's told her she could play first again. She's tall. She catches the ball. "I won't stick you at third or short next game," he told her. "But I'm gonna put you in left field for a few innings. The shortstop and third baseman will be right in front of you. Watch them. I want you to get comfortable on that side, because you are good enough to play anywhere."

She sighed: She guessed she could try it.

Colleen. Not so athletic. But scrappy as a terrier. She'll give the Marlins a decent chance on any ball hit to her. Brad enters her name in the spreadsheet, taking away some left field innings and putting her in right field. But she'll have a special right field assignment: Play shallow, right at the edge of the infield dirt, and watch for ground balls that get through. *You can still throw the runner out at first. You're almost playing second base, even at the same time that you're covering right field.* That's a special assignment; for Colleen only.

His big decision: Lori. Lori at first base. Two innings. She's one of their least athletic girls. Doesn't know the game. But she *catches the ball.* And she's learning. He worked with her at practice about running to cover the base when the ball's hit to somebody else: find the base, run to it and get your foot on it. No need to watch the ball or the other fielders. Find the base, and then there's plenty of time to see the throw and catch the ball. If she can grow into that position . . . Brad doesn't know what difference that would make. But it would be nice.

And finally: Kacie. She's got no business playing third. But she showed alertness last game; she's been paying attention. So—third base, one inning. She'll be excited. And who knows? Maybe she'll make a play. And wouldn't that be great?

That's the lineup. Print.

Pos/Inning	1	2	3	4	5	6		LINEUP
P	Kelli	Kelli	Jamie	Jamie	Kelli	Kelli	1	Renni
C	Maddi	Lissa	Maddi	Lissa	Colleen	Maddi	2	Courtney
1b	Courtney	Lori	Lori	Courtney	Lissa	Lissa	3	Jamie
2B	Colleen	Meghan	Kacie	Meghan	Lori	Colleen	4	Kelli
SS	Jamie	Renni	Renni	Kelli	Jamie	Jamie	5	Kacie
3b	Renni	Maddi	Lissa	Kacie	Renni	Renni	6	Lissa
LF	Meghan	Courtney	Courtney	Lori	Courtney	Kacie	7	Maddi
LC	Renni	Jamie	Kelli	Renni	Maddi	Courtney	8	Colleen
RC	Lori	Kacie	Colleen	Maddi	Kacie	Lori	9	Lori
RF	Kacie	Colleen	Meghan	Colleen	Meghan	Meghan	10	Meghan

* * * * *

Hi all

Cubs 11, Marlins 8. We lose. But I saw plenty of good things. Lori made her debut at first base and handled most of her chances cleanly. She should be proud of herself. All three catchers blocked tough pitches, and NONE of the Cubs' runners reached base on dropped third strikes. Meghan did a good job getting balls back to the infield, and I could see that our outfielders— Courtney, Colleen, et al—were alert and backing up plays. Most of all, the base running is coming along. Twice Renni took advantage when the Cubs weren't paying attention. Jamie stole three bases. I also saw Colleen and Kacie picking up my signals well; I'm trying to get the Marlins to not stop once they reach a base, but to try to see if they can get to the next base.

Not everything went well. We lost. I do get frustrated by errors—mental and physical. But mostly, we lost because the Cubs had a few good hitters that got big hits, and their infield just played well. So, we need to improve, but the Marlins gave a good effort today.

Brad omits one moment: Fourth inning, Diane nudging him, nodding toward Renni at second base.

Renni's got her cap pulled down; he can't see her face. All he can see is the visor: She's looking straight down at the ground. Brad squints at her, then turns back to Diane. "She okay? Is she crying?"

They peer across the field: Yes.

"Why? Did she screw something up?"

Diane shakes her head. "Not that I noticed."

Brad watches carefully. He sees Renni's chest shudder. He wonders if she's hurt. Did she twist an ankle? Did a baserunner run into her? He's about to call time-out to see if she's okay, but Diane puts her hand on his arm: Wait.

"Look alive Marlins!" he says instead.

After the inning, he takes her aside as she trudges off the field. "Renni."

Instantly she starts sobbing.

"Hey . . . what is it? Did you get hurt?"

She shakes her head, then covers her face in her glove.

"Hey, hey. What is it?" He hasn't seen her this way. He's come to know Renni as the happy-go-lucky girl with the devilish grin and the impish body language that speaks so clearly: *This is so much fun and it'll be even cooler when I make the next awesome play.* Renni?

Her voice comes out small. "I'm. Doing." Her fragile frame shakes. "Horrible."

"Renni," Brad says, "I didn't see anything wrong." He's telling the truth. "You're doing great. What do you think you did wrong?"

She looks down at the dirt, which starts to darken with wet dots. "I. Caused. My. Fault . . ." Her chest bucks and shudders like a car out of gas.

"Hey, hey."

Girls flock around him. *Who's up fourth? What position am I playing next inning? Are we winning? Can I run really quick to the snack stand?*

Hang on.

He tries to usher Renni away from the bench. Some of the girls back off.

He gets down on one knee so he's not talking down at her. "Renni, everybody's been making mistakes. Mistakes happen. But I—if you made some tiny mistake, I missed it." He senses the silence, the audience behind him. The Cubs are finishing up their warmups. Brad turns and straightens, calling out the lineup for the inning. "Lissa! Lissa, come on, you're up!"

Lissa grabs a bat and throws her helmet on. Diane kneels down with Renni as Brad heads out to the third base coach's box.

With Diane talking to Renni, they have no first base coach. Diane looks around quickly: Heather—keeping score—Heather can coach first base. Heather springs from the bench and arrives quickly, scorebook in hand, ready to go. "Just remind the runners to watch me for signals," Brad says. "And to take their leads on every pitch. And what to do on fly balls." Brad laughs. "Anything you think they might forget. Or not understand."

Heather sprints across the diamond. From the first-base

coaches' box she claps her hands. "Let's go Marlins!" she calls. "Let's go Lissa! Starts us off!" Brad feels himself relax.

Brad watches Lissa bat, looks across at Heather, scans the fielders, tries to listen to Diane even as she moves Renni out of earshot. He should have told Renni how much confidence he has in her. Or maybe that would have made it worse. He is not prepared for this. Will Coach Phil's book address this? How often does this happen? How can he be more . . . adequate? Next time?

* * * * *

The Cubs' coaches yell a lot. "*Caitlin!* What do we do when we see that throw going to second?" Hand to ear. "That's right, we *back up! Come on now.*" "Emily! What are you *doing*? Didn't you see the runner? Come on, use your head!" "Hey Lizzy, no daydreaming out there—you have to *run* when that happens!"

Theatrical palms-up gestures.

After the game, the coaches banter fraternally. "Good game. Great job. Your girls played well."

Brad confides that he's new to this. It took about five tries, he confesses, to figure out his position assignments.

"It's easier when you get to the playoffs," one of the Cubs' coaches says. "By then, the girls have all improved. Plus, in the playoffs you get to play your best players for the whole game."

They commiserate: *Twelve-year-old girls. That one play—where nobody covered first? That's ALL we worked on last week! Omigod, did you see my players swinging at pitches over their heads? I swear I am tearing my hair out.*

Brad listens and grins conspiratorially. Eyes rolling skyward.

"I know, I know," their head coach says. "It drives you nuts. And will somebody please remind me—WHY do we do this?"

Chapter 8
APPROACHES

Pitcher's Pub. Early evening. Von goes over his mental checklist. Plenty of limes. Olives. Lemon wedges in the pan. Toothpicks in glasses. Salt dish for margaritas.

Von likes listening to Brad and Mike argue. Tonight they're going on about stock investing. Not surprisingly, they disagree completely. The place is still almost empty, so he'll be able to listen in. It should be amusing. Possibly educational.

Mike's approach is to examine the charts of recent stock prices. He searches for shapes and patterns that tell him when to buy or sell. Basically, he tries to understand the *market*. Brad, on the other hand, tries to understand *businesses* and their value.

Mike grins in patient exasperation. "Okay. Value. So you buy a stock when it's 'undervalued,'" Mike says, using air quotes. "And you know it's undervalued because you can look at the company's business fundamentals and future business fundamentals, project its future cash flows, account for stuff like pension fund obligations and assets like goodwill, and calculate the value of the company. Which is higher than the price. So you buy. Then, at some point in the future, everybody else will eventually perform the same analysis, understand the value, and buy at a higher price than you did. Do I understand that correctly?"

Von looks over from behind the tap.

Brad squirms. "Well, yeah." It sounds like a confession, warily made. But, yes. That is what he tries to do. He tries to understand the value of the company; a value that others do not see.

Mike looks away to roll his eyes.

Brad takes exception. What *he* doesn't get is the idea of investing in things you don't understand at all. He needs to believe in his investments. He cannot base investment decisions on these chart shapes, which look to him like some combination of astronomy, astrology, and palm reading.

Von laughs. Neither approach sounds convincing. Mike throws up his hands. "That's the *only* thing that's understandable. It's how you figure out what the rest of the market is doing."

"So you're outsmarting the market."

"Dude," Mike says. "I try to understand the dumbshit collective mass market and be smarter. That's not hard. You, on the other hand, try to be *almost as smart* as the smart professionals who spend their lives analyzing information on this stuff."

"Yes," Brad says. "I mean—sorry, but I do in fact try to be smart."

"But—Brad—you have to play the game," Mike says, less patiently. "And it's *their* game. It's their game, and you have to know how it works."

In his approach, Brad allows, there's a lot that he'll never understand. He doesn't understand how the generic-sounding "mission statements" in the annual report will improve production efficiencies. The meaning of the corporate self-assessments and strategies elude him: *The spirit of our 4,300 employees is our greatest asset . . . Our innovative culture enables us to elevate product quality and introduce new solutions . . . Our global network will enable us to continue to execute at a high level.* He cannot understand the competitive forces that make one bank or insurance company better than the next. But he can understand a company that—he raises his pint glass—makes booze. Or cars. Or office buildings. He understands biotech companies.

"Biotechs," Mike says. "Okay. I guess you might be onto something there."

Yes, Von says. "Brad would have some insight there."

Mike wags his head about, half-conceding, but not without a last dig. "Enough to stay away, in most cases."

* * * * *

Normally, these softball games make Gwen anxious. Maddi says she's having fun, but she is not the most athletic girl; she's maybe average at best. When she's at bat, or when the ball gets hit in her direction, Gwen holds her breath. For all the testimonials about how sports builds confidence and character and leadership and just about every attribute a kid needs to succeed in life . . . Gwen never forgets that sports come with the likelihood of failure, the chance of embarrassment, the potential for trauma.

On this fine spring Saturday, though, Gwen finds herself looking forward to Maddi's game. She's not sure why. Maybe she's just grown comfortable with the routine. She and her husband have gotten this down. Camp chairs, picnic blanket, snacks and a few toys for seven-year-old Leah, and of course Maddi's equipment. They've learned to double-check that.

Or maybe it's just the day. It's early May; the long-awaited breakthrough has arrived. Sunshine plummets through the forest, catching on young buds, spreading a barcode of shadows on the woodland floor. Forsythia have gone on a decorating rampage; yards and hedges blaze with their sudden yellow detonations.

At the field, they stake their claim to a patch of grass down the left field line. The other parents and families surround them. They're all learning each other's names, and they exchange pleasantries about the weather and school and such.

As the game begins, Gwen hears a familiar voice behind her. It's her friend Stephanie. She's standing at the waist-high chain link fence with her two young daughters and a big guy who she realizes is Conner. Conner: *Coach* Conner, in a bright teal Marlins' cap, who seems to have returned from his overseas assignment. Gwen shoots her hand up to wave.

Stephanie looks relieved to see her. She leaves Conner in charge of the girls and picks her way through the lawn chairs and blankets to join them. Conner's just back visiting for a quick break, she says. It being such a beautiful day, they'd decided to get outside and check out their future team.

How's it going? With his business deal?

Stephanie shoots a glance back at Conner. She lowers her voice. Not so well. It doesn't seem like anything's about to wrap up over there. She's not sure about all the issues, but these biotech deals get complicated, and recent meetings have not gone well. "Anyway," she says, "not to bore you. How are the Marlins doing? And Maddi—how's Maddi's season going?"

Gwen's not sure how to answer this question. Maddi's had fun so far, and the team has improved. On the other hand, the Marlins have a 0-2 record. And in the last game a girl started crying. Really crying.

"That's inevitable," Stephanie says. "Unless—do you know what it was about?"

A lot of the parents hadn't even realized the girl was crying. Then they'd collectively scratched their heads and speculated over it. By the end of the game they'd figured out that the girl—Renni—had forgotten to back up a base and when somebody made a bad throw she wasn't there to salvage the play.

"Poor thing." Stephanie cringes. "But it sounds like she takes the game seriously."

Gwen thinks she should let Stephanie get back to her girls. She glances back over her shoulder. Conner's hunched forward, resting his forearms on the top of the fence. He peers through dark shades at the teams mingling on their benches.

"He looks like he's ready to step right in." Gwen smiles. "Got the team hat and everything."

Stephanie huddles closer. She wishes he hadn't worn the hat.

"Why?"

Stephanie casts a quick glance behind her. "I just wish he hadn't. I'm not sure why." She gets up to rejoin Conner and her girls.

As the game begins, Conner cheers loudly, booming out *"Nice play!"* every time the Marlins record an out. Before long, word gets around that the *real* coach is watching, and Conner becomes a subject of curiosity. Some of the parents get up to introduce themselves and ask questions.

Gwen catches bits of it. Conner's big voice carries. "I think they're on the right track," he says. "Looks like they're having fun." At one point, though, he wonders to nobody in particular if the Marlins' batter might bunt. "It's the perfect situation for it."

This draws interest. "What's the perfect situation?" somebody asks.

Conner notes that there are no outs and a count of two balls and one strike. He gestures toward the field, pointing out that the other team's infielders are positioned at normal depth; they're not expecting a bunt. "I've always loved the— what they call the 'small ball' game," he says. "It's an aggressive brand of ball. It's a fun way to play."

Stephanie rejoins Gwen as Conner chats. She rolls her eyes at Conner holding court behind them. Gwen puts her hand on her friend's arm. "It's fine," she laughs. "It's all good."

Stephanie is interested to observe the level of play. Gwen explains that the girls occasionally impress with crisp innings.

They even flash occasional brilliance: running catches, long hits, and this girl Jamie really seems to know what she's doing. These are outweighed, though, by interminable innings filled with walked batters trudging around the bases; easy throws dropped; pitches skipping—*spling!*—to the backstop; heaved throws borne aloft like tornado-tossed farm animals destined for parts unknown.

The other team—the Reds—scores five runs in the first inning.

Conner interrupts his conversations periodically to funnel his hands around his mouth and shout "*Let's go Marlins!*"

Stephanie is curious about Brad. Does he seem like a good coach?

The parents, Gwen says, generally agree: Brad doesn't project authority and gruff-bearded certainty like most coaches, but he does a good job communicating with the parents, and manages to maintain good humor when the Marlins bumble things. It's nice, Gwen says, when she hears Brad shouting out praise for tiny inconsequential things: *Nice backup! That's how to be alert! That's how to cover the bases— good job!*

During the fourth inning, the Reds' lead grows to 10-2. A few times Gwen notices Brad clutching his head in despair. After a dropped throw he stomps his foot on the ground. He folds his arms across his chest and paces back and forth. Then, the Marlins' second baseman picks up a ground ball and freezes in sudden confusion and looks about the infield and— almost a full second after the runner has crossed first base— throws the ball over the first baseman's head. Brad whips his hat off. He holds it, trembling for an instant, and then puts it back on. He does not yell, but he retreats to the bench and watches the rest of the inning from a hunched-over position.

By the next inning he's up clapping his hands again. The Marlins manage to score some runs, and their fielding goes more smoothly as the game goes along. In the last two innings, the Marlins score at least three more runs, versus only one for the Reds.

But it's not a close game.

When the last out is recorded, the parents hoist themselves up to fold lawn chairs, gather picnic blankets, and brush themselves off. They grin and nod at each other. "Oh, well," is the much-echoed phrase.

* * * * *

Hi all

15-6. Ouch! This one was a bummer. I will point out some positives. Colleen was alert on every play, and as catcher she blocked a lot of difficult pitches. Lissa collected two sharp hits. The Marlins ran the bases well; Jamie and Renni took extra bases on several opportunities.

I was losing it for a while there. I was surprised at myself. I understand that this is not about winning, and I'm fine if they give efforts like they did in the first two games . . . but just the way we lost—it burns me up. I was upset especially because of the way things got unglued in a few innings and the girls stopped doing the things they know how to do. I guess I have to apologize; the Marlins looked like a very poorly coached team. Maybe that's what got me upset.

We'll keep at it. Have your girls ready for a good practice on Tuesday!

* * * * *

For Christ's sake. It's 1:19 a.m. Brad closes his eyes, turns over to a new position, stays there for a while, and then opens his eyes: 1:34. He's received an e-mail: . . . *she likes to play the infield. I hope you can play her at second base more often, and her grandparents will be at the game next weekend, so a few more innings at second base would be nice* . . . and it bugs him because he gives more infield time to his poorer players than any of the other teams' coaches. He wonders about all those parents that look at him with blank expressions and shades and don't seem interested in introducing themselves. He sees Renni watering the dust with her tears and wonders what he should have said. He sees soft pop-ups eluding the hopeful outstretched hands of his Marlins. *Poor coaching,* he thinks. And oh yes: Colleen had something she wanted to talk about . . . and how can he get them to ditch those cell phones? It plays in a loop, right there on the inside of his eyelids.

He's sweating. He throws off his blankets. The clock reads 1:58. Brad switches on the light. Come on: They're eleven and twelve years old. Read. Don't get near those softball books from the library. This is absurd: *Get a life*, he tells himself. Or maybe a job. Oh, yes, that.

More thoughts that won't lie still. Brad knows biotech. He knows the science. He knows the procedures. He knows regulations, sources of capital, trends. He has connections. And then, finally—possibly—he has an idea.

He swings his legs over the side of the bed. He stands up, fully awake. In his study he turns on the light, finds a piece of scrap paper. He'll set up shop as an investment consultant; an independent industry analyst providing expert advice on biotech stocks. It makes sense. And wouldn't it be great, to have a simple, defined objective: Help investors make money. No conflicting tensions: Help investors make money. Now, the questions start: How does this happen? What's the next step? Is this another pipe dream?

It's 2:16 now. A breeze lifts the curtains. So far, they've had mostly delicious spring weather. Now, though, they could use a good rainfall. In the garden, the tomatoes are barely ankle-high. The peppers are spindly. Brad can't imagine any great bounty emerging from those wispy stalks.

Back to bed. Brad pulls a blanket back up. Oh: Something else he needs to remember. He can't quite grasp it . . . it's something about Renni. He needs to make a note of it—jot it on scratch paper, back in the study. Which seems so far away. Oh well. After practice. Of course. He'll remember.

* * * * *

It happens at all levels of play. Fielders react late, baserunners take advantage. And the chain of futility unspools, fielders taking turns unloading wild and untimely throws to unfortunate destinations. Coaches clutch at their heads: *Good God what are they thinking! This is out of control—stop! Stop!! STOP! Do NOT throw that ball around!*

Foreheads wrinkle; heads hang. But nobody really understands: *But you said not to hold it.*

They need to know what to do beforehand. They need to be able to envision it. So here he is at practice, lecturing a bunch of bored girls. "Have you ever heard a coach yelling at everybody to 'not throw the ball around'?"

Heads nod, a few hands go up.

"But you have to throw the ball *somewhere*, right?"

Heads nod.

"Let's say there's a baserunner and she's . . . more than halfway to second base," Brad says, "and the ball's still in the outfield . . ." He looks out toward left field, envisioning the situation. "If it's an easy throw . . ."

He stops himself. Rules can be followed. But he wants these girls to learn judgment. They need *guidelines*, not rules. So here's Coach Brad's guideline: "If that runner gets any-where near a base—if you're not sure you can get her out—

then the throw goes a full base ahead. So if she's almost to second, the throw goes to third."

Noses wrinkle; heads tilt. "Not second?"

At least they're paying attention. "We're trying to limit the damage. If your throw gets to second after the runner, she may be on her way to third."

The girls ponder that.

"We saw Jamie do that in practice the other day."

Nobody remembers that.

"Hold that lead runner. Just hold her. Don't make the desperate try to get her out on a close play. Just make the safe play and keep her from advancing."

He positions them in the field. He scatters balls in the grass all over the outfield, makes them turn their backs to home plate. He shouts out instructions for the drill. He'll run the bases. It's just like the cutoff drill, he figures, except they have to make judgments to throw to different bases. He wonders if they can see this. He jogs to a spot about halfway between second base and third base. "So if I'm here!" he shouts, "where should the throw go?"

No answer. The girls look at each other.

Brad holds his hand to his ear. "How many say third?"

Courtney and Maddi raise their hands, but quickly retract them.

"I'm almost to third!" Brad shouts. "So the throw has to go home."

"Wait. What? What if . . ."

He's hoarse. He needs a breath. Maybe they'll get it if he just starts.

"One out! I'm the runner!" From home plate he starts running, about half-speed. *"The ball is hit . . . through the infield . . . to . . . LEFT-CENTER FIELD!"* Brad watches Kelli break for the nearest ball. Taking the turn around first base, he turns on the speed on his way to second as Kelli comes up firing. Her throw goes straight to shortstop Maddi, standing

next to second baseman Lori on second base. Nice throw. Except Brad is already passing second, on his way to third.

Brad stops, turns around. "Kelli!"

"What?"

He changes his mind. "Lori! Maddi!" Second baseman and shortstop.

"What?"

"Where's the cutoff? Who's taking the relay?"

They look at each other. Maddi looks around the field. Lori slaps at a gnat on her cheek.

"Maddi, on that ball you have to take the cutoff throw. Not cover the base. So, as the cutoff, where do you stand?"

She points to a spot between Kelli and second base.

Which would be correct if they were trying to throw to second base. "But Maddi, I was already at second base. If that throw goes to second, I'm going to third. I was already on my way there."

Maddi nods.

"So where does the cutoff belong?"

Nobody knows.

"Now think—it's the cutoff drill."

He can hear one of them saying "Oh—yeah—oh" . . . and then Colleen comes up with the answer: Between Kelli and third.

"Yes!" Brad says. "That throw goes toward third."

Maddi nods.

"Lori?"

Lori nods.

Brad surveys the field. In right field, Courtney stands delicately balanced: legs crossed, weight on one leg, one arm propping the other at the elbow, chin resting on knuckles. Kind of a sculptural study: *The Softball Ponderer.*

"Courtney? You got this?"

She unfolds her limbs. "Yeah."

"You look like you have a question."

Oh. Nothing. She was thinking about something else.

"Kacie?"

Kacie's honest. "What if the runner, like, slows down?"

"Just get it in as quickly as you can. Get it to the cutoff—the relay."

He doesn't push it. "Okay!" he shouts. Doggedly he stations himself on second base. "READY? STILL ONE OUT. RUNNER'S ON SECOND! A BALL IS HIT OVER THE INFIELD . . ."

* * * * *

He's still only met about half the parents. He's barely made contact with a few of them. Much to his irritation. Brad understands that people are busy and that junk piles up in inboxes, but is it too much to ask to please answer a goddamn e-mail to say, "yes my daughter will be there" or "no my daughter will not be there"?

At the end of practice he sees Emmie heading off toward the parking lot. Emmie had a late start to the season and he wants to make sure that she understands everything. He also wonders if her parents ever received his message about schedules, practice attendance, and other notifications. He's learned about her involvement with the school play as well as her gymnastics schedule, and thus far Emmie's attendance has not been bad. It's just that she either shows up or not: Not once has he known whether or not to expect her.

He catches up to her as she reaches the car. "Emmie," he says.

She spins around, surprised.

"How'd the school play go?"

"Um," she says. "It was good."

"Did you have a big part?"

She shrugs. "Not really."

Her dad sits in the car. Gruff goatee, shaved head, dark

shades covering his eyes.

Brad moves to the driver's window to introduce himself. "Glad to have Emmie."

Brad is met by a beard, shaved head, shades. Slight nod.

He persists. "Is she having fun so far?"

Quick shrug. "Surewynot."

"She's had good practices."

"Good."

Brad figures he'll leave the guy alone.

"Maybe she can help you get into the win column," the man says.

Brad searches the face for humor. Beard, shaved head, shades. *Surewynot,* he wants to say. "Brad, by the way."

"Nice to meet you."

Brad waits: *Name, perhaps?*

"By the way."

Brad nods.

"Think you could send us a schedule?"

Brad feels his face wrinkling. *What? Are you kidding me?* He's sent the schedule to everybody. He's sent the schedule to everybody twice. He's pestered to make sure that everybody has the schedule. "I've sent it at least twice," he says. "And I'm sure you're on the e-mail list." Brad checks his phone for the list of team contacts. He recites the address.

"That's it."

Brad shakes his head. He does not understand.

Another shrug from the guy. "I haven't received anything."

Brad will try again. No big deal. In fact, he realizes, it's a bit of a relief to understand that there might be an e-mail glitch, because the lack of response from Emmie's parents is starting to make him angry. He repeats the e-mail address. The guy nods.

Brad heads back toward the dugout to retrieve the equipment bag and the stray balls.

Colleen is there, her small arms cradling a load of softballs.

She bends forward to drop them in the ball bucket. "Coach."

Brad checks: Does she have a ride?

Colleen nods and points toward the parking lot. One last car. A hand waves from the window. Brad waves back.

"Thanks Colleen. Go ahead now, before—"

"Coach, can we work on catching—practicing catcher?"

Brad loves watching Colleen play catcher. She doesn't have the strong arm to gun down runners on the basepaths, and after almost every pitch she has to tighten the catcher's shin guards, which are way too big for her. But she blocks pitches. She blocks those low pitches in the dirt; she flings body parts at them with badger-like ferocity.

But they never have enough time for catchers' drills. Brad is not sure he can put aside ten minutes to work with three girls on catching. "You're doing a really nice job at catcher," he says. "You blocked some very tough pitches in the last game. Those probably saved us at least a few runs."

She asks if she can stay after practice.

"Now? Today?"

She pumps her head up and down, but Brad is mindful of the waiting car. He lets Colleen tote the ball bucket while he shoulders the equipment bag.

He greets Colleen's mother—Vicki—at the car window. Vicki greets them with a smile, but shakes her head at Colleen's request. "I'm sorry. We need to pick up your brother from lacrosse." Colleen heaves a sigh. "Okay," she says, "then how about next practice? Or Friday?"

"Colleen, honey."

"Friday works for me," Brad says.

Vicki smiles with a concerned squint. "Can you really do that?"

"I can meet Colleen any time between three-thirty and five."

Vicki looks at Colleen.

Colleen high-fives Brad. "See ya Friday, coach."

Chapter 9
SATISFACTION

GAME 4: WIN!

Yay!

First win. Marlins 14, Cardinals 5. After a rough first inning, the Marlins dominated. Shout outs—where do I start? How about Maddi, with three hits? How about Kacie, who made all the correct relay throws from the outfield? When we do that correctly, we limit damage and prevent bad innings. How about Lissa, who hit a bomb over everybody's head? It wouldn't be like me to overlook the base running, and so yes, I'll note that all of our runners got good jumps on their steals. Courtney and Colleen both took extra bases when the Cardinals weren't expecting anything, and my favorite play was when Renni walked and got to second when she saw the pitch get away from their catcher. The Marlins are running the bases well. We've still got a lot to work on, but this feels great.

* * * * *

After the game, Brad finally meets Maddi's mother, Gwen. "That must feel satisfying!" she says.

Brad shakes her hand. "It's really not about *winning*, but yeah, this feels good."

"I'm Stephanie's friend, by the way. I work with her. I'm the one who got her to coach the team." She grins. "Or, rather: Got *you* to coach the team."

"Thanks a lot!" Brad groans.

She laughs. "Steph watched the last game with me. Against the . . . Reds."

Brad knew that Stephanie and Conner had been there. "Oh-oh." He cowers in mock fear.

"No no no." Gwen waves dismissively. "She said it looked like you were doing a good job."

"Phew."

"She also says it's not about winning. She was getting agitated at the other coach."

Brad can picture it. He and Stephanie tended to agree on things like this.

Maddi catches up with them, softball backpack slung over her shoulder. Brad high-fives her. "Heck of a game, Maddi. You really swung that bat today."

"Thanks."

He asks Gwen for news on Conner, who had come by to say hello after the horrible game against the Reds. He seemed like a good guy, but Brad hadn't had the chance to chat or ask about the big business deal.

Gwen doesn't know. All she knows is that it's some biotech thing; some financing arrangement for a big research project.

Brad wonders: Is Conner on the business side of things, or is he a science guy?

Palms up: No clue. "I think he generally does quite well."

"Sounds like it." Brad remembers how it had seemed so simple at one time. It was about science; inventing new medicines. But then, no, it wasn't. As he climbed the ladder, he went to more and more meetings. The more meetings he went to, the more confused he became. Meeting agendas were rarely about science. They were about press coverage, stock analysts, partners, insurers. They were about perceptions: *nobody cares about that disease right now.* They were about relationships: *If we go ahead with Version B they'll be more comfortable and we'll get them for another round on the MS drug later.* And then, public relations, which seemed to be less about communicating than about creating *ambiguity: We need those results fast; if we're ahead of schedule that'll sound like a win . . . we're going to call those results inconclusive . . . and we can truthfully say that they matched expectations . . .*

He needs to pack up the equipment bag. He needs to pry up the bases and stow them in the storage shed. He smiles. "I bet Conner can't *wait* to wrap things up and get to work with these fine athletes."

Gwen lowers her head, murmurs as her eyes shift about. "I'm not so sure."

Huh?

She laughs nervously. It's a loaded comment; a precipice approaches. Gwen retreats to safer ground. Stephanie and Conner, she says, look forward to coaching the Marlins.

* * * * *

The girls know how to steal bases. For most of the Marlins, stealing second is not hard. Not many catchers in the league can throw out runners stealing second. Stealing third, on the other hand, is hard. It's a shorter throw from home to third; catchers have no problem with that throw. The solution: The delayed steal.

At practice, Brad keeps his instructions short: "Take a lead on the pitch. When the catcher throws the ball back to the pitcher, run."

Without further explanation, he lines the girls up at second base. He positions Diane as the pitcher; himself as catcher. He catches Diane's pitch and holds it, waiting. Courtney ventures off second base; maybe three steps. "Longer lead," Brad calls. He throws the ball back to Diane, and Courtney retreats, back to second base. "Next pitch," Brad calls. "Delayed steal." He watches Courtney jog into a short lead as he catches the next pitch. Brad lobs the ball back to Diane in the pitcher's circle. Diane catches it, and then Courtney runs.

"Girls!" Brad calls. "Don't wait for the ball to get back to the pitcher—to Coach Diane! That's a great way to get thrown out! Start running as soon as the ball leaves the catcher's hand!"

Maddi's turn. She takes her lead nonchalantly as Diane releases her pitch. Brad sees her standing there looking bored: Is she paying attention *at all*? Is she going to run? To Brad's surprise, she takes off as soon as he releases his throw to Diane.

"Excellent! Great job! I wasn't sure you were going to go—that was great!"

With this successful demonstration, the girls' confusion dissolves. They become eager for their turns: *This is easy.*

Except for Kacie. She stands with both purple sneakers on second base. Her teammates encourage her: *Take a lead.* Then—*Now! Go now, Kacie.*

"Kacie," Brad says. "Is something confusing?"

She nods as she shields her eyes from the sun's glare. Unlike the other girls, she doesn't mind confessing her confusion.

Brad trots out to second base so he doesn't have to shout. "Take your lead to about . . . there," he says, pointing.

She moves to where Brad pointed.

"After Coach Diane pitches the ball."

"After the pitch?"

"When the ball leaves her hand."

She nods. Got it.

Brad returns to his spot as the catcher.

Kacie takes her lead.

"Kacie, wait. Wait until Coach Diane pitches it."

"Oh." Kacie's working on a wad of purple chewing gum.

Diane takes an abbreviated windup; slings the pitch.

Brad can see Kacie leading off from second. He tosses the ball back to Diane.

Kacie tenses at the knees.

"Kacie."

Kacie starts to run.

"Stop! Kacie."

Kacie runs to third. She smiles, almost triumphantly. "What?"

Brad sighs. "You have to go when the throw leaves my hand."

"I did."

"The second—as soon as it leaves my hand."

"Okay."

"You waited until it got back to Coach Diane. This is about timing, not speed. If you go as soon as the ball is thrown—"

"To the catcher?"

"Yes."

"Okay."

"I mean, no. To the pitcher."

The girls in line at second base start to giggle. Jamie awaits her turn.

"Kacie, watch Jamie."

Jamie executes the delayed steal flawlessly.

"Excellent!" Brad says. "See that?"

Heads nod confidently. Then something occurs to him: "And by the way. Hey. Jamie. You can use this concept any time. Any time the fielders are lobbing the ball around, not paying attention; round the base and see if you can keep going."

Jamie looks intently at Brad; she sees it.

Not everybody can. Hands go up.

"Look," Brad says. "If it's safe to round the base—it's like taking a lead. And then, if one of their fielders drops the ball, or if somebody's not paying attention, or if nobody's covering the next base, maybe you can get there."

Every time? What if they like, see you? What if there's no chance?

Brad holds up his hands. Okay. It's not a rule. It's a judgment. "If the other team's player has the ball right next to you, if all the bases are covered, stay on the base. But if the ball's not close to you, round that base; look for opportunities."

Is he confusing them? Is he taking this too far? The delayed steal is hard enough.

After practice, Kacie asks Brad to explain the *"late steal"* one more time.

"You mean the delayed steal?"

Yes. That.

He goes over it again. He's happy that she's asked. Other girls have questions. *Who do we play next? Are they good?*

Kacie stands over him as he packs the equipment bag. She's picking at a fingernail, which, Brad notices, is also purple. "Coach. Do I have to do that in a game?"

Very likely. Uh, maybe. Wait. Do what?

"The late steal."

* * * * *

Their next opponent is the Braves. The Braves are 3-0. After three games, their pitcher, Claire Boniface, has given up a total of one run. She's struck out more than half of the batters she's faced. There are limits on the number of innings a girl can pitch each week, and the Braves' other pitcher has given up runs, but they've powered through their first games by scores of 12-1, 14-2, and 9-3.

The Marlins know this. Brad hears them talking about how they don't want to bat against Claire.

Before the game, Phil Braden comes by to greet Brad. "How are your girls doing?"

Brad figures Phil already knows the Marlins' record, but the record is the simplest way to answer the question: "We're 1-3."

"But how are they doing? Getting better?"

Brad notes that he's been very pleased with a few girls.

"Your girl Jamie can play."

Brad thinks she's one of the better players in the league.

"We're not so hot," Phil says.

"You're 3-0."

Phil makes a face. "Yeah, but . . . we've got Claire and we've got some good players, but between you and me, some of them haven't improved at all since the first practice. Two of my girls don't even come to practice."

"Sure," Brad replies. "But, like you said, you've got Claire."

Phil leans close, lowers his voice. "I tell you what, even *she* worries me."

"Why?"

"I don't know. But the other day before the game she just started crying. I have no idea why. She seemed fine when she showed up. Nothing happened that I could see. But then, halfway through her warmups, she started bawling. Absolutely bawling. I tried to talk to her, but she wouldn't tell me nothing. She went ahead and pitched the game, and nobody could touch her. After the game I tried to ask her about it again, but she wouldn't say anything."

Brad notices the Marlins huddling in the outfield. One of the Marlins seems to have hurt herself, twisted an ankle or something. Brad nods his head as Phil talks—he doesn't want to blow off Coach Phil, but he needs to get going with warm-ups, and now as he looks out to the outfield he sees Kacie down on the grass. Kelli and Maddi come trotting in, wondering where to find an ice pack.

Phil's got his medical kit right there. He flips Kelli an ice pack: "Here you go."

Kacie sits up on the outfield grass. She's fine. Still, Brad needs to look after whatever it is. This anecdote about Claire is interesting, but he needs to attend to his player.

"I honestly don't know what it is," Phil says. "I'll find out, though. I have to be careful; these girls are just kids and they're vulnerable. We coaches have to be aware of that stuff."

* * * * *

The game starts with a ground ball to third base. Renni fields it cleanly and delivers a strong, confident throw to Lissa at first base. Right on the mark. One out.

Except.

Lissa—*Lissa!?*—drops it. And can't find it.

The Braves' runner advances to second.

Brad turns his palms skyward in supplication.

Next batter: grounder to Emmie at second base. She picks it up deftly, but instead of making the simple throw to first base, she tries the long throw across the diamond in a vain attempt to cut down the runner going from second to third. Third baseman Collen goes down to her knees to block the bouncing throw as the unconcerned runner arrives. There should be two outs. One at the very least. But there are none, with runners at first and third. The Braves proceed to score four runs.

For the Braves, Claire's as good as advertised. If some problem is eating at her, Brad sure can't see it. She appears utterly composed, her tanned face a picture of concentration. Pitches come sizzling off her hip and smack into the catcher's glove. The first two Marlin batters strike out on timid swings. Kelli manages a foul pop, which the Braves' first baseman catches easily.

After a slightly better second inning—the Braves score two more runs—Brad still holds out hope that the Marlins will find their groove, but the Braves' first batter to start the third inning reaches base on a bunt. The next batter hits a fly ball to short left field. Lori studies it carefully, then thrusts her arms out as the ball thunks onto the grass like a coconut on the sand. Renni and Maddi—playing shortstop and third base—both run toward Lori to receive the throw to the infield. Nobody covers second base or third base, and the Braves' coaches wave their arms flamboyantly, urging their runners along.

As they prepare for each pitch, the Braves' batters check constantly for signals. From the third base coach's box, Coach Phil delivers an elaborate, Marcel Marceau-like system of signals. Arm tap on sleeve, tug on the cap brim, hand swipe across chest, three claps, tap on the cheekbone. The Braves' players have somehow digested this system.

The third inning comes to a merciful close. The Braves lead 10-1.

Brad feels his face clench. He's nearly quivering as he strides to the bench. "Bring it in!"

"Am I up next?"

"NOW!"

Brad kneels in front of them. "What did we work on for an HOUR last practice?!?!" He spits the words at them. The girls look down at their gloves. They haven't seen him this angry.

"Cover the bases!" Fist pounds palm. *"Cover the bases! Always look for a base to cover!* We've worked on it and worked on it, and you *know* what to do!"

It seems absurd, but Brad actually believes that the Marlins are the better team. He's been watching the Braves in their warmups between innings, and he can see why Coach Phil is concerned: They're not that good. Sure, the Braves have the star pitcher. "Other than that," he says, "our team—you—are better. *Way* better. You girls should be creaming that team."

He searches the huddle, sending out visual challenges. The girls avert their eyes, looking down at their cleats.

A realization comes to him: They're playing their parts. They're facing the star pitcher and there's a natural and known arc to this story. It doesn't occur to them that they can make this turn out differently.

He lets a few seconds ride. Then softens his tone. Palms down, fingers spread: calm. "*Know* what the runners will do. Before the pitch is thrown. You can figure that out because you—we—know how to run the bases better than anybody." He continues in a rhythmic meter: "It's about being *aware* and being *alert*—you have to *know* where to *throw,* what the *runner* might do—*before* the pitch is made. It's about being prepared for what *might* happen before it happens."

A few heads nod.

Brad exhales. "Hey. You can play. You're better than this." They can recognize him again now; it's just him. "Now, let's get some runs."

But the Marlins go quietly: two strikeouts and a weak ground ball back to the pitcher.

Brad trots off the field from the coach's box. The Braves lope to the bench, chatting confidently. But as Brad passes the Braves' bench, two words leap from the white noise to bold, large-font clarity: "Mercy rule." Brad pays attention as the Braves settle on the bench and begin their fun, silly chants. Another phrase emerges: ". . . *mighty Braves.*"

* * * * *

They're at Pitcher's Pub. Brad yammers at Mike. He's talking about the Marlins' loss to the Braves. Mike shakes his head with patient tolerance.

"I can't believe how much I care about this," Brad says.

Mike can. "That's who you are."

That sounds like a compliment.

"You can't deal with this. This failure."

Not so complimentary. "I didn't say I was failing."

"Whatever."

Brad understands Mike's shrug: 1-4.

"Not to be brutal," Mike says, "but hey, you're out of a job, voluntarily or not. Not a disgrace, but it didn't exactly make you feel good. Failed marriage. Not a lot of smooth sailing for a few years. You want to feel like a winner."

"It's not about winning." It comes out automatically: Error message from the operating system. Brad sits up straight, cocks his head at Mike. "And by the way. Can I use you as a reference? I didn't know I was such a fucking prize."

Mike brushes it off: "You need to feel some sort of winner's satisfaction. Okay. So it's not about winning; maybe it's about *you*."

It's not about that either, but on his way to that disclaimer, Brad gets caught on the *"winner's satisfaction"* part. What, like winning the Super Bowl? Whatever it is, has he *ever* felt it? A quick review of his life: graduations, girlfriends, job promotions. Marriage.

Surely these were important. Or not: They were mile markers. They evoke no surges of pride—no "winner's satisfaction." They are bullet point credentials, but they are inert, statistical. From his hockey days, he remembers watching *other* teams celebrate, jumping all over one another, tossing gloves and sticks up in the air. He remembers watching, leaning on the boards by the bench, wondering what that might feel like. Has he ever known "winner's satisfaction?" Has he even come close? Surely, everybody's had *something* . . . and if he can't come up with something, he must confront the logical conclusion: He is a loser.

* * * * *

Brad pages through his memory.

When he was thirteen years old, he won the kids' ping-pong tournament at their church retreat, but that was because he was one of the older kids, and the other kids stunk. As the kids' division winner, he qualified for the adult tournament.

In the first round he faced Don Robertson, one of his parents' friends. Mr. Robertson had a serve that hurdled the net and hit the table like a greyhound. Every stroke exploded with wicked topspin.

Brad was overmatched and quickly found himself losing, 2-11. He tried to steady himself. He reminded himself that he had quickness and good hand-eye coordination. He decided to direct shots to the man's backhand if he could. He would pursue every shot to the floor.

He won a few points. 4-11. He stood coiled and ready. In one volley he went almost under the corner of the table to rescue a drop shot. He held up against a succession of volleys, winning a few more points. He got the score to 7-13, then 10-15. He was getting used to the serves and the topspin. Everything centered on the little white ball. The rest of the world receded into distant, underwater sounds.

People started kidding Mr. Robertson, giving him a hard time. To Brad, though, it had become deadly serious.

He returned a smash for a point; the applause was instant. He heard people talking to his parents. An oddly familiar voice called out: "Watch it, there, Don. This kid won't lose easily." Brad couldn't place the voice. No matter. He was *on.* Every nerve and fiber was in perfect concert, acting and reacting, controlled and leaping.

And he was gaining. From 13-17 to 16-18; and then almost even: 19-20. One more point, and then deuce.

The next rally was short. A topspin shot by Mr. Robertson hit the top of the net, tiptoed along the net like a tightrope walker . . . and fell . . . on Brad's side. To the table. Then off. It seemed to happen in slow motion. The ball looked large enough. Its trajectory was predictable. But there was a flash of indecision—a momentary mental stutter—before Brad could move his feet. He knew this in a shard of an instant. In that same, freeze-frame moment, he began berating himself, even as he watched the ball fall.

The ball's airy-light impact on the floor made an eggshell sound that was so tiny that it had to be final. Game over.

Brad's shoulders slumped. Then Mr. Robertson was there, smiling broadly, clapping him on the shoulder. Brad looked away as he shook hands. Not to be rude, but because he was struggling to stop the quivering, to stop the blurred, onrushing loss of shape and structure in his face. Trying to keep his mouth in a straight line, even as he felt his throat clenching up. Then, his chest started heaving and something gave way and tears came flying out of his eyes.

Everybody could see.

The adults clapped their hands.

There was no place to hide. And then he heard that voice again—that familiar voice. He felt a hand on his back. He looked up to see—of all people—Coach Dub! Brad had not known that Coach Dub went to their church. He'd never seen Coach Dub anywhere but the rink. But there he was, standing close, whispering through clenched teeth: "You should be proud of yourself. Because you. Were. *Magnificent.*"

Brad had come wrenchingly close. Earned a few kind words.

Maybe he'd taken too much positive mileage out of those kind words. Because that pattern—coming up short—had turned out to be the story of his life.

* * * * *

No, Brad does not know what "winner's satisfaction" feels like. Among the packing peanuts in his storage box of lifetime memories, he's come up with this meager moment from a *church ping-pong* tournament game. That he didn't even win. This is his offering.

He scrunches his lips grimly at Mike. "Maybe you can tell me what you mean by that. You know? Maybe 'winner's satisfaction' is one of those experiences reserved for people like you. Maybe you get it every day. Maybe your video-avatar characters are all satisfied winners. Your clients can't survive without you. You're a goddamn genius. That must be it, right?"

"Whoa, whoa." Mike looks around. "Did I—hey, easy."

"For such a satisfied winner, you're just such an . . . a-hole."

Mike shrugs. "Sure. Okay."

Von laughs: "Tell us something we didn't know."

"Wanna register your club membership?" That comes from Spence at the end of the bar.

"Which club?" Mike laughs. "Are we talking winners? Or a-holes?"

"Either or both," Spence says. "The winners club is . . . smaller."

Laughter ripples around the bar.

Brad releases the tension from his shoulders. They were talking about girls' Little League softball. So, forget it.

"Seriously, though," Mike takes it up again. "No, I don't hardly know what it feels like. I just mean you're probably hungry for some . . . great . . . feeling. When's the last time you had something like that?"

"Another beer will have to do, for now," Brad says.

Good enough, Mike agrees.

Spence's glass is almost full; he's all set. But he wants to hear about the Marlins and the Braves.

Brad jerks an exaggerated smirk at Mike, then swivels to face Spence. "So," he says. "The Marlins are down, but they're starting to play." Brad hesitates. "Like they can."

He explains the mercy rule: If one team is leading by ten

or more runs after four innings of play, they win. Game over. It was not invoked. Because after the third inning, Brad says, the Marlins show life. They hold the Braves scoreless for two innings and scratch out a few runs to make it 10-3.

Brad feels a surge of pride as he speaks. He hears his tone settling into a taut cadence.

In the sixth and last inning, Courtney gets her bat on the ball. The Braves' infield botches it. Brad claps his hands at Courtney. The Braves, he swears to himself, are *not that good*. They've got the star pitcher, that's all. Give 'em a chance; they'll make mistakes, too. Courtney steals second. Then Colleen, showing great patience, works a walk.

Brad signals for Courtney to steal third, even though the Braves' catcher has been firing laser-darts all over the field. So Courtney goes on the pitch, the catcher rifles it to third and the third baseman's got the ball in her glove, way ahead of Courtney. Courtney turns around and scrambles back toward second. The Braves' third baseman throws to second, but the throw sails over everybody's head and scoots over the outfield grass. Seeing the new opportunity, Courtney turns back for third, where she sees Brad waving her home. The throw home arrives late and bounces past the catcher, and in the meantime Colleen heads from first base to second, and then all the way to third as the Braves retrieve the ball from the backstop.

The Braves' coaches yell furiously: "Hold the ball! Hold the ball!" Whooping shrieks go up from the Marlins' parents, who finally have a reason—meager as it may be—to make noise.

Jamie's up next. First pitch: Jamie pummels it and the ball soars over the outfielders' heads. Colleen scores easily and Jamie makes it to second. On Kelli's groundout, she advances to third, where Brad claps her on the helmet.

In the pitcher's circle, Claire gets ready to face the next batter. Brad talks to Jamie in low tones. About the delayed steal.

She looks at Brad: "We can't do it to steal *home*."

"Sure you can."

"But they're standing *right there.*"

"It's the same thing. It's about paying attention. They're not paying attention. And by the way, you're fast."

"Not *that* fast."

"It's not about how fast you are anyway. It's about timing and it's about paying attention." Brad walks down the third-base line, showing her how much of a lead to take.

Several pitches go by and they're still arguing.

"*I can't.*"

"*Just do it.*"

"*I can't.*"

"Jamie. The whole delayed steal concept came from you."

She looks at Brad. "*What?*"

When they first started the base running drills, Jamie had been the one who kept running when balls were thrown back to the pitcher. "Remember that? That's where the whole thing comes from. I just stole it from you."

"But that's practice," she says. "This is a *game.*"

"Come on." Brad feels himself getting angry. "This pitch."

Jamie takes her lead as the pitch is delivered. It's a big lead, almost a quarter of the way home. The catcher gathers the pitch, glances at Jamie, and then lobs it back to Claire in the pitcher's circle.

Dirt clods fly from Jamie's cleats. Claire's got the ball in the pitcher's circle. Out of the corner of her eye she sees Jamie barreling down the line. She looks again, cocks her arm. But it's too late. There's no throw as Jamie runs across home plate and sprints for the bench. She high-fives Lori, who's waiting to bat and isn't quite sure what's happened. Brad watches Jamie take off her helmet. Her face is red. She wanted that run. So did Brad. He pumps his fist as cheers go up from the Marlins' parents, while the Braves' coaches yell "*Come on! Pay attention!*"

Brad knows it's stupid to have used that play; to have

shown it. The Marlins lose 10-6 and that run makes no difference. But Brad wanted the Marlins to show something. He wanted them to prove something to each other. He also wanted, one more time—and how shamefully small of him, he knows—to hear the Braves' coaches yelling at their girls.

Chapter 10
LATE STEAL

Mid-May. The green grass sparkles like a summer lake. Sunshine pours out of a high sky, splashing on bright softball uniforms. An ice cream truck cranks its rumpus-room tune through the neighborhoods. Parents have broken out flip-flops and shorts.

Brad arrives at the field with a sense of dread. The Marlins can play. He believes they can play as well as any of the other teams. But they're 1-4. Out of six teams, the Marlins rank fifth.

	W	**L**
Braves	4	0
Cubs	3	1
Reds	3	2
Mets	2	2
Marlins	1	4
Cardinals	0	4

Today's opponent is the Reds. The Reds are a tough team, and the Marlins will be without Kelli and Jamie. Their two best players.

In Kelli's absence, Lissa will have to pitch. She won't throw as hard as Kelli, but she was the clear winner of his improvised cornhole-softball-toss contest: She's the pitcher (and he'll want her as his cornhole partner if there's an end-of-season team party). He's got Emmie catching for two innings. She wants to try it. She's athletic and she pays attention. So, why not? He's got Lori back for another try at first base. He's assigned Courtney a few innings at third base. She pouted when Brad told her. But she'll try it.

He's braced for disaster. He would not be unhappy if a rogue thunderstorm moved in and postponed the game.

The pre-game agenda includes a quick infield practice, and then they move to the outfield to run the pickle drill.

Brad challenges them. He'll run the bases. They'll have eleven rotations. They have to get him out at least five times.

The Marlins run Brad back and forth between the rags they use for bases. They pursue, gauge his speed, time their throws, cover the empty base. Brad talks trash as he dodges about: "No way! I'm too quick! You coming after me?"

The Marlins have improved. They execute the drill correctly. As a result, Brad finds himself running out of breath. His legs get wobbly. Renni catches a throw and comes after him. His change of direction is sluggish, and he falls down. Renni falls down on top of him as she applies the tag.

"Out!" she shrieks.

Parents laugh and point.

"Got him!" Renni thrusts her arms aloft. "That's four!"

Brad stays down on the ground, rolls over to look up at the sky. He sits up. It's time to visit with the umpire, present a lineup card, finish raking the infield dirt. He gets to his feet and trots in toward home plate. He swivels about with one last taunt: "You didn't get five!"

"Not fair! One more! We win something!"

"Okay! Hey, don't worry; I'll make it up to you."

The umpire and coaches gather at home plate to shake hands and review ground rules. That leaves maybe twenty seconds before the game starts. Brad's still gasping for breath from the pickle drill. He calls the girls to the bench, waving them in frantically.

They sort themselves out around him.

"Hey," he says. "How can we possibly win without Kelli and Jamie?"

No response. Heads looking down at gloves.

"I've got news for you. All of you can play this game. Not just Kelli and Jamie. If you girls do what you know how to do, this is a game you can win."

* * * * *

Their first inning goes smoothly. The Reds' first batter taps a weak grounder back to Lissa. The second batter strikes out. The third batter lines softly to Lori at first base. Lori catches it, drops it, picks it up, runs and steps on first. Three outs. Brad claps his hands. "Good inning Marlins! Bring it in!"

In the second inning, the Marlins strike. It starts with a walk to Kacie. One out later Lori drives a ground ball that skips past the second baseman, kicking up dust until it finds the outfield grass. As she heads for second; Kacie looks up and finds Brad in the coach's box, waving at her to keep coming. She rounds second and makes it to third as the Reds get the ball back to the pitcher. Brad waits with a high five. "Exactly right! Just like in practice!"

A groundout by Emmie scores Kacie and moves Lori to second base, and then a solidly hit drive by Courtney drives in another run.

Brad's excitement is short-lived. In the next inning, the Reds' first two batters are retired on pop flies to the infield. The next girl strikes out, but the catcher, Emmie, can't handle the pitch, so on a dropped third strike the Reds' runner heads for first base. Trying to atone for her error, Emmie launches a throw to first that sails over first baseman Lori's head. Lori watches the ball's path, fascinated, as it touches down and continues its journey over the right field grass, and the runner takes second base. Brad keeps his mouth shut, but he can't keep himself from stomping his foot.

A walk to the next batter is followed by a ground ball to second base, which Colleen can't handle. It gets past her and she turns to chase furiously, her oversized cap flying off as she runs. There should be three outs, but instead the Reds' girls run gleefully around the bases. One of them crosses the plate. The next batter hits a ground ball to third. Maddi fields it cleanly. A throw to first base ends the inning, but for some reason Maddi looks around the infield and gets confused by all the moving bodies. She holds the ball as the batter reaches first. Brad feels his face clenching. His foot—there it is again—comes down hard on the ground; he can't help it. Something hot surges through him; it gets worse when the next girl clubs a solid hit over the infield. Two more runs for the Reds. The inning ends, mercifully, on a pop fly to Colleen at second base.

The Marlins file indifferently to the bench. Brad calls out the batters for the next inning. He's mildly proud of himself for maintaining calm. These girls don't get it. They don't care. Why should he? Coach Conner and Stephanie can come back and take this goddamn chore off his hands *any day* now.

* * * * *

In the fourth inning, trailing 4-3, the Marlins break through. The girls are getting their second and third at-bats now. They're making contact. And they run the bases.

Renni reaches on a solid base hit. On the next pitch she steals second.

Courtney walks. As she jogs to first, the Reds' catcher drops the ball. The coach says something to the catcher, but she doesn't understand what he says, and moves closer to hear. On second base, Renni watches the conversation. With the ball lying unattended on the ground, she takes off for third. The Reds' coach starts pointing and stammering as if he's just seen a disturbance at the surface of Loch Ness: *Right there! Right there!—hey!*—but Renni cruises into third. At the same time, Courtney advances from first to second. The Reds' catcher finds the ball. The Reds' coach clasps his head in his hands. "Come *on* girls," he pleads. "Will you please *wake up!*"

Lissa knocks a ground ball past the pitcher and into center field. Renni scores easily. Courtney reaches third base well ahead of the bouncing throw. Lissa rounds first and bluffs like she's heading for second. A chorus of shouts goes up from the Reds' parents and coaches: *"Pay attention!"* The third baseman notices Lissa, hesitates, then uncorks an ill-advised throw to second. The moment she releases the ball, Courtney breaks toward home.

Now, the Reds' players hear voices thundering something different: *Home! She's going! Throw it!* The shortstop throws home in a vain attempt to get Courtney. On the throw home, Lissa takes second. The throw bounces away from the Reds' catcher, and Lissa keeps going, all the way to third. Amid the hollering, the Reds' catcher does not attempt a throw.

The Marlins' parents roar their approval. The voices of the Reds' coaches boom like broadsides from a frigate: "Do NOT throw that ball all over the place! Do NOT throw that ball all over the field!"

Before the inning is over, the Marlins ring up five runs. Marlins 8, Reds 4.

In the fourth inning, the Reds come right back with three of their own. They're tagging solid hits. Not much the Marlins can do. Brad calls out praise to Meghan and Renni for getting their relays right, covering the bases. "Exactly right! Good backup!" They're limiting the damage.

In the fifth inning, the Marlins tack on an insurance run.

Then, in the top of the sixth (and final) inning, purple-helmeted Kacie draws a walk. A ground ball down the first-base line results in an out, but Kacie chugs safely to second base.

Brad has taken Kacie aside during practice. Many times. He's tried to explain that bases are not safe havens; places to set up camp. He's told her to think of them as time bombs that will explode if you can't figure out how to get to the next base. Now, he can see the surprise and delight in her cheeks as she arrives at second base . . . and rounds it. Brad shows his palms—*hold*—and she retreats to the base.

"Exactly right," Brad calls. They make eye contact; she nods.

Two pitches later, Brad leans toward her, hands on knees, tapping. That's her signal: delayed steal.

On the pitch, Kacie takes a lead off second. She watches the catcher catch the pitch. She returns to the base.

Huh? Brad says nothing, but scrunches his eyebrows.

Hands on knees. Tap, tap. Same signal.

Kacie takes her lead on the pitch. This time, as the catcher returns the ball to the pitcher, Kacie starts lumbering for third.

"She's *going!*" A chorus of calls sounds the alarm, but the pitcher is looking toward home plate and does not understand what is happening behind her.

Kacie stands on third, breathing hard, face heaving.

"Great job!" Brad yells. A raw lump rises in his throat, and it's because this is *Kacie*. Kacie, who has not—until now—understood that she can run the bases, she can steal bases, she can *play this game*. She's standing right next to him. He knows that too much loud yelling—even congratulatory yelling—will confuse Kacie. So he bends close to whisper. It comes through his teeth, a fierce hiss: *"See what you can do?! You know how to play this game!"*

She takes her stance on the base, hunched over toward home, hands on forward knee. She looks up at Brad, mouthing the words: "Can I steal home?"

Brad grins and then laughs. "Not now." He pats her on the helmet. "But I know you can."

Kacie eventually scores on Renni's line drive to left field. Final score: Marlins 10, Reds 8.

After the game, they huddle on the grass. "Girls. Great game. What is it that the Marlins do?"

Four voices: "Base running!"

"What kind of base running?"

Nine voices: "Aggressive!"

"That's what won this game for you. Remember how we talked about coaches yelling to 'not throw the ball around'?"

Nobody's chatting, nobody's fussing with their equipment bags, sneaking glances at cell phones. For this moment, the Marlins give Brad their full attention.

"Well, the Marlins are going to make a lot of coaches yell about that." Brad pauses. "The Marlins won this game missing two important players. You can play."

Hands go up. *I'm going to be late for next practice. I forgot the delayed steal signal.*

This reminds him . . . "Oh—and—hey girls—girls." He fights for one last moment of attention. "A big first . . ." They're slinging their bags over their shoulders.

Brad hoists the equipment bag, speaks briefly to Diane and then the Reds' coaches as they head off across the field.

Kacie's mother waits by the foul line. She's a bit stout, like her daughter. She's packing up her lawn chair; bends down to greet Kacie.

Brad can hear Kacie's small voice asking some question.

He hears her mother's brief exclamation—"I *did* see!" Then, "Wait . . . what—what was it? . . . the *late steal*?"

Chapter 11
MY GIRLS

An envelope arrives in Brad's mailbox. It's a one-page letter:

> *It has come to the board's attention that, because of your late installment as coach of the Marlins, you were never screened as per league procedures. Please fill out the enclosed form, as well as the Criminal Offender Record Information (CORI) form. This is all standard procedure that we require for all team coaches. Thank you very much.*

* * * * *

The Marlins are *getting* the relay concepts. Balls hit to the outfield are thrown back to reasonably well-positioned cutoff infielders. They still get confused about when throws are supposed to go to third base rather than second, but they're getting better.

They're good at the base-running drills. Brad introduces a few wrinkles: He leaves the pitcher's circle to walk around, beckoning one of the fielders over for a quick conference. Brad wants his runners to notice: *There's a base uncovered—take that base!* Brad drops a throw from one of the infielders and turns lazily to say something to somebody and he's thinking: *Pay attention—take that base!* Most of them—even Kacie—catch on quickly.

Brad goes home feeling good. The Marlins' record is just 2-4, but they're showing signs; they're improving.

Brad eats his dinner alone. Leftover chili, which is not half bad, he thinks. The evening sun stripes the kitchen table. It's absurd, this good feeling that comes from having a good practice. But there it is.

He replays an image of Courtney leading off second base, crouched with her hands in front of her, ready to advance, a picture of alertness and confidence—*Courtney, confident!*

Then a thought presents itself. The next base-running skill, Brad realizes, is sliding. You can't really run aggressively if you don't know how to slide. But . . . sliding. He doesn't know how to teach sliding. Nobody ever taught him how to slide. As a boy you just slid. You read about Willie Mays stealing bases and you imagined your own fearless self and your own clever fadeaway *hook* slide and you just tried it. Teaching it? He'll have to demonstrate. Damn: He doesn't want to demonstrate it. He's an increasingly creaky AARP-eligible guy and he might very well pull a muscle or wrench some body part of which he has heretofore been unaware.

Done with the chili. He puts the bowl in the dishwasher. It occurs to him: If *he* is in fact scared to slide, then the girls will most certainly be scared.

* * * * *

"How are the Marlins doing?" Mike has grown accustomed to Brad's rambling softball narratives.

Brad flutters his hand unsteadily: So-so. He's not sure he wants to get into it this evening.

"Anybody beat the Braves yet? How's my girl Claire doing?"

My girl. Huh. Well, Brad says, she is doing well. Claire's the best player in the league, and since she's a pitcher, she dominates the whole schedule. These girls' softball teams all have good days and bad days—except for Claire's team. Claire's team only has good days.

The pub's mostly empty. Brad sits up and takes the bait. "Lemme ask *you*: How *is* 'your girl' Claire?"

"She's awesome."

"She's *awesome?*"

She's doing well, Mike clarifies. Claire's always been a little distant with him, but recently she's been more relaxed. Telling him about school. About friends. And yes, about boys. Even asking for advice.

By the cash register, Von's looking down, sorting bills. "I thought she was smart."

Mike lets that one go. "It's been . . . it's been good."

"How's it going with her mom?" Brad asks.

Mike takes off his ball cap and rubs his forehead with his forearm. "Now that. Is. Complicated. You know. I like to keep things uncluttered."

"Oh. That plan."

Mike speaks slowly, selecting words like cards from a poker hand. "She's cute."

"You want to dump her."

"Uh, no. I don't." Mike studies the head of foam winking at the top of his beer. "It's weird; there's nothing wrong. She's a sharp gal and I've got no big problem with anything."

"But you don't want the complication." Brad takes pride in not just finishing but *starting* Mike's sentence.

Mike looks up at the TV. Brad follows his gaze and he realizes that ESPN is showing a college softball game. It's the NCAA tournament: Auburn against . . . Texas.

Mike uses his fingers to tick off a list of items: "She's relaxed. She's easy to talk to. She doesn't put pressure on me to do stuff. She puts up with me."

Brad nods. Mike hasn't mentioned the part about sex yet.

Mike exaggerates a shrug: "And the *sex* is pretty good."

Brad waits for the exhale.

"But it's like . . . nothing's enough. Nothing's enough to keep me from wondering what the hell I'm doing with her. Like, why am I here? What am I doing?"

"Is this about that woman we met here the other night? Suzanne?"

Mike shrugs. "She's cute, too. And sharp."

"So . . . are you—?"

"Brad." Mike looks him in the eye. "Look. I'm trying to—I've invested a lot of time and energy into getting the right balance of . . . things. With Jo."

"Just wondering," Brad says airily. He doesn't care to dig into it. He finds himself distracted by the softball game on TV.

"I can't get away from that question," Mike says. "About what I am doing."

"Okay, so why does anybody do *any*thing?"

Mike lifts his index finger: "Exactly right!"

Oh. "Well, people get married because they're in love. They want to have a family."

"Ahh," Mike waves his hand. "Stupid."

Stupid. "Really?"

Von overhears and interjects: "Some people get married because they're having too much sex."

Mike raises his glass in Von's direction. "So I hear." But his smile fades. He sips thoughtfully, watching the bubbles rise in his glass.

Brad's agitated: The Auburn center fielder has just made a stupendous diving catch and there's no reaction in the pub.

"I shouldn't say stupid," Mike continues. "Here's the thing. Say it's Saturday, and I'm looking forward to something a little special. For her. Doesn't have to be expensive or highfalutin, but something fun, something a little out of the ordinary; mostly I just wanna do something for her."

"How unlike you."

"Very unlike me," Mike agrees. "But here's the thing. I want to talk ideas for what cool thing we can do and Jo's like: 'What do *you* want to do?' So I look at her and say: 'No, what would *you* like to do?' And she doesn't know; we could do this or that, but nothing seems to be . . . *compelling*. At all. I mean, anything. If she wants to go to the fucking *opera*, I'm willing to discuss. I'll get the tix. If she wants to stay home and eat ice cream and rent a movie, that's cool, too. If she wants me to come along on some couples' date—which I *hate*—well, hell, I can accommodate. But we keep coming back to square one, and after a while I'm thinking 'what's the point?' I mean, it's like we're just *existing*."

Brad squints, trying to connect things. "Maybe she just wants to talk." On TV, the Texas pitcher explodes into her delivery.

Mike starts to come back with something snide, but Brad cuts him off: "Women like to talk, you know."

Mike blinks, shapes his mouth as if to talk but holds it back.

Brad senses some opening; a fault in Mike's impenetrable walls. "Sometimes people—not just women and not all women, but women more than guys—it feels good for them, just talking."

Mike looks skeptical. "So. Just shoot the shit. That's my big proposal?"

Brad thinks about that. Something about women: "It's not 'shooting the shit.'" He has to gather himself and try to explain—maybe a little less aggressively—hopefully without losing this rare moment of advantage. With women, he says, you don't talk about sports, and you certainly don't talk about women, but beyond that it's not *shooting the shit*, it's about talking in some emotionally engaged way. For which, he knows, Mike has no patience. "Maybe," he says, "she'd like hearing you talk about *you*. What do you ever tell her about

133

you?" It occurs to Brad as he speaks: What does *anybody* really know about Mike?

Mike shrugs it away. "Since when do you know anything about women?"

Brad returns fire. "What the hell do *you* know? You ever do a video game starring Zima the Warrior Princess? Or—whatsername—Xena?"

Mike ignores the question. "Look," he says, "I'm trying to not just go along with things just because they're going along."

Brad takes a moment to parse that out. "Well, don't," Brad says. "Your digital avatars wouldn't just *go along* with things, would they?"

"Yes they would. Once they're programmed with a few predispositions and motivations and defining characteristics, actions and reactions are pretty easy to figure out."

Brad pauses to consider that, even as he realizes that by hesitating, he's ceding leverage.

Mike tilts his head. "Take yourself as an example. *You* wanted kids. All that stuff."

"Uh . . . what?"

"That was the point of things. And then it went away. So you split. Right? Isn't that why you and Steph split up?"

Grunt. "You're going pretty far back. And it wasn't as simple as that. I mean, sure, that was part of it. But actually, the kid issues—they came to be mostly about whether I wanted to *adopt* kids."

"Ahhh." Mike's index finger signals recognition. "You wanted your own."

Brad had envisioned his own, not somebody else's. He figured parenting would be hard work. He thought he could do it—he could commit to the squalling and the sleep deprivation, the stupid plastic toys and the puking—if it were *his own* kid.

"You wanted kids from your own seed."

"Sure." Brad swigs at his ale. He'd rather watch the

softball game on TV than talk about this. An Auburn batter hits a grounder to shortstop, and the fielder scoops it and zings a throw to first base.

"You wanted their hang-ups—their complications—to be inflicted by *you* instead of somebody else."

"*What the fuck?*"

"I mean, isn't that the reason you two called it quits?"

Brad tries to identify the quick answer. "No. Yes. Shit." He tries to trace how the conversation has twisted around to this—Mike regaining the familiar instructive raised index-finger posture. He takes a mental step back, then moves forward with another try. "Once it became clear that we couldn't have kids, I thought we might have some resolution, but then for Steph it was *still* about having kids. And after that, we just never had any fun anymore." He's running out of breath. He's perplexed that they're talking about this. "Once it got to be all about kids, after that, nothing, even sex— especially sex—was about fun. Anymore." He stops, breathes. *There,* he thinks. *Good enough?* And then: "I couldn't figure out what it was about anymore."

"Exactly." Mike nods triumphantly. "*Bingo.*"

Brad's face wrinkles into a sour lemon pucker. He's confused. Then he remembers their argument about desertion in the colonial army. He remembers thinking how it should have been easy for Mike to understand: *What's all this killing about? You fools can have this war; see ya later.* So what's going on here, with Joanne? Is Mike choosing to not desert—is he actually trying to *understand* some perspective that doesn't make perfectly logical sense?

Brad looks for Von. He nods upward at the television. "Does anybody watch these games?"

Von shakes his head. "Want me to change it?"

"No. I was just curious."

"They're pretty good, aren't they?"

"*Really* good." Brad turns back to Mike. "Let's just watch

this fucking softball game."

"All right."

"Before somebody comes in here and hears us talking."

* * * * *

Emmie watches Coach Brad drag something over the grass. It's a canvas tarp, filthy, corners joined to form a ragged bundle. A few unkempt yellowish strands hang out. It looks like hay or something. And then she realizes: It's hay. *Hay?* Coach Brad lugs it as far as the infield dirt. Right around third base he spreads out the corners and starts kicking hay around, forming a mound.

Sliding drills, he announces. Coach understands that many of them don't like to slide, or can't slide, or might be afraid to slide. "But you have to know how to slide." He gestures at the mound of hay. "This should make it easier."

Emmie has prepared herself for sliding. It was in the book about softball techniques. She read the text and studied the pictures. Run hard, throw your legs forward. Fold one leg underneath so your two legs form the shape of a '4.'

The team lines up at second base. Coach demonstrates once. His slide drives a furrow through the hay, and he pops back up, strands of straw hanging all over him.

"The base is right here," Coach says. "I'll be right behind it. Your job is to slide and drive this stuff into my face." He warns them not to think too much about technique: "Just run fast, get yourself down low, and *slide.* Throw your legs forward." He makes a sweeping motion with his hand. "Maybe pretend like you're trying to do a flying side-kick."

Renni goes first. Emmie pays attention. Renni's a good athlete and she grasps most of the drills quickly. But she slows down a little bit just before she slides, and so she thuds onto her butt and stops short in the hay. The Marlins start laughing and Renni turns first to grin at them and then at Coach, who's nodding his head. "Not bad," he says, "but next time don't slow down."

Renni returns to the line. She's brought a fistful of hay, which she throws at Maddi, who laughs. It wasn't a great slide, and if it wasn't easy for Renni, Emmie knows it's not as easy as the book made it sound. She wonders if Renni would make a good gymnast, but Renni—she's too crazy. It's hard to picture her on a balance beam with all that mischief bubbling up.

Some of the girls—Kacie, Courtney—edge back toward the end of the line. "I can't do this," Courtney mutters. This does not deter Emmie. Courtney says that all the time.

Lori's next. Lori is heavy and slow. Parts of her body wiggle and flap as she makes her way along the baseline, but her slide is surprisingly reckless and takes her smoothly through the hay. "I got to the base!" she shouts.

Lori, Emmie realizes, wants to do well. She is *not* athletic—maybe even less athletic than Kacie or even Meghan. But during games, Lori is constantly asking what the score is. She cares: She wants to win.

Jamie's turn. She runs hard, like she's mad at the base. She hits the dirt hard, sending a big pile of hay flying. Emmie is not surprised. Jamie is the one; the one who's good at everything.

Lissa's turn. She doesn't run hard, and she shrieks as she approaches the hay, but her slide is passable. She returns to the end of the line, brushing straw stubble off her sweatshirt, fiddling and swatting to make sure there's nothing in her hair. "I'm so dusty!" she cries. Lissa's okay at practice, but Emmie is quite sure that if they went to the same school, Lissa would not speak to her in the halls.

Emmie's turn. She runs confidently. Her slide is not perfect, but she comes to rest in the hay with her foot close to the base. And she knows how it could have been better: She could feel herself keeping her upper body too upright.

"Nice job," Coach says. "Come in a little lower, so you're

sliding—horizontally—and not *sitting*. But for your first slide, that was really good."

Emmie heads back to the line. She's identified the correction she needs to make. She'll get this.

After school, even on cold days, Emmie has been taking her glove and a tennis ball behind the school to play catch with the brick wall. She's taken her bat and a softball and stood by the baseball backstop, tossing the ball up, swinging, launching the ball against the fencing. Over and over. She's learned how the feel of the impact changes depending on what part of the bat hits the ball, and at what part of your swing. When she gets it just right, there's a satisfying feel of . . . *perfect*.

Perfect. In gymnastics she strives for perfect. Her coaches and parents use that word a lot. It's interesting; it's funny. It's funny because she wanted to play softball to *not* be serious. And she is *not* serious about it. But there's that feeling. That feeling, when it flows, when it's right. It feels like . . . like *nothing*. It feels good.

* * * * *

After six games, Phil's Braves are still undefeated. Only two games, a 7-3 victory and their 10-6 win over the Marlins, have been remotely competitive. Claire is blossoming just as he knew she would. At the beginning of the season Phil spent extra time with her, working on her fielding, and on a flaw he found in her delivery. When her stride veered off toward the first-base side, she couldn't push straight through her delivery, causing her to lose velocity and accuracy. "When your stride's off," Phil explained, "your pitches won't go as fast."

With that small fix, Claire has absolutely dominated, throwing a two-hitter and two one-hitters. She's struck out almost half the batters she's faced.

With all that, Phil worries. A good coach always finds

something to worry about. For one thing, he knows that his other players need to step up. When Claire's doing her thing, innings go smoothly. Errors give the other team a baserunner here and there, but they mostly just lead to another strikeout against some poor terrified girl on the other team. As a result, the Braves' players play relaxed; every ball hit to them is a chance to play a part. There will come a day, though, when Claire is missing, or just off. When that day comes, it will feel different. It will be harder. The other girls need to get better.

Thus far, the only girl that has noticeably improved is Kristal Jernigan, his worst player. At the team's first practice, Kristal could not throw, catch, or hit. Now, though, she's already caught two pop flies, and she can play a passable second base. She can barely throw it to first base, but her confidence is soaring. Phil takes great pride in that.

Other than Kristal, though, Phil can see that some of his players have not improved at all.

He worries about Claire's father. Phil has never met him and doesn't know anything about the guy. Usually it's the dads who introduce their daughters to the game, and in Claire's case he probably pushed her. But something is wrong. There was that day when Claire started crying in warmups. And then again last week, at practice she started crying. About nothing. It was just an odd thing, and Phil bent down in front of her so her teammates wouldn't see. The Braves counted on Claire—needed her—to be that *big girl* in so many ways. Phil didn't want anybody to see her crying. In Phil's experience, these emotional issues were usually connected to parents. And the less the girl wanted to say about it, the more likely that was the case.

Phil reassured her, but he knows that this might become an issue. It angers him. No parent should put that much pressure on a twelve-year-old girl.

In addition to complacency and Claire's parental issue, Phil worries about the other coaches in the league. Next week he has to be out of town, but the Mets' coach is refusing to reschedule their game. The guy keeps asserting in his e-mails that sometimes coaches just have to miss games; that's what assistants are for. Phil can't honestly say that his assistant is also out of town, but it just seems like a reasonable request to reschedule. Phil knows that the Mets' coach probably knows that Claire will also be away that day for a tournament in her other league, but Claire's absence is *not* the reason Phil wants to reschedule. Oh well. They'll figure it out.

What bothers him more was the way the Cubs' coach, in the last game, instructed his batters to step in and out of the batters' box, present fake bunting stances, waggle the bat in front of the plate. It was all within the rules, but that sort of distracting tactic is not right for this level of play.

So far, the Marlins' coach—the replacement guy, Brad—is the only coach who doesn't seem contentious about Claire, or rescheduling, or other petty stuff. Phil likes Brad. The guy seems to know softball. He's too quiet, though. And he doesn't seem to know how to motivate his girls. You can be a great strategist and even a great teacher, but you can't be a great coach unless you know how to motivate your players. In their game against the Braves, except for a few moments at the very end, the Marlins did not look particularly motivated.

* * * * *

With a win over the Cardinals, the Marlins raise their record to 3-4.

Brad is happy enough; he'll take the win. They played a messy game, but at this point, he understands: That happens. They had their usual disaster inning, with Lori dropping an easy throw at first base, and Maddi dispatching a throw on a mysterious itinerary past second base.

Later in the game, something happened.

It's the fifth inning. The Marlins can run the bases and

they're proud of it. They've got Lissa on second, Colleen on third. She looks up at Brad, mouths the words: Can I *steal home?* Brad shakes his head: No. Nonetheless, on the next two pitches they scrutinize the pitcher and catcher: Are they paying attention? After every pitch, the Cardinals' coaches call out: "Watch that runner on third."

And then a pitch caroms off the catcher's shin pads. The girl twists about, searching frantically, then recovers the ball. She looks up the third-base line at Colleen, who's taken a threatening lead off the base.

"Nice job," the coaches applaud. "How to keep an eye on that runner."

This inspires the catcher: After the next pitch, she spies Colleen taking her lead, holds onto the ball, and stalks up the baseline.

A steady stream of encouragement accompanies her: "That's it. Walk her back. Walk her back." The girl bluffs a throw. "All the way back, that's it."

Colleen retreats warily, as if the catcher were a snake.

After the next pitch she takes her lead again. And again, the catcher comes after her, and keeps coming, almost all the way up the line toward third. When Colleen's foot touches third base again, the catcher is satisfied: threat averted. She turns, trots toward the pitcher's circle.

Colleen sees what Brad sees: home plate, uncovered.

The catcher approaches the pitcher to hand her the ball and remind her about something.

As Colleen takes off running, the vocal artillery booms from the Cardinal bench: *Hey! Look! She's going!*

The catcher hears the alarm. She whirls about; sees Colleen running. She snatches the ball from the pitcher and runs a few steps toward home to tag Colleen, but it's too late. Colleen crosses the plate without sliding.

The Marlins spring up out of their seats, cheering, jumping up and down. The Cardinals' coaches are angry. Meanwhile,

Lissa has advanced from second to third. She watches intently as she takes the turn around third.

The Cardinals' catcher hangs her head. She's standing between home and the pitcher's circle, still holding the ball, watching her coaches gyrate like tortured serpents. She looks at the pitcher, who holds her glove up to receive the ball.

As he takes this in, Brad suddenly realizes that Lissa—right next to him now—sees an opportunity. As the catcher raises her arm to throw, Brad knows what's going to happen and almost wants to stop it because he feels sorry for the catcher, but he's coached the girls to do this and Lissa's already in motion. The ball takes a relaxed arc through the air, ending in the pitcher's glove. And Lissa's in full sprint, almost home. The pitcher looks up to take it in: Lissa running, catcher standing helplessly, home plate uncovered. Lissa scores. One pitch: two steals of home.

Most of the Cardinals are not sure what's just happened. One of their coaches comes onto the field, arms showing full and dramatic wingspan. "That's a bunch of bull!" he barks. "What do you guys think you're doing!?" Both of the Cardinals' coaches appeal to the umpire—and it's Von working the game. Von shrugs and clarifies; it's all within the rules.

They turn to Brad: "Do you guys want to do this run-around-the-bases crap, or do you want to play softball?"

Some of the Cardinals' parents start to boo. *Come on! Play softball! Fancy stuff. Is that really what this is all about?*

Brad folds his arms across his chest. "It's a close game," he says. "We need runs."

"Then tell your girls to hit the ball!"

"Or maybe you could have one of your players cover home," Brad says.

One of the Cardinals' coaches stalks to the Marlins' bench. He finds Lissa and points his finger: "Hey! Hey you! You get back to third base!"

Lissa gets up obediently and starts putting on her helmet.

No way. Brad strides angrily toward the Cardinals' coach. *"Don't you tell my player what to do!!"* he yells. The vehemence in his voice surprises him. Diane shepherds Lissa back to the bench. Brad confronts the coach and thrusts his neck forward. "You teach *your girls* the *rules!*" There's a vague awareness of Von's voice calling for calm. "You teach *your team! I'll* worry about mine! Last time I checked, base running was a huge part of this game! *TEACH IT!*"

Diane tries to step between them. Von maneuvers his way into the jammed scrum, speaks to the Cardinal coach, who holds his hands out to his sides.

Brad is making a scene now. He doesn't care. With Diane holding her arm as a bar across his chest, he jabs his finger at the air: "Our player just made a heads-up play! She was the most alert player on the field!" He should stop there, but the flood walls have been breached. He's swept along by the exhilaration of reckless release, a cascade roaring and foaming from his mouth. "She should be congratulated instead of getting yelled at by clueless coaches who *don't know her and don't know the rules and don't know how to teach the goddamn GAME!*"

His chest heaves. His insides steam like the walls of a spent volcano. It's a bad look. And in front of all these people. *Come on: It's Little League softball.* The heat of his reactions caught him by surprise. He does feel bad for the Cardinals' catcher, who's not sure what she's done wrong. But he's proud of Lissa. Ain't *nobody* gonna undo her great base running move. He's proud of Colleen. He's proud of all of his girls. That two-word phrase sounds foreign, or maybe just new—but it's what they are now: *His* girls. *His girls.*

Chapter 12
INVESTIGATIONS

Phil is not on the league's board of directors, but he likes to attend their weekly meetings. Not everybody on the board likes him, but he likes to think that they all respect his commitment to coaching, if not his knowledge and acumen. His key ally is the chairman, Bob Remersdorf. Years ago, he helped Remersdorf on a legal issue when things weren't going so well. Phil can count on Remersdorf to stick up for him when issues arise.

They meet in the Community Bank building downtown. Remersdorf's family owns the bank, and Bob was the president at one time. He resigned several years ago, but he keeps a seat on the bank board and takes the liberty of using the conference room for softball league meetings.

Phil takes a seat against the wall as the board members settle in at the conference table. He reads a magazine as they start off with formalities, committee reports, unfinished items: fall fundraiser, summer league umpire list.

Then they turn to the agenda. Les Peterson starts things off. "It's interesting that Phil Braden is with us tonight," he says.

Phil stiffens. "Why's that interesting?"

Peterson looks at Phil over the top of his wire-rimmed

glasses. "About your—the Braves' roster."

"What about it?"

"Claire Boniface."

"What about her?"

Peterson leans back, clasps his hands on top of his gut. "Couple things. First of all, why is she on the Braves?"

"Because she was drafted."

"No." Peterson takes off his glasses and uses them to point at Phil. "If you can jog your memory just a tiny bit, you'll recall that she was *assigned* to your team. Yes, there were other girls assigned to teams—but they were daughters assigned to the teams their parent was coaching."

"Okay."

"Except you are not Claire's father, and neither is your assistant."

This stuff, Phil knows, can be tricky. Coaches coach their daughters. That is not the case for Phil's Braves, since Phil's daughters are now in college. Coaches' daughters are held out of the draft so the coach won't have to expend a draft choice on his own daughter. Since neither Phil nor his assistant Bruce has a daughter playing in the league, it had seemed fair that the Braves should also have a girl assigned to their team—a girl they didn't have to draft. A similar arrangement had been made for the Marlins: Maddi Tomsworthy's mother's best friend was the assistant coach—at the time of the draft—so Maddi was assigned to the Marlins. After much consideration, Katherine Remersdorf was assigned to the Braves.

And then there was Claire. The arrangement, Phil says, was that Claire's mother's boyfriend was going to be an assistant for the Braves.

"But he isn't."

"I think they broke up."

"When?"

"I don't know. I don't keep up with that kind of gossip."

Peterson pauses, cocks his head to one side. "Putting aside

the fact that you already had a player assigned to your team. Do you even *know* the guy, this boyfriend? Know his name? Ever met him?"

Phil only knows *of* Mike. "Sure," he says.

"All right. Whatever," Peterson says. "My concern is that the situation was never even close to where Claire should have been held out of the draft."

"Then why'd you arrange it that way? I didn't make the rules."

"That's my concern," Peterson says. "I'm not saying we need to redo rosters halfway through the season, but we have to make sure that this type of thing doesn't happen again."

"Okay."

"Because it's not fair."

Phil takes offense. He hears some version of this same argument almost every year, and it's mostly because people don't know one *tenth* of what he knows about softball. In this case, if Claire had been assigned to any other team, she would not have improved as much as she had. "Isn't this about teaching the game?" he says.

Heads nod around the table.

"Well, I'm teaching her the game."

"Oh, sure," Peterson says. "And if Emily Dunmore were your pitcher it would all be the same to you."

"I'm just telling you; I'm teaching her the game."

Peterson waves at the comment, shooing it away. "My second concern." He stops. "Phil, I know you spend time working individually with Claire. I trust that it's just at the beginning or the end of practice." He looks at Phil. "Right?"

The league maintains a policy that, other than just before or after practice, and at the field, male coaches are not to spend time alone with any player (other than their daughters) on their team.

Yes, Phil says. Well—there was one time—inside a gym when practice got rained out. Yes, he knows the policy; he'd let it slip that one time. He apologizes. He does point out, though, that it was just because he cared. Few coaches would have cared enough to take the time.

There's a moment of appreciation. "Not to pick on Phil just because he's here," Peterson says, "but about this point in the season we always send out reminders about that policy."

Right. Murmurs of assent; notes taken. Remersdorf will send the e-mail.

"My last concern," Peterson resumes, "—and it's *our* concern, not just mine—has to do with the number of innings girls are allowed to pitch."

"Not just Claire," Phil says.

"It applies to everyone. But I think Claire's the only girl used exclusively as her team's pitcher."

"I do not have her in there exclusively," Phil says. "Absolutely not. I've had Haley Fiore in there, I've had Riley Pisca—Piscatewitz . . . Riley—just the other day. Two innings."

"Phil."

"Yuh."

"Claire's your pitcher."

"I've been working with her as our pitcher. The truth is, I have a hard time getting the other girls to pitch. Haley damn near started crying when I asked her to pitch. I'd even have this other girl . . . Bella . . . pitch, but I can't *force* her."

Peterson looks around the room.

Don Jenkins speaks. "Whatever the circumstances, Phil, we're considering a limit of ten innings per week."

Phil nods. That would cut into Claire's innings, but not much. "How about in the playoffs?"

Looks go around the table. They haven't addressed that yet.

Jenkins continues. "For players who also pitch in other leagues, the limit would be six."

Six? *Six?* Now, *that* seems unreasonable. "Why six?"

"Our concern is twofold." Peterson resumes the lead.

"First, we're concerned about not hurting their arms. If the reality is that the girl's working her arm to death between two different leagues, we have to be aware of that. Second, this board has always believed that girls need to learn multiple positions, as part of learning the game."

"I think you left out the part where you don't want my team to win," Phil says.

"Phil." Jenkins again. "It's not about winning."

"I get that," Phil says. "But if it's not about winning, then why is everybody so concerned that my team is 7-0? Are you trying to legislate for a league where every team gets a 500 record?"

Voices vie with each other. Then Pete Magnuson speaks. He hasn't said much, and as the former high school softball coach, his voice carries some weight. The floor yields. "Nobody's legislating anything. To a certain extent, Phil, it's about fairness. We're discussing the fact that our coaches seem to have differing priorities. Some of that is just inevitable. But it's an issue."

Phil clips his pen into his shirt pocket and stands up. "Anything else I should know?"

Glances bounce around the table.

"Okay," Phil says. "Have a good evening."

* * * * *

To the Board

Gentlemen: It's (Cardinals) Coach Marty. I would like to bring to your attention some issues concerning the interim coach of the Marlins. First of all, in our recent game against the Marlins, this man screamed obsceni-ties at me for several minutes and had to be physically restrained. It was embarrassing and inappropriate for the spirit of our league. Second, he has apparently taught his girls some tricky but overly aggressive base-running tactics that push the rules (and which, btw, is not good teaching, since this stuff won't work at higher levels of play). Again, I find this inappropriate. I regret to say that other issues have come to my attention as well. Coach Brad—who is not gainfully employed—may be violating our rule about working with girls alone. This is typically not cause for alarm, but I've heard something about him taking down his pants in front of the girls at one practice. I know that one Marlin player has already quit softball. I respectfully suggest that the Board consider or reconsider his fitness to coach in our league.

Sincerely,
Martin Hazelbach

* * * * *

The Marlins run the over-the-shoulder drill. Brad wants to run it briefly, as a warmup. He's got bags of candy in the car. He hasn't forgotten his promise—from one of the early blacktop practices—of some kind of candy.

Throws are off. Throws are dropped. Brad struggles to find reason for encouragement, and he's momentarily rewarded as Meghan—Meghan!—gets one to settle into her pink glove. Kacie—she's getting better—twists around for a throw, but she gets dizzy looking up for it. The ball ticks off the bill of her purple cap. She drops to the ground. Everybody laughs.

Next girl. Who's up? Come on. *Whose turn is it?* Courtney steps up. "Sorry."

Courtney manages a clean catch over her shoulder. She runs toward her waiting teammates, but does not know where to throw: No girl presents a target. Lissa and Kelli are near the front of the line, but they're talking and don't notice Courtney approaching.

"Come on!" Brad fumes. *So much for the candy,* he thinks. He needs to change the drill. He thinks: He still can't depend on them to throw to the right bases. Okay. *There's* something to work on.

Brad bats. Some of the girls field; the rest run the bases.

He positions Emmie at shortstop, Kelli in left center, Kacie in left field. He launches a fly ball to shallow left field and watches it thud to the ground. The girls look at each other, and it's funny. Runners are moving, but Emmie falls down as she runs to pick up the ball. Howls of laughter; Lissa—the runner—laughs so hard that she wobbles and falls down between second and third.

"All right, come on!" Brad hollers. "Let's see if we can accomplish something here! Let's just try to focus!"

He assigns the girls to new positions. From home plate he surveys the field and hits the ball over the outfielders' heads. From left-center field, Colleen makes an accurate throw to Courtney—the relay at shortstop—who sees Renni heading for third. Courtney delivers a perfect throw to Kelli at third. They've got Renni nailed. Renni halts, and turns back toward second. Kelli gives chase. Courtney stands watching, but doesn't bother to cover third. Kelli throws to second. Renni changes directions again and heads for third. Nobody's covering.

Brad feels something starting to churn inside him. "Who's supposed to be covering third?"

Nobody seems to know.

"Courtney, why are you standing there watching? There's a base to cover." The churn becomes a boil.

Courtney looks down at the ground. "Sorry."

Renni stands on third base. She bends over, coughing and wheezing.

"COVER THE BASES!" Brad shouts. "How long have we

been doing these drills?"

Heads go down.

He kicks at the grass. Lets the silence ride. Don't they understand? You cover a base, you prevent a runner from advancing, maybe you save a run. Which just might be the difference between a win and a loss. He lets out a loud breath. Reminds himself: They're eleven and twelve years old.

"Okay," he says. "Most of you know what you're supposed to do. But if we don't do it right in practice we probably won't do it right in a game." He surveys his team, all of them looking like shamed dogs. "Nice running, Renni," he says. "Are you okay?" She's standing on third base, holding her stomach and looking down at the ground, but she nods and straightens.

The Marlins resume their positions. Emmie gets set to run. Brad hits a fly ball; it's headed over Kacie's head. "Deep!" he shouts. "Back!" Kacie steps forward, hesitates. She starts to backpedal, and then nearly falls down as she realizes it's over her head.

Renni scores. Emmie rounds first as purple-clad Kacie waddles furiously after the ball. Emmie heads for second, and then takes the turn for third as the throw comes into the cutoff.

The Marlin infielders maneuver, working the relay system. Standing at third base, Kelli gathers the bouncing throw. Emmie charges past, makes the turn for home. Kelli pivots to throw home. She's got plenty of time. She can hear Brad: *"You've got her!"* She looks for the catcher. Emmie's helmet looks big, though. White with bright blue and green streaks. Kelli stays calm, but she can't take *too much* time, and then—suddenly hurrying—she releases her throw, which flies off to the right. Past everybody; it hits the backstop. Emmie crosses the plate, where Renni greets her with a high-five.

Brad retrieves the ball. He congratulates Emmie on her aggressive base-running. Kelli stands, hands on hips, puzzlement creasing her face. It was an easy throw. She looks at her hands, as if expecting an explanation. She looks at Brad, who shrugs. "It happens," he says. He looks out at the field, and he's about to shout something out, but then stops himself. He sighs. The throw from the cutoff should have gone home. Not to third. But he's already explained this.

* * * * *

After practice, Mom's late again. Fortunately, Meghan doesn't have to wait long; the car arrives and Mom's in there leaning toward the passenger side, smiling and waving.

Meghan gets in.

"How was practice?"

"Good."

"Anything fun happen?"

"No."

Mom lets an exasperated breath escape.

"I mean, nothing unusual." Meghan puts on her mitt and flexes it in her hand.

Mom curls her lips in against each other. "And how was school?"

"Good." Her group received a B-plus on their evolution project.

"Okay," Mom tries to sound bright and happy. "That's not—that's pretty good."

"It's good," Meghan says flatly. "The project went well." Realizing that she might sound peeved, she decides to go ahead and talk a little: accommodate. They've finished the evolution unit, she says. It was interesting. Only as she says these words does she realize that yes, it was in fact interesting. Meghan was interested to learn about species like sloths and opossums, which found strange ways to survive. Now they're working on a unit about communities.

"Communities? Communities. What kind of communities?"

They were learning about how groups and species—

including humans and animals like bees and wolves—had to rely on each other to perform different roles.

Mom keeps her eyes on the road.

"Some animals have assignments to keep watch or build nests," Meghan says. "They don't all just hunt and defend themselves."

"Well, yes, that's true," Mom says. Meghan waits to see if Mom comes up with some example of some species or culture that Meghan's never heard of. Meghan likes knowing that there are all kinds of roles. She likes this about softball, and since she's talking, she takes a bold step and announces her belief that a softball team is a good example of a community with lots of different roles, and that *she* can fit in a role as a good baserunner.

"Baserunner?"

Meghan looks up warily. Nobody thinks she can do anything, but she's learning and so far she's done fine in baserunning drills. She knows that you have to get on base first, but she can get on base. She can get walked and yes, she can hit the ball. "I'm a good baserunner," she says.

Mom smiles. "I'm sure you are."

Meghan sinks down in her seat. She hates the constant corrections and investigations, but sometimes it's worse when Mom just goes along. You can tell when she doesn't believe you.

* * * * *

Brad receives two e-mails from the league. The first one is addressed to all coaches (he's finally been added to the circulation list):

This is just a reminder to all coaches: in order to avoid any possibility of any impropriety or perception of such, it has been our longstanding policy that coaches should not spend time alone with any girl on their team. Exceptions to this policy arise—girls need rides, girls sometimes arrive early or leave late—but time spent with players is to be in the context of team practices or games.

Brad has not been aware of this policy. He understands why it's a good idea. But: Colleen. Twice now, her mother has dropped her off at the park to meet Brad. Both times they went out into the park and spent about thirty or forty minutes, working mostly on catching. Nothing fancy, just repetitions. They worked on blocking bad bouncing pitches, with Colleen blocking the ball like a hockey goalie rather than stabbing at it with her glove. Then Brad stood behind her where she couldn't see him and tossed pop-ups in the air; Colleen had to tear the catcher's mask off, find the ball, and catch it. She practiced long tosses from home to second base, and then farther. Then Vicki thanked him and they drove off, Colleen's hand waving out the car window.

The second e-mail is addressed to Brad, acknowledging receipt of his CORI form. Plus:

. . . In addition, we would like to meet you, and to discuss a few issues that have arisen. If convenient, we would like to meet with you after our board meeting next Tuesday. We meet at the First Community Bank (2nd Flr conference room); we should be done with our agenda by 8:30. If this is not convenient, please let us know of a time that might work for you.

Robert Remersdorf, President

Brad feels his face angling and crinkling. *Issues.* Well: The nutty screaming episode against the Cardinals is the obvious guess. But is it messier than that? He checks the monitor again for the precise reading: "a *few* issues." Not just one.

He blows out his breath. *What bullshit. Whatever it is.* He never asked for this gig. He's done his best. To figure this crap out. To help these girls: help them have fun, learn the game—and yet, somehow, *a few issues have arisen.* Probably some political sidebar bullshit. Once again: It's the peripheral something that's always there, waiting for him.

He contemplates a beer. Or something stronger. Something to divert his thoughts, as the rising spring breeze coasts through his empty house.

* * * * *

It's easy to spot them at the high-top in the corner: Justin, pudgy with dark beard like the young Santa; Craig, thin and blonde in wire-rimmed glasses, with the mild look of a folk-singing youth group discussion leader. Brad realizes how much he's missed them. When he asks how they've been, they roll their eyes and groan. They've been at the lab all night.

Brad feels an involuntary smile freshening his face. It almost feels like he could step right back into it: rushing to proof reports and press releases; exchanging glances of excitement from new patterns in the samples; puzzling over outliers. Even when things were bad, the people around you could keep you going: Just the inertia of their presence and the camaraderie of shared missions provided a sort of ballast.

Craig is Brad's successor at Rylix. When issues arise, Craig says, he still finds himself trying to figure out what Brad would say.

Justin rolls his eyes. He mimics Craig talking like Brad: *"You gotta to get to KNOW this enzyme. You gotta OBSERVE."*

Craig laughs. They all envy Brad, Craig says. He gets to relax for a while, and then he'll land on his feet when the right thing comes along. As for them, they're all sneaking in lunchtime interviews. Poking around. The company's had no new breakthroughs, nothing showing enough promise for press releases. No deals on the burner. Supposedly the whole industry's scrambling for partners, but the money's gotten picky; every promising drug shows potential red flags, or maybe the venture guys have learned to show a little more restraint.

They've all seen the writing on the wall. The old crew has dwindled. Gillian found a good fit with one of their rival companies. Mia's in San Diego, working on pancreatic disease therapies.

Mia was the one who'd spoken up about the tweaked test results. Her words had never made it out. Brad had intercepted the journalist, reminded him about a favor owed, and the writer changed the story to something about a rumor from an undisclosed source. It wasn't long before the Executive Committee came asking. Brad thrust himself into the position of responsibility. And taken the hit.

Craig rests his chin on his knuckles. It's a matter of weeks, he guesses, before Rylix closes its doors.

Which is why they've met. There are opportunities out there. Two in particular. The first one's a startup. They don't even have a name yet, but it's a small team cutting loose from Rocgen. "They're still figuring out their plan," Craig says, "but it's real. It's gonna happen and it could be a great fit for us. And," he says, "they know who we are. By reputation."

From his coat pocket Brad produces a pen and a wire bound notepad. He uncaps the pen. "Whose reputation?"

Craig holds up his hand. He's getting to that, but he needs a refill. They look around. There's a shift change, with new staff reporting for duty. The new waitress sees them as she ties her apron in the back.

Wow. Blonde hair done up in a small fountain of tresses, impossible hourglass figure. She arrives to take their orders, and then flashes a dazzling smile as she departs.

"Mostly they know about *you*," Craig says. "But yeah.

They're interested."

"Sounds good," Brad says.

"Would you be in?"

Brad hasn't told them about his prospective investment consulting business. He's had a few meetings with financial advisors and portfolio managers. He's enrolled in an accounting class for the summer—not that he'll be a balance sheet expert, but he'll want to improve his fluency nonetheless. Yes, Brad says. He'd be in.

"All right," Craig says. They raise their hands for high fives all around.

It occurs to Brad: When did high fives become universal? Didn't they evolve from an old *low five* 'gimme-some-skin' exchange? *Meghan*, he thinks. She still wants to catch the ball with the palm of her glove facing up. She wants to *see* the ball find its home in the open pocket. Brad hasn't been able to correct this, but it's suddenly obvious that when you give a high-five you do not look at your own hand; you look at the other person's hand. He'll remember to show this to Meghan: He'll high-five her and ask what she was looking at; she'll see— he hopes—that she should look at the ball and not worry about her glove.

Brad opens his notepad to jot a reminder.

"You need contact info?" Craig says.

Brad closes the notepad. "Just writing myself a note about something."

The waitress arrives with their refills. She makes eye contact with each of them as she sets the pint glasses on the table.

The second opportunity, Justin says, "is not as fresh and exciting, but it might be more . . . solid." Peninsula Thorex is exploring a merger with a German outfit, and if it goes through, they'll be establishing a U.S. pediatric oncology unit. It all hinges on the deal going through, but their old Rylix gang would surely be a prime candidate to get things started.

The waitress returns to check on things, and then brings them glasses of water. She has to extend her arms—bare, smooth, and eggshell brown—to find room for the glasses on the table. "Anything else I can get for you?"

They're good. "Thank you," they say, almost in unison. Justin reaches for his water; his hand bumps his beer glass. He recovers quickly and saves it from falling. He shakes his head. "I was a little distracted."

Brad and Craig grin. *Yeah. I guess.*

"I was *not*. Staring." Justin focuses on his water glass and holds it. "I mean, okay, I was distracted. My attention got thrown off from the intended target."

Craig chuckles. "Got thrown off," he says. He takes off his glasses; wipes them on his shirt as he grins at Brad. "It's what we've been trying to do to this very stubborn protein," he says. "Throw it off." He puts his glasses back on; tosses a sidelong nod toward the waitress. "If only it were so easy."

Brad remembers these frustrations; these challenges. And it comes to him: *Kelli.* Kelli's bad throw home at their last practice. Justin almost knocking over the water glass. *Attention . . . thrown off the target.* That was Kelli's problem: She was looking at the runner, instead of her target. She was right behind the runner heading home, and couldn't help watching the moving runner with her bright helmet. She's used to throwing the ball where she's looking; it screwed up her throw. Lesson: Find the target. *Block out* the runner.

He jots another hasty note in his notepad. Then he tells them about his softball coaching gig.

Justin and Craig laugh.

"What's funny?"

"Nothing." Justin just has a tough time seeing it. "You don't look the part," he says.

Brad does not want to picture what he looks like, but he suspects that Justin's probably right. He never did find a pair of those tractor-grade coach shoes.

Craig, on the other hand, sees coaching as a great fit for Brad. "Because Brad's a great scientist." He turns to Justin. "Doesn't matter what you look like."

"Great scientist. Sure," Justin says. "Since when do great scientists make great coaches?"

Craig shrugs. It's about figuring out how to get things—living things—to behave differently. How to condition reactions and processes; how to coax and manipulate.

"I see what you're saying," Justin says. "But it's a weird analogy. Geeky. I can see why you were a science major."

"Yeah. Well." Craig takes a pull at his beer. "I'm not sure why *you* were."

Whoa. "Good comeback," Brad says.

"At any rate, *Coach*," Justin says, "how would you feel about this second potential opportunity?"

Brad hesitates. Certainly he's interested. He raises a cautionary note, though, about the merger: These arrangements seem to make sense for companies, but then people find themselves operating a lot differently than they'd expected.

Of course. They'd thought of that.

So which one sounds better to Brad?

Brad doesn't know. "They're both interesting. Obviously, we need to see how things develop. Keep me posted."

Justin expects an update on Peninsula next week.

They cross-check calendars for their next meeting. Brad's schedule, of course, is very flexible, but he'll have evening practice on Wednesday, games on Tuesday and Thursday.

"Shit," Craig says. "Tough schedule."

"You should see these girls," Brad says. He's surprised to hear himself. "They can play."

"Really."

Brad corrects himself: "Well, sort of. Some of them."

They finish their beers and settle the bill, leaving a generous tip. It's been a productive meeting.

* * * * *

Phil heads to the field to watch the game between the Marlins and the Cubs. The Cubs are very good, and these two teams are the Braves' next two opponents. His Braves have already beaten both teams, but Phil likes to monitor things.

The Marlins have only eight players for the game. That's the minimum number. He goes over their roster in his head. Among the missing: Renni Hornsbee, a smooth-fielding infielder. Phil has coached her sisters. Also missing: Lissa McQuillen, another skilled all-around player who's grown an awful lot; Maddi Tomsworthy, a girl he remembers as having potential; and some other girl that he can't quite remember. More important, their weakest players are all there. With just eight players, they'll have two outfielders instead of four. There will be a lot of open ground. Anything hit to the outfield will hurt the Marlins.

The Cubs have a full complement. They're a tough team, stocked with big girls who can hit.

Coach Brad deploys his Marlins in an odd outfield alignment. Instead of a right-center fielder and a left-center fielder, which would provide the best coverage, he has a center fielder and a left fielder. Right field is empty. The second baseman, though, is positioned a bit deeper than usual. They're gambling, apparently, that balls hit to that side can be handled in the infield. Which actually makes some sense, Phil thinks; most of the strong hitters hit balls to left field and center field. Phil also notices a fat, awkward-looking girl playing first base; another gamble.

In the third inning, one of the Cubs' batters blasts a rocket over the left fielder's head. Two runs score and the batter trots easily into second base. Brad claps his hands as if his own team has just scored two runs. "Exactly right!" he yells. "Colleen, exactly right on the cutoff!" "Kacie, great job getting that ball in!" "Emmie, that's exactly right!" He's talking about their relay. And Phil sees that they executed correctly, with the shortstop relaying the ball to third base. The correct base. Simple enough, but they did it quickly and they did it right.

Overall, the Cubs dominate. Phil takes note of Brittany Caldwell, who smashes two balls deep into the outfield. One of them, interestingly, is caught; the other goes for a home run. The Cubs' infield looks sharp. Final score: Cubs 14, Marlins 6.

Phil remembers, though, that the Marlins' shortage of players probably cost them four or five runs. Other than that, they did not play badly. He takes note of one interesting play by the Marlins: While stealing second base, one of the Marlins' runners saw the pitch get past the catcher, and—without slowing down—kept going all the way to third.

Phil enjoys watching these girls play and learn. He finds these games entertaining. He is not concerned for the Braves. He isn't sure exactly how he will allocate Claire's innings count, but the new innings limits are not yet in effect. Claire will be needed against the Cubs, but now he wants to use her against the Marlins as well. If the innings limit takes effect before the game . . . well. He'll figure something out. He can experiment with other pitchers against the Cardinals, maybe the Mets. Against these two teams, he'll need Claire.

Which reminds him: He needs to call that guy Mark— Mike—Claire's mother's boyfriend—about helping out. Bob Remersdorf advised him that it would be a good idea to at least give the guy a call. Bob's heard that Mike and Joanne had in fact *not* broken up, but that Mike does not want to coach. So, just in case anybody decides to make an issue of it, Phil will be able to say that he approached the guy—and *expected* the guy to coach—but the guy backed out. Just in case anybody has a problem.

Chapter 13
SCRIPTS

With dusk closing in, a scent of lilac wafts through the open windows. Somewhere down the street, a screen door bangs shut.

Brad wears a film of sweat and infield dust. His position assignment grid sits on the table, damp and stained purple where Kacie's popsicle dripped on it. He contemplates his e-mail to the Marlins.

The Marlins faced Claire Boniface this afternoon. The Braves took their eighth straight victory.

After the game, in the huddle, Brad pointed out a few things done well: good base running, a few good plays.

Maddi raised her hand, wanting to know the final score.

"11 to 8."

"Oh. That's not so bad."

The rest of the Marlins agreed. Lissa thought it was "something like 15 to 2." Other voices chimed in. A wave of conversations began to rise.

Brad let it flow for a moment before getting huffy. *"Not so bad!?"*

The noise died down.

Something about Mike flashed through his head—some tiny thing about those stupid computer game characters.

"These games are not pre-determined," Brad said. "This is not a script; it's not like the Braves are *supposed* to win. You girls do too much talking about what you can't do; why you can't bat against Claire Boniface—you're beating yourselves before the game even starts. I'm telling you, you can beat that team, even when Claire pitches like she did today. I'm not lying when I say that. Next time we play them, I'm expecting a win."

They didn't believe him. He's not sure that *he* believed him.

Heading off the field toward the waiting cars and parents, the straps of the equipment bag bit into his shoulder. When he got to the parking lot, a bunch of balls jumped out of the ball bucket and sought shelter under his car. He derived some perverse satisfaction from noting how the balls had succeeded in finding the most difficult spots to reach.

His second beer goes down, cool against his throat.

Hi all

We lost, but the girls continue to improve. Big shout-out for Emmie. She joined us late and started out a little behind, but she's really come on recently. Today she handled plays all over the field and she knocked in a run with a solid hit. Second shout-out goes to Kacie for a nice catch in right field, and for backing up bases on every pitch. A shout-out also goes to Jamie. Jamie does so many things to help us, but today she showed something new, pitching a solid and scoreless (!) inning. She'll get more chances to pitch.

A toxic feeling snakes around inside him.

As he headed off the field, one of the Marlins' parents intercepted him. Brad didn't recognize him; he's met more moms than dads.

Stout guy, windbreaker, buzz cut, heavy-set jaw. Brad

reached out to shake his hand.

"Hey Coach," the guy said. "You're doing a good job."

"Thank you."

"But, hey." He rubbed his face. "Why do you keep putting that fat girl at first base?"

Brad stiffened. He was talking about Lori. Brad shrugged up the straps of the equipment bag on his shoulder. He decided not to defend Lori. "Which girl is your daughter?"

"Renni."

"What a great kid," Brad said. "One of my favorites."

"Well thanks. I think she's one of your best players."

"She is clearly one of our best players. Great baserunner, slick fielder. She doesn't yet have a lot of power with the bat, but she puts the ball in play just about every time."

"Yuh." He tapped Brad on the arm. "Well then, lemme ask you. Why does she play outfield one inning and third base one inning and first base another inning?"

Brad looked around to see if Renni—or anybody—was within earshot. There were too many reasons, but he decided to give it a shot. He wants the girls to learn different positions. All of his players have to learn to play the outfield. Left-center field gives them chances at well-hit fly balls. He's trying to get girls to step up to new responsibilities. He'll give them chances to earn promotions to new positions. Yes, it would be simple if he just gave one position to every girl. But that would mean some other girl wouldn't be rewarded for her progress. "Renni plays a lot of positions well—"

"I'd suggest short and third—"

"She may even get some innings at catcher at some point." Brad looked around again and found Renni in one of the cars, just a few strides away. She was slumped down in the back seat. When she saw Brad looking at her she sat up and waved, coughed into her hand, looked at it, and made a face.

The guy shook his head. "I respectfully disagree with that approach."

"I'm going to be fair to Renni," Brad said. "If anything, I might favor her at the expense of the others. But I have a responsibility to eleven girls here."

"Well, that's right. I agree with you. So why not keep it simple, put the best girls at the important positions. That way they'll win games and have more fun."

Brad could feel noxious stuff squirming around inside.

"Isn't that how the other coaches do it?"

"I don't know how other coaches do it," Brad said. "I think I know how I can help these eleven girls learn and have fun." He felt indignation stirring, untethering. "Look, don't get me wrong. I'd love for this to be all about winning."

The girls were leaving the field, some of them calling "Bye, Coach!"

Brad saw Renni waving at one of her teammates. She opened the car door. It was not a good time to be arguing with her dad. "Hey, I hear you," Brad said. "I do get your point."

The guy spread his arms, shrugged, and turned away.

Brad's been trying to shorten his e-mails. But he continues:

> . . . *I'll also note that many of the other teams only play their best players at key positions. I'm sorry, but that's just not how we're going to do it. Players who improve—I want them to know that they can earn new opportunities. That kind of improvement will help us and give us flexibility. For instance, if Jamie only plays shortstop, then nobody else can learn that position and feel good about that. More important, it means that I can't let Jamie try pitching, where she may well discover a new favorite position. These girls are 11 and 12. I'm going to give them chances to succeed or fail (and learn) as they earn them.*

Next game: Mets. Go Marlins! See ya there.

He pauses to reread. He wants to make this clear. But he wonders: Is he way off? Would it be better for everybody if he just did it like the other coaches? He positions the mouse, clicks "send."

Who'll be missing for Thursday's game? Meghan. Meghan? Hot damn! Brad opens a new excel sheet to begin the lineup puzzle, which has suddenly become a whole lot easier.

He knows he should be ashamed of himself. For his glee. Meghan's a nice girl who wants to play. She's just . . . not . . . and then he feels even worse for the fleeting thought of Meghan's mom, who happens to be a concerned . . . and attractive and apparently successful strawberry-blonde lady, divorced and . . . whatever. Brad can't help it: He's glad that Meghan will miss the game. So maybe he's a real prick. Maybe that's why all these parents blow off his e-mails without responding. Anyway. He'll have right field assignments for Lori, Colleen, maybe Kacie. They'll all be ready to take on the special assignment that's been reserved for Colleen until now. Renni? Shortstop and third? Renni, as he thinks about it, is probably their best fielder, along with Jamie, of course. Renni also contributes an important element of levity, but she picks her spots and she's serious once the games start. She'd missed the last practice—some sort of doctor's appointment—and Brad felt the difference in some altered, less natural balance between focus and laughter. At any rate, Brad thinks, Renni will get time at short, third, and left center, maybe first. What's her dad's problem?

E-mail responses start showing up. A few short, positive notes.

"Go Marlins!"

"Thanks for noticing Kacie's backups. She's explained backing up to me."

And then, this one:

Thank you for your note, and your excellent commu-

nications. It helps me and my wife arrange our child-driven schedules. And thank you for spending your spare time coaching our daughter (Lissa). With that said, I want to make a suggestion. I know it sounds funny, but maybe you could yell a little more? At some point these kids need to know that an authority is holding them accountable. It seems you don't like to yell at them, and I think that's a great approach in an ideal world, but at some point they need it. Maybe I should just speak for Lissa. She needs to be yelled at. If she's not paying attention, or if she's not trying hard, or if she shows an attitude, please don't hesitate to get a little angry. As a Little League coach myself—coaching Lissa's brother—I've found that a little anger really gets their attention! My honest opinion is that you're doing a good job, but I also think you're coddling these girls. They need to be accountable! Tough loss today; good luck next game!

And this one. Unrelated. It takes a minute before Brad realizes that it's not a parental response.

Conner Baird has informed us that he is now available to resume his responsibilities as the Marlins coach. You can either return your equipment and materials to us, or we can put him in touch with you to make arrangements. We sincerely thank you for your contributions to this softball season.

Best Regards
Robert Remersdorf
Softball Little League President

Chapter 14
REPETITION

Brad harbors no hard feelings toward Conner. None of this is *his* fault.

Conner's set to take over. It turns out, though, that he can't make the next day's scheduled practice. E-mails fly about. Threads tangle and untangle. Clarifications are sent and revised.

Brad will run the practice. After that, he and Conner will meet at Pitcher's Pub. Brad will provide a briefing: what the girls can and can't do, what they've worked on, what to expect.

Their record—Brad's record—stands at 3-6. Fifth out of six.

	W	**L**
Braves	8	0
Cubs	6	2
Reds	4	5
Mets	3	5
Marlins	3	6
Cardinals	1	7

* * * * *

Last practice: Brad slings the equipment bag over his shoulder. Colleen waves as she gets out of her mother's car and volunteers to tote the bucket of balls. They walk along the chain-link fence around the field.

Colleen betrays no knowledge of any coaching change. Brad figures that a lot of parents might have given up on the fouled flurry of e-mails. As he ponders what Colleen does and doesn't know, he sees her becoming agitated. Her wrinkled nose tells him that something's bugging her. "Why do we run the pickle drill so often?" she says.

Brad laughs.

"What?"

Brad starts to recite the list of benefits: They can all play catch, but will they be able to make that throw at the correct time, while running? Will they remember to present a target for the thrower? Can they catch the ball with a runner coming right at them? Will they remember to always cover the uncovered base?

"But we never use it."

He halts, readjusts the equipment bag straps on his shoulder. If a group of players can do that drill well, he explains, they know to look for bases to cover, they know how to make quick decisions and difficult throws. So even if they never use it, it helps girls learn the game.

She wrinkles her freckled nose. "But we do it *so often.*"

"Colleen. *You* do a great job. But we need everybody to get it."

"Okay," she says. But she's still waiting for something.

They reach the fence gate and enter the field. On their way to the bench they greet Maddi and Emmie, sitting on the grass along the foul line. Courtney and Renni play catch. Brad lets the equipment bag slide down off his shoulder.

It's not much good, Brad continues, if one or two players

know how to do it. The whole team has to get it. When the Marlins can all do the drill, the whole team will be better, and have more confidence. It doesn't make anybody a star, but it means the Marlins know what they're doing, that they can play the game. "That's why we're here."

Colleen looks at the ground, and then squints up at him.

"It just . . . matters," Brad says. There.

But then with her small voice she persists: "Why?"

The Marlins arrive. Lori waves as she walks toward the bench. Lissa emerges from a car. They need to get started. "Colleen," he says. "Geez: *Something* has to matter."

As the girls arrive they pair up quickly and move to the outfield to play catch. A few of them linger to chat near the bench.

"Grab a ball. Start throwing," Brad says. "You can chat while you warm up." It's just another practice.

Meghan pairs with Jamie. He can hear Jamie saying, "Nice throw, nice catch." He does not hear Meghan respond, but he glances over and sees the pink glove and notices that she's holding it with the fingers up. "You're looking good!" he calls, but she either doesn't hear him or thinks he's talking to somebody else.

Lori throws with Lissa. He wonders if those two get along in school, if they even say hello to each other in the halls. Lori lets one fly. It makes a solid smacking noise in Lissa's glove.

"Hey," Brad says. "Where'd you learn to throw like that?"

"I know!" Lissa says. "She's hurting my hand!"

"Lori. Nice throwing. You been working on that snapping thing?"

Lori smiles, shrugs.

"Keep backing up."

"Backing up who?"

"Keep moving further apart. Make some longer throws."

Her next throw goes flying over Lissa's head. Brad has a ball; he flips it to Lissa so she won't have to retrieve Lori's errant throw. "That's okay, Lori. You had some zip on that one."

Lori smiles.

Nothing new on the agenda. A couple of different infield drills, cutoffs, a little bit of base running. Pickle if there's time.

Today they run cutoff drills with live situations: Brad hits flies to the outfield, with runners moving. There are a few sloppy throws, but the girls set up correctly and throw to the right places. At one point, he needs to hit one to right center. Jamie's the runner, lined up next to him like a track runner in starting blocks.

He tosses the ball up, swings. He gets a bit too much on it. The ball comes off the bat squarely and rises—too fast—toward right-center field. Toward Meghan; over her head. *Back, Meghan!* he shouts.

She tenses for a moment, realizes it's over her head, and then starts running after it, arms outstretched. From home plate, Jamie takes off. She rounds first, checks to be sure that it clears Meghan's head, and streaks for second.

Fielders spring into motion. Courtney's at shortstop; she moves to cover second base. Renni's the second baseman; she runs into the outfield to take the cutoff throw. He notices Kelli, moving from left-center field; she can see that Meghan can't throw it all the way in to Renni, so she positions herself as an extra relay person.

Meghan gets to the ball. Throws it to Kelli. Who catches it, turns, and lets fly with a strong throw to Renni. Renni catches it, looks up to see Jamie tearing around second base. Maddi's on third base, waving her arms. Renni's throw bounces once. Jamie slides.

Maddi fields the throw and sweeps her glove low across the base, catching Jamie on the leg.

Out.

Brad lets out a whoop. Thrusts a fist in the air. "*THAT! WAS!*" Both fists. "*BEAUTIFUL!!*" He'd begun to doubt that they'd ever get to this point. He pumps his fists over his head, again and again, and can't stop. *"Yaahh! That's what I'm TALKING about! Yeah!! AWESOME!!"* Maddi jumps up and down. *"Perfect tag, Maddi! Kelli—how to help out! That's alertness! Renni—that was perfect!"*

It's just one time. One repetition. Who knows if they'll ever do it like that in a game? But it feels good. He gets ready to launch another fly ball. He can smell the grass and the rising dust. He's got a slight glow of sweat going. One repetition. Is all. But for this one moment, it feels like an accomplishment.

* * * * *

They quit practice a few minutes early.

"Bring it in!"

Some of them trot, others walk. They gather loosely, some of them chatting, some of them stuffing their gloves in their packs. They have questions: about drinks of water; about *who do we play next game*; about *I have to use my cell phone to call Mom . . .*

"Girls. Take a knee."

A few girls are still talking as they gather around.

"Girls." He raises his voice slightly: "I've got news."

The chatting dies slowly, like a boat drifting after the engine's been cut.

"The good news, for you, is that you might not have to do any more pickle drills or base-running drills."

They shift uncomfortably.

"Some of you may remember that I'm the *temporary* coach of the Marlins. Kind of a sitter."

They fidget.

"Your real coach is ready to take over. His name is Conner. Starting this weekend, in your game against . . . the Cubs, I think, he'll be your coach. My . . . uh . . . my ex-wife, Stephanie, will also be helping out. I don't know exactly—"

"You won't be the coach anymore?"

"No."

"Will we—"

"I've talked to Coach Diane, and she'll still be working with you."

"Will Heather still keep score?"

They like Heather. She's a young adult and she's pretty, like they all want to be. She's always positive and pleasant and when she thinks something's funny they laugh along with her. Brad doesn't know if she'll still keep score. "Girls," he says. "Give me a minute here."

Brad notices a wad of chewed-up gum in the grass. He studies it as he speaks. He didn't expect that this would be a big deal, but now he wonders if they feel betrayed . . . like maybe he never really gave a crap. "I'm going to talk to Coach Conner to let him know what you girls have been working on. I know you'll all be respectful to him and listen to what he has to say. I want to tell you that I've had a great time with you girls, and I've learned a lot. I haven't done this before, and I've tried my best to help you have fun. I hope you've had fun and maybe learned a thing or two. You girls can play this game, and I'm glad I've gotten to know you." His toe works at the chewed-up gum, which grabs on to his sneaker.

Hands in the air. *What about Skittles? You owe us treats. . . . Is Mr. Conner somebody's father? . . .*

"And I'm not just saying that. I really hope . . . you have a great rest of the season." It comes out a bit lumpy at the end. He makes a kicking motion to get the gum off his toe. "So," he says. "Go Marlins. I'll see you around."

* * * * *

He won't miss the equipment bag. That's for sure. He won't miss all the worries—whether he's being fair, whether the girls will do *anything* he says, whether the parents are happy or pissed off. But he'll miss it. He'll miss it more than anybody will miss him. They've played almost half the game schedule; it's been more than half the season in terms of time spent, including those first frigid practices on the pavement.

He's got the equipment bag and the bucket of balls, and he's almost to the car.

"How come you came to this practice?"

It's Colleen.

Brad smiles. He's glad to have that small voice there. "Well, you need a coach to run practice."

"But you knew you're not the coach anymore."

"I'm helping the new coach. Coach Conner. And my ex"— he corrects himself—"and his girlfriend."

She ponders that, in the way she might ponder the taste of a new food in her mouth. She finds it unsatisfactory. "I wouldn't have bothered if I were you. Coming to practice."

"Yes, you would have."

"No, I wouldn't have."

"Colleen. I just felt like I should come to practice."

"Nobody would have expected you to."

"Maybe I felt like I should say goodbye."

Colleen offers no argument. But she's still thinking.

And as they approach the waiting cars, Brad feels like there's more to say. Shards of thoughts wander around and flash in his head like fireflies. He can't catch them. "Well," he says. "Practice is fun."

Colleen looks up, incredulous.

"You don't think it's fun?"

Sure. But practice is practice.

Brad sticks with it. "Maybe I wanted to see you girls do the cutoff drills right." He sticks his tongue out. "So there."

Colleen laughs.

"What? What's funny?"

"Coaches aren't supposed to, like, stick their tongues out at players."

"Maybe." Brad exaggerates a shrug. "But I'm not a coach."

Chapter 15
REAL COACH

Conner's come straight from work. Still in his slacks and dress shirt and shiny shoes. Tanned and tall, dark-haired, clean-cut. Brimming with authority—more authority, Brad suspects, than the temporary substitute Marlins coach.

They shake hands. Conner hails Von at the bar, and Von dries his hands on a towel before giving a hearty shake to Conner.

They take a table in the corner, next to a Guinness beer poster. They chat briefly about Conner's towering business obligations. Conner thanks Brad for filling in. "I feel bad—like I'm yanking something away from you." Conner's baritone voice tolls like a gong in a chapel. It makes idle chatting feel almost momentous.

"Quite all right," Brad says. They joke a bit and roll their eyes about the "privilege" of coaching a bunch of girls trying to play softball.

Brad reviews the roster for Conner. Some of them can play. Most of them, he says, are improving. They all have things to work on. He finds himself trying to explain how the simplest, easiest plays can go haywire; how they sometimes start flinging the ball to bizarre locations, like maybe they've invented a new game . . . but then there are those sudden moments when somebody understands something and two girls execute something just right—and suddenly the whole team looks like a well-coached unit.

Conner nods along. "How's the pitching?"

Kelli, Brad says, is a good pitcher. After the Braves' star and possibly the Reds' pitcher, she's as good as anybody. She's working on a change-up, but still has trouble throwing it for strikes. "You ever try one of those?"

Conner shakes his head. He does not know much about the windmill delivery. Pitching will be Stephanie's department.

"Well," Brad says, "if she can get that change-up down it'll be a major weapon."

"How about catcher? Got a strong arm behind the plate?"

Brad shows Conner the grid of position assignments from their last game.

From his shirt pocket Conner produces a pair of reading glasses. He wipes the lenses and fits them to his face. He squints and frowns slightly as he reads. "Looks complicated."

"It's like a sudoku puzzle. Takes about twenty-four hours each game."

Conner chuckles as he peruses. Once he gets to know the girls, he'll figure out their positions.

Brad goes over their signals: steal, delayed steal. They've got a code word for bunting. "About half of them will recognize it in a game. If you change it, no big deal."

Do they bunt a lot?

Brad shakes his head. "Almost never. We've tried maybe three times, with very mixed results. Only a few girls are good at it. Even fewer of them want to."

Conner strokes his chin. "Do you have a 'take' signal?"

Nope.

"They just swing away?"

"I talk to them. I'm trying to get them to understand how to manage their at-bats, but mostly I want them to learn how to recognize balls and strikes. And how to swing the bat."

Conner nods. Sagely. "I'm a proponent of the small ball game," he says. "It's the key to an aggressive offense."

"Absolutely. The girls have heard a lot about being aggressive."

"I like to force mistakes."

Yup. "Make 'em throw that ball."

In high school, Conner says, one year his team used the hit-and-run in almost every game.

Brad never even played high school baseball. He needs to step away from this one-upmanship. "Of course," he says, "when the other teams get aggressive, the Marlins make mistakes, too."

"Right." Another thing to work on. "Sorry. I was getting stuck there," Conner says. "On the small-ball thing."

"No sweat."

It's going well enough. They order a second round. Brad decides to venture a casual question about Conner's business deal.

Conner exaggerates a glum face. "*Must* we talk about that?"

Brad pauses with his pint glass halfway to his mouth. "I guess not," he laughs.

Conner takes in a measured breath. "Long story short. I don't know how much you know about the biotech business. But this just wasn't a good deal. There was plenty in it for us, but I would have had to give away too much control. I couldn't do that. So." He heaves a deep sigh. "I don't have much experience with victories of restraint. But I just said no."

When they finish their beers, Brad hands over the plastic sleeve with the score book, the medical release forms, the medical safety handbook, the roster with contact information, and schedule. "If you ever have questions about anything, just ping me."

"Don't be surprised if you hear from me."

Back home, Brad steps out onto the back deck. A

whispering breeze tickles his forearms. He heads for the park. He takes a familiar route, along the edge of the forest. A full moon washes and polishes the night sky.

Conner's all right, he thinks. Maybe he'll turn out to be the coach the Marlins need. Brad suspects that the parents will have fewer suggestions.

Across the field, he hears the basketball rim rattle. There's a light on over the basketball court, a silhouetted figure shooting free throws. Shot after shot splashes through the cords of the net. Brad notices the guy's release: After a slight hop, the shooting hand snaps forward; the non-shooting hand swims back along his side, bringing his two arms to about 10:20 on the clock face.

* * * * *

Mike has learned to see shapes, how to pick them out from their confusing contexts. He's learned how to foreshorten; he's learned how branches twist and grope and reach. He can recognize key spots where textures change, angles clash, where lines get delicate and dissolve.

But he continues to struggle.

It's not a technical problem. It's in his head. He's scoured the art section of the library: *Approaches to Art, Freeing the Mind for Art, The Soul of Art, The Inner Artist.* The pages are steeped in spirituality, with lots of focus on breathing instead of drawing. He finds himself skimming, glossing over suggestions about choosing your best time of day to work. He considers and then moves past the wisdom-soaked words that hang like ancient silk tapestries on exhibit: *"after drawing the simple cup every day for years, one may then attain the vision to really see the cup."* One passage snags his attention briefly: *Everything that one draws, all that one creates, is a recreation of the creator.*

In his own analysis, Mike can see that his problem with

trees comes down to an internal conflict. Part of him wants to sketch the forest: the *forest,* with its messy breakage and rot; its random tangles. Another part of him wants to draw *trees.* Trees: He wants a beech to take the form that a beech ought to take, a maple to look like a maple, a birch like a birch. But it's never like that in the forest. It's one thing to capture the forest from afar. From the outside. Smooth clumps of broccoli under blankets. It's recognizable; it makes sense. The problems come when you know too much about the details, and try to draw it from the inside.

He shows a sheaf of drawings to Joanne. They sit together on the sofa in Joanne's den. She leafs through them, smiling. "You're very good," she says. "I mean, for somebody who's never had formal instruction, you've really gotten good."

For somebody who's never had formal instruction . . . Mike nods along.

"One thing, though," she says. She pauses to consider a pencil sketch of three maple trees. Silver maples. A few broad strokes convey the general idea of tangled forest in the background, but he's rendered the three maples with great precision. He's taken care to understand branching patterns. He's studied bark textures in great detail. The small grouping is suitable, he thinks, for a museum diorama.

"Somehow these look too . . . *right,*" Jo says. "I mean, the accuracy is amazing. But they look a little like . . . specimens. In the woods, aren't they more . . . more irregular?"

Mike nods vigorously. "I think you nailed it." A sketch of a botanically correct tree is just not interesting. But even when he decides to draw a broken-off tree, it still comes out looking clinical. "There's no . . . no *art*"—he winces to use the word—"there's no art to it."

Joanne sets the drawings down on the coffee table. She continues to peruse at a leisurely pace, like she's browsing a catalog.

Mike leans forward, fingers clasped. He likes the way trees

in the forest seem to take on personalities, albeit a lot of them seem quite disturbed. The problem, he says, is that he keeps drawing them without all their distortions. He doesn't know why. They just come out that way. He reaches across and shuffles among the sketches. He turns to a sketch of a gnarled apple tree with a broken branch. "Even this one looks too studied," he says. "It looks like an arrangement. Like a portrait, or still life."

He does not know how to draw the *forest,* up close in its chaos and wildness, with the different trees defiant, or broken, or both, or somehow . . . natural.

Jo flips back and forth among the pages.

Mike doesn't think she understands what he's trying to say. She seems unimpressed.

Joanne looks up. "Have you thought about Phil's e-mail?"

Mike has received an e-mail from Claire's softball coach:

I realize that I never actually contacted you directly. I trust that Joanne spoke to you earlier this spring about helping me coach her daughter's softball team. I'd heard through Jo that you were probably not interested, but I thought I might reach out to you again, just in case you might have changed your mind. I could use the help. I can tell you that it's fun. There are headaches, but I'm here to take care of those. If you have any interest, please contact me at your earliest convenience.

Mike can see that Jo's done talking about drawing trees. He looks away from her, and then back.

"I know you don't have a lot of time," Jo says.

"I don't."

"I know you don't like a lot of complications."

"I don't know that I want to work with these other coaches, either."

Joanne cocks her head to one side. "Do you know them?"

"Never mind." The Braves' coaches have nothing to do with his reluctance.

"You know," Jo says. "If you decide to do this I can almost guarantee you it will be messy. If you don't want messiness, I understand. But—" She stops herself.

"What?"

It looks like she's about to shut it down, but then she decides to continue. "You can't live a spot-free unwrinkled life."

Mike resents the accusation—is it an accusation? Of what? It's at least *some* kind of condemnation of his life choices. Something in her words makes him think of Brad, and his thoughts bunch up.

Jo lets her words hang and drift. After a few moments, she offers another thought. "It might be good for Claire," she says. "For you and Claire."

Mike sits back. He pillows his hands behind his head. He's seen Claire studying her stances and strides in front of the big mirror in her room; doing wrist-flick exercises as she moves about the house. He's heard about her games. He's made a few encouraging comments, but he does not know her well.

He is not infatuated with Joanne. He's not school-boy-in-love; he's not about to propose or anything. But he does want to do something for her. So, coaching: Maybe it's not out of the question.

* * * * *

Diane was sorry to see Brad replaced. But she's glad that Conner and Stephanie asked her to stay involved. And she can see that she's needed. Stephanie, in fact, is still hobbling, and she's swamped at work; she'll miss the first two games.

Diane is happy to help. She's been enjoying the season. The Marlins are having fun and the team is competitive, even though its record—after the loss to the Braves—stands at just 3-6.

Before his first game, Conner saunters about during warmups, hands behind his back, watching the girls. Evaluating. He comes back to the bench, takes up the scorebook and starts writing. He tears out a sheet and hands it to Diane. "Any suggestions?"

Diane scans the position assignments. Jamie at shortstop. Check. Kelli pitching. Check. Courtney in right field. Hmm.

"Did you talk to Brad?"

Conner nods. He has. But just watching the girls, he has some ideas.

Diane searches the page. "Is this just for the first inning?"

Conner shakes his head. "We'll start with this, and see how it goes."

Diane looks from the paper to the field. The girls have grown accustomed to playing several different positions each game. That is not always the best way to do it. But at least some of them—Lori, Renni, Maddi—like it. She'll talk to Conner as the game goes along. He seems to have some conviction. There are many different ways to do things. And Conner is the coach.

The girls pay attention to Conner. He towers over them; a big guy with a big voice. When they make good plays, Conner is effusive, more effusive than Brad. But when ground balls elude them, when balls are not caught, Conner is quick to reproach: *You gotta be ready! Hey! What are you doing? Don't ever throw behind the runner! Never!*

The Marlins look nervous, but they do as they're told.

Diane cringes a few times. At second base, Emmie starts to her left, then stops as a ground ball scoots past. Diane has been noticing Emmie's improvement: She's been gaining confidence, getting quick starts on balls hit near her. On this play, though, Diane sees uncertainty.

Then, when one of the Cubs' hitters sets herself to bunt,

Conner sounds the alarm so loudly—"*BUNT! Gotta COVER!*"—
that Colleen and Lissa, playing catcher and third base, look at
Conner instead of charging after the ball, then try to peel out
for it when they see him pointing. Colleen picks it up belatedly,
but makes no throw.

"Gotta be *READY!*" Conner shouts. "Come on now—on
your toes!"

Diane moves next to Conner. "I think you scared them."

Conner throws up his hands. He sucks in a hard breath
and shakes his head vigorously. "They have to learn," he says.
"They've got to learn to be ready at all times."

"Absolutely," Diane agrees. "Some of them will try your
patience." She turns to wander along the bench, then stops.
"All of them will."

"Yeah—" Conner laughs lightly. "And this is just my first
game."

"Just . . ." Diane makes a calming, palms-down motion.
She smiles. He means well.

The game ends in a 9-9 tie. But the Marlins could have
won. This rankles Conner.

Afterward, they gather on the grass in the outfield. This is
where Diane stows field rakes and bases in the auxiliary shed;
packs up the equipment bag. With Brad coaching, from the
shed she would look out at the huddle and see Brad nodding
at girls, girls' hands raised. This time, she sees Conner
gesturing, karate-chopping the air. The girls sit stiff and still.
He has their full attention.

* * * * *

One incident bothers Diane. It wasn't even an "incident," but
two days after the game, it still bothers her.

It happened in the fourth or fifth inning. Jamie at bat. By
now, everybody in the league knows that Jamie is a dangerous
hitter. The Cubs' coaches motioned their outfielders to back

up. The Cubs' infielders shouted encouragement to their pitcher. "You've got this!" "You're the pitcher!" "No worries, Michaela!"

Diane remembered her playing days. Back then the chatter wasn't just cheering for teammates; it was more directed at the opposition: *Nooo batter, she's no batter! Hey batter— swing!* Nowadays such talk would be frowned upon as unsportsmanlike. So the Cubs cajoled and encouraged: "No problem, Mikki, just lay it in there . . . you've got this . . ."

There was a fitting, party-ribbon flutter to it: Bird calls on a spring day. Then, from within the peaceable sylvan world, the tone changed: ". . . she can't hit, we won't lose . . ." Diane smiled faintly—and then something snaked through: ". . . *she can't even buy new shoes!*"

Diane heard surprised laughter. She saw parents looking at each other: *These girls and their silly rhymes!* Wait. What? Diane looked at Jamie's cleats. They were scuffed. Not worn out. Were they too small? Was this just a rhyme? An inside joke? Or something else?

Jamie showed no reaction. She took her practice swings easily. The chatter continued. Coach Conner hadn't noticed anything.

Jamie hit a fly ball, not deep. It was caught. Jamie trotted back to the bench and placed her bat on the bat rack.

Diane looked around the field. She detected no issue and decided to let it go.

But she can't shake it from her thoughts. She wonders about Jamie's parents. She's never met either of them. She knows nothing about Jamie in school or at home.

After dinner, she asks Kelli if she knows many of the Cubs' players.

Kelli looks up from her bowl of ice cream. She has a few friends on the Cubs. She's familiar with almost all of them.

"Good kids?"

Kelli nods. "I guess so. I mean, why?"

Diane hesitates. She doesn't know if she is ready to open this topic. "Last game, did you hear one of them chanting a rhyme that sounded a little weird?"

Kelli pauses, her spoon loaded. "What do you mean?"

"When Jamie was batting?"

"Mom, what are you talking about?"

All right, Diane decides. "Here's what I heard."

Kelli nods along as she eats. She did not hear the chant, but she is not surprised. "Jamie doesn't have a lot of friends," she says. Jamie, she explains, is . . . mean. Too competitive. She plays rough in sports. She uses bad words. She uses the 'F' word a lot.

Diane has never heard Jamie cuss, but she can imagine it. Jamie plays with a vengeance. "Do you think that chant was supposed to be fun, or was somebody trying to demean Jamie?"

Kelli's done with her ice cream. "Demean. If that means 'be mean,' then I wouldn't be surprised if that's what the chant was about."

"Do you know who might have said such a thing?"

"Mom." Kelli puts her spoon down. "I don't know."

Diane is not sure what she can do. But she remembers her playing days. When she was meaner. Back then she carried a strong conviction: Good teams stand up for one another. The next time the Marlins play the Cubs—or any team . . . she'll be paying attention.

Chapter 16
CHOICES

Mulch blackens Brad's hands. With his forearm he wipes the sweat from his brow. He's planted four eggplants, and they're showing promise. He gauges the distance between the eggplants and the cukes. He realizes that the cukes have already made their invasion plans: to sneak close, reach out, strangle the eggplants, and then overrun the territory. He remembers his plan: to get the cucumbers started on climbing missions rather than territorial domination. He's browsed online, considering stakes, cages, trellises. He doesn't know what will work best, but he's eager to try something. He remembers that Stephanie used to use lattices, or trellises— whatever they're called—for roses and clematis. He'll have to give her a shout.

* * * * *

Brad settles into bed with the laptop. Outside, the trees toss and murmur.

He'd been at the pub earlier. Just briefly, for one beer and a bit of banter with Von and Spence. At one point Spence mentioned something about Mike and his new babe.

"What?" Brad said. "What new babe is that?"

"That gal that he was hitting on the other night," Spence

said. "Your friend's friend."

"Oh." Brad smirked on one side of his face. "Just a little flirting."

"What makes you say that?"

Brad had asked about Suzanne, and Mike responded with his scornful *you-must-be-kidding-me* look.

"And he told you nothing's going on."

No, Mike had not *exactly* said that nothing was going on, and upon reflection, Brad realized that Mike had been evasive; he'd said something about working on the "balance" in his relationship. But, still. Mike does not like to complicate things. "He was just flirting," Brad said. "A little excitement. Yeah, that's what he told me."

"Well, um. Brad?" Spence put his hand on Brad's shoulder. "He lied."

And Brad remembered: Mike *had* seemed unsettled about Joanne. Whatever: It's none of his business. But it bugs him that he's so clueless about this stuff.

He browses the internet, checks e-mails. There's one from Craig, but it's just a brief update to say that he hasn't heard anything new.

Brad is almost relieved to hear this. Recently he's been more and more excited about his prospective investment advisory. He's thought it through, estimating startup costs, envisioning pitfalls, researching the industry. So far it's stood up to scrutiny. His qualifications give him an advantage. He's not just another analyst with an MBA. He'll be able to spot red flags; he'll know how to read between lines; he'll be able to understand and sort through the details and complications underlying the sunny press releases and annual reports.

Even Mike thought it made sense. "What are you gonna name it?" he'd asked.

Brad hadn't gotten around to naming.

"How about, 'long shots'?" Mike said. "Or maybe 'pharm prospects'."

Brad grinned.

He's been prepping for a required test; he's looked into registration requirements. He's got his business plan together. He's got promising leads on his new office space.

With all that, he knows that he will have to deal with stuff—stuff that has nothing to do with a company's research or products or market. He'll need to be ready. He'll have to *get it*: about egos and relationships and all the crap that finds its way into every endeavor in the world. He can't be caught off guard. Like he was at Rylix.

He remembers one meeting in particular: He was there to present important trial results. They had promising findings on a cure for an emerging form of meningitis. He'd prepared a tidy summary that pointed to a clear conclusion of likely success. The resulting cacophony stunned him.

"Nobody's even heard of this disease."

"Did you get a look at last month's JAMA?"

"Whatever. It's not even on Greenberg's radar. If it's not on his radar, it's not on mine."

Brad spoke: "This is our most promising product."

"Even if it works, Medicare won't kick in for it."

"Why do you say that? And when did this become a Medicare issue?"

It felt like being invisible in the middle of a food fight. "*Any questions about the trial results?*" Brad said.

"Greenberg's just one person."

"He's our person."

"Why is that? Aren't we good with PGV? How about Ray Simonetti at Copper Beech?"

"Simonetti's on the outs over there. You saw it yourself. That scene at their hospitality suite in San Diego last month."

Brad fought for focus. "We're ready for Stage Three trials," he said. But the conversations made their detours and flowed on around him.

"Matsui's got that diabetes drug moving."

That came from Larry Tarlton. Tarlton wielded influence, and Brad had been expecting his support. But then it became clear: Tarlton and Evan Mitchell, who had become the prime advocate for Brad's project, did not like each other. If Brad's team's project were to succeed, credit would go to Mitchell. So Tarlton had swung his support to a rival project.

"Would you please stop calling Matsui's thing a drug? Do you even get it, that it's an alternative delivery system?"

"All I know is it's going to work. And it sounds exciting."

"This drug—our drug—will work," Brad said. "I just told you why." Wasn't that what the meeting was about? They needed funding for one more trial round. If they got past that—like he'd *just* said—they had about a 70 percent chance, and the licensing arrangements would be simpler than anything they'd done in years.

"What about the press? We need press coverage. On something that works."

The arguments launched and wobbled and sagged, struggling under the weight of their political payloads. Brad tried to trace connections, tried to make sense of the strands of alliances and external concerns, tried to identify an opportunity to talk about their product.

He'll have to be ready to play those games. In the meantime, his business has potential.

* * * * *

It's late. He sets his laptop to the side, picks up the book he's been reading. At the end of the chapter he checks his phone for the time, and makes one last e-mail check. There's a new message. It's from Diane.

Hi Brad!

I hope you're enjoying some free time. I wanted to get

in touch for two reasons. First, you should know that I received an inquiry about you from the league. The Board wanted to know about some incident where somebody said you made a player cry. They also wanted to know about that girl, Ashley, who quit after the first few practices. I told them that the girl who cried—it was Renni—had just started crying because she'd made some mistake, and you and I tried to console her. I told them that Ashley just quit, and that it was probably best for all of us—and her. I told them that you were a great coach, and that the Marlins were lucky to have had you!

Quick update—Conner and Stephanie are fine. They're different in that they spend more time working on individual things like girls' throwing motions and their swings. That's fine; it's just different. They also manage the count for the hitters—they use signals for taking pitches and fake bunts. This confuses the girls, but it's a valid strategy and the girls will get used to it.

The Marlins tied the Cubs 9-9 (it got too dark to keep playing) and then beat the Reds 13-11 in a sloppy game. One other game (Mets) got rained out. Lissa's played really well. Renni told me she misses the sliding drills. I think she's been sick or something (horrible coughing!), but she's still mostly fun and upbeat. I think Maddi was sad because she didn't get to play the infield last game. One thing I know you'll appreciate: Courtney stole second, and when the pitch got by the catcher she went all the way to third. When Conner yelled out to congratulate her, she shouted "That's how the Marlins run the bases!" That made me laugh—you taught them a lot!

Hope all's well
Diane

PS—one thing you should know: The Cardinals' catcher in that game when the coach raised a stink is the coach's daughter. I think that's why he got so pissed. He thinks she's a superstar in the making!!

And then another message pops up. Finally: The one he's been waiting for.

It's from the board of the softball Little League. It's been two weeks since he'd responded to their e-mail about "issues." The message gives away nothing. It does include an apology for the slow response. And a time to meet: next Tuesday evening.

* * * * *

Business at the Pub picks up in May. Along the downtown streets the crabapple blossoms grow heavy. The breeze swirls their petals around, littering the sidewalks with cotton candy confetti. People—guys—want to get a little drunk. They need to get out. They come to the Pub.

Brad and Mike sit at the bar, looking up at the TV.

Von banters with them between trips to the kitchen and trips to tables. "Heard about you, Brad," he says. "About Conner coming back."

"Heard about *him?*" Mike says. "Did you hear about *me?*"

"What?" Brad says. "What about you?"

Von flings a sidelong nod at Mike. "Meet Mr. Brave."

"No shit?"

Mike waves his hand dismissively. He's an extra body, he says. He'll help with field prep, warmups, maybe serve as a fielder-prop at practice.

Von clangs the tip bell: "To Coach Mike of the Braves!"

Glasses clink around the pub. People laugh. Somebody exclaims: "Yeahhh!"

Mike gives a disgusted half-grin, shaking his head in embarrassment. "Hey, fuck you guys. Jeeesus Christ."

Von leans forward, elbows on the bar. "Sorry, Coach. I mean, sorry, Mike."

Brad nods at Von, then turns to Mike. "So," he says, "why the change of heart?"

"I dunno," Mike says. "I mean I *really* don't know. I think Jo likes the idea."

"That's new." Brad feels a swell of relief: *Jo* likes the idea. So much for the new babe.

"What's new?"

"That . . . motivation."

"What are you saying?"

Von cuts in: "That he's normally a selfish prick?"

"Something like that."

Mike shrugs. "Maybe I just need to get more . . . involved. In something."

Brad watches the bubbles rising in his beer. Mike will be good for the Braves. Back when he and Mike played hockey together, other than Coach Dub, Mike always understood the game better than their coaches.

Von removes an empty pint glass from the bar. He looks at Brad. "You gonna miss it?"

Brad remembers that Von had encouraged him to coach. Yes, he will miss it.

Von hesitates, holding the empty glasses. "Is that girl Heather still going to keep score for the Marlins?"

Brad doesn't know.

"Hope so." Von grins. "She's a cutie. No offense—I like you—but I don't mind it when you send her to meet with me and the other coaches before the game."

"Didn't seem to help us with any calls."

Von bends over the sink to wash and rinse the glasses.

"You're different, you know. You were different."

"How so?"

"Base running."

Brad allows that he was a stickler for base running.

Mike laughs. "As in fanatic."

"Your girls really ran—run—the bases aggressively," Von says.

Mike scoffs. "Shit."

"What did you find to be the toughest thing?" Von asks.

Toughest thing to coach? Plenty of candidates there. Brad ticks through his mental file cabinet of frustrations and failures.

"The toughest thing to coach," Von says, "is the simplest thing." He pauses. "How to throw."

Brad agrees.

A lot of these girls have played the game for three, four, five years, Von says, and even some of the decent players still don't throw right.

"So what's the solution?" Mike says.

Von's idea: "Tell a girl to bounce a tennis ball as high as she can. In many cases—not all, but many—the girl will instinctively raise her throwing arm up, step forward, and slam the ball down, and it'll bounce high." He demonstrates with an imaginary ball. "That's the throwing motion. You have to tilt it up so you're throwing forward instead of down, but that's the throwing motion, with the arm coming down like a whip, instead of flapping like a fin."

Brad processes the images in his head. He can see it. "How effective is this? Does that work for . . . maybe . . . half the girls?"

Von shakes his head as he mixes a martini. "No. Some. Not half."

Brad recounts his own technique. "Crack the whip. That's what I've been preaching. To use your arm like a whip. I actually took off my belt to demonstrate that concept."

Von impales two olives on a toothpick. He pauses before sliding it into the drink. "You took off your belt?"

"I wanted them to remember it. Also, that was at the first practice, and I needed to get their attention."

Mike and Von grin at each other.

"Did your pants fall down?" Mike asks.

Brad grunts. "Ha. Unfortunately, my waistline's a little snug."

"I don't know." Von leans over the bar to inspect Brad's waist. "I think you're doing pretty good there."

"Thanks." Brad sucks in at the waist and looks up at Von. "In that case, I'll have some more of them fries."

* * * * *

For their second meeting, Brad finds Justin and Craig at the same high-top in the corner. Much to their chagrin, the pretty waitress is not working. Brad shares his plan for his new investment consulting business.

Neither of them seems particularly surprised.

"I figured you had something in the works," Justin says.

Nothing's certain just yet, Brad says, but he wants to be forthcoming. He thought they should know sooner rather than later. At the same time, he says, he's still interested in whatever new possibilities they might pursue.

Craig jiggles his leg up and down. "When you quit," he says, "It wasn't just about protecting Mia, was it?"

Brad sighs; he's not sure. He'd stepped forward to take the hit. He'd helped Mia. He'd felt like a man of principle; almost heroic. But even beyond that, was there something else? Had he *wanted* to get out?

He'd always understood that rules got bent. They got nicked; they got broken. In the real world, such stuff is unavoidable. But a few things had lodged in the back of his mind and kept making noise. Like the decision—a few years earlier—to dump their rheumatoid project.

"Well, lots of projects—lots of good projects—get dumped," Craig says.

"Right. But get this." Brad's not sure he wants to divulge this. "That project got dumped—even though our initial findings were very promising—because it was a *cure*. It got dumped in favor of an improved *treatment* that showed decent but not great promise. RA treatment. Same disease."

Brad and Justin and Craig and their team had built up knowledge, tested theories, and were just getting hot on the trail of a potentially ground-breaking cure, but Rylix decided to allocate its resources instead to the *treatment*. Why? Because the treatment would earn an ongoing stream of profits from every patient; the cure would only capture a one-time payment.

It takes a moment to digest. Justin stares, then slumps at the neck. "Wow."

Craig shakes his head slowly. "How'd you learn this?"

"Lou Disetovich." Brad had argued bitterly about the decision, and it had strained his relationship with Lou. Months later, Lou came clean: He was on Brad's side, but between treatment and cure, they could only have one, especially if the cure was effective. He had to deal with the other departments, and finance won out.

"What a—that is so . . . fucked," Justin says.

They share a few moments of grumpy silence.

"In all fairness," Brad says, "it wasn't Lou and it wasn't really even Rylix." It was just the money talking. The capital guys had more confidence in the treatment, mostly because there was precedent in some other treatments that had been reasonably successful. "They said they were chasing too many 'next big thing' projects; game changers. They were looking for something that sounded a little more . . . grounded."

"Whatever that means," Craig grumbles.

Brad continues: "They figured the treatment would

probably have a quicker approval process. And they had to cut something. So it wasn't really quite as bad as it sounds."

"Okay," Craig says, "but that kind of shit—is that what this is all about? Is that what we tell our recruits?"

Brad nods in sympathy. "Craig," he says, "you're beginning to sound like *me*."

Craig looks at him. "Is that a bad thing?"

Brad lets out a heavy breath. "No. But I'm just telling you. That shit goes on. It was messing with my head."

Craig nods grimly. "I get it." He shifts in his seat, glances about restlessly. "But I don't *want* to get it," he says. He doesn't want to understand the business perspective—the *shareholder* perspective, or whatever—he doesn't want to make sense of it. He wants to be mad about it.

Justin sips his IPA. "It's a good reminder," he says. "Doing what we do, you feel like you're on the inside. And then. Well. It's the inside of *their* world."

There are a few updates on potential opportunities, but it's a quiet exchange. Two beers. They talk about schedules, but it all depends on when they get new information.

* * * * *

The First Community Bank sits in the middle of downtown. It's a 19th-century brick building, three stories with an arched stone entrance. A worn marble staircase takes Brad to the second-floor conference room. Seven guys sit around a polished mahogany table.

Good evening. Welcome. Have a seat. Please.

One of the guys at the near end of the table stands up to pull a chair out for Brad. *Sit. Please.* It feels almost comically mob-like.

At the far end of the table, Brad notices the name plate for "Robert Remersdorf," who introduces himself as "Bob." Silver hair, tanned complexion; golf shirt showing off a workout physique. He opens the evening with an apology for never having met Brad.

Brad's anxious to know about the issues that seem to have arisen.

"Right." Bob gets down to it. They had to conduct a CORI inquiry on every coach. The CORI came back clean. As for the issues . . . his fingers scrub his chin. "To be honest, I think a few people—I won't name names but you know who I'm talking about—just didn't like your aggressive base-running tactics, so they tried to dig up dirt."

Dig up dirt? "The Cardinals' coaches tried to 'dig up dirt'?"

"Somebody said you pulled down your pants in front of the girls."

What?

Bob makes a dismissive noise: "Tsch. It's nothing. I suspect that was your 'use-your-arm-like-a-whip' demonstration."

Brad wonders how anybody knows anything about this.

"Von told us about that . . . that interesting technique of yours. Von the umpire-bartender-picture framer."

Picture framer? Right: *Von.* Von owns that frame shop; he's got a bunch of things going.

"So. No dirt there. After that, we just had to wait for a few e-mail replies."

Brad had received an enthusiastic review from Diane. And much to his surprise, he'd also received strong support from several parents, including Renni's dad and Lissa's dad.

"So," Bob concludes. "You're the coach."

So it was all about nothing. Brad clicks his pen closed.

The board members sit watching as Brad closes his notebook. They seem to be waiting for him to say something. He obliges; they're all buddies now. "Good to meet you all," he says. "I was a little creeped out that there were concerns."

A couple of them soft-toss apologies.

"I have to say it was fun coaching," he adds. "I was really surprised—shocked, really—by how much I enjoyed it."

Bob leans forward on his elbows. "Brad. You're the coach." After a moment, he adds, "Of the Marlins. If you want to be." Conner's job responsibilities have blown up again. The Marlins need a coach. It's all changed. Again.

Brad takes a moment to adjust his mental balance. He hears himself say something about "thinking it over." He starts to get up, but then stays seated.

He's done his favor. He's done what he said he would do. He doesn't owe anybody anything. Reassessments lurch through his head. There's that heavy equipment bag. The constant uncertainties: *Can she not hear, is she pretending she can't hear, or is she just not getting it and hoping he'll move on and forget about it?* Teamwide e-mails, unanswered by parents. *Put those cell phones away!* Bewilderment: *Why did she not step on the base?*

It's been a good experience. But what else could happen? He'd grown attached to the Marlins, but to them he's just another forgettable grown-up, yakking at them from outside the bubble of their world—the world of eleven- and twelve-year-old girls. That's the reality.

But he wants to coach the Marlins. Of course he does.

Chapter 17
ADJUSTMENTS

Conner stops by to drop off the equipment, scorebook, and paperwork.

Conner's Marlins have won one game and tied one, improving from 3-6 to 4-6-1.

The bag thuds on the porch. Conner's got a minute. They sit down on Brad's old wicker chairs.

"I'm really sorry you've gotten jerked around," Conner says.

"They told me you got busy again."

"That's true." Conner sits with his hands in his pockets. "That's the official reason."

Brad waits.

"To be honest," Conner says, "Steph and I were arguing too much. She was only even at a few practices, but we were arguing. About coaching. *They don't understand what you're saying, I've got a better drill, concentrate on this thing first, don't let them get away with that.* You don't need to hear all of it, but let's just say that in addition to my schedule, coaching the Marlins was another thing that was hard on our relationship."

For some reason, Brad does not feel uncomfortable.

"Which," Conner says, "is important to me—to us. Our

relationship."

Brad clasps his hands together. "Want a beer?"

Conner hesitates.

Brad gets up and heads inside. "I'm having one. Come on. I need to pick your brain for a few."

Conner agrees to one, but warns that he can't hang around long.

Brad comes back with two bottles.

"Oh, crap." Conner palm-smacks his forehead. "Steph's garden trellises," he says. "I forgot to bring them."

Brad waves it away. Not an emergency.

"She said you wanted them, and she never uses them anymore. I'm sorry."

Brad hands Conner an open bottle.

"Stephanie, softball," Conner says, accepting his beer. "I keep getting in on your gigs."

Brad returns to his seat. "I've been thinking about trying to get in on yours."

Conner gives him a puzzled look.

Brad explains his biotech background. "I sucked at the business end of it," he says. "I couldn't do what you do to save my life."

Conner nods, takes a swig of beer. "You were a lab guy."

"Research director."

"I couldn't do *that* shit to save my life. I can't even pronounce the names of all these concoctions you guys come up with."

Conner works on the financial side of the industry. For him, it was never going to be about scientific discovery or medical advancement. It was always going to be about deals, finance, relationships.

"I guess you're good at that," Brad says.

"It's what I do. I guess I do all right."

"So." Brad fidgets with the label on his bottle. "You got less pressure these days?"

Conner grimaces. "You know—that deal? It could have happened. I had the Euro dudes on board. They were going to go along with our broader pipeline, but then this fucking Joe Eagle Scout in our company started blabbing shit about a few outlier test results and they started getting uncomfortable, like they didn't want to deal with more than a few projects at a time. That idiot keeps his mouth shut, and the deal gets done, and all we're talking about here is the fine print."

"Maybe the guy was trying to keep you out of trouble." It crosses Brad's mind that Conner—his ex-wife's boyfriend, of all people—might turn out to be a useful networking connection for his advisory business.

"It was a non-issue. It was of zero inconsequence." Conner clears his throat. His company, Conner explains, casts its nets broadly. They try to develop as many drugs as they can. That potential Swiss partner likes to focus narrowly, targeting specific diseases and its variants. "They would have made us cut out about half of our pipeline," Conner says.

Brad crosses his legs. Some companies like to amass projects. He's always preferred the narrower approach, focusing on their interest in the particular scientific inquiries, the complexity of the molecular issues, the potential for breakthroughs.

"The broader approach—it just increases the chances for success," Conner says. He hesitates. He doesn't understand how the research scientists maintain their energy. "I mean, correct me if I'm wrong, but I'm guessing that a lot of you guys have whole careers without ever bringing a drug to market."

Brad nods reluctantly: The success rate is very low.

Conner takes a pull at his beer. "I couldn't do that. Working with failure after failure."

"We plug away," Brad says. "And when something doesn't work—or say we find out about bad side effects—it still furthers the knowledge and sometimes opens up other ideas. Might not be cause for celebration—maybe it's not 'success'—

but we get something out of it. It's not wasted."

Conner nods. "Okay. But, still."

"Well, it sounds like you made the right call. On the deal."

Conner heaves a sigh. That's what he tells himself. He's been trying to adjust his definition of success.

Brad slouches down in the couch. "How'd you do with the Marlins? With the girls?"

"They were okay." Conner jiggles his knee. "Jamie—well, Jamie can *really* play." He pauses. Kelli, he says, has been making progress with the change-up. "Talk to Diane. She's been working with Kelli at home. Sounds like it might be almost there."

Brad motions at him to continue.

"Let's see. Lissa can play. And on the negative side, there's Meghan, Lori, and that other girl, the other chubby one. . ."

"I mean, chemistry-wise," Brad says. "Were you able to . . . connect with these girls?"

Conner sits up. "One thing you should know: Maddi might have quit. After the first game, she missed the next game and every practice."

Brad thinks: One game and a few practices. "Maybe she's sick."

Understood. But Conner has a bad feeling. He thinks she's quit.

Why?

"That first game: She just didn't seem into it. Maybe because I didn't let her play third."

Brad nods. He's tried her there a few times.

"She belongs in the outfield. Maybe second base now and then, but she can't play third."

Hmm. Maybe not *yet*, Brad thinks. He makes a mental note to talk to Gwen.

"Now, Emmie . . . interesting case."

Brad leans forward. He never really connected with Emmie.

"I guess you know about her gymnastics."

"Only that she *has* gymnastics."

Conner raises his eyebrows. "Emmie went to the Junior National Championships last year. Gold medal on the balance beam; second in uneven parallels." He nods, channeling his lips. "Nationals."

Brad digests the word. Did everybody know except him? His lack of curiosity confronts him.

"She's a great athlete. Attendance might not be great."

"I'm glad I know." Brad wonders if he'd reached out. Apparently not enough. He still thinks, though, that he made decent connections with some of the girls. Colleen, Courtney. Renni was an easy girl to connect with.

"Now, there. There's something." Conner holds up his index finger. "There's something going on with Renni. She's only missed two practices, but they were both for medical appointments. I don't want to speculate," Conner says, "but you have to wonder what's up with that."

Conner looks up at the porch ceiling. He's barely learned their names. "It's a bunch of eleven- and twelve-year old girls," he says. "Pre-teen girls are pre-teen girls. That's what it is."

Conner's right. With the exception of the Braves, one girls' softball team looks pretty much like the next. Sure, the girls all have their individual quirks and some play better than others. But they're a bunch of pre-teen girls, and a few months of softball won't change that.

"You know," Conner says. "I was kind of looking forward to the playoffs." He picks at the label on his bottle. "And by the way, I can still help out a little. You know. On the bench. If you need it."

"Of course," Brad says. Most of the other teams have three coaches. Diane will be there to help at most games and occasional practices. Heather will keep the scorebook. But of course he could use more help. He laughs. "Once you get past the fact that it's a total pain in the ass, it's kind of fun."

Conner agrees. "And, we accomplished some things," he says. "We were 1-0-1. And the game they tied; they could have—they *should* have won that one."

Brad's beer is empty. "Did Von—at Pitcher's—did he ever tell you about his T-shirt?"

Conner shakes his head.

Brad tells him about the "Girls' Softball" T-shirt and the saying on the back: "It's all about the ice cream."

Conner likes that. He examines the label on his bottle. About half of it has come off; he picks at the remaining part.

Another beer?

Conner lets out a sigh. "Maybe one more."

* * * * *

Brad sends out a teamwide e-mail announcing his return. He knows not to expect any sort of immediate or enthusiastic response. These are busy families juggling kids and errands, lessons and birthday parties, overdue books, zig-zagging schedules. He sends one individual e-mail:

Hi Gwen

As I said in my teamwide e-mail, I'm glad to be back for another shot at this. I'm wondering how Maddi's been doing with this stuff. I ask because Conner told me he hasn't seen her in a while. I hope she's okay. Please tell her that I'm proud of how much she's improved and expect to have a lot of fun over the rest of the season. And that the Marlins need her.

* * * * *

Mike drives to his first softball practice with Claire. It's the first time he's been alone with Claire.

205

He likes Claire well enough. They don't have actual conversations, but she's polite; she answers when he speaks to her. She laughs—or at least smiles—when he cracks a joke.

In the car, he asks Claire about Coach Phil, and about some of the other girls on the Braves.

Claire minimizes her words. The girls are mostly okay; Coach Phil's okay.

"You've been learning new things?"

Mm-hmm.

"About softball—about how the game works—or individual skills like pitching and hitting?"

She shrugs. "Umm. My hitting's getting better."

He hesitates: He doesn't want to grill her. "You've been working on hitting?"

Mm-hmm.

"How about pitching?"

She takes her hand from her face to look at the fingernail she's been chewing on. Her change-up, she says, is not consistent. "I still throw it too high a lot."

Mike doesn't know much about pitching mechanics. He wonders: What does a second assistant coach even do?

Claire doesn't know.

Mike wonders why he was asked to do this. And then, why did he agree? Some of it has to do with Brad's constant chatter about his coaching gig. Then he remembers: It's about Jo. It's something she wants, and something he can do for her. Maybe a little clutter will be okay.

For the first practice, his plan is to observe. Get to know some of the girls a little bit, but mostly just observe.

When he arrives at the field, Phil greets him enthusiastically and introduces him to Bruce, his main assistant. Bruce is a big dude with a jutting chin. He gives Mike a clipped, sentry-like nod. Mike watches and shifts his feet as the girls start playing catch. He asks Bruce what a third coach is supposed to do. "I'm not sure why you guys wanted another assistant."

Bruce nods his head—shouts out instructions for the girls to start throwing—then turns back to Mike. There are times when he or Phil might not be there, he says. Also, an extra coach can help them have more stations for different drills in practice. Finally, in games it's best to have one coach at first base, one at third, and another one on the bench to warm up a pitcher, keep score, make sure the girls are ready when it's their turn to hit.

"Sounds simple enough," Mike says.

After a quick team briefing, Phil sends Bruce and six of the nine girls off to work on bunting. Phil takes Claire and two other girls—a catcher and the other pitcher—to the side of the field to work on something. Mike goes with Bruce to watch him run the bunting drill. After a few minutes, he hears Phil calling him over.

Claire's crying. She watches as the other pitcher, Haley, practices her pitching stride. Except for the wetness shining on Claire's cheeks, nothing looks wrong.

Phil takes Mike out of earshot: "This has been happening. Do you have any idea what's going on?"

Mike does not. He's seen no sign of anything wrong at home. He wonders if this is about him. "Do you think it's because I'm coaching but I'm *not her dad?*"

"No," Phil assures him. "This has been happening."

Great: first practice. Tears. Inadequacy.

Mike takes Claire aside. He asks what's wrong, and is not surprised to receive no response. Okay. Mike looks around, gesturing at the expanse of green grass. "I mean, is it about something going on here? Is it even about softball?"

Claire starts crying harder, hiccupping as she shakes her head no.

Mike weighs a few thoughts. First practice. *Try something.* "Claire. I know we've never talked about personal stuff. Personal things that might bother you."

Claire wipes her nose.

Mike lets the silence coast for a minute. "Would you tell me if I guess right?"

Claire sniffles.

Friends—something at school?

Nope.

That wasn't a real guess; just something to get the process going. This wouldn't happen regularly or even semi-regularly unless it was about something bigger—some issue that's *always* there. Something about home.

Nope.

Something not at home.

Hesitation.

About . . . your . . . father?

Ding ding ding: Sobs start lurching and bumping into each other in her chest. She nods 'yes' and plunges her face into her hands.

Mike squats down, looking at the grass. This is not good territory for the mother's boyfriend. "Claire," he says. "This might be an uncomfortable conversation. But I bet we can handle it. Maybe we can try it on the way home after practice. Can you make it through practice?"

Claire brushes a strand of wet hair from her face. She heaves a sigh, and then one more, her chest shuddering dry. She turns to coach Phil.

"Claire, are you gonna be okay?" Phil asks. "You wanna go home?"

Claire shakes her head. She holds up her glove, beckoning for the ball. She swallows. "I need to work on my change-up."

The rest of the practice consists of ground balls, fly balls, and a brief round of hitting practice.

On the way back to Jo's house, Mike probes at the issue, getting nowhere as Claire sits leaning against the passenger door. He wonders if he's ready for this conversation.

Claire sits up. "I'm sorry I cried today," she says. It wasn't anything that happened, she explains. It was just . . . her face starts to lose shape again, and Mike fears that she'll start crying just as they get home.

After a few moments, though, she recovers. Yes, it's about her dad. She shakes her head, throws her hands up in futility. "He's just such a mess." He's really smart, she says, but he starts things, he screws up, he quits, and then he doesn't get off the couch all day long, until it's night, when he gets drunk. He's moving in with his mother and he swears he's all straightened out, but he's said that so many times. "I guess it's stupid," she says, trying to sound blasé. "I don't know why I even let it bother me."

Mike winces, knowing how it feels when your chest constricts and strangles your words; and how it feels when families don't work. He wants to ease her out of it; he thinks he should comfort her but he knows she doesn't feel that close to him.

She ekes out a wobbly sentence: "It makes me sad." She wipes her face. "And mad."

Mike ponders as he drives. He appreciates Claire's decision to share this. He decides to take a long route to Jo's house. Maybe, he thinks, past the frozen yogurt place. Then he thinks better of it. However much Claire might want to talk, he needs to earn it. Not buy it. They can go for a fro-yo some other time; not now.

When they arrive at the house, Mike hesitates before getting out of the car.

Claire looks like herself again. Mike has his hand on the door handle.

"The thing is," Claire says, "he says he has this new girlfriend." Mike realizes that she's spent the whole ride thinking about her dad. "He seems to really like her, and I hope it works out." She brushes her hair back; makes a slight harumphing noise. "I just have my doubts."

This is not good subject matter. Mike knows even less

about this than he knows about softball pitching mechanics. But he's surprised to realize that he wants to continue this conversation. Maybe not *now*. But soon. They exchange glances. She sets her lips firmly; it seems like an acknowledgement. And then they get out of the car.

They walk breezily into the house. Jo's in the kitchen. She calls out her welcome.

"How was practice?"

"Good," Claire says.

"Good," Mike says.

* * * * *

Brad has forewarned them in an e-mail. At the next practice, the Marlins' *players* will design two drills: one for pre-game warmups, another for practices. Brad wants their ideas. It might be good, he thinks, for them to talk about what *they* think they need to work on.

After warmups, they huddle around him.

"We're glad you're back, Coach."

That's Renni. She's grinning, as usual.

Her teammates laugh and start teasing Renni with comic exaggerations: *Ohmigod we're sooo glad you're baack!!*

"Not like thaaat," Renni maintains her smile. "It's just—well. *I'm* glad you're back."

"Well thank you, Renni," Brad says. Her parents had e-mailed him about some recent medical tests; he means to speak with her after practice.

The Marlins are ready for their assignment. They've got plenty of ideas, apparently, for new drills. Hands go up. *Hitting. Base running. Running to the ball to catch it.*

Brad tries to cut through: "Hey, I'm glad you have ideas. But you—you as a group, not you as individuals—need to come up with these drills. You have to discuss and you might have to compromise." From his pockets he produces a note pad and a pen. "Who wants to be the scribe—the person who writes down what the group decides on?"

A few hands go up. Brad scans the hands and settles on Maddi, but she quickly withdraws her hand, and he hands the pad over to . . . Courtney.

Both drills have to address something they think they need to work on. Brad suggests that they not be too complicated. "If it's fun, all the better."

The girls tromp off across the field and plunk down in the outfield. Brad takes a seat on the aluminum bench. Across the expanse of warm grass he can make out voices. He can pick out Jamie's voice even from this distance, and then Colleen. Every now and then a petal of laughter flutters across the field. Courtney stands up. She waves her arms around, demonstrates a few different stances. Renni stands up, mimicking her; the laughter surges briefly. Lissa and Kelli turn their heads, glancing over their shoulders at Brad.

After fifteen minutes they start getting up, brushing and whacking at their shorts.

Courtney submits the note pad. Three pages filled with writing.

Geez. Wow. He can't read all this right now. "Why don't you describe them to me?"

"Uhhh . . . but I don't want to," Courtney protests. Renni is chosen as the spokesperson.

"Umm. Well . . ." She wrinkles her face, trying to follow Courtney's notes. The other girls giggle. Renni starts, stops, tells her teammates to *stop!* and *shut up!* Apparently there was disagreement. Some of the girls like the drills they already run. Others had all kinds of ideas, but couldn't describe them. In the end, the drill is for girls to take turns in line with Brad simply hitting or throwing balls just out of their reach, so they'd have to run for them.

"Especially over our heads," Jamie says. She gives him a serious look, from which he gathers that she's *had it* with pop flies falling in behind back-pedaling teammates.

"Right," Renni says.

Okay. Not bad, Brad thinks. Then, a thought: "How about we mark off an area where you can't let it fall?"

Renni's in: "That's what *I* said."

No no no no. Colleen's excited. "We make two teams, and one team takes turns throwing the balls and the other team has to prevent the balls from landing in some marked-off area."

Brilliant. "Did the rest of you not like that idea?"

I don't get it.

Boring.

Let's just try it . . .

Brad cuts in. "How about I take this idea—Colleen's idea—and tweak it just a little? It's great that you've thought of something to work on. I'll tweak it, and after that you can think of other ways to modify it if you want."

They look at each other. Heads nod mildly. Consensus.

Now: How about a pre-game drill?

There's been even more debate on this issue.

Girls start shouting out their choices. Renni raises her voice and motions with her hands for them to calm down. The decision was to run—she grins her demented mischief grin—the . . . *"pickle drill!"*

Applause: *"Yay!"*

Grumbling: *"Boo!"*

"That's just WRONG!"

"Yes—yes!"

All at the same time.

It turns out that the officially recorded choice was for basic infield drills and shagging flies. *"But I like the pickle drill,"* Renni protests. The chorus of voices rises anew.

"Okay!" Renni sits down, pouting conspicuously.

Brad promises to consider all suggestions. He folds the papers and stashes them in his pocket.

Practice goes smoothly. The girls pivot crisply to make throws. When the ball gets away they hustle after it. They move from one drill to the next. Everything looks better. Conner must have done something right.

To finish up, each girl will make one over-the-shoulder catch; he'll make all the throws.

Brad keeps them waiting as he fishes around in the equipment bag. Carefully. There are eleven "balls," which are actually wads of paper towels taped into lumpy packages. Each contains a bag of Skittles and a handful of candies—caramels, Jolly Ranchers, Starbursts. Each girl takes off running, looking back over her shoulder. His throws are right on: He's floating them at just the right distance, with just the right amount of loft. Colleen goes first; she yelps with delight when she discovers what she's caught. Meghan needs a second chance. Brad makes it a bit easier, and she hauls it in. One after another, the Marlins catch up with the trajectory of the precious white object, which falls easily into their treasuring gloves. Then they gather in a group, sorting happily through their surprise stashes.

"What are these for?" Courtney asks.

"I owed you. Remember?"

Oh . . . *"Right! You also promised that we could go get ice cream. You owe us candy for that time we did the pickle drill . . ."*

Practice is over. Brad rounds up the balls, packs the equipment bag. Then he remembers: "Renni!"

She's standing right behind him with an armful of balls for the ball bucket. He squats down next to her. She feeds him the balls and he drops them in the bucket.

He asks if she feels okay talking about her medical tests. "I mean, is it something serious? Do they know what it is?"

The doctors aren't sure, she says, but they're testing for a few diseases. She can't remember their names.

Any?

One of them is supposedly not very common. Most people haven't even heard of it.

"Try me."

It's two words. "Something about a system. Then fiber-something."

Cystic Fibrosis. The words crystallize in the air before his eyes. Their crusty ugliness frightens him.

She brightens: "Yes! That's it!" As if they'd just discovered that they have the same birthday.

Brad stands up straight. He does it too fast, gets a rush in his head and feels dizzy. CF: typically diagnosed in infants. But not always. It creates a sticky mucus in your lungs so you can't breathe. It invites bacteria and infections. It kills. "Renni . . ." he falters.

"I'm fine, Coach."

Brad can't think of what to say. "Keep it that way."

"Don't worry." She smiles. "I'll be fine."

She waves as she trots across the field toward the cars.

It's a fine evening. From the cars, parents call to their daughters, their voices floating through the spring evening. Renni joins a few of her teammates. They share gum and giggle and then run, flitting after each other like barn swallows as their parents' calls become more insistent: *We need to pick up your brother RIGHT now!*

A few parents wave to him from the cars. They seem very far away. One of them asks how practice went. Brad hears himself shout out a quick reply. Another voice: "Glad you're back!" At least he *thinks* that's what he heard.

The equipment bag feels even heavier than he remembers. He shrugs the straps up to a more secure perch on his shoulder. He watches the girls run and shriek in the gathering dusk.

Later that evening, Brad sits at the kitchen table. He picks at a piece of chicken cutlet. An e-mail shows up:

Coach

Emmie will have to miss next practice and probably the one after that. In fact, she might miss many of the remaining games. She's got a very busy schedule this spring, and it doesn't seem like it would matter much for her to miss some games. We're leaving it up to her on a game-by-game basis. Just letting you know.

On one hand, it seems that the e-mail glitch with Emmie's parents, whatever it was, has been solved. On the other hand, is she quitting? It's always been foreseeable—maybe inevitable—that Emmie might quit. She's overscheduled. She doesn't need this item on her agenda.

He cracks open a beer.

He can hear Renni's voice: *I'll be fine.*

He wants to believe that. It sounds believable. Couldn't it be?

It's been two weeks since he last met with Justin and Craig. They might know somebody who knows about CF. Somebody at Vertex, but Brad doesn't know them, and it sounds like there's something unusual about Renni's strain of the disease.

Brad drags his sleeve over his face; daubs at his eyes. *Goddammit.* His rib cage shudders. *Fiber-something.*

He blinks, and then something lets go. He feels it coming on; the blurred, soggy swarm behind his face; things clogging and swelling. Which is stupid: stupid, stupid, stupid. He's known her for a few months, is all. But it's Renni, and this, he thinks—maybe now, finally, this is where it's not about him. A fat teardrop wets the tabletop, and then another, and he thinks of Renni's tears watering the dirt when she made some meaningless mistake that nobody had even seen.

Mike was right. Up to now, it has been all about him. It's all been a big show. He's set it up so he might prove to the world that his ideas *work*: His insight and his oh-so-inventive methods *work* . . . but he's no different; it's all about him. Until now. Until this moment, with its immovable hardness; with this wetness on his face, on his sleeve, on his table.

Chapter 18
PROPS

It's taken forever, but finally it arrives: warmth. *Lazy* warmth; reliable warmth. You lie back in the grass and clover and look up at the sky and hear a lawn mower droning somewhere. And then, all too quickly, it's moved on; changed again. The air feels heavy. It's hot.

Lissa does not want to be there. The heat is unbearable. In fact, *none* of them want to be there. Except for Jamie, maybe. Sweat beads form and grab at Lissa's shirt. In the outfield, she and Kelli gossip while Lori bats. She and Kelli have a group project for Social Studies and nobody understands the stupid assignment. It's not even *about* anything—that's how dumb it is. Jake and Theo, the other two kids in their group, say the same thing, but Jake's trying to think of some ideas. Jake, they agree, is a good kid. And cute.

When Lori's done, it's Maddi's turn to bat. She strokes a few ground balls. Jamie's the next batter. She puts on her helmet and stands off to the side, watching Coach Brad pitch to Maddi. With each pitch she gets into her stance like she's batting. She times the pitch and swings hard. Lissa does not like Jamie. She's such a grump. She's so *competitive*. Like she wants to hurt you or something.

Maddi finishes her swings. She rotates in to right field;

Lissa rotates from the outfield to third base. Jamie's up. Lissa knows well enough to pay attention.

Jamie spanks a hard ground ball up the middle, then hammers a high drive over Kelli's head in the outfield. Jamie can hit, that's for sure. In fact, Lissa realizes, Jamie is probably one of the best all-around players in the league. Whether you like her or not, it's good to have her on your team.

In the last game against the Cubs, Lissa was vaguely aware of some not-nice chatter directed at Jamie—something about buying new shoes—and Kelli told her later that her mom spent their dinnertime grilling her about it.

Jamie keeps swinging. Balls rocket into the outfield. Increasingly indifferent girls jog after them.

Lissa stays in her alert crouch, on the balls of her feet like Coach Brad taught her. When people say *on your toes*, Coach says, they're really talking about the balls of your feet. "When the pitch is delivered, I don't want to see anybody standing flat-footed."

Jamie smokes a ground ball to Lissa's left. Lissa springs after it, but it's out of reach.

Coach Brad reaches into the ball bucket. "Just a few more," he says.

As Coach delivers the next pitch, something looks a little weird and Lissa starts to say something.

Jamie also flinches—"Wha—" but then just goes ahead and swings.

The ball explodes. *Explodes.* Shards of stuff spray all around. A clump of something—is it a *dead animal?*—flies a short ways before whumping onto the dirt near Coach Brad. Some stuff lands on Lissa's cheek, and she thinks she feels something in her hair. She does not know what it is, but it feels like somebody's brains or something. She screams. This triggers an echoing chain of screams from the other girls all over the field.

"Nice hit!" Coach Brad yells. He flicks his toe at the clumpy thing lying near his feet.

There's a collective sorting; recognition comes slowly.

Jamie blinks, looks at Coach. "What was *that?*"

From second base, Renni runs into the infield, pointing and yelling: "*Grapefruit! It's a grapefruit!*"

"*What?*" Girls become frantic as they check their hair. "*That is SO gross!*"

Lissa sees Jamie staring at her, squinting. *Oh no*—did something weird get stuck on her face? The set line of Jamie's mouth gives way to a grin. "You have some on your nose."

Lissa jerks her hand to her nose. There's a giblet of pulpy wet stuff. "Aaggghh!" She wipes her face, becomes hysterical inspecting her arms and shirt. There's sticky stuff on it. "*Yuck! That's disgusting!*" Then she points back at Jamie: "Your helmet! There's some in the ear hole!"

Jamie freezes for an instant, then yanks off her helmet and throws it on the ground: "*What th—it's ALIVE!*"

Kelli runs into the infield. She throws her head back and laughs. Jamie scans the infield and points at the disgusting grapefruit rind: "There it is! Somebody—get—get that gross thing outta here!!"

Not knowing what to do, Lissa lets out a loud, stupid, noise-splat of a scream. The sound erupts out of her; it is not recognizable as anything of her own. But it's okay; she starts laughing. Kelli finds a piece of pulp and rubs it on Lissa's face, and Lissa does not resist but just keeps laughing. She leans away weakly and then staggers and sinks down to the dirt on the field. She's got sticky juice and pulp on her face and shirt— and now she's freckled with dirt—but she was just about soaked in sweat anyway. Her teammates are running about, making noises, emptying their water bottles on each other.

Coach laughs as he points at Jamie. "Wow, you hit the *snot* out of that thing!"

"Grapefruit snot!" Maddi yells.

Jamie points her bat at Coach Brad. "I'll get you back," she vows.

Coach Brad holds up his palms innocently. "I didn't know it was going to *explode* like that!"

"*I* wanna hit one!" Renni yells.

The rest of the Marlins follow suit: "*Can I hit one? No—me! Can I?*"

Renni picks up the flattened, dirt-covered rind of the ruined grapefruit and brandishes it at Courtney. Courtney shrieks and bolts for the outfield. As she runs she pulls her bubble gum out of her mouth and throws it at Renni, who dodges but continues her pursuit and fires the fruit carcass. It glances off Courtney's leg. The rest of the Marlins scream and point and laugh.

Lissa finds herself standing with Coach Brad and Jamie, watching the chasing and shrieking. He's only brought one grapefruit, Coach says. At the store he thought it was probably a dumb idea, but got one anyway. Now he wishes he'd brought more.

Lissa checks her shirtsleeves for grapefruit pulp. She wonders if they're going to finish batting practice. They still need to get turns for two more batters, and then they were going to do sliding drills. For now, though, Coach lets everybody run around, and Lissa can see why. They're all laughing. And not complaining about the heat. Maybe he's thinking that on this muggy day, that's good enough.

Lissa looks at Jamie. "Wow," she says. "You really creamed that thing."

"It felt so weird." Jamie grins. "It felt like nothing."

The three of them stand together, watching the Marlins chasing each other over the hot grass. The shouts and laughter from the outfield burst and flutter like splashes and butterflies of sound. Then, after a few more minutes, Coach calls them in; back to finish practice.

* * * * *

At the end of practice, the girls chug from their water bottles, gather up practice balls, and shoulder their backpacks.

Courtney and Lori wait for Brad in the infield. They've arranged to spend a few extra minutes after practice. Courtney wants to work on her throws from third base. Brad wants Lori to take some extra throws at first base.

A parent lingers. It's Lissa's father, Chris. He waits for the field to clear and then makes his way toward Brad. Brad looks across the field, sees Lissa getting into the car. He waves, and she waves back, laughing and calling out something that he can't quite make out.

Brad sets himself at the plate, bat on shoulder. He's about to start hitting ground balls to Courtney, but as Chris approaches he changes his mind. He gives a ball to Lori as she heads for first base. Lori will simply toss ground balls to Courtney. Courtney will field them and fire back to first.

"Coach."

"Hey, Chris."

"Got a minute?"

"Sure." Brad motions Chris to walk with him to a spot in foul ground behind Lori, where he can back up errant throws.

Chris hesitates.

"Courtney," Brad calls across the field. "Good throws, or you might hit Mr. McQuillen." He gives Chris a good-natured nod. "Mr. McQuillen has a cracked rib." Chris doubles over, pretending to favor his side. "And if you hurt that rib, he's coming after you!"

Courtney grins.

Chris and Brad watch as Lori starts tossing grounders to Courtney. Brad stands ready with his glove.

Chris wants to talk about Lissa's position assignments. Lissa does not like playing the outfield.

"Well," Brad says. He speaks loud enough for Lori to hear.

"Everybody has to play the outfield. They all need to know how to play outfield."

"But Lissa; I think you know she's one of your better infielders."

"She certainly is," Brad agrees. He watches Lori catch a low throw, and claps his hands. *"Nice scoop on that, Lori!"* He turns back to Chris. "But I have to give other girls chances to earn infield time, too."

Maybe at second base, Chris suggests.

"And third."

"Well—" Chris lowers his voice so the girls won't hear. "That's the thing. *Third?* And"—he glances quickly at Lori and mouths the word—*"first?* Don't you think those positions should be just Jamie, Lissa, Renni—maybe one or two others?"

"Nice throw Courtney!" Brad shouts. He apologizes to Chris—yes, he's listening.

The next throw bounces away from Lori. *"Tough hop on that one, Lori!"*

Chris picks up the ball, tosses it to Lori.

"Thank you," she says.

"Lissa's one of our best," Brad says. He gestures at Lori. "I'm trying to get Lori more comfortable, though." He raises his voice. "This girl just keeps getting better and better, *dontcha Lori?"*

Lori turns with a grin as she tosses another grounder to Courtney. Chris gives Lori a friendly nod.

"Lissa's important," Brad continues. "She won't be thrilled every single inning, but if first and third are her favorites, I will certainly keep that in mind."

"All right," Chris mutters. "I appreciate that. That was it."

Brad makes sure to shake hands before Chris leaves. "See ya Sunday," he says.

Lori keeps tossing grounders. "Great job," Brad says. "And by the way, I think you're starting to really understand this game."

"Yup."

So am I, he thinks. "Thanks for letting me use you."

Lori interrupts her throw, holds the ball, turns to look at him. "For what?"

* * * * *

Brad has taken the necessary deep breaths, rehearsed his lines, picked up the telephone. Hedge fund managers, mutual fund managers, pension managers, venture capital guys. These people know money. They know discount rates, intangible assets, one-time charges, credit facilities. They do not know science. To Brad's surprise, relief, and elation, most of his calls elicit welcoming responses.

And yes, they would be happy to meet. Yes, they could use some guidance with their investments, deciphering these reports and test results and press releases with all this strange language about *proteases* and *inhibitors* and *kinases*.

He's also renewed his biotech contacts. He's been in touch with former colleagues, collaborators, rivals. Investor relations directors. Brad will need them. When he calls, they pick up. They remember him; they respect him. They want to know where he's been; they've heard he left Rylix. "You did well to do what you did," one of them says. "I don't know who to talk to over there anymore."

They all want to talk. At Rylix, Lou Disetovich and even Larry Tarlton want to talk. And they understand: Brad will give them an educated and fair audience. He will analyze and report objectively, knowledgeably, and independently. They may not always be happy with what Brad reports to his institutional investment clients, but if test results are good, Brad will understand and report; if results are promising, Brad will understand and report; if their disappointments are surmountable, Brad will understand that, too.

So. Brad has a niche. He has the contacts. He's on the cusp.

* * * * *

Phil is glad that he asked Mike to help out. At his second practice, Phil asked if Mike had figured out anything about Claire's mysterious crying jags. As Phil had suspected, it was a parental issue. It always was.

"But it's not the typical thing," Mike said. "Not a pressure thing. She just gets sad."

"About her parents' divorce?"

"About her dad."

Phil was raking the dirt around home plate. He sensed reluctance to discuss the issue. Maybe that was just as well.

"She'll be all right," Mike said.

That was good enough. They could talk more about it later. Phil realizes that he has confidence in what Mike might say. In their last game, with two outs and a runner on third, their third baseman fielded a ground ball, but rather than make the well-rehearsed throw to first base, she'd thrown home, where his catcher struggled to hold on to the throw and then failed to apply the tag on the runner coming in from third. Phil had turned to Mike in exasperation, wondering why his player would choose not to make the simple play.

Mike seemed completely unsurprised. "Unless they're really thinking ahead, they want to make the play that's in front of them."

"But—"

"The runner distracted her. She was *right in front of her*."

Phil threw up his hands in futility, but he could see that Mike was probably right.

That had happened in the first inning. In the second inning, one of his players—Annabelle, one of his *worst* players—arrived late. Her expected absence had lightened his concerns, heightened his anticipation of the game. But then there she was; he'd have to juggle his position assignments. It could be tricky. He didn't want to assign her to right field for *every* inning, but he didn't think he could afford to play her in the infield.

He huddled over the lineup grid with Bruce and Mike.

"Let her choose for herself. For an inning or two," Mike said.

Bruce didn't like that idea. "She's been whining and begging to play first base. Can we survive an inning with that?"

"She won't choose any position where she's afraid she might fail," Mike said.

Phil dragged his finger over the position sheet. One inning wouldn't kill them. He was pretty sure that they'd win the game. Claire would strike out half the batters anyway.

Bruce grunted. "I mean. Okay."

Phil let Annabelle choose her position in the third and sixth innings. And Mike was right: she chose left field in the third, right field in the sixth. Phil made a mental note to get that into his book.

* * * * *

With just a few weeks left, the Marlins sit in fourth place.

	W	**L**	**T**
Braves	10	0	--
Cubs	6	4	1
Mets	5	6	--
Marlins	4	6	1
Reds	4	7	--
Cardinals	2	8	--

A win over the Mets brings the Marlins to 5-6-1. And third place.

Hi all:

To be honest, I was expecting this win. These girls can play and they're beginning to understand that. I continue to see good base running. Kacie's becoming a good baserunner; she's taking leads, rounding bases and picking up signals, and she's alert for opportunities.

Several nice fielding plays by Renni and Colleen and a GREAT backup by Lori saved us a run!

I want to say something about the play where Meghan and Courtney collided going after a fly ball. It fell in for a double, and it's true that both girls failed to call the ball. Coaches are supposed to be unhappy about that. But I loved it. I hope everybody noticed how both girls were tracking that ball. They were going after it hard; both of them wanted a shot at it. It takes confidence to do that, and that's something Meghan, in particular, is gaining.

So, of course some things could have been better, but the girls are having fun and I don't want to get too picky. We've got the Braves on Saturday—go Marlins!

* * * * *

On Friday evening, Brad receives an e-mail from Phil Braden. The Braves need to reschedule their Saturday game. They won't have enough girls. Would Sunday at 4:00 be okay for a make-up?

Brad needs to check with the Marlins' parents. Late spring

schedules are full of land mines. School play. Recital. Bat Mitzvah. Lacrosse. Soccer. Brad sends out a mass e-mail.

On Saturday morning, the responses trickle in. More yeas than nays. No for Lissa, no for Lori. But yeas for Jamie, Renni, Courtney, Maddi. And for Emmie, who he has not seen since his resumption of coaching duties. Perhaps he won't have to plead with anybody's parents. By 9:30 it looks like they'll have at least nine players.

Brad e-mails Phil: Sunday at 4:00 will be fine.

The response is almost immediate:

That's great. Thanks for your flexibility. We'll see you Sunday.

He e-mails the rescheduling announcement to the team.

Today's game has been rescheduled for Sunday, 4:00. See you at the field. 3:30. Go Marlins!

About half an hour later, Brad's cell phone chirps. It's Diane, her voice tight. "I don't like this. They're trying to pull something."

"Huh?"

"Shouldn't it just be a forfeit? If their players can't show up?"

The thought of making that case had crossed his mind. But the Braves' coach, Phil, is buddies with some of the league's board members. So Brad doesn't know that he'll win that case. It would be a battle, and he's not sure how he would feel if they were to *prevail*. Because it's girls' Little League softball. *Let's all just not make unnecessary fusses. We'll play 'em when they're ready for us.*

He's already put out the word. The reschedule is set.

* * * * *

From the back of her SUV, Stephanie unloads her assortment of garden trellises. Decorative-looking iron trellises, rectangular wooden trellises, and a couple of A-frames that she's never used.

Brad leans them up against the SUV. He and Stephanie stand together, inspecting the line of them. Briefly they discuss the relative pros and cons. Perhaps the A-frames might be his best solution.

"Conner told me about the loss to the Braves," Stephanie says.

Brad heaves a sigh.

"I also heard from Gwen. It didn't sound good."

Brad nods. It was ugly.

She'd heard more about the Braves than the Marlins, she says. Gwen had explained to her that the Braves had had two games scheduled for Saturday, including their originally scheduled game with the Marlins. But Claire Boniface would not have been allowed to pitch both games, because of the league's restrictions on the number of innings that girls were allowed to pitch on a given day or week. The Braves had rescheduled the Marlins' game for Sunday—a different day and a new week—so that Claire would be available to pitch.

Brad had suspected something—that it was all about Claire. He'd decided not to make a stink about it. He'd actually thought it might be good for his girls to get used to facing the ace pitcher. But the game turned out to be a lopsided 13-2 loss, and it felt every bit as bad as the score. The mercy rule had been invoked.

Stephanie nods grimly. She'd heard.

It surprises Brad, how unbothered he feels. He asks if Conner had said anything about the game. He'd seemed upset afterward.

"Here's the thing," Stephanie says. "Conner needs to be a hero."

"Oh?" Brad hopes he sounds surprised. He starts loading

the extra trellises into the back of the SUV.

Stephanie lets out an annoyed sigh. A few weeks ago, when Conner was coaching, something happened that just . . . bothered her. She'd overheard part of a conversation with a parent—Renni's mother—and it sounded like a biotech-related conversation. She'd heard Conner say, "Let me see what I can do." Now, it is possible that they were talking about a softball problem or a scheduling issue. On the other hand, she heard the word "treatment" and a jumbled phrase that sounded something like "advanced stage" and she can't get it out of her head. It wasn't exactly a promise, but there was this reassuring paternal tone. *I'll take care of it; it'll be okay.* What was he talking about? What was he going to *fix?*

"Sorry." Stephanie grins ruefully. "I'm worried."

"About your relationship?"

"I'm worried about *him.* He's just . . . He needs to be a hero." Stephanie crinkles her face, like she's wincing. Then, with an exasperated sigh, she flings her hands up in the air. "Okay. That deal he was working on in Europe? It sounds to me like he handled it well. It wasn't a good deal. It didn't make sense. But he was depressed. His attitude is '*I get deals done.*' But do you do a deal to do a deal, or to help your company?" Stephanie purses her lips. "For Conner, it's a whole different equation. He believes that the higher he climbs on the ladder, the more he can help the company. And the way to climb the ladder, in his thinking, is to get deals done."

Brad listens. He wonders if this is a common way of looking at things—if his old colleagues and rivals think this way.

"Whatever." Stephanie forces a smile and smooths the back of her hair. "You don't need to hear all this."

"It's okay. I'm sure people have heard shit about me."

Stephanie shuts the rear door of the SUV, rattling the license plate. "You know what? Not as much as you might think."

"Oh," Brad says, trying to find a way to make light of the moment.

She comes back to the front door. "Oh—and there's something else Gwen said."

"What's that?"

Stephanie climbs into the car.

Brad comes to the open window. "What?"

She gives him a sidelong look; heavy-lidded, a little sly. *"What?"*

"She said some of the Marlin mothers have said nice things about you."

"Really? Who?"

"Apparently someone thinks you'd make a great dad."

Brad scowls. "Thanks for the trellises."

"Also, so you know, one of the Braves' moms told Gwen that the Braves' coaches are fixated on going undefeated."

"Well." Brad stands with his hands in his pockets. "They might." With their latest win, the Braves' record stands at 12 wins, 0 losses. The Marlins have won 5, lost 7, and tied one.

Stephanie smirks as she starts the car. "Conner probably wishes he coached *them*." She waves as she drives away.

* * * * *

Jamie usually looks forward to Coach Brad's sliding drills in the hay. At practice, though, instead of hay, Coach sets two water balloons, jiggling nervously, on the grass. One is supposed to be the base, the other one sits about four feet in front of it. When you slide, you have to pop both balloons. Then Coach replaces them with two new water balloons. Jamie doesn't see the need for this, but it's a muggy afternoon, it feels good to get a little wet, and she takes pride in her sliding. She busts both balloons every time. Water shoots into the air. Her second slide soaks Coach Brad's shirt and face.

Kacie pops both balloons on her first slide. Jamie wonders

if anybody else is noticing. Kacie's fat. Kacie is afraid to slide, and she's not usually very good at it. Jamie pumps her fist: "Nice slide!" She hears similar shouts from two other girls.

Kacie jumps up from the wet grass, holding her arms out awkwardly, like a cormorant drying its wings. She lets out a squeal: "I'm SOOO wet!"

Jamie wonders, though: Don't they need to work on other things? Other than sliding? Coach Brad squats, setting water balloons in the grass. Jamie stands above him, arms folded, coach-like, across her chest. Weren't they going to work on bunt defense?

"Hang on."

Kelli comes charging in fast. Her slide breaks the balloons and sends up a shield of water.

Coach Brad dodges. "Great job!" he shouts. He turns back to Jamie. "I think the team needs to not hear me talking so much today."

Jamie looks at him. This doesn't make sense.

Instead of running another drill and barking at everybody to pay attention, he just wants everybody to have fun. "Hey," he says. "You girls are going to gab and mess around. We know that for sure. When I've got something to say I say *Okay! Listen up!* about five times. I'm just not up for that right now."

"Why don't you just yell at us?"

Coach Brad sighs. "I wish everybody took this game as seriously as you do. But they don't. So I at least want everybody to *want* to come to practice. This may seem like a waste of time, but look at your teammates. They're having a blast, and some of them are learning to slide better. You saw Kacie's last slide."

True enough. But Jamie can't understand why some of these girls don't want to get better. "If they want to come to practice—"

"Jamie, there's girls on our team about to quit any day."

So? Ashley quit after three practices, and Jamie figures that that was best for Ashley, and best for the rest of the team.

"Let's say we lose another player. That leaves us with ten. Now, next weekend Courtney's out of town. If one other player gets sick or something, we have eight. We're not going to win many games with eight girls."

Jamie looks down at her cleats. "I guess."

Courtney comes in sliding a bit too soon, popping one balloon but not the other. A bit of splash shoots up and catches Brad on the side of his face. This raises a chorus of shouts. Courtney thrusts her fist in the air as she trots back to the line. Coach grins and wipes his face. "I want everybody to want to keep coming. Having fun and learning a little bit." He shrugs. "For today, that'll be good enough."

Jamie starts back toward the end of the line.

"Jamie, if you want to stay late, we can find something to work on. Hitting. Bunting." He pauses. "You ever make a diving catch?"

"No." She wonders how you could practice that.

Coach isn't sure. But it could be fun, he says. "Possibly useful."

* * * * *

Renni and Colleen join Jamie after practice. Three wet girls and one wet coach.

Brad has them start on their knees. He'll try tossing balls to their left and right, just out of reach. To catch them, they'll have to use their knees to push off to the side and catch the ball as they fall. If they can do that, he'll try more difficult throws. They'll have to lunge harder from their knees. From there, they can eventually work up to starting on their feet, from a low crouch.

The wet parts of the field are ideal. Jamie finds that it's not that hard to push off sideways from her knees, and snatch the toss while she's falling. After just a few tries, they're launching harder: diving. Brad worries about how they land, but Jamie says she hardly feels anything when she hits the ground. Renni makes it a point to set herself up near the wettest parts of the grass, and then slide as far as she can after she dives.

Actually catching the ball, though, proves difficult. And Brad struggles with his throws. They're either too far, too close, too hard, too high, or too low. Jamie snags one on her first try, but can't come up with another. On her fourth try, Renni manages to flap her glove shut on an almost-flat-out dive, and holds the ball aloft from the wet grass. "What are you?" Jamie yells. "A salamander?"

"Yes!" Renni shrieks.

Colleen has a few almost-catches, but can't quite get one. She keeps trying.

Chapter 19
GOOD ENOUGH

Brad and Conner take a booth in the corner. They wave at Von, glance up to check the score in the Bruins' game.

Brad initiated this meeting. In their recent game against the Reds, Brad asked Conner to tone down the volume and Conner nodded, but then he'd stalked around in conspicuous silence. And then he'd had a minor run-in with one of the Reds' parents. The Reds' pitcher had hit a rough patch, walking three straight batters. This girl was probably the second-best pitcher in the league; not at Claire Boniface's level, but probably more advanced than Kelli. As she struggled to find the strike zone, the girl's father called in a stream of corrections from behind the backstop, and when she kept missing with her pitches, he became angry and sarcastic. The other parents grew quiet as they tried to tune out the obnoxious voice. Conner strode behind the backstop to confront the man. Brad and Diane and Heather stayed by their bench, casting glances at the two men as they jabbed fingers and thrust their chins at each other. Brad's feeling was that it was a shame and the man was embarrassing his poor daughter, but it wasn't his player; it wasn't any of his business. The episode, thankfully, had been short-lived.

Brad wanted to talk.

"For starters," Conner says, "I'm really sorry about that little . . . 'scene' last game."

Brad puts his hand up. "Don't worry about it. Please." It's not what he's come to talk about. Brad wants to remind Conner that, while he agrees with most of what Conner says, the girls can only absorb so much. Brad brings up an example from their last game. Lori had just snared a throw at first base for an out. Brad was happy to see her succeeding, gaining confidence, playing an important position. Conner, though, noted that Lori had set her whole foot on top of first base. "Lori," he called. "Just your heel. Just touch the side of the base with your heel." Standing next to the first-base line, he demonstrated the proper stance, glove outstretched toward the throw. He nodded back at his foot, emphasizing how she would catch the ball a split-second sooner if she placed her heel against the side of the base instead of on top of it.

"Lori, nice catch," Brad said.

"Right," Conner affirmed. "The important thing," he told Lori, "is that you caught the ball."

At this, Lori smiled. She'd caught the ball, she'd made an out, and she was damn proud of it. She liked first base.

Conner remembers. "If we're going to play her there, we have to teach her the position."

While it is possible that Lori was ready for this new lesson, Brad doesn't think so. Lori needs to think about one or at most two things at a time. She's been learning: Practicing decision-making about when to cover the base and when to field the ball; learning to show a target and stretch for the throw. "I worry about giving her too much," Brad says. "I think you forget how much you know. I'm sure it's hard, but just—just remember that it overwhelms some of these girls."

"Possibly," Conner concedes. "There's just so much they need to know."

Brad is relieved. *Constructive*, he thinks. They can drink a few beers and relax. "Just don't forget how little they know," he says. "And sometimes they take it better when we talk to them on the bench instead of while the game's going on."

"I don't know." Conner squints doubtfully. "I think it helps to address the issue right at the moment, when it's fresh in memory."

Brad hesitates. That sounds reasonable. His concern, though, is that the girl is trying to pay attention to the game. Also, he says, she might not like being corrected in front of everybody.

"Sure, but Brad. If I can help them, I gotta give it a shot. They have to know. That's what we're here for." Conner pushes forward over his elbows. "You know," he says, "we didn't lose a game that I coached. You're the coach—I can't be the coach—but I did achieve some success."

"I'm just reminding you," Brad says, "that we're bottle feeding here."

That's for sure: total agreement on that.

"Okay, how about this," Brad says. "Try to remember what you were learning when you were eleven. On that stuff—you know, not swinging at those high pitches, stuff like that—go nuts; be the teacher. But on some of these finer points? If you could just check with me first. I work with them in practice. They hear stuff from me and I try pretty hard to keep it simple, so they only have one or two 'next steps' to keep in mind. So during games, before you get into any long explanations, any fine points, check with me first. They're not going to do everything just right, and we have to live with that. But if they're hearing too many different things from different coaches—if we're confusing them—then we're making it harder, not easier."

Conner channels his lips and then nods. "Sounds reasonable. And you're the coach."

That was all they needed to cover. Now. There's a new IPA on tap. Conner pushes back his stool. "I'll get two."

* * * * *

On the outfield grass, Courtney runs the pre-game drills. Brad can hear her voice rising and falling as he rakes the infield dirt. He has turned this responsibility over to the girls, thinking they might pay attention if somebody other than him runs the drill. And they're running their own player-designed drills: That should also help. Brad knows they need better pre-game routines—something to get them ready so they can avoid some of their first-inning horror shows.

Courtney was reluctant as always, but Brad told her: "You're my choice." He's told Jamie—the best player—that she needs to support Courtney, pay attention, and do everything exactly as Courtney says.

Conner arrives and trots out to watch them. When Brad calls the girls to the bench, he exchanges glances with Conner. Conner gives a crisp thumbs-up: They're engaged.

The Marlins don't get off to a great start, but it's not bad. After two innings the game is tied at four.

Brad spends the game clapping his hands, shouting encouragement, occasionally stopping one of his players coming off the field, pointing out some small thing: *Make sure she sees you for the cutoff throw. Remember to round that base.*

He resolves to *not* yell out any instruction, and he renews this resolution because the air rattles and throbs with the rickety flow of Conner's shouted instructions. "Courtney!" he calls after Courtney dumps a weak foul ball off to the right. "Use your hips!" He demonstrates the imaginary perfect swing from his position in the first-base coach's box. "Bring your hands through here . . . then swivel those hips. Hands and hips. Hands and hips!"

Courtney connects with solid contact, but her looping liner settles easily into the shortstop's glove.

In the next inning, Colleen, perfectly positioned as the

cutoff, receives a relay throw from the outfield, but she is slow to uncork her throw to second base. Conner leaps up, calling out: "Colleen! Quicker on that pivot!" He makes a catching motion, followed by a half jump. "Crow-hop! Catch and pivot! Catch and pivot!"

Between innings, Brad likes to wander the field, dishing up small reminders to his players as they take their warmups. This time, he stays in the bench area, beckons at Conner. "All good stuff," he says. "But remember—let's not confuse them. Don't give them too much to think about."

Conner nods. "Yeah. But the thing is, I can help. I can help Courtney with her hitting. Hitting a grapefruit won't do it. She's gotta use her hips."

"Conner," Brad says. "Like we talked about. You're right. But I don't think Courtney can digest that during her at-bat and change her swing and hit a line drive. I mean, keep it simple. So they can keep up."

"Sure." Conner wanders along the bench, looking out at the field.

The Marlins get good pitching from Kelli, Jamie, and Lissa. Solid plays from Renni and Colleen. Big hits from Courtney and Kelli. It all adds up to a 10-7 victory over the Mets.

In the post-game huddle, Brad congratulates the girls: "Now that feels good, doesn't it?"

"YES!"

It's a full-throated shout, unanimous and spontaneous. It rings with the joy and certainty of children.

The Marlins are as good as any team, Brad tells them. He thanks Courtney for running the pre-game drills. Good job. Next game that job goes to—Brad scans the circle of girls with his finger . . . "Colleen."

Colleen slumps over as if she's been shot.

Brad acts surprised. *What? It'll be fine.*

* * * * *

Afterward, he catches sight of Emmie walking off by herself. He sets down the equipment bag and jogs to catch up and walk beside her. "Good game," he says.

"Thanks."

He's e-mailed her parents: *I hope Emmie's having fun . . . I understand she has several commitments; I hope she can make it tomorrow . . . please keep me posted on her schedule . . .* and once again he's received no reply.

"Can we talk for a minute?"

She stops. Families stream past them. Parents at the car doors.

"I know your mom's waiting, I just need—"

"That's not my mom."

"Not your mom?"

Emmie shakes her head. It's a sitter.

"Okay. Still, just a few minutes." Hastily he starts tossing questions. *Having fun? Too many things going on?*

She responds with standard nods.

"How's gymnastics?"

"Good."

"That's your thing."

She nods.

"More than softball."

She nods yes again as she looks toward the car.

Brad looks around, finds the sitter waving from the car. He holds up three fingers. "Three minutes?"

The woman nods and smiles. No problem.

Brad crouches down to talk to Emmie. "I hope this is fun, too."

"It's okay."

"Just okay."

She shrugs. "I'm not as good at it as I am at gymnastics."

"The better you are, the more fun?"

She nods. Brad nods. Who could argue with that?

"How come you decided to play softball?"

"I wanted a sport. Or something—I mean my *own* sport."

Brad takes a careful breath. *Keep going*, he thinks.

"Something that's *my own* thing. But . . . I'm . . . not good."

"I think you're a pretty good softball player. And getting better every week." This is true. She's shown athleticism from her first day. More recently, she's handled several plays in the field, and in the last game she pulled off a nifty base-running play; the Mets' infielders had everything under control but Emmie scampered from second to third base when she saw the Mets' third baseman tying her shoe, not paying attention.

Emmie shakes her head. "But I'm *really* good in gymnastics. It takes a lot of time and work but I got good at it."

Brad does not want to put her on the spot. But he needs just another minute . . . or two.

"I want it to be fun," she says, "but I also want to be good."

Right. Brad searches her face. "Maybe it's more fun if we win more games." It comes out as a question.

She nods dutifully. "I'm trying for the championship in gymnastics."

"I hope you win it." Brad stands up, and they resume their approach to the car. "Emmie."

Yes?

"The Marlins are trying for a championship. Once the playoffs start."

"I mean a *real* championship," Emmie says.

Real. "You mean, something that matters? Matters to who?"

She shrugs. "Lots of people. People come to the meets—the seats get pretty full sometimes."

They're almost within earshot of her sitter. "I guess it must matter if it gets in the newspaper," Brad says. "And the bigger the paper, the more it matters."

Emmie nods.

Brad gets it. "But the Marlins matter, too. In a different way. We don't play in some big fancy stadium, but I can tell you for sure that it matters to Jamie; it matters to Colleen and Renni and Kelli and even Kacie and Meghan. And they need you. So if it matters to them . . ." Brad's running short of time and talking fast, and he doesn't want it to feel like browbeating. "We miss you when you're not here." That's better. "We've got . . . not that many weeks left. For a few weeks, Emmie, I want you—I *ask* you—to stick with this. Whether we win games or not, let's just try to improve and feel good about ourselves. And I'm telling you that it matters, because if it doesn't matter, then pretty soon practice doesn't matter, and then the next batter doesn't matter, and then the next game doesn't matter, and then Renni and Courtney and Colleen don't matter and I don't matter and you don't matter and then what are we all going to do?"

Brad catches his breath.

"I'm sticking with it," Emmie says.

Brad taps her on the shoulder. "I'm glad. And I promise it'll be fun. A different kind of fun."

"It's fun enough," she says.

* * * * *

Brad jogs back to the bench. He still needs to stow the field maintenance equipment. Somebody's left a batting glove under the bench. He needs to talk to Renni's parents and spots them chatting with some other parents in the parking lot. He can't find the scorebook. Maybe Heather still has it. He hopes. He gets down on all fours to reach under the bench for the batting glove.

Some guy makes his way around the chain-link fence into the dugout area. Chubby guy, crew cut and sun visor. Brad turns, straightens. "Hi," he says.

"Listen," the guy says. "Was it really necessary to keep stealing bases in the fifth inning?"

Brad looks at him. What is this guy *talking about?*

"Do you realize"—the guy jabs his finger at Brad—"your runner, when she slid into third, almost killed my daughter?"

Brad remembers that the Mets' third baseman fell down when Colleen slid into third base. Colleen's foot might have hit her shin.

"And given the situation, I think it was not only unnecessary, but unsportsmanlike."

Brad feels his cheeks flush with anger. He can jab his finger right back at this guy. He takes a step forward. He wonders if the guy's putting on a show for somebody. He looks around and sees Heather coming his way with the scorebook. "We were playing softball," he says.

"Gimme a *break*. It's just so just *pathetic*—guys like you coming out here to act like big shots. There's a lot more to kids' sports—"

"Heather," Brad says. She's just on the other side of the fence, making her way around. Showing a bit of leg in her shorts and white tennis shoes. "What was the score in the fifth inning?"

Heather pauses, leans her head to the side as she opens the book, and comes around the fence into the dugout. She smiles at Brad, then at the angry Mets' parent. "Let's see." She is sleek and competent. Doe-eyed calm under her festive pile of auburn hair. "The Mets got one in the top half, and then it was 7-6, and then we got two in the bottom half."

There's a pause. Heather takes the pencil from behind her ear, drops it, makes a dopey laugh as she bends to pick it up. The guy's attack stalls.

"I hope your daughter's okay," Brad says.

Immediate concern from Heather. "Oh—oh—did she get hurt?"

The guy hesitates. "She's okay. It's just—her ankle . . ."

"We've got ice packs," Heather says.

"She'll be okay. I didn't realize the game was that close."

Handshakes all around. A pleasant smile as he shakes

Heather's hand.

Brad and Heather watch him leave. Brad wonders how much Heather saw or heard. She grins. She crimps one side of her face and performs a cartoon mimicry: *"It's so pathetic. . . there's a lot more to kids' sports . . ."*

Brad laughs and thanks Heather. "I think he might have been grandstanding for somebody."

"Seeking glory."

Brad looks at Heather. His fetching comrade. "He got the glory of a nice smile from you," Brad says. "Hope you don't mind."

"Whatever it takes." She hands the scorebook to Brad. She leans toward him, bright teeth showing, face forward and tilted slightly like she's about to share a secret.

Good Lord. How unfortunate, Brad thinks, that he's about twice her age . . . but he doesn't need to think about that. He remembers something. He looks about the parking lot. Renni's gone.

* * * * *

Last game: Cubs. In the outfield, Colleen shouts out instructions for pre-game drills. Brad listens as he finishes the field prep. He recognizes Conner's car pulling in. On the bench, Heather fills out the lineup in the scorebook. Colleen's voice drifts across the grass. *"Pickle drill! . . . one line over here . . . then you move to this base . . ."* Brad and Diane catch each other's glances and grin. Colleen's one of the smaller girls on the team, but she can be a bullhorn boss when she wants to.

Conner waves as he makes his way from his car. Brad has a few moments, so he hikes across the field to watch the pickle drill. Colleen squats, just as Brad does when he runs the drill. He watches Maddi chase a runner, make her throw, then cover the base that she just threw to. Emmie takes the throw. The runner—Meghan—changes direction. Emmie gives chase.

Meghan runs with her usual wispy chicken strides. But she looks excited, like something newly hatched; she's watching—Emmie throws it to Lori—to see when they might make their throws. Finally, an error: Maddi can't handle a hurried throw. Meghan stops. She's almost touching Maddi's base—*safety!*—but she hesitates for a split-second . . . and . . . turns back for the other base. Where Maddi's throw arrives quickly.

Out.

"Good recovery!" Brad shouts. "Nice job!" At long last: They've *got it.*

One thing: He motions Meghan over to talk. "Meghan," he says quietly, "nice running. But you were right there at Maddi's base. Why didn't you just take it?"

He can barely hear her answer. "Sorry?" He cups his hand to his ear.

"I was trying to score."

Oh, he thinks. Right. Maddi was covering imaginary third base. The other base was home. He'd forgotten. *Still*, he thinks. Yes, scoring is the objective, but she was *two feet* from safe . . . and the happy realization comes over him: Where he saw safety, she—Meghan!—saw something else—she saw a chance. "Right," he says. "Good answer."

With a win, they'll get to 7-7-1.

It is not to be. The Marlins come back from a 5-2 deficit to tie it at 6 after four innings, but the Cubs' hitters come through for two runs in the fifth and sixth.

Hi all:

I guess a win would have been nice, but the girls played a good game.

The Marlins' record is now 6-8-1, and we're tied for third place. Playoffs start next Saturday. The schedule is not out yet, but I'll keep you posted.

Today we got nice hustle plays by Colleen and Kacie, who's really been playing well recently. Spectacular leaping stab by Lissa; great hitting days for Jamie and Renni. I think we're ready for the playoffs.

Brad chooses not to mention one thing, mostly because he doesn't understand it. It happened in the fourth inning.

Jamie pitching. He'd meant to pitch Kelli for four and then Lissa for two innings, but Diane suggested a few innings for Jamie. It's her second inning, and she walks the Cubs' leadoff batter. The Marlins cheer her on: *You can do it, Jamie! Looking good, Jamie! You got her!*

Despite the encouragement, she walks the next batter. The next Cubs' batter comes to the plate smiling, saying something to Colleen, the catcher.

Jamie's first pitch is a ball. The chatter rises slightly: *No problem, Jamie. You've got this!*

Jamie delivers ball two. The Marlins are incessant: You've got this . . . right in there, Jamie . . . fire it in there . . . you're the pitcher . . . *this batter couldn't touch you in a million years*!

That last one—Brad thinks it came from Lissa. Kind of strong. Then Kelli, from her crouched stance at shortstop: "Come on, Jamie. No batter, Jamie. No batter *at all!*"

And from someone else at the same time. Again, with a bit of extra emphasis: "She'll NEVER get a hit off you!" Brad looks over to check with Diane, but she's watching intently and seems not to have noticed.

He can see an effect. He is certain that the Cubs' hitter changes her demeanor. She looks around the infield, and the volume of Marlins' chatter rises. The girl puts her head down as she takes her practice swings.

Jamie's next pitch is a strike. Brad can hear Marlin voices rising all around the field. He can hear Kacie, Lori, Lissa, Renni. *She can't hang with you, Jamie!* The next pitch results in a ground ball back to Jamie, who fields it and calmly throws it to Lissa, covering third. One out.

Brad looks again to Diane, but Diane is looking out at the field, shaking her fist as she calls out, "Great job, Marlins! Great job out there!"

The inning ends, scoreless. Brad waits with high-fives as they come to the dugout. Some of them are literally skipping as they run. Except for Jamie. She walks with her head down. Her teammates slap her with their gloves as they run by.

Brad peers closely. He's not sure at first, but then, yes— she's crying. He doesn't know why.

* * * * *

Brad wanders into the Pub. The Braves have an evening practice, so Mike's not around. He's pleased to find Spence there, quietly tracking the Bruins' game on the screen over the bar. Brad takes the stool next to him, and they get started on all things hockey.

Brad marvels at a clever pass. They watch the slow-motion replay, and Brad notes how a subtle realignment of the passer's hands caused a defender to change his angle, and opened a passing lane. "These guys are so damn good," he says.

His own hockey skills are diminishing. Brad can still handle the puck and anticipate plays, but his balance is not so good anymore. His hand-eye coordination is off a few ticks.

Von overhears. "You ever get Mike to lace up again?"

Brad blows out a deflated "*pfh*."

"You just wanted to kick his butt."

Maybe. Brad understands that he's been trying to goad Mike, which is probably not possible. Ever since he'd walked away from the game as a teenager, Mike has resolutely refused to come back to it. Brad has never understood this. Because Mike loved hockey. *Loved* it. Brad's done his best badgering; wondering why Mike would completely give up on something he loved.

The question seemed to amuse Mike. "Why did I quit hockey? You mean way back when?" He gave a scornful shrug: "It was a cluster—"

Brad tried to get in Mike's face. "Lemme tell ya. Everything's a cluster. Doesn't mean you blow off the world and disown everybody you ever knew."

To which Mike shrugged again. "Lots of clusters out there. Isn't that why you quit Rylix?" When Brad hesitated, Mike said, "Don't tell me you'd ever go back."

"I guess that's Mike," Von says. "When he lets go, he lets go."

"Give him credit," Spence says. "We should get him to talk to Kevin."

Von rolls his eyes. He turns to Brad. "Do you know Kevin?"

Brad does not.

Kevin, Spence says, was probably the best high school basketball player in the history of the town.

Von leans forward, forearms on the bar. "In the state tournament, he totally carried us. Totally. Game's not even close without him. And then he missed a few free throws near the end."

Spence nods along at the memory. "Even after he missed, it was still a tie game. And there were still twenty seconds left."

"Right," Von says. "Anyway, we lost the game."

"Never got past it." Spence rolls his eyes. "The guy's nuts."

"How so?" Brad says.

"Thirty years later the guy's still punishing himself. Pumping free throws—he probably shoots a few hundred a week."

"I don't know that he's nuts," Von says. "I mean, there's no question he's got his issues these days, but I don't know that that has anything to do with the free-throw shooting. I think he just likes shooting baskets."

"To what purpose? Why would anybody dedicate that

much time and energy to friggin' basketball free throws?"

"I know." Von shrugs. "But maybe it just feels good. Maybe he just likes that sound—that 'swish'. Maybe it's therapeutic."

"That's what I'm saying," Spence grumbles. "Therapy. In other words, he's nuts."

Von crouches at an imaginary free throw line. As he flexes upward and forward into the release, he hops slightly with one foot. As his shooting hand snaps forward, his left hand swims back, leaving his limbs posed at about 10:20 on the clock. Von holds the pose as he looks at Spence.

Spence raises his eyebrows, impressed. "Not bad. That's the stroke."

"Just so you know," Von says to Brad. "This guy Kevin . . . would be Kevin . . . *Boniface*."

* * * * *

Brad replays the last game in his head. In the end, he and Diane were pleased. The Marlins made some good plays. They competed. After the game, Conner shook Brad's hand. He'd been relatively quiet during the game. He didn't like losing, he said, but yes, for the most part they'd played well.

Brad sighs. Yes, but. There was an easy pop fly dropped by Maddi, who compounded the misadventure with a demented throw over the second baseman's head. There was Lori's bizarre refusal to run for the next base with Renni's hit bounding into the outfield. A different course of action on either of those plays would have gained a run . . . or two, or maybe even three. Would have meant one more win. Instead of 6-8-1 they could have finished 7-7-1: Five hundred. That would have been nice.

Chapter 20
PLAYOFFS

The Marlins finish the regular season in third place.

	<u>W</u>	<u>L</u>	<u>T</u>
Braves	15	0	--
Cubs	8	6	1
Marlins	6	8	1
Mets	6	9	--
Reds	5	10	--
Cardinals	4	11	--

Heading into the playoffs, the first-place Braves and second-place Cubs earn first-round byes; the third-place Marlins will face the Cardinals in Round One.

The Cardinals finished 4-11, but they'd started 1-9 and then won three of their last five games, and their late-season losses were all close. They can play.

Brad has grown accustomed to lineup preparation. This one is different. All of the girls have had their opportunities at their coveted positions, and they've all batted in different parts of the lineup. Now it's the playoffs. The other coaches will play their best players in the important positions all game; the bad players will play the outfield and sit on the bench.

Diane has been through this before. She confirms Brad's suspicions.

You've been fair all season. In the playoffs, though, you play to win. We know who our best players are. We need to keep them at the key positions. Pitch Kelli. Jamie and Renni at short and third; Lissa at first. Courtney's gotten good enough so she can play some first, some third base. Meghan, Lori, and Kacie will have to sit extra innings and play mostly right field; I wouldn't try Lori at first again. Colleen, Emmie, Maddi—they're in between. There should be some innings for them at catcher and second base. Whatever you think works best, but those are my thoughts.

Brad fusses at the position alignments. They'll need a skilled player in left-center field every inning. Emmie and Maddi won't run down balls for difficult plays, but they will catch balls hit near them. So, second base and left-center field for Emmie. He's less certain about Maddi. Colleen brings jaw-clenched grit; nothing gets past her. She will play second base, catcher, and outfield. Possibly third base for an inning.

Meghan will sit out two of the early innings. Kacie and Lori will sit for two innings. He designates Maddi to sit the fourth; Emmie to sit the fifth. He needs one more sit-out: It has to be Meghan. She's shown effort and alertness recently. But Meghan will have to sit an extra inning. It's the obvious choice; it's the correct decision. He can almost feel the sting.

* * * * *

A misty drizzle dampens the grass. Both teams pile up errors and unearned runs; girls chase after ground balls, scampering through the infield.

After three innings, the Marlins hold a 5-4 lead. It's anybody's game. The Cardinals' coaches, Brad suspects, are envisioning a glorious, validating finish to their season.

Two consecutive five-run innings win the game for the Marlins. Jamie, Kelli, and Courtney deliver hard hits that elude the Cardinals' outfielders. With the bases loaded, Lori—look at her swing that bat!—pounds a hard ground ball that gets through the infield and drives in two runs.

In the field, Emmie repeatedly runs from the outfield to the infield to cover bases and back up. Meghan crouches before every pitch, pink glove open, ready to move.

The final result: a surprisingly easy 15-8 win.

Afterward, Conner shakes Brad's hand again. He'll have to miss the next game.

"Okay." Brad conceals his relief.

Conner has to be out of town.

"Overseas?"

"Um." Conner hesitates. "No. Not that far."

"Fun stuff?"

Conner rolls his eyes. "Meetings. It's you goddamn research guys. Think it's all about the science."

"Oh. Wait." Brad can't resist. "It's not?"

"In this case it's about the money, which is in fact needed to deploy the science," Conner says. Then he picks up on Brad's dig. He drops his shoulders. "Don't get me started." He punches Brad in the arm. "Got that, fool? It's about the money."

"Got it." Brad laughs. "Hope it goes well. We'll keep you posted."

* * * * *

Mike isn't sure how he feels about his fellow coaches. He gets along with them well enough. He's been pleasantly surprised to find, though, that he likes the girls. Twice so far he's pulled girls aside to give suggestions; both times they seemed to listen.

He is doing a good thing for Claire. It surprises him to understand that he *wants* to do a good thing for Claire. A few times now she's asked him to help her work on pitching. Once before practice, and then twice at home when he was visiting Joanne.

One day she wanted to work on a new "drop ball" pitch that her pitching coach had introduced. Claire explained the mechanics and how it was supposed to work. The problem, she said, was that it curved, but it really didn't drop very much. The two of them went to the park. After a brief warm-up, Mike squatted down to catch. Claire's pitches came in hot. It was difficult to observe the mechanics of her delivery, but Mike called out how the pitches were spinning, and a few other things he could see—*Did you dip your shoulder on that one?*

As they walked home, Claire tossed the ball up in the air and caught it. Then she tossed it hard into her glove. Then up in the air. Mike reached to intercept it on the way down. Claire protested, and he grinned and flipped the ball back to her.

He's doing a good thing for Joanne—for his relationship with Joanne. Heck, he's doing a good thing for himself. He's glad that he decided to coach. He and Claire have something to talk about now, and she engages him in conversation.

On the way home from practice one evening they stop at the Flavor Frond for frozen yogurt. Claire heads straight for the pineapple; Mike inspects the options before deciding. "Go a little easy on the toppings," he says.

Claire takes a table while Mike pays, as if following a years-old routine. They sit down, chatting easily, and naturally the topic turns to the Braves.

"What do you think of your coaches?" Mike asks.

Claire's mid-spoonful. "You're a good coach," she says brightly.

"Well, thank you. How about Phil and Bruce?"

Claire thinks for a moment. Coach Phil likes rules. "He knows we won't make good decisions most of the time. So he makes rules about what to do."

"Would you prefer that he let you make mistakes?"

"Yes."

"Why?"

Claire takes another spoonful; Mike wonders if he'd let her get too much. "Because that's how you learn," she says.

"Who told you that?"

"My dad."

"Your dad sounds like a smart man." Mike sits back, wondering if he wants to talk about her father.

Claire digs into the cup, trying to load the spoon with Heath Bar bits. She sees him watching and smiles as she mines the yogurt.

It catches Mike off guard. He's come to think of her as the star pitcher. Right there, though, she looks like a little girl; like any other twelve-year-old girl. He returns the smile. "What else did you learn from your dad?"

"Um." After she takes her spoonful, she takes the spoon out, turns it upside down, and sucks on it some more. "He told me to practice a lot. Until my motion is, like, automatic. That way I'll be less likely to fail."

Mike breathes evenly, nodding slowly. He doesn't want to get into anything heavy. As she raises her next spoonful, he reaches out to jiggle her elbow—her spoon elbow.

"*Hey,*" Claire steadies her spoon, pouts at him. "*Quit that.*"

* * * * *

Joanne is surprised and pleased that Claire has shared her thoughts with Mike; that the two of them seem to be cultivating a relationship.

They sit relaxed at the deck table, shading their eyes against the sunshine. Glints of light bob in their wine glasses. "Same here," Mike says. "Surprised and pleased. I was scared at first."

A breeze comes up. Jo lets the moment ride. "She loves her dad," she says.

As he's spent more time with Claire, Mike has found himself thinking of his own family. The dark and stale bedroom where his mother stayed in bed watching TV; the vulgar bodily sounds and lurching movements and collisions of his dad downstairs at two in the morning. From a very young age he was able to see how things were—how messed up they were—and how he did not want to be.

"You're back to drawing trees," Joanne says. "What is it about trees?"

Mike still doesn't know. It is interesting, though, to understand how different kinds of trees grow differently, reach for the sky differently, reach for the soil differently, repair themselves differently. Soil, light, water . . . they all need the same things, and yet they all have different ways of getting them. "In some ways," Mike says, "they're actually social—in the ways they seem to make room for each other."

"Do they?"

"Sure. Trees don't grow branches that stick in each other's space. Where the forest gets crowded, they stay skinny until they get up high."

"Interesting."

Mike is proud to share what he's learned. After so many forest walks, observing and inspecting leaves and seeds and bark, after so many consultations with three different field guides, he fancies himself knowledgeable if not quite expert.

Depending on the particular patch of forest, he continues,

different kinds of trees are like families from different cultures. Old spruces and pines stand tall like weathered aristocrats in dimly lit council chambers; school-uniformed youngsters pass cigarettes outside. On the other hand, hawthorns and redbuds and wild crabapples intermingle, leaving discarded tires and broken tricycles in each other's yards.

Mike finds it interesting. He assumes that Jo wants him to share it with her. He doesn't share this stuff with Brad or any of his guy friends.

"Why not?" she asks. "Is it not masculine for guys to talk about trees?"

"Some topics are better for conversations with women," Mike says.

"So . . . trees. Women think trees are interesting?"

"It's not *trees*," Mike says. "But you can't talk to women about the things we *like* to talk about, which are mostly sports and women and all the cool stuff we did when we were young."

Jo rolls her eyes. "So these guys you call your friends . . . you only talk about sports and women?"

"We also tell dirty jokes."

Jo sighs in mock disbelief.

"Guys have serious conversations," Mike says. "We have our introspections and emotions. It's just . . ." He looks down into his wine. "There's just some stuff. That maybe I'd rather talk about with you."

Joanne reclines in her seat, looking up at the bright sky. She turns to him with a sidelong smile. Lazily she extends her hand.

Mike takes it and kisses it. This trees-versus-forest hang-up, he says, keeps showing up. "Trees start out a certain way. There's a way they're supposed to be. But then they come across other trees, and things get twisted and distorted and tangled."

"Sounds kind of like softball coaches," Jo says.

"That actually occurred to me," Mike says with a laugh.

Mike tells her how he and Claire were talking about the Braves' coaches. After he'd asked what she thought, Claire returned the question: What did *he* think of Bruce and Phil?

"And what did you say?"

"I said Phil's a good coach. But she wanted more of an answer, and I said maybe he takes himself a little seriously." Mike sits back, smiling. "She agreed."

Joanne refills his glass. "Do *you* take yourself seriously?"

"That's what *I* said. I said, 'Claire, that's what people say about *me. I* take myself too seriously.'"

"And?"

Mike smiles. "She said that I take myself seriously, but not coaching softball."

"Good for you." Joanne refills her glass and sets the bottle down. "Sounds like you passed."

"I might have." Mike pauses. "But yeah, in some ways I probably take myself too damned seriously. Brad's right." He works his lips together, looks out over the yard. He has never understood all these pointless *hobbies* people take up. He's never been one to waste time on people or pursuits without understanding why. But here he finds himself babbling on about trees and drawings as if they mattered, and now there's this . . . this little coaching gig. "Maybe I can be a little less . . . *purposeful*," he says. "About a few things."

* * * * *

The Marlins' next opponent—*again!*—is the Cubs. They've got two of the league's best hitters, and several other girls who can hit for power. Brad can picture screeching line drives leaving vapor trails over his outfielders' heads.

Position assignments are much the same as for the first game, but instead of Emmie and Maddi, this time Courtney and Colleen will each have to sit out an inning. Other than that, he starts tinkering, but quickly throws up his hands and hits the print button: The girls are just going to play the game and they'll make some good plays and some bad plays and they'll either win or they'll lose.

* * * * *

Gwen has enjoyed the softball season. It's been a pleasant surprise. Maddi has been excited to get promoted to important positions, like catcher and third base. She's gotten along with her teammates well.

But Gwen feels nervous. She thinks she knows why.

In that first playoff game against the Cardinals, Gwen parked her lawn chair among the families along the left-field foul line. The Marlins' bench was across the field, on the first-base side.

In one of the middle innings, a sharp ground ball came bouncing down the third-base line. The third baseman—Colleen—extended herself to make a difficult backhand catch. Her throw didn't quite make it to first base, though, and the first baseman had to leave the base to catch it. It was a good try, but the runner was safe. Later that same inning, when a throw came in from the outfield to third base, Colleen hesitated and had to rush to cover the base. The ball and the runner arrived at almost the same time, and the ball ticked off her glove and the runner scored.

Colleen's shoulders sagged.

"Tough play," Gwen heard Brad calling. "It's okay. Two outs. Next play goes to first. Let's get this one."

Watching her from behind, Gwen saw Colleen's chin sink down into her chest. It was not her daughter, but Gwen cringed. Childhood athletic failures sprang at her, still just as raw as if they'd happened yesterday. Pitch followed pitch. The next batter walked. Colleen kicked the ground, and Gwen could see her shoulders quivering.

Coach Brad left the bench. He trotted quickly behind the backstop and around the chain-link fence and back onto the field behind third base. Gwen heard a brief exchange between Brad and the Cardinals' coaches, and then Brad moved to the foul territory behind third base and crouched down. He spoke in low tones.

"Colleen? Colleen. Stay ready for the next pitch, but please nod your head if you can hear me."

Gwen was the parent closest to Brad. She could barely hear him.

Colleen nodded without looking up. The side of her cheek, Gwen could see, was red and streaked. Her shoulders shook.

"Colleen, you made a tiny mistake. One really tiny mistake. Let it go."

A hush fell over the lawn chairs; parents strained to hear. Gwen wasn't sure where Colleen's mother was.

"Every practice and every game, you give it your best. And I know you're going to try as hard as you can on the next play. And that's all you . . . that's . . ."

He stumbled over a few words, stopped. A broken rhythm hung in the air. Brad paused as Kelli delivered the next pitch. Foul ball.

"Hey. Colleen. What you've contributed all season makes you *bigger* than one mistake. You are bigger than one error or one bad inning. *Way* bigger. One mistake cannot possibly hurt you; it cannot beat you up because you are *so* much bigger than it."

Colleen nodded. Her shaking subsided slightly.

"Everyone makes mistakes. I make mistakes," Brad said, looking around surreptitiously. "All you can do is try your best on the play that's about to happen. That's what you always do. And that's why you're such an important part of our team."

Brad extracted a nod from Colleen, then got up, ran back behind the Cardinals' bench, behind the backstop, and back to his place on the Marlins' bench. Two pitches later, the batter struck out. Inning over. The Marlins trotted in from the field. The applause was louder, Gwen thought, than normal.

It's that moment, Gwen realizes, that makes her nervous. Up until now, she's hasn't cared about the outcomes of these games. But now she wants—she *desperately* wants—the Marlins to win.

* * * * *

It's a perfect late-spring Sunday. The hot infield dirt glares in the sunshine. The girls wear shades; a few of them daub blacking on their cheeks. They think it looks cool. Brad and Heather meet with the umpire and the Cubs' coaches at home plate. Brad can hear Maddi barking out directions as she runs the pre-game drills in the outfield.

Renni leads off. She lets one pitch go by; then steps into the next one. The ball jumps off her bat on a line. It goes straight into the glove of the Cubs' third baseman. Lissa's the next batter. She falls into an 0-2 count, then starts fouling off pitches. Hanging in. Staying alive. Then she finds one she likes and drives it over the shortstop's head. The excitement vanishes as the Cubs' left-center fielder takes just a few steps to her right and hauls it in. Swinging hard at the first pitch, Jamie smokes a high-hopper, but it's right at the pitcher, who fields it and tosses casually to first base.

All three batters hit the ball hard. Three outs. The Cubs' coaches clap their hands and pump their fists and raise their hands for high-fives as their players run off the field.

* * * * *

The Marlins are also up to the task. After one inning, the game is scoreless.

After two innings, the Cubs take a 1-0 lead. After three innings it's 3-1 Cubs.

The Cubs have been tough all season. And their improvement has been impressive. One girl in particular: Brad swears she was one of their weaker players, but she's grown noticeably and she's clubbing the ball with authority. Another girl who's apparently missed some of the Cub-Marlin games—Brad doesn't remember her—adds yet another formidable hitter to their lineup.

The Marlins break through in the fourth. Renni smashes a double; Lissa reaches on a soft ground ball. A hard grounder by Jamie gets through the infield and then scoots through the softer defense in the outfield. Two runs score. Then, after stealing third, Jamie scores on a ground ball. The Marlins lead, 4-3.

In the fifth inning the Marlins get two more runs as the Cubs' fielding begins to crack. Once the errors start, they tend to pile up fast.

Trouble arises in the bottom of the fifth. For four innings Kelli's thrown strike after strike. But now, suddenly, she can't find her release point. Brad calls out to remind her of the mechanics they've worked on. *Cock that wrist! Toe drag!* She nods and tries to *concentrate*, but pitch after pitch comes in either too high or low in the dirt. Behind the plate, Colleen scrambles doggedly to block and smother pitches, taking bad hops off the shin guards, one off her mask. She keeps the ball in front of her.

With one out, the Cubs have loaded the bases, all three runners reaching on walks. They score a run on a bases-loaded walk, then another on groundout. The Cubs' bench is alive, girls up and leaning against the fence. The Marlin lead is down to one run: 6-5. The next batter is a girl named Brittany, one of their star hitters. It's her third at-bat, and she's locked in on Kelli. This girl can hit.

With two balls and no strikes, the pitch comes in. Kelli's delivery looks awkward, a bit off. No matter. The pitch looks juicy. Brittany strides into it, her hands moving forward in perfectly orchestrated timing.

But the ball fails to arrive. It seems frozen in the air.

Brittany's wrists release, whipping the head of the bat around in a powerful arc.

The ball hovers and then drops quietly into Colleen's glove.

Wow. Hush. Diane turns to Brad, mouth agape, and they marvel: It has to be the best change-up Kelli's thrown.

The next pitch is Kelli's regular fastball again. Brittany swings and connects, but not with the fluid momentum that she had before. The ball loops softly toward second base, where Maddi gathers it in. Three outs. The Marlins have limited the damage.

On the bench, the Marlins grin and high-five with the coaches. "You girls are awesome. Awesome, awesome, awesome." Brad laughs as he taps Kelli on the shoulder: "You really earned that one. Best change-up ever."

She grins as she flicks her ponytail back behind her head. "I couldn't throw a strike anyway, so I figured why not try the change."

* * * * *

In the sixth inning the Marlins strike again. With Colleen on third, Lori lifts a soft liner that loops over the second baseman's head. That's good for another run, and a 7-5 lead.

Lori's trademark is her wandering, pale-eyed smile; almost cluelessly content . . . but as Brad looks out at her, she's not smiling. Her fists are clenched; her chest is heaving. He has not seen this; he had no idea.

"Look out there!" he yells to the Marlins on the bench. "Let that Marlin player hear it!"

The Marlins respond, chanting "Lo-ri, Lo-ri," as they wave imaginary high-fives out to their teammate.

It's not over. Going into the bottom of the sixth inning, the Marlins lead by two runs, but Kelli's still struggling.

The first batter walks on four pitches.

After a groundout, Kelli gets ahead of the next hitter with two quick strikes, but the batter fouls off a series of strikes and works a walk. Two pitches later, the Cub runners steal, safely arriving at second and third. The Cubs' bench buzzes, girls cheering giddily in anticipation of a jubilant, dramatic victory.

With runners at second and third, the next batter swings at the first pitch. Brad exhales as the ball travels on the ground to Jamie at shortstop. The Marlins relax as sure-handed Jamie fields it smoothly. But as she gets ready to throw, the ball slips out of her hand. Brad can't help it; his foot lands hard on the ground. The lead runner scores from third on the play, cutting the lead to 7-6, with Cub runners now on first and second. Brad feels his face clenching. Mouth open in helpless bewilderment, he turns to Diane, who nods grimly.

The sight of Jamie kicking the dirt jolts Brad back to the moment. "Hey!" he calls. "Forget about it, Jamie."

She doesn't seem to hear him. She is bewildered and angry, possibly shaken.

Brad watches dumbly. He considers calling time-out. Von's the umpire today—and as Brad glances at him there's the sudden vision of a haunted former basketball star measuring up free throw after free throw, doing an endless penance for a meaningless, thirty-years-gone misfire.

But the girls just have to play. Brad cups his hands around his mouth. "Jamie. It's all about the next pitch. Doesn't matter what just happened. We *want* them to hit it to *you,* Jamie. You're too good to *ever* hang your head." He feels his voice catch at the end. Nothing he can say will change what's about to happen. He folds his arms stoically.

The Marlins are still winning. It doesn't look good, but the Cubs' batters still have to perform. He can hear their coaches instructing their hitters: *Wait her out. Do not swing unless there are two strikes.*

With runners already at first and second, Kelli walks yet

another batter, loading the bases with just one out. Another walk will tie the game. A base hit will win it for the Cubs.

Kelli keeps looking over at Brad and Diane. Her face is red. She takes a deep breath as she looks in at the batter. Brad and Diane clap their hands. "You're the pitcher, Kelli. You know what to do. You can do this. *You can do it with your eyes closed.*" Mechanics. Arms and legs. Wrists, follow through. But Kelli is tired. Diane clenches her fists together under her chin.

The girl approaching the plate is one of the Cubs' much-improved sluggers. After taking a ball and two strikes, she sees a pitch she wants. She keeps her weight back, then steps into it, unleashing a violent swing. The ball sizzles like an uncoiling rope into the hole between shortstop and third base.

There it goes: One can only watch.

Vision anticipates the future. The ball hurtles along a clear, slightly curving path to the outfield, where wide-open fields await. Brad sees Jamie pushing off to her right—her strides digging at the dirt, determined but futile. He can already sense a cruel wound inflicted, a wound that will forever scar his twelve-year-old star player.

Vision corrects on the follow-through: Only after the fact is one aware of the blurry form moving at the periphery of vision. From her position at third base, Renni has launched herself to her left. As if she might disrupt the inevitable streaking flow of events. The coordinates converge. The laser trajectory is interrupted; the ball disappears. Renni lands hard, face-down on the infield dirt. Ball in glove. Instantly the Cubs' coaches become frantic—"Back! *Get back!*"

Things move in garbled slow-motion: Renni, struggling for footing. In front of her, the Cubs' runner, mouth open, screeching to a halt; turning, scrambling back toward second. Renni looking up; Emmie standing on second base, glove open, mouth open. Screaming something that nobody can hear.

Renni gathers herself on her knees, identifies the opportunity. Brad can see her face and wonders in astonishment if that's a *grin* he sees. Calm throw to second. Double play. Game over.

The cheers that erupt are drowned by a rush in Brad's head. Renni and Emmie run to hug each other. Jamie jumps on both of them from the side, knocking them over. Her face is red, wet, and raw as a beating heart. Lori runs about the infield, not sure what to do but apparently ready to pursue the next Cub runner in case the game's not over. Parents all stand: clapping their hands, exchanging high-fives, taking footage with their phones.

Brad's already thinking about the next game. It'll be against the Braves. For the championship. It was never supposed to be about this. For the most part, he's managed to not let it be about this. But he won't deny it: Next game, it's about winning. And that's okay because it's not about *him* winning; he wants the Marlins—his girls—to win. Or maybe not; maybe it's about him. Whatever: one more game. He wants to win.

Chapter 21
WINNERS

Sure enough, the Braves breeze through their playoff semi-final, beating the Mets 7 to 1. It'll be the Marlins vs. the Braves for the championship.

Brad believes the Marlins can win. They have a chance.

He decides to avoid Mike for a few days. He does not want to face Mike's taunting bemusement: *Come on. Be real.* It's easy to see himself tightening into resentment: *Yeah, we'll see!*—making Mike's next line an all-too-easy gaslight: *Don't take it so seriously. It's all in fun. Come on: it's a girls' softball game.* That would be correct, of course. But it's best, he figures, to steer clear.

* * * * *

Emmie looks for Coach Brad. She needs to tell him something. He's in the dugout, checking the scorebook with Heather, glancing out toward the outfield, where the Marlins are warming up.

"Coach."

He looks startled. Then he laughs and says, "There you are. I was just looking for you."

She's worried, she says. She's worried about pressure.

"What? What's this about *pressure?*" Coach smiles, holds his palms up like he can't believe something. "Pressure? Emmie, you're the star gymnast. Pressure ain't nothing to you. It sure didn't seem to bother you last game. And by the way: Last game was pressure. Compared to that, today's gonna be easy."

Heather jostles her shoulder. "Come on. You're a good player. Just have fun out there."

Coach Brad swats playfully at the visor of her hat. "It's a great day. Great chance for good things to happen." One of the mothers waves as she walks past the backstop. Brad laughs—"And the women are watching."

Emmie squints up at him.

Coach laughs. "Just something stupid that guys say—or think—sometimes. When they think there's some kind of glory in reach."

"My parents are watching," Emmie says.

"I'm sure you'll make them proud," Heather says.

"Coach," Emmie says. "Just so you know."

"Oh-oh. What?"

"This is their first game."

"Hmm. Well."

"They got almost none of your e-mails."

Coach pretends to be impatient. "Emmie—girl, what you talkin' 'bout?" Then serious again: "I only sent out one—okay, two—e-mails since last game."

"That's not—I'm talking about all season." All season long, she explains, she's intercepted his e-mails. She didn't want her parents to get them, especially the schedules. She didn't want them to come to her games. But when they found out that this one was for the *championship*, they'd insisted on coming.

After their victory over the Cubs, Emmie had gone out onto the back deck. She'd just sat there, watching the dusk descend. The blossoming dogwoods and lilacs got blurry and grainy, like when you open your eyes underwater. She'd felt the temperature on her skin. The little sweat beads, gleaming like cool jewels. One thing she knew for sure: If she ever saw Renni or Jamie—maybe any of the Marlins—in some school or in some store in town, they would be friends. She'd won plenty of gymnastics competitions. But that last game against the Cubs—the memory was already burned in. She could remember screaming without knowing what was coming out of her mouth, standing on second base, pleading for the throw. She could still see Renni rising up to her knees, and the clearest part of the picture was the wicked flash of triumph and mischief—*gotcha!*—in Renni's eyes. And she—Emmie—she didn't remember *thinking* at all. It wasn't even about knowing—it was just—it felt like . . . how strange!—it felt like *nothing*. It felt like they were a star dance couple, making everything effortless, like they were all the same person, only with more arms and legs.

Her parents thought it odd for her to be alone out there for so long, and so they'd come outside and settled into chairs and talked. And decided that they were coming.

Emmie wants it to be known. "This is *my* sport. Not my parents'."

Coach squats down next to her. They're both aware of the rest of the Marlins tossing and chatting in the outfield, the occasional shout, the parents gathering, but it all seems very distant. "I'm glad you've had some fun this season," Coach says.

"I did."

"I bet you'll remember it for a long time."

Emmie wants to win. If they don't . . . well. She'll go home. Since she goes to private schools and has to do gymnastics all the time she won't see much of her teammates anymore. She's a gymnast. But that last game felt good. Coach is right. She'll remember it—and the Marlins—for a long time.

* * * * *

Conner's not coming. He's e-mailed his apologies: He won't be able to get back in time. He hates to miss out; he wants to help, but he simply cannot make it.

Kacie and Lissa run the pre-game drills. Then the pickle drill. With Brad as the runner. At this point he expects them to get him out. He is not disappointed. They execute efficiently and relentlessly, running him back and forth: Stop. Change direction. Stop. Back. Start. After Colleen tags him for the third straight out, he falls down and stays down. "That's enough," he gasps.

The protests rise in predictable fashion. *"Oh come on! That's not fair! Come on. I didn't get a chance to get you out."*

Lying on his back on the grass, Brad lets the shouts wash over him. The heaving in his chest calms as he regains his breath. He studies the cloud formations above, debating whether they look more like whipped cream or white cotton candy. Then he sits up.

* * * * *

The Marlins lead off the first inning. Braves' pitcher Claire looks as scary as ever. Only one Marlin hitter even manages a foul ball. In the bottom half of the inning, the Braves' bench buzzes as their leadoff hitter steps in. After getting ahead with a one ball-two strike count, Kelli's next two pitches skip in the dirt. Three balls, two strikes, and the Braves anticipate a leadoff runner on base. Kelli's next pitch comes in rising, near the top of the strike zone. It surprises the hitter, who swings awkwardly and misses. One out.

The next batter hits a weak ground ball right back to Kelli. The third Braves' hitter hits a pop fly; right to Jamie, who gathers it in easily. The Braves' part of the inning is over, just as swiftly as the Marlins' half.

* * * * *

Von enjoys umpiring in the playoffs. He likes the tension. At this point, the teams have improved, and the games matter. This matchup between the Braves and Marlins starts out crisply. The early innings are scoreless, error-free. Pitch after pitch comes through the strike zone. There are few borderline calls, no groaning complaints. The game moves along quickly.

Minor controversy arises in the bottom half of the second. With one out, the Braves get their first baserunner, on a bouncer between shortstop and third base. After waiting out one pitch, the runner takes off for second. She makes a perfect slide into the base, clearly ahead of the throw, which bounces in the dirt. But . . . the Marlins' shortstop—Jamie—goes down to her knees to smother the throw, and a collision results. Dust rises, bodies tangle. For a moment, Von can't see the ball.

Coach Phil starts to applaud, but stops suddenly in mid-clap. In the suspended silence, as he cranes about for the best angle, Von feels all eyes turning to him. As the two bodies squirm to untangle, the runner rolls—just a bit—off the base. Jamie—still sprawled on her side—reaches to re-apply her tag. Carefully Von scans the still-writhing jumble; he finds the ball nestled in Jamie's glove. "Out!"

Coach Phil rolls his gaze skyward. One of his assistants fails to stifle: "Oh, *come on.*"

The Braves' next batter strikes out to end the inning.

In the third inning, one of the Marlin hitters—Von is familiar with Colleen—faces a two-strike count. The next pitch comes in hard, but in the dirt. The girl swings, misses, and starts to run immediately. The Braves' catcher deftly scoops the ball on the bounce. Colleen is well on her way down the line. She touches first base as the Braves' catcher holds up her glove to show Von that she hasn't dropped it—she *caught* it— as Von is about to pronounce the runner safe . . . but then Colleen does *not stop* but instead rounds first base, going full tilt for second. The Braves' catcher continues to show the ball in her glove. According to the rules, however, when the third strike hits the ground *at any time*, it's a *dropped* third strike. So: The Marlins' runner will be safe at second on a strikeout-dropped-third-strike . . . and then, from the Braves' bench Coach Phil starts hollering and the catcher jolts herself to attention as they all realize that Colleen has *still* not stopped running and is now rounding *second*. The catcher bluffs a throw to third, though, and the opportunistic little runner retreats to second.

The next Marlin batter hits the ball sharply—the first well-hit ball of the game—but the ball disappears quickly into the Braves' second baseman's glove. The inning ends when Claire strikes out the next batter.

* * * * *

Brad can see the Marlins gaining confidence. In the bottom of the third inning Kelli strikes out the first hitter. The next batter grounds out. Claire Boniface drives a fly ball fairly deep to left-center field, but Emmie ranges confidently to her left. Easy as a summer day: The ball settles into her glove.

After three innings, the game remains scoreless.

Damn, Brad thinks: These girls know what they're doing. Kelli pumps strike after strike at the Braves' hitters. Umpire Von woofs out "STRAAAHH!" over and over. Brad pumps his fists at the air. After every strike, Emmie calls out, "One more, one more! Nothing but strikes!" In right field, Lori pounds her glove on every pitch, poised on the balls of her feet.

One of the Braves' runners leads off second base; Maddi charges in from right-center field to cover the base in case of a throw.

"Great job, Maddi!" Brad calls. "When you do that, it reminds every one of us to stay alert!"

Emmie leads off the fourth inning with a strikeout. Meghan's up next. Chances do not look good this inning, but Meghan has actually had a few hits this year, and she's standing in the batter's box looking small and overmatched but determined as a mother raccoon. The first pitch is a strike. The second pitch is on the way. Against Claire's roaring fastball, Meghan's swing looks like a fluttering soda straw, but the straw makes contact. Not *good* contact: The ball drops weakly into foul ground near the Marlins' bench. Strike two. "You can do it!" Jamie screams from the bench. "You can do it!"

On the next pitch Claire seems to ease up a bit on her fastball. Meghan steers her bat toward it. Contact is made. The ball plinks into the air. It drops into the infield. It bounces, and then rolls. Meghan runs. The Braves' first baseman charges in, picks it up, and whirls to make her throw to the second baseman covering first base. But she's not there. Meghan crosses the bag. Safe.

It's not much of a threat. Along the Braves' bench, there is no concern. Brad sees Mike and Phil sharing a small chuckle. But the Marlins have a baserunner.

And something is different. Meghan usually stands with her feet splayed. Looking wispy, vulnerable to the breeze, a stuffed animal in the wilderness.

Not now. She's tensed and alert, knees bent and twitching. Watching the pitcher; looking across the diamond at Brad.

Brad is tempted: Steal? No way. Meghan is not fast. She runs with a grandmotherly trundle, with the bright swooshes on her cleats making little tumble-dry whirls. But unless she can get to second, they'll need at least two more base hits to score a run. That's asking a lot against this pitcher. One out. Emmie up, Renni next. Renni will make contact. He's not so sure about Emmie. Brad decides to wait a pitch.

Strike.

Or two.

Strike.

"Take your leads," he calls to Meghan.

Meghan nods. Emmie swings hard at the next pitch. And misses: Strike three. Meghan leads off first base, looks in at the catcher. The catcher bluffs a throw, and Meghan retreats to first.

"Two outs now," Brad reminds Meghan. "Run on any contact."

Renni's up. Renni's a good hitter. She has a chance . . . but they need Meghan to move fast on the basepaths—and they'll still need two straight hits to score.

Renni swings at the second pitch, lifting a soft liner that rises and wavers over the right side of the infield. The Braves' second baseman runs after it, glove outstretched. Without hesitation, Meghan begins to run. The ball carries. Meghan nears second base; she's found Brad in the coach's box and she's looking for a signal. Brad watches the ball. He sees the second baseman in pursuit. Their paths grow closer . . . until the ball clears the fielder's glove and lands on the outfield grass. Meghan rounds second, and Brad waves frantically: *Come to me, please get here, please hurry, get here, come to me!* She's trundling hard, her face pink and hot, unable to see the play unfolding behind her.

The Braves' coaches yell, the Marlin bench screams, Braves' fielders scramble about to restore order and get the ball in. Brad holds up his hands to stop Meghan at third.

But she doesn't stop. She turns for home without even slowing down. *How could she have missed him? He was right in front of her, hands up in unmistakable "STOP" command!* The Braves' infielders relay the ball effectively, and it's heading home, well ahead of Meghan. Brad clutches helplessly at his head.

The catcher handles the throw, turns to tag Meghan. Meghan halts and turns back for third. The catcher pursues her. Meghan is in a pickle.

She's been here before.

Meghan runs straight at the third baseman standing on third base, and Brad can see the certainty: Meghan knows that her onrushing approach and her bright helmet will distract the fielder.

The catcher's throw to third sails . . . and skims the top of Meghan's helmet, confusing the third baseman, who barely manages to knock the ball down. And Meghan is just two steps from third base—two steps from *safety*. Brad stands dumbly, suddenly passive, watching it unfold in slow motion. Meghan stops. *Third base.* Brad's brain screams, but it doesn't seem have any control over his voice. *Right there!* But the words don't come out. *You'll be SAFE! Back to third! It's right there!* Meghan sees it . . . and turns away, heading for home.

She wants to score.

The third baseman, like Brad, is surprised. Suddenly she feels rushed—there's no time to set her feet after she retrieves the ball—and she hurries her throw. It bounces wide of the target. It hits the backstop as Meghan clatters across home plate and heads for the bench, where there's a writhing collage of pumping fists and leaping bodies and gaping, screaming mouths. Jamie and Kelli rush to hug Meghan, who disappears among high-fives and a hail of hands beating on top of her helmet.

Brad claps his hands, vaguely aware of the hollering from the Braves' coaches, even less aware of Renni standing next to him, having advanced all the way to third base on her own. He's stuck on an odd moment of awareness: awareness that this hero-welcome is an entirely foreign experience for Meghan; that she will remember this moment for the rest of her life.

The Marlins have scored a run. The Braves have not.

Lissa takes a defiant stance in the batter's box. For the Braves, Claire takes care of business. She fires four sizzling fastballs, three for strikes. Inning over.

But on the Marlins' bench, there is no more fear.

The Braves file in to their bench. The silence is broken by a coach's voice: "Are you girls gonna *get your heads* in this game?"

* * * * *

Phil Braden takes pride in his teams. Not so much in their talents, but in the way they play the game: always heads-up, always prepared. But on this day, with this team, he finds reason for alarm. With two innings left, they trail. Only by one run. They have time. But he does not like what he's seen.

He recounts the transgressions. In the second inning, one of the Marlins reached base—not just first base, but *second base*—on a dropped third strike when his catcher stopped paying attention. Then, in the fourth inning, one of the Marlins' worst players—possibly the worst player in the league—plunked a harmless dribbler down the first-base line and it was just like a bunt, but nobody covered first base and the runner was safe. *Oh, brother!* They've gone over bunt coverage at almost *every practice all season long.* Just minutes later, that runner scored the game's only run on yet another sloppy play. *"Wake up!"* Phil yelled angrily. For some reason, his girls were not playing with urgency. Phil threw his hat down on the ground. "Are you girls gonna *wake up*!? You need to *get your heads* in the game! This is a close game; you need to be ready! Every pitch: You need to be ready!"

His words fell on deaf ears. The Braves' hitters dragged their bats to the plate that inning. They swung lazily, it seemed. After a strikeout, Phil did notice one of his batters looking carefully to make sure the third strike was caught. He was glad the girl seemed to have been paying attention, but they needed more than that now.

Phil realizes that his team hasn't been behind for more than a few innings in the entire season. After the fifth inning, he calls them in for a quick huddle. *Positive; stay positive,* he tells himself. He reminds them that they've won fifteen games, and lost none. "That doesn't matter right now, but I want to remind you girls that you've been the best team all year; you earned those victories. This one's not gonna be any different.

Just play like you know how."

And finally, in the fifth inning, the Braves break through. It happens swiftly. With one out and a runner on first, Claire shoots a line drive into center field for a double, sending the runner to third. The next girl is Kate Remersdorf, one of his prime hitters. Kate sends a fly ball down the left-field line, and it falls, well beyond the left fielder's reach. The Braves' bench springs to life. Two runs score before the Marlins' pitcher regains the ball in the pitcher's circle. Kate stands on second base. The next batter grounds out to the pitcher, but order has been restored. Heading into the sixth and final inning, the Braves hold a 2-1 lead.

* * * * *

Back in the third inning, after striking out, Jamie came back to the bench muttering. She made direct and meaningful eye contact with Brad before she put her bat in the rack. Brad followed her down the bench: "What's up?"

Jamie noted that she'd swung at a strike.

Okay.

But it ended up outside and in the dirt.

"She throwing something weird?"

Jamie nodded. She hadn't seen that pitch before.

Diane had seen it, too. "Drop ball," she said. "It dropped and also had a pretty good curve on it. I think she's thrown about three or four of them today. That last one was the best."

Brad thanked them. "Let's keep an eye on that," he said.

"She'll probably throw it with two strikes," Jamie said. "And no balls or one ball. When she's ahead."

Brad nodded and pointed to his temple. "Good thinking."

It's the top of the sixth inning now. With a one-run lead to protect, Claire hits a rare rough patch and walks leadoff batter Kacie—Kacie!—on five pitches.

Lori approaches the batter's box. She takes three hard

practice swings before stepping in. She assumes her stance, peering around her front shoulder at the fearsome pitcher.

"Lori!" Brad stands in the coach's box, flashing Conner's signals: bunt. He can't risk a steal with Kacie running, but they have *got* to move her to second base. For all her improvement, Lori still lunges at bad pitches and swings weakly at good ones. They need contact.

Lori's shoulders sag. She resumes her stance, experiments with the spacing of her hands on the bat, but then the pitch comes in and pops in the catcher's mitt before she's squared around. "Ball!"

"Lori!" Brad calls.

She looks down the line at him. She looks confused.

Brad calls for time. From the coach's box he jogs down the baseline to Lori. He leans down, hands on his knees. "What's up?"

Lori doesn't want to bunt. In fact, she informs Brad, she *can't* bunt.

Yes you can. Brad reasons: "Remember how it's like catching the ball with your bat? Well, you're good at catching."

"But I haven't practiced bunting in a long time."

This is true. But still. "Lori, you can bunt."

She looks down, avoiding his eyes.

"Lori. We need you to bunt so Kacie can get to second, and possibly third if they don't play it right. We have to have this ball in play on the ground."

"But I can just hit it."

Brad hesitates. There's so much to explain.

"I've really been working on my hitting."

Brad understands. And he realizes that she thinks that he doesn't have confidence in her. He searches her pink over-heated face, reminds himself that it always looks pink and overheated, but he's afraid—*please God no!*—that she might start crying. He tries to explain: In situations exactly like this, major league baseball players—even star major league baseball players—have to bunt. There's not enough time to explain all the reasons for this age-old strategy. "Lori. I know you're a good hitter. This is just a thing teams do to win."

"Coach." Von joins them. "Brad." They're taking too long and Von has to break it up.

Brad straightens, nods at Von. "Try it, Lori. Two pitches."

Still reluctant, Lori agrees. She steps in and squares around as Claire begins her delivery. There's a solid metallic clink as the ball bounces off the bat barrel, drops into the dirt, and dribbles down the third-base line. Perfect. Lori heads for first, Kacie toward second—their two slowest runners, but they're moving. The Braves catcher and third baseman converge as their coaches holler for them to let the ball roll. They stand over it, walking alongside it, and the ball rolls foul.

Brad looks up to see Kacie rounding second, Lori on first with a proud smile. But it was a foul ball. Strike one.

Lori jogs back to the batter's box. Brad waits for her, holding the bat. "Swing away," he mutters.

"What?"

"That was a heck of a bunt. It was—it was really *brave* of you and I'm impressed. But you can swing away now."

"Wait. What about the Braves and me?"

Brad laughs as he shakes his head. "Swing away."

Brad resumes his position in the coach's box, not sure why he's no longer having her bunt. Clearly she can bunt. Bunting is the correct strategy, if they want to maximize their chances of winning. Conner would be stammering in protest. Bunting is the thing to do. At this point, though, Brad understands that it's about winning now, but it's not *completely* about winning. It's also—still—about Lori having fun hitting, trying to do what she thinks she can do. It's sort of partly about how this might affect Lori if she thinks her coach didn't let her try to hit because he didn't believe in her. Nothing's completely or purely about anything, and the motivations are all jumbled, but he's told her to swing away and they'll all just have to see what happens.

On the next pitch, Lori knocks a solid line drive over the first baseman's head, down the right-field line. Lori's running; she's almost to first base as the ball lands . . . foul. Barely.

Brad can see Lori smiling as she jogs back to the plate. She's feeling good. Claire takes a surprised look at Lori: Lori, who suddenly seems dangerous. From the Braves' bench, Brad hears Mike call out something to Claire. Thoughts race through Brad's mind, even as he shouts encouragement. One ball, two strikes.

Brad looks at Claire, who's set to pitch, hands in front of her as she gauges the target. Her hands jiggle nervously in her glove. Brad looks at Lori, who looks calm and determined as she peers out at the pitcher. At the last moment, Brad realizes that Claire was doing something to change her grip on the ball. Things are moving too fast.

The drop-curve comes in straight, then breaks sharply, down and away. Lori lunges hard after it. She nearly falls forward as her swing flails at air. Strike three. But just as the pitch eludes Lori's swing, it also eludes the catcher. It hits the dirt and skips to the backstop. Lori runs. First base is occupied, so the dropped-third-strike rule is not in effect, but Lori does not know this; she just runs. From first base, Kacie runs. The Braves' catcher recovers the ball as Von hollers, "The batter is out!" But Kacie has advanced to second. She's there because Lori's loud foul ball convinced Claire to throw the tricky drop-curve. It's the same result as a good bunt: Mission accomplished. Brad and Diane and all the Marlins clap their hands.

* * * * *

When the Braves overtook the Marlins in the fifth inning, Gwen almost sensed relief among the Marlins' parents. There had been optimistic murmurs: "These girls have really come together." There had been brave talk. But nobody really expected them to *win* this game.

In the final inning, Kacie walks, but the Braves' star pitcher looks as invincible as ever. The next Marlin batter—Lori—strikes out. Kacie manages to advance to second when the catcher can't handle strike three, but after another strikeout the Marlins are down to their last out.

Maddi comes to the plate.

Gwen feels her insides churning. Nobody wants to make the last out. What can Gwen do? She needs to call time out, stroll across the field, reassure: *Relax. It's a game. You've played well. You've had a great season. It's just about having fun, right?*

Maddi stands in the batter's box, kicking at the dirt, looking for comfortable footing. She takes her practice swings, and then from her crouching stance she looks out at the star pitcher. She watches the first pitch whiz by: Strike one. She repeats her practice swings, gets into her poised crouch. The next pitch smacks into the catcher's glove. Silence. *Ball*, the umpire calls. All around her Gwen hears breaths exhaling, hands clapping cautiously: *Good eye! That's how to look it over!*

The next pitch is a strike. And then on the next—possibly final—pitch, Gwen sees Maddi step into a pitch, and for a terrible split-second Gwen holds her breath, and then the ball shoots straight back, rattling the chain-link backstop. Foul ball.

More hands clap around her: *"Good cut! She's not afraid! Right with her Maddi, you're a hitter!"*

Gwen's fingers cover her mouth. Her shoulders are tight. Maddi swings her bat back and forth. She seems miles away. Gwen realizes, despite her unfamiliarity with the game, that Maddi is *focused*. She crouches in her stance without fear. Her timing on that swing, Gwen hears someone say, was just right. And Gwen saw: It was a swing with an expectation of success.

Gwen says nothing, fearful that Maddi might hear her and

become distracted. She looks around her, marveling at the sudden importance of the next few seconds. She has no idea how Maddi might react, what she—the helpless parent—might have to do. She smiles as bravely as she can. "Come on, Maddi," she hears herself say.

Still two strikes. Maddi crouching. Pitcher in motion. Maddi lifts her front leg, striding forward from her back foot.

The next sound is small and muffled. The ball bounces off Maddi's thigh and scrawls a trail in the dust.

Gwen is confused: Maddi runs. Hard. She rounds first base, turns for second, and looks for Coach Brad in the third-base coach's box. The umpire steps forward, waving his arms about: "Dead ball!" he shouts. "Ball is dead!"

Maddi is awarded first base, but has to stop there. Kacie—now standing on third—has to go back to second.

Gwen struggles to process. Her little girl has just been struck by a hard object traveling at high speed. Without hesitation—without showing pain—her reaction was to run as hard as she could. She ran to the base and then tried to keep going, trying to get to the *next* base. Gwen peers across the field, trying to see Maddi's face through the bars of her helmet, but cannot discern anything.

Next batter: Jamie. On the first pitch, she swings hard. The ball swerves and straightens, finds the outfield grass. It bounces high, and then again before the Braves' left fielder can knock it down.

Kacie is not a fast runner, but she gets a good start from second base as soon as the ball is struck. It's not a close play at home plate. But Kacie—a chubby, unathletic-looking girl—slides anyway, raising a small cloud of dust. Kacie regains her feet quickly as the catcher fields the throw. She runs happily to the bench, where—given new life—the Marlins cheer and shake their fists. Maddi stands on third base, clapping her hands. Jamie stands on second base, fists at her side, head jutted forward, neck muscles straining, screaming something crazy and primal and unintelligible.

The Marlins' next batter strikes out. But in the middle of the sixth inning, the score stands 2-2. Maddi has escaped. Gwen doubts that it will come down to her again.

* * * * *

It's the bottom of the sixth inning. Kelli's tired. Her stride is weak. This throws everything off, just a tad. She tries to make adjustments. Nothing works; she can't find the strike zone.

In a steady voice, Diane calls out her encouragement. *Strong stride, Kelli. Follow through.*

But her pitches continue to miss. For five innings her pitches have flooded the strike zone. The Braves have managed just two hits and one walk. But now, Kelli is off.

The Braves' hitters have been instructed to be patient. The first batter walks. The second batter—probably their weakest hitter—walks. The third batter hits a shallow fly ball to Renni at third base for the first out. Kelli's next two pitches are just outside.

Brad confers with Diane. "Got any brilliant solutions?"

"I've gone through everything. She knows them all."

Brad sets his knuckles to his chin. He looks at Kelli, then turns back to Diane. "Lemme try something?"

Diane nods. "Anything."

"Time!" Brad signals to the umpire and trots out to the pitcher's circle. He stands with his back to the bench. Diane can't hear what they're saying. She sees Kelli nodding; hears her say "outside." She wonders if Kelli feels pressure the same way that adults do; if she's weighing the adjustments she might make; if she's *in command* like the Braves' pitcher, or if she's just playing a game she likes.

Brad leans down, hands on his knees, talking quietly. Kelli shakes her head. "Eyes closed" . . . "can't" . . . "not in a *game*" . . . "maybe" . . .

They speak for another minute, and then Brad skips back to the bench.

"What's up?" Diane asks.

Brad nods toward the Braves' bench. "That guy, Mike. I remember one time he and I were watching a game and we noticed the pitcher changing his angle."

Diane nods as she takes note: Kelli has moved over to the far end—the third-base end—of the pitcher's slab.

Kelli's next pitch—from her new angle—heads outside, well off the plate. The batter swings and misses.

The Braves' assistant coach shouts from the first-base coaching box. "Wait for your pitch! That was *way* outside!"

Kelli looks over at Brad and Diane, who clap their hands in acknowledgment.

The next pitch crosses the middle of the plate. Strike two.

With two strikes, the hitter can no longer be selective. Something's up; the last two pitches looked different. The next pitch comes in a bit outside. The batter swings. And misses.

Two outs.

"How to get it back!" Brad shouts. But Diane knows. Nothing has been solved. Two of Kelli's last three pitches should have been balls. But she'd gotten away with them.

The first pitch to the next batter is a ball, just outside. The Braves' runners are in motion: Double steal. Colleen, catching, receives the pitch and fires her best throw to third, but the runner is safe.

Kelli's next pitch is inside: Ball two. Diane and Brad stand with their arms folded, spectators. The Marlins shout out their encouragement.

Kelli looks down at the slab, gauging her position. She looks toward the bench, mouths a question that neither Brad nor Diane can understand. Brad looks at Diane. He's about to call time, but Diane puts her hand on his arm. She reminds him of the rule: Coaches are only allowed one visit to the pitcher in an inning. More than one visit and the pitcher has to be removed. There's nothing they can do.

"You've got this!" Brad calls. "Make your adjustments."

"Whatever it takes!" Diane shouts. "You're in charge. You can do it!"

Kelli works her toe against the slab. She looks in at the hitter, rocks back, starts her forward stride, and then—instead of swinging her arm up and around the windmill arc—simply releases the pitch.

The unexpected sequence confuses the batter; disrupts her timing. She makes a hurried, flat-footed swipe with her bat. The ball hops weakly back to Kelli, who scoops it up and delivers an oh-so-casual toss to Courtney at first base.

Three outs.

A murmur travels through the crowd. For the first time all season, a game will have to be decided in extra innings.

Brad laughs as the girls trot off the field. "*Quick pitch?* Where the *hell* did you come up with that one?"

On the bench, Kelli sips from her water bottle. Diane approaches her daughter with a grin and a hard high-five. And then a hug.

* * * * *

Seventh inning. Even Claire might be tiring. Lissa works a walk and steals second. They need her to get to third. Brad weighs a steal or delayed steal.

Time out: Braves. Brad is surprised to see Mike—not Phil— jog out to the pitcher's circle. He gathers his catcher and in- fielders in a huddle around Claire. Brad can see his hands gesturing. Is he talking about the delayed steal? Do they have a plan to lure Lissa into an unwise decision?

Mike grins at Brad as he trots off. Then he stops, hands spread wide. "What an awesome game!"

"Yes it is." Brad welcomes the camaraderie, but stops short of high-fiving him.

He does not know what the instructions were. He'll have to hold Lissa at second for at least a few pitches while he watches to see what the Braves might be up to.

After the next two pitches—a ball and a strike—the Braves do not seem to be paying attention. It seems safe. Brad catches Lissa's glance and gives the signal: Delayed steal.

Claire delivers her pitch. The catcher receives it: Ball two. Lissa leads off second base.

The catcher stands up lazily; Lissa tenses to go.

The catcher makes her return throw to the pitcher.

Lissa takes off for third.

But the catcher's throw is not to the pitcher. Instead, it goes directly to the Braves' shortstop, who has moved close to third base. Directly in Lissa's path. Lissa tries to stop, but she's a dead duck. Ball in glove, the shortstop tags her.

Coach Phil springs from his seat, fist clenched and raised: "*Yaaahhh! That's a great job!*"

"That was *perfect!*" Mike calls.

Runner—potential winning run—erased. It's Brad's fault. He should have suspected something. But he didn't.

The inning ends when Colleen taps a weak ground ball to the first baseman.

Brad tries to keep a brave face. He cannot let despair show.

In the bottom half of the inning, Kelli continues to adjust on every pitch, and she mixes in a few change-ups, which—to her surprise—she is able to throw for strikes. She walks a batter, but the Marlins handle two ground balls—to Kelli and Jamie—and a pop fly to Lissa at first base.

In the eighth inning, Courtney steps in to the batter's box. She sees a pitch that she likes. She braces her weight on her back foot . . . and at the last, perfect instant, drops her hands, strides forward, snaps her wrists. The ball reverses course, clears the Braves' outfield. By a lot. Brad can see Courtney rounding first, looking up to find him. He watches the Braves' right-center fielder pick it up, drop it, pick it up again, and he waves Courtney around toward where he waits at third. She puts her head down, rounds second. She's wide-eyed as she looks for Brad, who can see the cutoff throw bouncing, not being fielded cleanly by the Braves' second baseman. Brad jabs his hand toward home. Courtney hits third base, turns for home. The second baseman collects the ball amid hollers from the Braves' bench. Brad yells "Go! Go!" and then as she runs past, "You'll have to slide!"

He almost laughs as he hears "Okay" fly out of her mouth as she runs. As it turns out, there's no need to slide: The throw home is well off the mark. Home run. Marlins 3, Braves 2.

There's the run they needed.

The inning closes without further incident.

Amid the excitement on the bench, Brad calls out assignments. "We're not there yet," he reminds them. "Concentrate on every pitch. Just like you've been doing all day."

The girls grab their gloves. Brad watches them trot out to their positions.

Is this going to happen? Something gnaws at him inside. He checks the assignments. He wonders if he should move Maddi or Colleen . . . but decides against it: He will not change a thing. Three more outs. It doesn't quite seem possible. Such things do not happen for him. Something bad will happen. He tries hard to banish such thoughts. It's the girls' game. They just have to play.

* * * * *

In the later innings, Von finds himself feeling sorry for the Marlins' pitcher. She's obviously tired. She can't find the plate. Von almost wishes the game could have been a more standard 9 to 4 score. The girl tries change-ups, slower pitches; she tries changing her position on the pitcher's slab, and then a quick pitch, which works once. But she's done. In the eighth inning she surrenders walks to the first two batters. Ball one, ball two

. . . and they weren't close. Ball three, ball four.

The clamor rises on the Braves' bench. With runners on first and third, the Marlins' first baseman fields a ground ball and throws the Braves' runner out at home plate. Von makes a theatrical punch-and-pull motion: "Out!"

Coach Brad erupts: "Yes!! Lissa! Maddi! GREAT job!"

But that's just one out, and the batter reached base, with the runner on first advancing to second. The next batter whacks a ground ball and the Marlins' third baseman makes a valiant effort, knocking it down, but the runners are all safe. Bases loaded. The next batter hits a short bouncer just in front of home plate. The catcher fields it and throws to first base for the second out. But on the play, the Braves' runner scores from third. The game, once again, is tied.

The Braves' girls looked scared earlier, but they're feeling it now. Their chants and cheers grow raucous. They're closing in on the victory they'd expected. With two outs and runners on second and third, Claire Boniface drives a fly ball into the outfield. It falls between two Marlin outfielders. From third base, the Braves' lead runner scores easily, well before the throw from the outfield bounces through the infield.

The celebration on the Braves' bench is immediate and loud. By a 4-3 score, they have prevailed. The Marlin girls remain standing at their positions, looking a little confused.

The handshake line moves swiftly, the Marlins walking sullenly, the Braves players following orders to contain their excitement. Von calls the coaches together. He needs to get to another game. "Gentlemen," he says. "Phil. Brad. Great game. *Great* game. I hope you had fun." Phil and Brad nod at each other. "Because," he adds, "it doesn't get better than that."

* * * * *

As always, Joanne keeps her cheering voice to a conversational level and takes care to comment on other girls' contributions.

When parents congratulate her, Joanne is quick to return compliments. This is her way of accepting good intentions while at the same time deferring, pointing out that *she* is not the pitcher. Yes, she understands that her daughter is the star pitcher, but that bestows no special importance.

The Braves' parents take pictures and videos, high-five each other in their camp chairs. Then they make their way to the girls, where they assemble for group photos. "Way to go Braves! You're the champs and you've earned it!" Some of them stop to chat with the Marlins' parents, and they all marvel at what they've just witnessed.

Joanne searches for Claire among the navy-blue Braves' jerseys, sees her hand go up to wave, and Jo waves back, mouth open in delight. Joanne watches from the edge of the crowd as Claire accepts accolades and high-fives, as she finds Mike and hugs him. Tightly. Joanne steps in with a big hug for Claire, and for Mike. After a few minutes, the high-fiving among grown-ups starts to feel silly. She notices Mike looking across the field toward Brad, where the Marlins huddle quietly on the outfield grass.

* * * * *

For a second, it occurs to Brad that he jinxed the game by letting himself imagine the scenario. But the game is over and he must now present himself in front of these eleven girls. "Bring it in!"

They look at each other, gloves still ready, watching the Braves high-five and jump about.

Brad has never been good at speeches. He gets down on one knee. He looks at the dirt.

Somebody asks about ice cream. *Do we still get that prize?*

"Girls. *Marlins*," he says. "We'll have some ice cream— some sort of fun event at some time. Soon. I promised you all a prize and I owe you that. So, yes to ice cream—sometime, but this was a very long game and I don't think it'll be today."

Brad has given no forethought to this. He tries to find words, but gets distracted by the seconds ticking amid the sudden silence. He wants to say something about the whole season, not just this game, and he remembers that first frigid practice on the blacktop, when it came time for the coach to say something, and so he starts in, but the sounds that come out of his mouth feel meaningless, like tasteless tofu: *blah blah good game blah blah proud of you, blah blah effort that counts.*

It's a hot day. Jamie, Maddi—their faces are red. Sweaty. Renni fidgets. He tries to see them—see their faces—clearly under their cap visors. Colleen's lip quivers.

Diane steps in. "You girls played a whale of a game," she says. "All of you gave it your best. I'm proud to be part of this team. You should all be proud to be Marlins. Because the Marlins were *magnificent*."

Brad looks up at Diane. He nods gratefully. Doggedly he starts again. There *has* to be more: more for them to take away from this. "You should be proud." His voice is a ragged croak. "Of yourselves. And each other. Because you." He gathers himself. "Gave." The words balk and stall like mules on a rope bridge. "Each other. Everything." *Dammit.* He fights to yank words from his constricted passages, but he needs to put a cap on this. "Everything." It still feels inadequate.

The girls start packing their bags. Some of them come to thank Brad and Diane for coaching. Parents linger to talk.

Diane senses Brad's emotion. She stands next to him with her arms folded. "These girls will be lucky if they ever get to play in a game like that again," she says.

Inside he's squirming, still trying to get a handle on what's going on. Parents—from both teams—offer congratulations. Here he is again: *Great effort, all they could handle, your girls should be proud.* Pride in his team surges, beaten down by what-ifs. The hollowness of disappointment gapes inside. "Close but no stogie," is what Mike would say.

It takes some time to pack the helmets and catcher's gear and bats and balls. He doesn't want to do it. Diane helps out. Heather helps out. Kelli stands by, slurping at a popsicle, chatting with friends as they stop by.

Some of the parents want to talk. Emmie's father comes by, takes his shades off. "I'm Pete. I was rude the other day when we met, and I apologize. I think we—I—we were going through a few things and I was just out of sorts that day."

"No need." Brad appreciates this gesture. "I understand. I know what that's like."

"This was all Emmie's thing," Pete says. "She didn't want any of us involved." He grips his lips together; it looks like he's holding something in. "I think this season has been a good experience for her. It's been worthwhile."

There's too much stuff swirling around in Brad's head, and this sounds like a rather sparse endorsement. Brad wonders if "worthwhile" was the only appropriate goal for the season. He wonders if "worthwhile" could ever equate with "successful."

"We were talking about it last night," Pete says. "Emmie's gotten so used to championships. First-place finishes." He takes a breath, looks around at the post-game mingling. "And at this point, I wonder if maybe a little failure—a little 'coming up short'—is a good thing for her to experience."

Brad searches for Emmie but can't find her. His ear samples the sounds of the words: *Experience failure; coming up short.* He wonders if *that* is what his girls will take away from this. "In my old job," he says, "we failed at just about everything we tried." He almost laughs. "But it wasn't wasted."

Other parents flock about. Handshakes from moms and dads. Hugs from several of them. He sees Diane directing Kelli in his direction and Kelli comes and hugs him. Several of the Marlins follow suit: Renni, Courtney, Colleen, Maddi, Lori.

He checks the area around the bench. He bends down to pick up a few last bubble gum wrappers. Then he zips the equipment bag and stands up. He looks down at the bag, then looks around at the dwindling scene of players and coaches and parents. When he walks away from this field with this heavy bag, it will be over. He doesn't want to leave. He's jubilant at the way *his girls* played. He's hurt by the wounded looks on these girls' faces.

He's glad it hurts. Because, yes, it came to be about winning, and it came to be about him, but mostly he wanted them to *give a crap*—about softball and about each other—and in the end, they all did, and so even if it's all forgotten in a few hours, in this moment it seems to matter a great deal.

* * * * *

In the happy milling around, Phil looks for Brad. He sees Brad put down his equipment bag so he can receive the parents coming to shake hands and chat. Some of the Marlins' players hug him. Some of the Braves' parents are there shaking his hand. Coach Mike claps him on the back.

Phil waits for his chance and then approaches Brad. "That was the greatest game I've ever coached in," he says. "And I've coached in a lot."

"I know you have," Brad says. "Congratulations."

"I envy you," Phil says. "You accomplished an incredible amount."

"Well," Brad says, "I thought we had a chance there. But I don't know that I'd envy *you* if we switched places."

Phil leans close, lowers his voice. "Who cares who won? I know that's easy for me to say, but I'm talking about what you—and all of these girls on both teams—were able to accomplish today."

Brad nods.

Phil wants to make sure: "I hope you can see that. Your girls—at the end of the game, when I looked over at your bench, what I saw was a bunch of winners."

Chapter 22
CLARITY

Brad's ready to open the biotech investment consultancy. Part of him, he suspects, will miss the lab; being on the inside, where he applied his own expertise and ideas to solve and discover, adjust and prove. As an outsider, as an analyst, he'll render judgments on these companies. It might feel a little detached. But that's probably good. And in his new role he will know one thing: It'll be about money. That will be clear.

Mike's warned him. "You sure you're up for this?" Typically paternal. But Brad knows what Mike's asking: *Is Brad ready for people telling half-truths, exaggerating, lying? Is he prepared to piss people off? Is he up for pressing the flesh at conventions where everybody's better-looking and better-acquainted and more important?*

"Can't wait," Brad said.

"Just making sure." Mike believes that Brad's business has potential. But Mike always warns Brad. And Brad never listens.

* * * * *

Pitcher's Pub. Brad and Diane. They need to plan their end-of-the-season team party. Brad wanted to buy her a drink; to let her know how much he appreciated her support. There were so many things: She'd remind him of some opposing batter's tendencies; how they needed to re-position fielders; she'd notice some bad habit that needed to be corrected; she'd get the girls on the bench to stop gossiping and *pay attention* to the game.

They sit elbow to elbow at the bar; they joke a bit about their "date."

Brad had considered flowers, but nixed the idea because it would have looked conspicuous in the pub. Plus, they're *coach* comrades. Can coaches give each other flowers?—that can't be cool. Beer will have to suffice.

Von congratulates them on the Marlins' season. Bob Remersdorf, he says, calls the Marlins-Braves championship game the "most thrilling Little League game he's ever seen."

"We would have taken a boring win," Brad grumbles.

"Yeah, but like I told you: It won't ever be better than that."

It's a breezy feeling. Three beers for Brad; two for Diane. They marvel at how much the girls improved, how Courtney gained confidence; how Colleen's alertness and hustle and determination made her such a valuable player. In the end, they agree, *even Meghan* contributed and experienced something that she'll remember. Brad compliments Diane on Kelli's progress—her nerve and her inventiveness—as a pitcher. They have fun debating which of Jamie's exploits stands out most.

One thing he's never asked about: Was Jamie crying during that last regular-season game against the Cubs?

Diane nods. One of the Cubs, she says, brought some *horrible* and inappropriate chatter against Jamie one day. One of the games when Conner was coaching. She'd taken it upon herself to sniff out the perpetrator.

"The Cuuubbs . . ." Von groans as he pours from the tap.

"You ordered the girls . . ." Brad chuckles— "to get *nasty*?"

"Boooo, Cubs." Von pours, wipes, rinses, mixes, checking up and down along the bar. "Booo, Cubs." Thumbs down.

Diane sets her jaw in a hard line. The Marlins were going

to stick up for each other, she says. She'd made that quite clear.

Brad looks at Von. "What *about* the Cubs?"

Von shakes his head as he bustles about the bar. The Cubs brought in somebody's older sister and a girl from another town for the playoffs. "Didn't you see some unfamiliar-looking girls?"

Diane and Brad look at each other: Come to think of it, they *had*. They'd wondered about it, but let it go. They'd been impressed at how much some of the Cubs had improved, how much they'd grown, and they'd figured that some of them had missed the earlier regular-season games. It had not occurred to them that anybody would cheat so blatantly. One of the Marlins' parents, it turns out, knew who the girls were and contacted the league about it. The league has since notified the Cubs' coach that he will not be allowed to coach in the future.

"We're glad the Marlins won that game," Von says.

Diane and Brad contemplate this soberly. Wow.

Diane congratulates Brad on his prospective business. It sounds interesting. "So," she says, "you stay in touch with the science, but you don't have to deal with the politics."

The political bullshit is everywhere, Brad says. In one form or another, it'll be there. But he thinks he can deal with that now. And yes, he expects less confusion among agendas.

That's an important thing, Diane says.

"I am a little worried," Brad says, "about being alone in a one-man shop."

"What about that worries you?"

Brad's not sure. "I mean," he says. "This season would have been a lot harder without a colleague."

Diane smiles at the compliment.

They know they have to talk about Renni. They've both heard. The test results have come back. Unknowns remain. They've caught it early. There's a chance. But: Cystic Fibrosis. Confirmed.

Diane nods sadly.

Brad looks down at the bar, shakes his head grimly.

Renni: mischief brimming. She made practices fun. She made games fun. She played with *joy*. Neither of them will ever forget her spectacular diving catch to seal that playoff win. Brad remembers the strange progression of perceptions, how he'd already seen that ball tracing a path deep into the outfield, how his awareness of Renni's bead on the ball almost seemed to bring something back in time. He knows it sounds corny, but Diane jumps in: "Yes, yes!" She shakes her head, reliving the wonderment. "I know it sounds weird, but it almost felt like she somehow redirected the course of things, making—y'know—*correcting* something that seemed to be inevitable."

They sit pondering their shared perception of that moment, wondering if it could somehow hold greater meaning.

"What do you know about this disease?" Diane says.

Brad knows the basics. Beyond that, at Rylix they'd explored it only briefly. He knew people who probably knew a lot about it. CF was on radar screens, despite the fact that it was a bit of an "orphan" disease—a rare disease that does not threaten the broad populace. He remembers a few skeptical discussions: Did they really want to allocate scarce resources to an orphan? Brad remembers some exasperated comments about the problem, the wily complexities of the gene.

Diane touches his hand. "We'll see her at the party."

Right. The party.

They toss around possible dates. Diane will bring salads and snacks, a few bottles of wine for parents. Brad: sodas, dogs, burgers, beer for the parents.

"And ice cream," Von says from the bar.

"Of course," Brad says. "Can't have a softball team party without ice cream."

There's still time for one more round, but they think better of it. It feels like a business meeting, and that's best. They shake hands, let it fall into a brief hug. Then they're out into the warm evening, heading off in different directions.

* * * * *

At the pub, Mike and Brad discuss the epic championship game. Mike punches him in the arm. "You were an aggressive bastard."

"*You* were a bastard for figuring out our delayed steal signal."

"I didn't know your signals," Mike says. "I figured you'd wait two pitches, and then run it."

Brad clamps his lips together. He *should have known*.

Mike claps him on the shoulder. "Phil worried about you. He'd say 'we have to pay attention—this team gets sneaky on the bases. They're always looking to run.'"

"The Marlins learned how to run the bases." Brad nods, reassuring himself. "The Marlins played their guts out."

Mike shrugs. "So did the Braves."

Brad doesn't want to be bitter. But the Marlins were the underdogs. The Marlins had more to overcome. Brad believes that the Marlins—*his girls*—got more out of the game—and out of the season—than the Braves' girls.

"Braves were awesome." Mike makes a fist, marks the air solidly. "Marlins were pretty good," he says. "Close but no stogie."

There's nothing to dispute. But the words land heavily.

Brad raises a challenge: "And how about you?"

"What about me?"

"Any stogies? Other than the brilliant coach thing?"

"Dude. I don't know. Just doing my thing."

"Right. Pretty comfy. Don't take on anything you might not be brilliant at."

Mike grins. And it's the same infuriating grin. Hasn't changed from fifth grade. "Dude." He spreads his arms. "Girls' softball. Relax."

Brad pauses, then sits back. There's no reason to get hot about anything. He's let it get out of context. He's allowed the game to become some kind of vehicle . . . to prove something; to correct something. He's allowed a part of himself to live vicariously through these young girls who were just playing for fun; he's let himself get greedy for the taste of some silly coach-glory—some 'winner's satisfaction' after all.

Still: Brad has grown tired of the "it's *girls' softball"* shrug-off. People cared. Mike doesn't know a goddamn thing about it.

* * * * *

Craig's e-mail sounds hasty.

> *Brad. This has come up fast. None of us is pursuing it, but before you open your new business I thought you might want to know about it. I don't know all the details, but the Cystic Fibrosis Foundation needs a new person—Boston-based is fine—for a pretty high-level role in allocating funds for research and development. I know CF is not our primary expertise but I'm betting they won't come across anybody better than you.*

Brad starts typing a response, then decides to call. Craig answers on the first ring. Yes, Brad says, he knows of this foundation. Yes, he understands that they focus exclusively on CF. It's about treatments and cures for CF—it's about beating CF. He is not a CF expert. But yes, he is interested. Very interested.

Chapter 23
NEW SEASON

March has arrived, weak sunshine throwing its cold-water bleach on the tawny grass.

He's got six tomato seedlings from the garden shop. Brad thought again about starting them from seed this year. He likes the thought of that initial, unpromising poke from the soil. At this point, though, either he's lazy, or just used to buying the seedlings. Either way—seed or seedling—you never know which ones will thrive, which ones will produce. There are a zillion factors. At this point, he gives them all a pretty good chance.

* * * * *

It was back in February; time for Claire to start preparing for softball. It was also time for Mike to get out in the woods among the bare trees.

This intrigued Claire. She wondered why Mike wanted to draw February and March, when everything was so much nicer in the summer and fall.

"Definition," Mike said. "When the leaves come in, everything looks defined. For some reason I like the tangled-up stuff that gets hidden."

One Saturday he took her to the hitting cages to hit off the pitching machine and shop for a new bat. Afterward they stopped at Panera. They took a booth and Mike showed Claire one of his sketchbooks. He sat sideways in the booth with his back propped against the wall. He'd meant to let her flip through at her leisure, but found himself pointing things out: where he had too many straight trunks, or too much busy confusion, or where the arrangement of the trees was too uniform. Claire nodded as she perused. Mike figured it would be pretty boring and academic to a thirteen-year-old. Claire flipped back and forth a few times, then settled on a page and slid the open book across the table. "This one's my favorite."

Mike looked across the table. "What do you like about it?"

Claire didn't know. But it was definitely her favorite.

"Well that's interesting," Mike said. "That one's my favorite, too." He also didn't know why. It had something to do with his trees-versus-forest problem. After so many failures, he'd found a way to suggest a jumbled forest context, with the main focus on three trees, interfering and tangling and pushing each other into unnatural contortions.

Branches jutted awkwardly. There were unfilled spaces, devoid of branches. There was a juncture where two of the trunks twisted against one another, like a kissing scene in one of those old black-and-white movies where you're not sure if she likes it or hates it. A few economically placed strokes and swipes suggested fallen trunks and brush piles in the background. Partly by accident, it came out that a viewer might be able to envision the trees as they'd wanted to grow, and wonder and then guess about the distortions, what had happened to form these interesting shapes.

Claire angled her head to different vantage points. A smile lifted the corners of her mouth.

Mike tried to imagine how she might be seeing it. He looked again at the drawing and realized that, when he took the parts together, as a whole drawing, it did not seem so broken; so ruined: It seemed workmanlike, almost tidy.

"Is that the three of us?" she said.

"Huh." Mike sat up, drummed his fingers on the table as he studied his drawing in a new light. "That's not what I was thinking when I drew it," he said. He couldn't quite identify which tree might represent which of the three of them, but certainly they were relating to each other, and it was interesting to see them in this way. "On some level, though,"— and here he knocked on the side of his head with his knuckles— "it's possible that that idea was in there somewhere."

Claire seemed to take this as a yes. "You should show it to Mom," she said.

Later that afternoon, when he showed her, Jo agreed with them: This was her favorite. The perspective looked up from the ground, up toward the sky, where the higher branches found room to straighten. Room to reach, and then soar; the way they were meant to. Was what Jo saw.

* * * * *

About a month ago, back in February, Brad saw Meghan's mother in the park. She was walking with a man, with her golden retriever on a leash. It was a brisk day. Remnant crusts of snow patched the soggy field. She waved to him before he recognized her, and then he struggled for her name . . . and found it: Julie.

She introduced her dog, Marco, and her companion.

"Adam Himmelman," the man said.

Julie explained that Adam was Meghan's doctor.

"I think softball was a good thing for Meghan," Adam said.

The three of them stood with their hands in their coat pockets. Adam looked at Brad, and then at Julie, and then he said, "Here," and took the leash from Julie. "I'll take him for a bit."

Julie watched Adam and Marco wander along. Turning

back to Brad, she said she was happy to report that Meghan wanted to sign up for softball again.

"That's great to hear," Brad said. And it *was* good to hear. Brad exclaimed about Meghan's starring moment as base-running hero in the championship game. He started to tell Julie about the time, just a week before that, when they were running the pickle drill . . . but then he noticed Julie nodding a bit too fast and he wondered if she didn't have time for this, and then suddenly she burst into tears.

She scrambled to apologize. She wiped her face with her coat sleeve, and she put her hand on Brad's arm. Brad stood there, a little bewildered, wondering if he was supposed to comfort her—a light hug?—but instead just asked stupidly if she was okay.

She nodded as she dug in her pocket for tissues. "Meghan told me about that." She paused to sniff back some snot. "You know, her doctor's appointments last year"—she nodded toward Adam, who had made it across the field and was walking along the distant chain link fence—"she was going through some emotional issues."

Brad nodded, not sure how long they might talk. He felt ashamed to remember his relief—was it elation?—upon realizing that Meghan would miss a game. "How's she doing?"

Julie calmed herself with a measured breath.

"I mean, has the doctor—has Adam helped?"

"It's so dumb. It's not like some fantastic thing happened," Julie said, and it took another moment for Brad to realize that she wasn't talking about the doctor's appointments. "I hardly even got very many pictures from the season." Her voice still sounded gloppy. "It was just a good season," she said. "It was just . . . it was really, really, really good for Meghan."

"Meghan certainly had her moments," Brad offered.

"Yes." Julie paused to wipe her face again. "And there are few enough of those." She gave him a helpless swollen look. Then she quit holding it together. She let go and laughed and blew her nose and it made a honking noise and she laughed some more, and Brad joined in and they laughed together: such a hilarious mess of a moment.

They hugged. It was awkward, but not terribly so. Then she walked away to join Adam. She turned once, holding her hair in place as the wind tried to web it across her face. She waved and smiled. Brad stood there and watched her get smaller as she crossed the field.

* * * * *

And then there was that Saturday morning, back in the fall: Turning down the cereal aisle in the Stop'n'Shop, she stood comparing the fine print on two boxes, two little girls climbing and twisting and hanging off the grocery cart.

"Steph," he said.

The smaller girl was about three; he put the older one at about five. Stephanie looked up and greeted him with an enthusiastic "Hey!" She thanked Brad again for taking over the Marlins. "From what I could see, you did a great job. You cared."

Brad asked after Conner.

Stephanie spoke slowly. "I guess he's . . . okay," she said. "Not that I'd know."

Brad pressed his lips together. What would be the appropriate response? "That's too bad," he said. Conner hadn't shown up for the end-of-season party, but there were no issues between them.

Stephanie glanced quickly at the girls. She and Conner were done.

"You always had bad taste in guys," Brad said. "Next time stay away from biotech losers and nobodies."

The older sister braced her feet on the bottom of the cart and leaned her head back so she could look up at him upside down.

Stephanie lowered her voice. "Conner had a rough patch. Maybe you know something about it. I think he's fine now."

Brad had heard a few stray comments, but hadn't delved.

"Conner needs to achieve," Stephanie said. "He needs to impress and be recognized. Well, a couple things didn't work out, and his wiring didn't hold up well."

Achieve. Yes, Brad thought. *Be recognized.* He decided not to jump onto this pile. Because he was no different: He needed these things, too.

Stephanie gazed absently at her girls as they clambered over the shopping cart. "Conner needs to be a celebrity. When he's not the home-coming hero, his system short-circuits. Or something."

He'd picked up a rumor about Conner moving. To the West Coast: San Francisco?

Stephanie confirmed that yes, Conner had lost his job. And an opportunity had arisen in the Bay Area, but then fallen through. As far as she knew, Conner was still looking around.

Brad nodded along, backing away, trying not to dig.

"But hey," she said. "Quit with the 'losers and nobodies' references. I never called you a loser or a nobody."

Brad rolled his eyes, grinned slightly to make light of it.

"I said—once—that you'd be a loser *dad,* and even then what I really meant was that you'd be a loser *adopting* dad."

Okay. "Gee thanks."

"I just want to get that straight once and for all." Stephanie smiled. "And by the way I might revise even that . . . I mean— you might not be so bad. You know. It's probably one of those things that you can get better at."

She had to go. But first she had to ask about Brad's job. Gwen had told her something about a new business.

New business? Yes, well. Plans had changed.

"Did it . . . not go well?"

Brad hunched forward over the cart handlebar. Long story short. Over the summer he'd done all the legwork, filed all the documents, prepared his forms, lined up contacts and prospective clients. He'd started looking for office space. Then, a flurry of phone calls had changed his course. His new job— he'd been there a few months now—was with the Cystic Fibrosis Foundation.

Stephanie raised her eyebrows.

It was going well, so far. He'd been meeting with companies and scientists all over the country. He was learning the territory: the disease, the therapies, the approaches, the stumbling blocks. Sorting among priorities in allocating funds.

Brad paused to remind himself to e-mail Renni's parents about an encouraging development. Bottom line, he said, it was something where the objectives were clear. There was an enemy to defeat. Brad felt himself on the verge of a longer explanation, but then he remembered the ice cream in his cart, which was probably melting. "Hey," he said. "Lemme know if you need anything."

Stephanie drifted down the aisle, scolding mildly as the girls reached out to touch all the boxes on the shelves. Brad knew he would avoid Stephanie if their paths crossed again at checkout. That second meeting always felt awkward.

But when in fact he saw her in the checkout line, he did not turn away. "I said to let me know if you need anything," he said.

"Yeah?" She looked up as she loaded her items onto the belt.

"Uh . . . you haven't signed up to coach some team, have you?"

Stephanie laughed. A happy, natural laugh, unspoiled by caution or irony or significance. Then she waved him away and went on unloading the cart.

Brad hesitated, momentarily immobilized by his startlingly clear recognition of her laugh—and it wasn't really *that* many years ago, he realized, that he'd been accustomed to that laugh. Then he found a different checkout line.

Her two girls, he thought, were cute. In just a few years, they'd be playing catch with their mom. That was going to happen. They'd get into it, whether they were coordinated or interested or not. Almost like they were born for it.

* * * * *

Jamie works frantically at the locker combination. She twists the dial violently, rattling it, tries to breathe evenly to slow her fingers . . . and—*damn!*—misses the number. Again. *Come on!* Then—finally!—she's in. English, Math . . . softball bag—the stupid thing's too bulky; she has to yank and pry it out of the locker. She needs to get over to the high school and even if she runs all the way it's a half-mile and it's snowing. There's no way she'll make it in time.

She wonders how Claire Boniface is getting there. She and Claire are still in junior high, but the high school softball coaches invited them to try out for the high school JV and they both made it. The season begins indoors in March. The first practice starts in about ten minutes. Jamie dreads being late. She'll get all these weird looks from these high school kids who don't know her and probably resent her.

She throws her backpack on, slings the softball bag over one shoulder. The corridors are heavy with traffic; kids clumping around in ski jackets and snow boots. Jamie starts to run. Kids make way for her and she doesn't care what they think. She bursts out the doors, starts running toward the street.

She hears her name. She turns, sees her friend Kelli and somebody she doesn't quite recognize—waving as they walk toward the curb, but then she hears her name again, and it's an adult woman's voice, vaguely familiar. She stops. And then—from the car right in front of Kelli—a hand out the window, waving. Coach Diane!

Diane pops her head out the window. "Do you need a ride?"

Jamie runs to the window, out of breath. "I have to get to the high school. Would it—could I—"

"Hop in," Diane says.

The three of them pile in. Kelli takes the front seat; her friend—Lissa!—shares the back with Jamie. Jamie and Lissa sometimes say hi in the halls; not so much recently.

Drops of melted snow slide down Lissa's spangly earrings. This reminds Jamie of something; she's not sure what.

Lissa turns her head, fiddles with the earrings as if she's listening to something in her fingers. She sees Jamie looking at them. She smiles.

"If it gets just a little colder," Jamie says, "you'll have icicles hanging off your ear."

Diane laughs as she lifts her eyes to the rearview mirror.

Kelli peers back around the side of the front seat. She notices Jamie's extra bag—her softball bag. "I heard about you!" she says. "You and Claire, right?"

"Right!" Lissa says. "That is awesome!"

Kelli turns to her mother and explains Jamie's situation on the high school JV.

They pepper her with questions. Is it the first practice? Who else is on the team? Who's the coach?

Jamie tries to calm herself, but her knee jiggles nervously as she watches cars take forever to make left turns, as the traffic light turns red. She doesn't know anything about the team, she says. She's a little scared. She doesn't know anybody.

"I bet they all know who you are," Kelli says. "They know about Claire."

Everybody knows about *Claire*, Jamie thinks. Claire has said hello to Jamie a few times, mostly last year after softball ended. They do not know each other well.

Coach Diane smiles into the mirror. "You're going to be late," she says. "But just—maybe five minutes. And don't you worry, you'll make friends fast. Once you start playing ball, all those girls will be glad you're on their team."

"That's right," Lissa says. "I hated you until you were on my team."

"Oh," Jamie grins. "Well, thanks. I guess. We made good teammates."

Lissa lounges down in her seat. "Well," she says. "It was an interesting team."

This makes Diane laugh. Kelli laughs, too. Lissa says, "What? *What?*"

Jamie wishes Kelli and Lissa could be on the JV team. They're both good players: Why weren't they invited? And Renni—Renni? She can still play—she's still all right. Right?

"She's okay," Diane says. "They're trying some things and her family had a bit of a scare a few months ago, but for now she seems to be all right."

A drop of icy water makes a trail down Lissa's earring, combines with a few other drops, and jumps down onto Lissa's coat. And Jamie knows what she was reminded of earlier. "Remember the grapefruit—that time in practice—"

"I was just thinking about that!" Lissa says.

* * * * *

Pitcher's Pub. Beers with Mike. They're good again. Brad had stayed out of touch for a while. Then one day he wanted to watch a ballgame with somebody, and he knew it was time to forget the damn thing, whatever it might have been.

Mike tells Brad about his drawing. He's been at it for a year. Brad had no idea.

Mike laughs. "As you know, I usually don't talk about things that I don't know a lot about."

"True. It's tough to be arrogant when you're ignorant."

He's improved a lot, Mike says, but he *still* struggles with forests.

This surprises Brad: Mike letting on about something he's

struggling with.

He can draw forests as distant masses within a landscape, Mike says. Or, he can draw *trees*, and he can render them in almost botanical accuracy. From inside the landscape, though, he's trying to learn to draw trees as parts of the forest chaos— so it looks random like in real life, but in a way that makes sense. He's starting to get it, though. He's completed a few drawings that he found satisfying, and there are a few that Claire and Joanne both like.

As he speaks, Brad notices how Mike's hand marks his statements in the air, thumb touching middle finger. He wonders if this is an acquired gesture. An *artist* gesture? Brad nods along. He tries to envision Mike with a sketch pad, squinting at trees. He remembers seeing Mike in the park on a spring evening, shifting from side to side, a little un-comfortably.

"Something about relationships," Mike continues. "The workshop instructor says, 'it's all about relationships, it's all about relationships, it's all about relationships,' and I think I'm starting to see it."

Speaking of relationships, Brad asks about Joanne.

Still going strong.

"Did you have a little . . . side fling going on for a while?"

"No." Mike seems genuinely puzzled. "*Side fling?*"

Brad shakes his head. "Cool. Didn't think so."

Mike tilts his head, like he's straining to hear something. "I won't say I haven't had thoughts. Because I have. But"—he turns up his palms to signify *clean*—"no. No side fling."

"Good," Brad says. "You two have a good thing going."

Mike agrees. And then, he continues, there's Claire— there's a nice little affectionate relationship developing be-tween them. "I guess that's how it happens," Mike says. "You try something and then you get tangled up in it and everything changes and you get twisted around."

Huh?

"I'm as surprised as anybody," Mike says.

First, drawing; now, some sort of emerging domestic commitment. As he's admitted, Mike doesn't usually do things he doesn't already know how to do.

"And get this," Mike says. "Here's another one for you." In his client's next war game, Mike has introduced the idea of *desertion* as a behavior alternative. Under certain conditions. "You were right," Mike says. "It's a very real possibility; of course it is. A lot of it happened."

"Quitting."

Mike shrugs. "Half the battle back then was keeping the army from quitting. These militia farmers didn't know squat about being soldiers. After a few months of misery, you probably start wondering why the hell you got into this."

Sure. Now *this* sounds more like Mike, asserting his knowledge.

Mike's client doesn't like it. "Hates it. They want it to stay focused on combat." Mike heaves a sigh. "But if you don't know why you're there . . . what a brutal existence." He's put a lot of thought into this. "*I'd* desert."

"Wait." Brad wants to relish the moment. "You're taking a stand on this?"

Mike shrugs. "Sort of. Desertion was a real factor, and I think I can make it a fun part of the game. We're going back and forth on it."

This is a lot for Brad to digest.

"*I'm* the deserter," Mike says. He shifts on his stool, turns to face Brad. He's always quit when things didn't serve his purposes, or when they didn't make sense for him, or when whatever they were supposed to be *about* didn't square up.

"Right," Brad says. "When it's a cluster."

Mike's fingers spread and his hands make erratic, excited gestures. "So, yeah, your desertion idea—I think there's some potential there. It'll still have to be entertaining. But I have some sway with the client. I give it a chance."

Now this—this earnest Mike—has Brad off balance. He looks about, as if wanting to hold on to something. There's a ball game to watch. They watch three pitches. Ball, swinging strike, foul ball.

"Just so you know," Mike says, "I'm sorry I pissed you off that time."

"Sorry, too," Brad says. The whole point of having an old friend like Mike is that you don't have to get into this kind of stuff.

But Mike goes on. "As I suspect you know, I can get pretty dismissive when I don't get it that somebody really cares about something."

Brad finds it strange and amusing to hear Mike apologizing.

Mike persists. "I didn't understand how much you were invested in that team."

Shit: What is he even *talking* about? Brad wasn't *invested*. He was trying. That's all.

"You were a great coach," Mike says. "You gave a crap. I didn't get that when I made that asshole comment."

"Asshole."

"Oh well. Should I stop making sense now?"

"Please."

Mike fondles his mug. "Another beer?"

"Another beer."

"One other thing."

"What?"

"I was going to wait but I might as well tell you now."

"What?"

"Me and Jo. We're getting married."

* * * * *

Softball starts soon. It bugs Brad, a little bit, that the league has not contacted him about coaching. But he understands: In most years there are more than enough parents to coach. This year is probably just a normal year (Phil Braden, of course, is a mainstay). But still. Brad wonders if they'd have been in touch with Conner if *he* had coached the season.

A few weeks ago, he saw Bob Remersdorf in the parking lot at the grocery store, waving. It was a Saturday morning, sunshine melting the snowbanks, tempting a few souls to break out light windbreakers. Brad figured Remersdorf wanted to talk about the upcoming season. He was grinning and he shouted something, something about . . . "coach guru . . ."

Brad waved back, smiling, only to realize that Remersdorf was waving at somebody else. Brad checked behind him. Phil Braden was getting out of his car. Bob and Phil called back and forth over the tops of the cars. Something about a reception. Something about the bookstore. Neither of them saw Brad.

As he drove out of the parking lot, Brad remembered: Phil's new book, *Coaching Winning Softball*, had just come out in print.

* * * * *

Waiting at the stoplight. Ten bags of mulch in the back of the car. In the early spring sunshine, it's just warm enough for the yearned-for novelty of open car windows.

A big SUV in the intersection waits for left-turning traffic to pass. The passenger window's open; a girl's hair swirls around crazily.

The recognition jolts him: Colleen. He hasn't seen her since the end-of-season party. Her hair is longer and from just her face he can see how much she's grown.

The SUV moves forward, passing in front of him. Brad hurries to wave, but the window won't come down fast enough; he rushes to jam his palm on the horn.

She sees him. Her eyes widen—he can see this even as she struggles to tame the wind in her hair. Her mouth opens and she shouts something that he can't hear. She shoots her arm and her head out the window to wave. Brad waves back, almost frantically. The car passes through the intersection and away down the street. It gets smaller, but he can still see Colleen's head thrust out the window, hair rippling and flapping over her face, arm waving back and forth.

He remembers talking to Colleen on their way off the practice field. That last practice before Conner took over. She was asking questions and he was trying to say something about how being at that practice mattered, without quite being able to say what it was about that practice that mattered.

* * * * *

Back at home, from the deck he surveys the yard and the remains of last year's garden. His hands are scratched and bloody from clearing out the stabbing stalks and rotted leaf matter from the year before. In a week he'll have new seedlings in the ground.

Thin sunlight slants through the silvery trunks of the bare forest. It's all a tangle. Maybe something Mike might draw, and Brad can see why: It's not impossible, he thinks, to make sense of it.

ACKNOWLEDGMENTS

I am painfully shy about asking people to read my writing and offer honest feedback. So, huge thank yous to Carol Paik, Steve Fraleigh, Seth Pappas, Heather Totty, and Sarah Woodworth. Thanks also to Anne Dillon and Matt Sharpe for their editing insights.

Of all the things to write about, I never expected to derive inspiration from girls' little league softball. Thank you to the Marblehead (MA) Softball Little League and all of its coaches, who kept it fun; and thank you especially to the players (including my daughter Frances, who got me out of the house), who all grew up too fast but left me with a trove of treasured memories.

And finally: Thank you to my wife, Barbara, for listening and support; and to Atmosphere Press, for guidance, and for seeing something in my rough manuscript.

From all of you, I've learned more than a thing or two.

About
ATMOSPHERE PRESS

Atmosphere Press is an independent, full-service publisher for excellent books in all genres and for all audiences. Learn more about what we do at atmospherepress.com.

We encourage you to check out some of Atmosphere's latest releases, which are available at Amazon.com and via order from your local bookstore:

Twisted Silver Spoons, a novel by Karen M. Wicks

Queen of Crows, a novel by S.L. Wilton

The Summer Festival is Murder, a novel by Jill M. Lyon

The Past We Step Into, stories by Richard Scharine

The Museum of an Extinct Race, a novel by Jonathan Hale Rosen

Swimming with the Angels, a novel by Colin Kersey

Island of Dead Gods, a novel by Verena Mahlow

Cloakers, a novel by Alexandra Lapointe

Twins Daze, a novel by Jerry Petersen

Embargo on Hope, a novel by Justin Doyle

Abaddon Illusion, a novel by Lindsey Bakken

About
THE AUTHOR

Photo by Joseph Puleo

Richard Paik lives in Marblehead, Massachusetts. *A Thing or Two About the Game* is his debut novel. Five seasons coaching girls' softball served as inspiration, while providing insight into the tribulations and rewards of this benign activity. He is currently at work on his next book, a collection of linked stories, none of which are about softball.

Learn more at www.RichardPaik.com.